Telluride

Telluride

a novel by Susan Clark Schofield

Algonquin Books of Chapel Hill 1993

Published by
ALGONQUIN BOOKS OF CHAPEL HILL
Post Office Box 2225
Chapel Hill, North Carolina 27515-2225

a division of
WORKMAN PUBLISHING COMPANY, INC.
708 Broadway
New York, New York 10003

LIBRARY OF CONGRESS CATALOGING-IN-PUBLICATION DATA
Schofield, Susan Clark, 1958–
    Telluride : a novel / by Susan Clark Schofield.
      p. cm.
    ISBN 0-945575-96-3
    I. Title.
    PS3569.C5253B46 1993
    813'.54—dc20   93-1072
                    CIP

10 9 8 7 6 5 4 3 2 1
First Printing

Acknowledgments

I want to thank my editor, Robert Rubin, my agent, Mary Evans, and all the people at Algonquin Books and Workman Publishing who turn writers' dreams into published books.

I am grateful to those who supplied valuable information: "Glider Bob" Saunders at the Telluride Airport, on weather, geology, and sunsets; Mark Greene, on opera; Charlie Colbert, on claims; Callie at Telluride's library and Cathy Greene, on Telluride and mining; Bob Walton at Big Al's Gun Shop, on guns; Anne Belcher and Gisela Epple, on German; and Warren Bechtel of Western Union, on telegrams.

Finally, this book would not have come to life without Tommy and Liz Armenta and Lisa Poinsot Kean, who made southwestern Colorado home, at least for a little while; MaryAlice Timmons, my first reader; Diane Martin, Louise Stilphen, Patti Murphy, and Heidi Somers, who cared for my children so I could work; and Jeff Clark, my husband and first love, even before writing.

For my parents
and in memory of Auntie Jean Fehr,
with love

Contents

Telluride

PROLOGUE

September 1878

Marie DuBois ran a saloon on Pacific Avenue called the Fallen Idle. She'd made enough friends among the miners who drank there that they'd helped her build a frame house with a shingle roof for herself and her daughter, Catharine. At the time, most of the houses in the boomtown known as Columbia, Colorado, were built of logs, with mud roofs. Some miners even lived in tents. So far, Marie and Catharine DuBois were Columbia's only ladies; the rest were whores. One day other ladies would come, with standards and airs to put on, ladies who would think Marie with her hobnailed boots and woolen trousers no better than a whore. But they would be wrong.

A block from the Fallen Idle, along Colorado Avenue, burro trains waited, loaded with ore to go over the mountains to Ouray for shipment by ox team to Alamosa and from there by rail to the Grant Smelter in Denver, or with supplies to go up to the mines. The supplies cost more than the mines pulled in, now, and the ore had to be high-grade, worth at least three or four hundred dollars a ton, to

3

make the trip even barely worthwhile. The little burros, with muzzles and tails sticking out either end of their loads, occasionally lifted a hoof and squished it back into the mud, or rotated an ear to some far-off signal beyond the splashing and shouting of freighters and the blasting above the town.

A young man named Zachary Coleman—Cole, people called him—guided his dapple gray cow pony through the traffic. He was tall and lanky, not yet grown into his height, with dark hair and blue-gray eyes; he wore the high-heeled boots and spurs and broad-brimmed hat of a ranch hand, not a miner. He hated mining. Sitting straight and stiff on his horse, he looked neither left nor right, as though angry, or in any case less than pleased with the grime and bustle that surrounded him.

It had rained the night before and the mud was deep, coating all who passed. Unhitched burros foraged in the garbage tossed from houses and saloons. Burros could survive anywhere, but mules and horses needed feed. They didn't come cheap, with hay at ninety dollars a ton; many a miner had only his feet to get him anywhere. Cole had bought his cow pony and paid for its keep with what he'd earned cutting trees. Now mud coated the horse's legs, clear up to its knees and hocks.

Cole stopped at the general store, a new frame building with a board sidewalk out front and a sign overhead across the sidewalk, for a treat for Catharine DuBois. He found only dried apples, which was all he ever found, if that. He stuffed a handful into his pocket, handed the merchant a coin, and rode on to see Catharine.

At the frame house with the shingle roof, the two of them sat on a flowered settee and he gave her the dried apples from his pocket. Her red-gold hair fell loose over her shoulders and her blue calico dress fit tight around her waist; when she sat, the snug fabric pushed her breasts up. As she ate the apples her small, full lips smiled at the corners and her leaf green eyes narrowed. She slipped off her shoes to show tiny, perfect feet with polished toes that she claimed to keep hidden from all but him. Today her toenails were scarlet.

"Buck Daunt was more broken up than Zachary when I told them that Anna died," he said, giving up on getting any apples. "Even Zachary took me back a little. I don't get it."

Anna had been Cole's mother. His father Zachary had come west with Buck Daunt from Georgia in search of gold. At the mining camp on Cherry Creek, both men had fallen for Anna, but it was Zachary who ended up marrying her, after getting her pregnant with Cole. Or so the story went.

"I don't like him," said Catharine between apples.

"Buck?"

"He's lecherous. Like you."

Cole laughed.

"Besides, he has a wretched temper. You should see the way he whips the burros. Mama says he beats the whores."

Cole shrugged. He'd known Buck so long that he didn't think of him one way or another. He was just someone who hung around the house like a bachelor uncle, though he'd never gone so far as to bounce Cole or his sister on his knee when they were little.

Suddenly Catharine stopped chewing and cleared her throat, a small noise. She seemed to have paled.

"Excuse me," she said, and left him alone on the couch with the apples for a few minutes. When she returned, her cheeks were flushed and she seemed a hint flustered, which was unusual. Cole had saved her a couple of dried apples, but she wanted no more.

He asked if she was all right and she nodded, but she wouldn't look at him. Again, she cleared her throat.

"You know," he said, "now that Anna's dead we can go away. Like we talked about."

"What does her death have to do with it?" She still wouldn't look at him. He tried to think of an answer and came up empty. It just did. He touched her cheek, dropped his fingers to the pale pink smoothness of her neck. She flinched.

"Don't you want to go away? Before winter? We can go someplace warm, like Texas. I have the horse." He touched the tops of her breasts, above the dress.

She stood. "I don't think so."

He stood too. He did not know what to say. At least she was looking him in the eyes now, but her hands hung at her sides and her expression was shielded, even cold. It reminded him of Anna, which came as a shock. Anna. His jaw tightened.

"I can't stay here," he told her. "Not another winter."

She went on looking at him. It was maddening.

"Well?"

She sighed. "Maybe you could send for me, if you get steady work. Winter is probably not the best time to find work, even in Texas."

"And you'd come?"

Her gaze flickered away.

Well, he thought. Well, hell, that was quick. So quick it didn't even hurt, yet. His mother and his girl, both in the same day. He considered saying something else, or maybe kissing Catharine goodbye, but he had nothing to say and the idea of a parting kiss left him cold. He could never kiss his mother, either.

Outside, the dapple gray snorted noisily, pawed the ground.

"I'm going," he said, a last call.

She might have looked pained, or sad, or even a little scared, but only for the barest instant. In any case, she held her ground. Damn her, then. Her and the whole town, too.

With jaw still tight and fists clenched and cheeks burning, all against his will, Cole walked toward the door and opened it to the muddy streets full of refuse and burros with ears turned toward far-off signals. He strode outside and swung onto his horse and yanked the reins toward the valley where his father would have gone with Buck Daunt to dig Anna's grave, and where he would go now to collect his things and ride out.

At the cabin an hour later, he stood over his mother's body while Zachary and Buck dug her grave outside. There was the faint sound of shovels striking the earth and heaving it away: Buck fast, almost frantic; Zachary slower, stronger, steadier.

The window in Anna's room framed a square of gold that failed to brighten the grainy dimness. When Cole had found her this morning, it had taken him a minute to realize she'd finally died. Through the window the autumn aspen appeared watery, but it was only the wavy glass, not tears. Now, as this morning, he had no need of tears.

He would not miss her. Not the clipped German accent, not the frosty eyes, blue-gray as his own. Not the platinum hair, as fine and light as his was thick and dark; not the way she'd kept it lashed back tightly from the artful beauty of her face. She'd never allowed herself to grow old, only sick, with an illness she'd declined to discuss, something too shameful for a proud woman like Anna Streich Coleman.

He would not miss the body, this body that had borne him, birthed him, suckled him, but always held him away—never embracing, never comforting, never caring, only resenting. How could he miss her, when in death she was no different than in life, or what had passed for life in her?

She was silent at last. Aside from the faint hacking of the shovels, all Cole heard was the rhythmic rise and fall of the heddle frame in the other room, where his nine-year-old sister, Gretel, wove gently away at whatever grief she might have felt. The loom sound was all that remained of his mother, but it was still too much. He stared back out the watery gold window, willing the sound to let him

be. Finally he tore his gaze away and forced his long legs, which had
gone sluggish with some of Anna's chill, to carry him across the
swept wood floor to the main room. He saw only a purple square
where before he'd seen gold, as the trees turned inside out in his
head. He did not see Gretel, though he heard the loom sound cease
and felt her dark eyes trace his steps. He held fast to the gold square
turned purple, to the relief of blindness, and reached the door to the
valley outside just as the square faded.

He breathed, at last, and looked around, his eyes freed from the
death room, from his sister's stare. The valley surrounded him, and
the cabin seemed to vanish as though neither it nor the rest of what
the prospectors built had ever marred the sunsparkled greens and
golds of autumn in Colorado's San Juan Mountains. It even seemed
that the mining camps were gone: Ophir, Alta, San Miguel, Columbia; the placer operations that sent torrents of rocky mud down the
San Miguel River valley; the prospects burgeoning into mines, rid-
dling the mountains, wounding, boring hungrily for the precious met-
als that men craved—and women. All gone. Or so he wished,
standing there in his father's valley with the sound of the shovels
behind him, behind the cabin. So he would always wish. All gone,
even Catharine and Marie and their fine frame house, leaving only
sapphire sky to crown the peaks and tingling air to rustle the flaming
leaves.

Cole walked to his horse, heaved his saddlebags across its back,
and tied on his bedroll, trying all the while to get Catharine out of
his mind. He'd left her at the door of her mother's house with a back-
hand wave, unwilling to look at her again, unwilling to risk the hope
that she might change her mind. He had spurred the horse through
the slop of Columbia's streets, out of town along the rushing, polluted
San Miguel River. He had pulled up here at the cabin in a sweat,
thrown his things together. He had been on the way back outside,

to say good-bye to Zachary and Buck, when he'd paused by his mother's bed. God knows why.

Now the shovels stopped. Cole walked through the sudden silence to the rear of the cabin, where Zachary and Buck stood on opposite sides of the open grave, breathing hard, streaked with mine grit and valley soil. Cole returned his father's warm, sad handclasp; Buck merely stared at him, something like hate in his eyes.

He climbed on the dapple gray horse and turned it south. At last he would be shed of this place, with the gold aspen flaming at his back and the mountains rearing above his head, with Catharine's leaf green gaze following him and the red-gold of her hair burning behind his eyes. He would climb the escarpment that formed the valley's southern wall, scale the high pass beyond, and head down through the foothills to where the land flattened and the sage grew thick and the Utes still roamed. He would think no more of Catharine, and he would leave Anna's burial to Zachary and Buck.

The horse's hooves pounded the earth, crushing the grass. Cole could feel the cabin and the town receding, and the way opening in front of him. He tilted his head, gazed up the steep escarpment. And then he heard Buck Daunt, hollering after him, in a rage: "She was your mother, you bastard!" So he still loved her, after all this time. The cry echoed, but Cole did not look back.

PART ONE

Bonne Chance

July 1891 to September 1892

1

Braunn Mining Limited

The in-town office of Braunn Mining Limited, which operated the Flosshilde and Bonne Chance silver mines, was a squat, granite building with small windows and a heavy door. It stood beside a grand five-story brick building under construction; next to the new structure the office looked as stolid and fortified as a bank.

Johnny Torres dropped from his tall, surly palomino in front of the office, raising dust when his boots hit the street. It was hard to tell whether more dust came from the street or from him. No rain had fallen on the San Juan Mountains for a month, and Johnny had just ridden over from Creede, more or less without stopping, and the dust coated his work clothes and black beard and long black hair.

He tried to brush off some of the dust and gave up, and wondered instead about getting a bath and a drink before looking for work. Trouble was he had about run out of cash—no work and the freezing waters of the San Miguel River might have to do for washing.

His heavy hobnailed boots thudded across the knotty boardwalk

13

and into the office, which was so cool, dim, and quiet that it took a few seconds to blink away the street outside. A balding man with a fringe of colorless hair and weasel features approached him with a faint look of distaste: it could have been Johnny's need for a bath or the fact he was Mexican, probably both.

"What is it?" said the man slowly, as though Johnny might not understand.

"I'm looking for work." His voice came out more American than Mexican. "I've been at Leadville and Creede in the last year. I do mostly blasting, plus double- or single-jack drilling. Graveyard shift."

Some of the distaste had gone, not much. The man seemed young enough, but his shoulders were hunched. "Go to the Bonne Chance tonight," he said. "Zachary Coleman is the shift boss there; it's up to him." He walked off and slid his weasely frame behind a desk. Johnny glanced around the office, one large room and a smaller room through a door. The sign next to the door said BUCK DAUNT, SUP'T. Some of the office workers eyed him; they probably didn't get many Mexicans here, and certainly none asking for a skilled job like blasting or drilling. He went outside.

Leaning on the railing, he stroked his palomino along the jaw. The horse must have been worn out; it made no attempt to bite. Johnny needed some rest, a hot bath, and a meal before work, which he figured to find all right from what the weasely office man had said. Mountains hemmed Telluride in on three sides, guarding or imprisoning, depending on a man's point of view, but in any case shot full of mines, with plenty of jobs. He'd see the shift boss. Something about the name the man had mentioned—Zachary Coleman—was familiar, but had nothing to do with Colorado. Maybe Texas. That's all he could remember, and it hardly mattered, anyway.

Men and women passed him on the boardwalk, mostly men. Lots of people came and went in these mining boomtowns, so strangers hardly merited a glance, but the people here tended to be Anglo in one way or another and he got enough glances. The women veiled theirs, but they always looked twice. The men tended to look from his dark face and black beard to the Colt hanging at his left hip: he was left-handed. He'd take the gun off soon enough; most folks didn't wear one in town. It had come in handy before, though—a little extra insurance whenever he got to a new place, which was often.

From the boardwalk, he listened to the banging of construction and watched society and the labor class mingle here on Telluride's main street, Colorado Avenue. There was a north side and a south side to this town, and a north-side lady would never set her slippered foot on a south-side street. He could picture it: on the north side there would be "at-home" socials, where the women would gossip about one another and their south-side opposites, if they were really that, in refined tones over tea and scones and dainty cakes. Their homes would be large and wood frame—or brick for the most fortunate. On the south side there would remain a few log houses with mud roofs, but not many now that Telluride had a proper image to maintain. Most would be frame buildings also, some with high, square false fronts. Life in the parlor houses and dance halls, boardinghouses and saloons would be livelier, closer to the edge, more like what had once been the frontier and could still be a precarious existence.

Johnny had come from a north side, years ago, but preferred the south. Unlike most, he could cross over. He'd spent years crossing over in Europe before the money had run out and he'd come to New York to join the throngs headed for the American West. Now, after weeks of drink, dance, and nights with the ladies in Creede, the money had run out again and he was here, searching for the barber.

Through thick horse and wagon, mule and burro traffic, he spotted it across the street, with a livery nearby. He climbed back into the creaking saddle, threaded his way to the livery, and watered, grained, and curried the horse, which did its best to trample his feet.

He paid the old man there to keep the beast until night. From outside the stable he saw that the brick structure next to the mining office would be a hotel called the Baroness, with an opera house next door, or what would call itself an opera house. Both buildings were nearing completion. He smiled, finally, and headed toward the barber's, past the stationer's, the hardware store, and a pharmacy, each with its sign straddling the boardwalk. His saddle-tired muscles began to relax at the thought of a steaming bath, a massage, and the sleepy aroma of a good long cigar.

Full dark had settled over the mountains by the time the palomino reached the Bonne Chance silver mine. There was no moon. Below the steep trail to the mine, Telluride sparkled with the night's revelry. Sounds, too faint to identify, lifted on the warm air: a distant popping, joined by longer tones, sometimes melodic, all fading as Johnny reached the flat expanse before the enormous mine.

The mountain reared above the Bonne Chance's three entrances, called adits, a towering black wall against the stars. A wash of dull light came from the main adit, and trammers dwarfed by the mountain shoved their ore cars along the tracks to dump a load and return for the next. Younger laborers, not yet miners, went about various menial tasks among the dark, hulking buildings outside.

At the main adit a Cornish miner said that Zachary Coleman had gone to the six hundred station. Johnny headed into the mine. Partially timbered walls of rock and dirt folded around him. Powder gas seeped from deep within, left over from the rounds the last crew would have fired at the end of their shift. As Johnny continued along the gradually rising tunnel, the timber began to reek of underground seepage saturating the wood. The Bonne Chance would have many thousands of feet of tunnels down there, all connecting in one way or another if the surveyors had done their job right. It would have consumed more trees than the largest forest fire to fortify the walls against sloughs and cave-ins. If the owner was lucky, the walls would be solid rock and the dwindling supply of timber wouldn't matter. But the mountain would always want to close the wound. Johnny walked on. He had what miners called a single-jack "dago" hammer slung over his left shoulder. It was a half-pound heavier than the regular four-pound hammers used for one-man drilling and had a narrower face. It delivered more force with each blow but could also break a man's hand more easily if he missed the drill steel. Johnny had missed the drill steel only once, as a boy, when his father's miners had first taught him to drill. They'd laughed at him and his cracked hand; his father had scorned him for sharing in such common labor. His father couldn't have swung a hammer for all the gold in Mexico, which was probably why his miners disliked him so much and never gave him a decent day's work. Johnny hardly thought of him anymore, except when he first went into the earth after a long layoff, like now. He thought of his mother often, and of his much older sister, Linda, even more. He hadn't seen Linda for twenty-four years, not since his early childhood in Spain, before Mexico, before mining, before his father had thrown her out.

Two hundred feet into the Bonne Chance he heard angry voices. As the tunnel curved a little, the six hundred station came into view, with two men nose to nose, or almost—one was much shorter than the other.

They saw him a hundred feet away and broke off arguing. When he got to them they were still breathing hard. The shorter, wiry one was breathing harder than the other, and for an instant the whites showed all the way around his dark eyes. He had a hatchet face with graying black stubble and a kink in his long, narrow nose. His skin was dark with mine grit. He spat a string of brown tobacco juice where the timbers met the floor and wiped his thin, harsh lips with the back of his left hand—a hand calloused and sinewy, with only the thumb and first two fingers remaining. He had a wiry strength to him, and something about the way he held his shoulders made him look like he'd lost his hammer and drill steel and needed to get back to the rock face.

Johnny guessed the other man to be the shift boss, but the wiry man with the hatchet face had had the last word. The taller man's clothes were a hair less ragged, his anger more controlled. He was solidly muscular, except for a fullness at the belly, and over six feet tall, an inch or two taller even than Johnny. He had thick, dark hair cut short, and a trimmed beard. There was anger in his brown eyes but Johnny saw that it would pass. Both men were at least fifty.

"I'm looking for Zachary Coleman," Johnny told them.

"This here's Zachary Coleman," the wiry man drawled, very Southern—Georgia, perhaps. "I'm Buck Daunt. You're the Mexican wants work, I expect."

So they'd known he was coming. Johnny nodded and told them who he was. Daunt was the super; Johnny remembered his name from the office in Telluride. But he was right about Coleman being the shift boss. Now it came back to him: Zachary Coleman, a name he'd heard in various saloons, along the trail, turning up throughout the Southwest. They hadn't been talking about this Zachary Coleman, though, but a younger one, more often called Cole, with a reputation as a shootist in Texas some years back. Johnny hadn't heard his name lately.

"I do blasting and drilling," Johnny said. "Single- or double-jack. I've worked in mines for more than twenty years, since I was a kid."

A hawkish smile cracked Daunt's face. "Talk to Zachary," he said, his obsidian eyes glinting. "I was just reminding him that he's got a job you can do." And he walked off, not moving quickly but looking like he did, his motions harsh, like his hatchet face, leaving Johnny alone with the shift boss.

Zachary Coleman looked Johnny in the eye. He was still angry.

"I didn't want to give no one this job," he said. He had the same

Southern drawl as Daunt. "But it's Buck's call and I ain't in a position to say no because it's gotta be done." He started along an intersecting tunnel, and Johnny followed. Three hundred feet farther in they got to a shaft and climbed down a ladder for another hundred feet. Now they were closer to the current drift faces, and the ring of hammers on drill steel and thuds of muckers heaving ore into cars filled the air. It seemed to come from all directions and none, bouncing off the walls where there was rock, disappearing into damp timbers where there was wood.

"There's no drilling or blasting jobs open tonight," Zachary continued, when they were once again on the relatively level footing of a corridor. They walked alongside some tracks, through murky dimness. Zachary gave Johnny three candles. He had lighted his lantern above the shaft and it made big traveling shadows along the uneven walls.

"There's a fast turnover, like always," he went on, "so a job might open up any time. There's always mucking or surface work." They stopped walking and he studied Johnny a minute. Johnny half smiled.

"I didn't think so," said Zachary. "So, if you need work tonight, the only thing we've got is breaking hung ore chutes."

This time Johnny laughed.

"You done it before?"

"Would I be here if I had?"

Zachary nodded slowly. They started walking again.

"It's up to you. I wanted to do it myself, but you can guess how that came out. Pay's six bucks an hour, twice the regular rate."

They climbed down another ladder and the sounds from below grew louder, clearer. Johnny listened for tommyknockers. Blasting hung-up boulders out of ore chutes was a quick way to die, though the mountain could kill a man by any means it chose, and often did. Cave-ins, sloughing walls, floods, fires, premature blasts—only the tommyknockers were there to bang out a warning, if there was time. Sometimes a man would be walking through a corridor, any corridor, nowhere near the drilling or blasting down on the drift face, and the tommyknockers would start up banging in his head, or on the walls, or all around. That's when he'd better listen closely, and clear out fast. You always listened to the tommyknockers, whatever they were. Ghosts, spirits, a sixth sense: miners offered many explanations, but those who did not believe, did not listen, or worst of all, could not hear, got taken early. Johnny thought of tommyknockers as the mountain itself, and he always listened.

He and Zachary had nearly reached the drift face, where the sounds of work jarred the eardrums. What the hell, he thought, and took the job.

2

Tommyknockers

Johnny Torres survived the first night, then the second night, and the first week and the second week. The shift boss seemed to hang around whatever chute he'd crawled into, but did not distract him with talk. He just hung around, as though if Johnny killed himself doing this work he wanted to go, too. Apparently Buck Daunt found out, because one day Johnny saw Zachary and the super outside the mine having words again, and after that Zachary was down working on the drift faces with the other men, none of whom had yet paid Johnny any mind.

After the first night, Zachary had taken Johnny to the boardinghouse where he stayed during the week and asked the landlady to advance him the month's room and board. The boardinghouse was an improvement on most bunkhouses, which were all right but lacked a woman's homemade breads and jams.

The house was roomy and cool with summer cross breezes, papered in various florals downstairs and whitewashed on the two

21

upper floors, with many detailed weavings and tapestries draped on the overstuffed chairs and beds or hung on the walls. The landlady's name was Emma Stotter, and she was quiet but genial, generous, and clean. She had three teenaged kids, one a girl and the other two boys. Her husband was the second-shift boss at the other big mine, the Flossie. Johnny suspected that Zachary paid for his first month, because Johnny was not supposed to live that long. Emma always called him John. His given name was Juan, and though no one else in America called him anything but Johnny, he saw no reason to complain.

He liked Zachary very much. After Daunt kept the shift boss from hanging around the clogged chutes the men saw each other less, mostly on their ride to and from work and at the bars, drinking. Every day except Sunday, Zachary returned from the mine to a huge breakfast at the boardinghouse, slept the rest of the day, got up in time for supper, then went out. He had a woman in town, Marie DuBois, though he never talked about her. Johnny only knew from Emma that she owned a place called the Fallen Idle on Pacific Avenue, the heart of the south side. Saturday nights Zachary drank and gambled, and on Sunday afternoons he rode to a valley several miles from town.

Johnny headed right for bed when he got off work, slept four or five hours, and got up for a midday dinner even bigger than Zachary's breakfast: chicken and dumplings and similar fare, seasoned with herbs that Emma grew, followed by a bottomless peach pie, when she could get peaches. Johnny could eat half a pie at a sitting. Every ounce of the sugar and flour and butter and peaches got sweated off at the Bonne Chance.

The other two miners at the house were Irish. They worked the day shift, so Johnny rarely saw them. He had generally taken off on a walk or a long ride in the mountains by the time they came down from the mines; at such times Emma supplied him with a meat sandwich or a hunk of cheese and a bottle of beer. Some evenings he came back in time to hit the bars or dance halls for extra nourishment. He knew one of the madams in town, Silvia, from his days in Leadville. But he stayed clear of her parlor house. Years back, he had courted one of her girls, her niece, and the girl had died.

By the end of the second week, clearing the chutes had grown routine. Some nights Johnny got to spell a drill team with Zachary, using a double-jack hammer and alternating swinging the hammer with turning the drill steel. He noticed that Zachary used a metal cleaning spoon rather than a wooden stick to tamp the powder and primers into the drill holes. Only old-timers did that, clinging to some odd tradition; the slightest spark from metal striking rock could set off the charges early, and no tommyknocker could give a man time to get away. Still, he liked working with Zachary and wished he could do it more often.

On the fifteenth night they were walking to the latest hung chute when they came upon a group of men laughing and talking. The men stopped abruptly and returned to work. Johnny and Zachary continued to the hung chute, which was clogged from the middle clear up to the raise above it. The raise was like a large ore bin, filled with tons of rock waiting for passage into the chute and on through to the ore car below. Johnny crawled inside the chute gate and up a little way, bracing himself against the timbers.

"You know," he called back to Zachary, "these chutes would work a whole lot better if you put the logs butt end out instead of sideways. Then you could make them longer, too."

Zachary said nothing and Johnny dropped out of the chute to the tracks below. Zachary steadied him as he landed, though he landed as easily as ever. Johnny grinned at the older man, who was for the moment his only friend. They both knew what those miners had been doing.

"Put ten bucks on six weeks," Johnny told him, "but don't tell them who's placing the bet. If there's no drilling or blasting work by then I'm calling it deep enough."

Zachary nodded. "Tap 'er light," he said, holding Johnny's eyes for an extra beat, and walked off to place the bet with the rest of his crew.

Six weeks from the day he got to Telluride, Johnny was still alive and breaking hung ore chutes in the Bonne Chance. Now he had a paycheck to cover the bet if he lost, so Zachary wouldn't have to sell his horse. He rode up the mountain that Sunday night and learned there were three plugged chutes. He cleared the first two and headed for the third, still coughing some from the dust and powder gas of the second.

The third chute looked easy. Two boulders blocked it, wedged up high, near the raise. Zachary took off and Johnny crawled inside. The chute was new, of the butt-end-out construction Johnny had recommended. It should not have plugged, but the two boulders were unusually large. He crawled out and assembled a couple of sticks of sixty powder, crimping the blasting caps with his knife. The powder by itself wouldn't hurt him, but one careless touch and the caps could fire, taking his hands and likely his life. He always took care with blasting caps.

He lashed together three fifteen-foot wood poles and tied the explosives on the end, running the fuse along the poles. Then he poked the poles up into the chute and with the greatest gentleness wedged the explosives between the boulders. The boulders were so high that Johnny had to stay far inside the chute to place the powder. He unrolled a length of fuse, dropped back toward the chute gate below, cut a V in the fuse with his knife and poured in some more powder, then spit it with his candle. As always, the ignition blew out the candle. The sputtering fuse provided only a dim, blinking light. It had a long way to go before reaching the powder.

Johnny fished a match out of his pocket and relit the candle. As he struck the match he thought he heard another noise, maybe a rock shifting. A splat of wet earth hit his hat. He didn't dare look up.

Tommyknockers started banging inside the log walls of the chute. Johnny scrambled down to the gate, but lost his balance, tumbled head over heels against the timbers, and dropped to the tracks in a heap. His candle went out again. In the blackness he heard the boulders let go and crash toward him. He rolled sideways. Rock burst through the chute gate, beating his prone body. He tried to get up. The huge boulders thudded next to him; rocks drove him to the track bed, bruising, cutting.

He yelled. He could not get up. The cascade of rocks pinned him, buried him, shattered his determination to rise and run, even to crawl.

Sonofabitch, he thought. Six weeks to the day and I can't collect on the damned bet.

But someone yanked on his arms and shoulders, hollered his name, yanked harder. He moved his legs, pushed against the tracks. His body was stubborn, painfully stiff, covered with sharp rocks and wet gob. His head spun again as the ground fell away. He had a sensation of halting, bumpy motion. He heard a blast, or felt it. It shook him as his father had shaken him as a child. It hurled him against something cruelly hard, and he yelled again.

Then he heard only the echo of the blast and his own name, clearly, and someone coughing. Lots of people coughing. He coughed, too, his back jerking against a rocky floor. And he heard a man ask in an incredulous Cornish accent: "He's alive?"

He opened his eyes and looked up to see a crew of faces peering down. Zachary was kneeling next to him.

"Six weeks," Johnny said through another couple of coughs. "Guess who won the goddamned bet."

Three days later, on a Sunday, the cuts and bruises were mending well, the tommyknockers had left him to dream in peace, and Zachary wanted to speed the healing by taking him to the valley where his daughter, Gretel, lived. So the two men scrubbed up at the barber's, curried and saddled their horses at the boardinghouse's stable, and headed out of Telluride. Colorado Avenue was dry now, baked into ruts after a recent summer storm. The horses kicked up clods of dirt as they wove around the usual wagon, burro, and ox traffic.

Zachary rode an aged brown gelding, docile and serviceable enough, but suited to no more than the five miles between his homestead and town, or a slow climb to the Bonne Chance. Johnny's young palomino needed a daily run and nearly raced up the slopes during afternoon rides; he was anything but docile and would as soon take a chunk out of his rider as accept a lump of sugar.

"Whoever broke that horse owes you some money," Zachary said as the last shacks of Telluride gave way to a wide, cattle-dotted pasture. They passed through the smaller town of San Miguel, and on out of the valley.

It was after noon and late August, with the sun blazing and the temperature over ninety, the air clear and dry. They rode along the river, which smelled less of garbage the farther out they got. The water rushed white in the narrow parts and dawdled in the meadows. The men cut off at the South Fork, into another huge, deep, canyonlike valley. Johnny recognized the route as heading toward the mining camps of Ames and Ophir, then Trout Lake and Lizardhead Pass beyond. Otto Mears had just pushed his Rio Grande Southern through here, completing the Ophir Loop, a hair-raising network of trestles that climbed the escarpment at the back of the valley before crossing the pass. The crews were now working on the descent to Rico. Johnny had ridden this path often, sometimes wondering who owned the homestead on the valley floor.

The horses slowed to a walk amid the soft, high grass, not rutted like the town streets or the trail along the main part of the river. Sandstone rock walls with pine and spruce clinging to their thin soil flanked the riders on the right, rising sharply to a broad, high mesa, where what looked like a castle was under construction. A wealthy man, the owner of the Bonne Chance and the Flossie, had ordered it built for a summer residence; he and his wife, rumored to be from Telluride, had lived year-round in Germany since the late seventies, leaving Buck Daunt to run the mines that Daunt had prospected and sold. The owner's name was Heinrich Braunn. Johnny had seen the mansion from trails higher up. It rose stone by stone, with masons and carpenters crawling over the growing walls like beetles on a rose. From the opposite mountainside a man could hear the faint clink of chisels and hammers, but down here on the valley floor all he could hear was the rushing river and the wind in the leaves, and maybe a magpie's harsh, rapid *queg queg queg queg* over the hum of flies and bees.

The men rode through stands of pine and white-trunked aspen with pale green leaves shimmering, and, along the riverbed, cotton-woods tinged gold on top and willows with swaying, spiky leaves. Zachary said he'd laid claim to as large a parcel of the valley as the law would allow. No one had ever challenged him or Gretel, or raided the timber, which he and Johnny now left behind for a broad meadow that fronted a modest log cabin and barn. Johnny saw a well-tended vegetable garden to the side of the cabin, and borders of blue lupine and white daisies growing along the front.

At the barn Zachary dismounted and led his horse inside; Johnny followed. They unsaddled their mounts and tied on morrals of grain. A pair of chickens and a rooster scurried in and out of the big sliding door.

Back out in the drenching sun of the meadow, the men saw a woman coming from the woods on the other side with a sizable rabbit hanging from one hand. She carried no gun, only a knife in a sheath at her waist. She neither smiled nor shouted a greeting, just strode through knee-high grass, moving with a tall woman's grace. She wore men's clothes: corduroy trousers held up by suspenders and a green plaid homespun shirt with the sleeves rolled to her elbows. No hat covered her dark brown hair, pulled loosely back into a thick braid that swung to below her waist.

When she got close enough, Johnny saw that her knife had a delicately carved handle, and the sheath was covered by what looked like a miniature tapestry with multicolored fringe dangling from the end. She handed the rabbit to Zachary and held out her hand for Johnny to shake. Her long, browned fingers felt cool and smooth.

"Gretel Coleman," she said in a low voice. "My father said he'd bring you around one of these days." She smiled then, for Zachary, briefly but warmly, and Johnny noticed her white teeth were a little crooked in the front.

Zachary took the rabbit out back to skin it, and Gretel took Johnny into the cabin and poured him a beer from a frosty jug. She poured Zachary a mugful, too, and carried it to him outside. The cabin was tidy and spare. Half of the front room was the kitchen, with a black wood stove and pump handle, and shelves and hooks for pots and pans, dishes and utensils. There was a sitting area in front of a large hearth with an ornate tapestry of the valley and the escarpment rising above it over the fireplace. On the mantle was a daguerreotype of a woman, a pretty woman, very fair, but with a grim set to her mouth and hair pulled back severely. Zachary's late wife? It must be. A bear rug covered the wide pine floor in front of the hearth, and an expertly woven afghan, white on white, draped the back of a faded red settee. Between the cooking and sitting areas was a carefully handmade pine table with four chairs.

Through two doors in the back wall of this main room Johnny could see bedrooms, one with a full-sized bed and pine wardrobe, the other with an enormous loom that crowded the smaller bed against the far wall. Both beds had counterpanes woven with the same artistry as the tapestry and afghan in the living room.

"You're the weaver?" Johnny asked when Gretel returned. "These pieces here, and the ones at the boardinghouse?"

"And at the dance halls and restaurants and the homes on the north side."

He drew on the beer, which was better than the local brewer's.

"And the beer?"

"I make that, too."

Johnny drank some more. Gretel was looking at the bandages on his arms and neck.

"What happened to you?" she asked after a moment.

"A cave-in at the mine. I was trying to break a hung ore chute. Your father saved my life but not all my skin."

She pulled a chair from the pine table and set it near the hearth. Johnny settled into the settee, his back against the white-on-white afghan, and downed the last of the beer. She got up to pour more and brought it to him, then sat lightly on her chair, and sideways.

He took another long swallow. The beer was truly fine, dark amber and almost bitter, with full taste at the tip of the tongue and as it slid down the back of the throat.

"You don't like beer?" he asked.

"No."

"You brew this for Zachary. He's lucky."

She shrugged.

"You should sell it in town."

She laughed, which took him by surprise.

"I like that," he said of her laugh. "Tell me, do you have a brother named Hansel?"

A shadow crossed her face, quick but very dark. "Of course not."

"Oh. But you do have a brother."

Her brows knitted again. She stood. "I don't know, to tell you the truth. He's been gone a long time."

She walked outside and Johnny followed, into the warm, dry sunshine. Zachary had finished butchering the rabbit and was wiping his hands on a rag. Gretel lifted the kettle of wet, red meat.

"As for names," she said, "I've never heard of a Mexican called Johnny."

"It's really Juan Maria Torres de Sevilla. Pretty bad, huh."

She smiled so that he could see her crooked white teeth. "I like Johnny better," she told him, and took the meat inside.

3

The Pass

Anna Streich Coleman had taught her daughter to be wary of men. She'd tried to teach her to hate them, but Gretel loved her father too much for that.

Weeding the vegetable garden the day after Johnny Torres first visited the cabin, Gretel thought he seemed exactly the kind of man her mother would have detested. Then again, maybe she had that backward: maybe Anna would have liked his smooth smile and the trace of a Spanish accent. She believed at times that she had known her mother better than anyone else; then again, that no one had known her at all. Even long dead, Anna remained a mystery: shielded, cold, walled off as if by a crypt, sealed even to her daughter.

Enough of such thoughts. Gretel yanked a bunch of weeds and tossed them into the tall grass, picked a pair of summer squashes and took them inside, shaking loose the dirt as she went.

Zachary brought Johnny around every few weeks. Johnny had gotten the job he wanted, on Zachary's shift, and now and then after Sunday dinners at the cabin he asked her out. He suggested things that she might enjoy: a walk in the mountains when the aspen ignited with gold, a run on skis when the first snow fell in mid-October, a sleigh ride in November. Always she refused him. No excuses, no attempt to buffer, but also nothing to deny his efforts at friendship. They did become friends, of a sort, perhaps mostly because he was the only person she saw regularly, except Zachary. He would shrug when she turned him down, or sometimes raise his dark brows in a brief, wordless question. Then he would say okay. He never flushed, or looked away, or showed any anger in his glittering black eyes. Later he would sit by the hearth drinking beer like Zachary, or bitter, steaming coffee like Gretel, or wine or brandy if he'd brought it from town, talking or silent, always at ease. He would run his hand through his black hair, which was long and wavy in the back and shorter in the front, and Gretel would wonder for an irritating instant if she should have said yes this time. Then the men would leave and, knowing she would not see Zachary for another week, or Johnny for another several weeks, she would feel more than alone, she would feel lonely, an unfamiliar, unwelcome sensation that she could not identify at first, but came to know and detest as it deepened with the blanketing snow outside.

The next day she would generally try to shrug it off by skiing. Most people used skis to get from place to place, but Gretel skied for fun, or to hunt. Her legs would pump the skis while her hands held the long pole for balance, and after a short while her fingers would thaw and redden and grow as warm as the summer day Zachary had first brought Johnny to her meadow. She would take off her woolen cap then, and loose strands of hair would reach for the sun, electrified, escapees from the braid that swung across her back. She would feel her muscles stretch and tighten, she would breathe the crystal-like air, and she would listen to silence broken only by the rhythmic rush of her skis as they cut trails in the virgin snow and convince herself that the loneliness was an illusion. She would believe this until she returned to the empty cabin and found herself imagining him there.

He had caught her eye. She could not deny it. Like her, he had many layers. On the surface he was a miner, thickly muscled under his work clothes, with permanent black lines around the cuticles of his nails, and when she leaned forward to serve him seconds his close-cropped beard smelled faintly of blasting powder and rock dust. He often discussed the Bonne Chance with Zachary, and Gretel learned more about mining, and about the increasingly harsh, penny-pinching ways of their old family friend Buck Daunt than she'd ever cared to know.

But he also had that smooth accent, and his intonations more closely resembled those of the north-side Europeans than the few Mexican laborers Gretel had met. Also, he behaved like a gentleman without fidgeting. Men out here fidgeted when trying to treat a woman like a lady. Under that she could see he was smart and pas-sionate. Get too passionate and you get hurt, she thought, and tried to live by that thought. But she liked it in Johnny. Her father was the only person on earth she'd ever felt passionate about—a fierce, pro-tective kind of passion—except maybe her brother, Cole, who made her feel something like hate.

Johnny never mentioned any brothers or sisters. Gretel knew that he had a strong interest in Telluride's opera house, which opened in December. She assumed he took other women to the perfor-mances, which were probably revues more often than operas. In fact, it occurred to her that he must do quite a lot with other women, and she resented that she should think of this. She had other worries now, anyway, for no sooner had the opera house opened than the Rio Grande Southern completed its loop from Durango through Rico and over Lizardhead Pass. Zachary reported a great explosion of revelry in town, while Gretel shuddered every time she heard the filthy black locomotives wheeze through her valley. It took them forever to grind and groan their way up the Ophir Loop to the top of the escarpment, while their sooty smoke gashed the still, blue sky. Their cinders blackened the snow along the track bed, and the passengers often tossed trash out the windows. It was as bad as when the crews had first invaded the valley to lay the rails.

As winter progressed, Gretel stayed inside more than usual, her skis and snowshoes abandoned in a corner. She took to brooding but denied it when Zachary suggested something might be bothering her. He did not dare probe beyond the suggestion. She realized in February that Johnny had not visited in more than two months. Finally, she asked Zachary where he was and Zachary said working. They'd started putting electricity into the Bonne Chance and had opened up two new drift faces. Johnny's deftness with the single-jack hammer kept him in demand for drilling in stopes too narrow for a man's shoulders. Supposedly the Cousin Jacks, the expert miners from Cornwall, were the only ones capable of drilling in these tight spots without leaving the skin from their arms on the rough rock walls, but Johnny was faster and stronger. He was also good at double-jack drilling, and Zachary said in March that he planned to ask Johnny to join him for the Fourth of July drilling contest. Gretel rolled her eyes. She hated crowds and noise and so stayed well clear of town over the Fourth, but right now the thought of green grass and summer breezes brought on an inward sigh.

"You usually love the winter," Zachary said one night.

"I know. It's a long one this year."

He belched under his breath from the beer. "Well, it's got longer to go."

And then he left, and she was alone again. Alone and lonely, with the loneliness now deeper than the snow, which showed no sign of melting and barely burned off under heavy March clouds that had hung listless and unmoving for days. Gretel went to bed, tired and bored and restless, unable to sleep and unhappy for the first time in ages.

Johnny came back in May, thinner but stronger, and acting as though he'd visited only a week before. Gretel could not keep from shifting her eyes to his shoulders and thighs, and imagining the muscles under the dark skin there. He had probably had his fill of sleigh rides with the ladies, she thought, and caught herself wondering what else.

She treated him curtly and, as the day wore on, pretended to study the scene outside the windows. In the meadow, most of the snow had finally melted, leaving the earth soft underfoot and the grass startlingly green. Last year's wildflowers had poked shoots above the ground and the aspen leaves were budding on the trees, while the evergreens hung heavy with new growth. Snowmelt from the sunlit mountains rushed in narrow torrents down the steep valley walls, and when the trains didn't intrude the river sounded swollen, pregnant, in a hurry to deliver its spring burden to the main fork.

Unable to enjoy spring's beauty, Gretel finally stopped glancing out and sat silently by the fire as the setting sun tinted the cabin with rose and the men talked about the mine. It seemed Buck Daunt had cut costs more than ever, not because of the Bonne Chance but because of the other Braunn mine, the Flossie, which now yielded low-grade ore or nothing except, at wide intervals, short, pockety veins of high-grade so rich the men could chip it off the walls and sack it without sorting.

"It's a tease," said Johnny. "It only makes Daunt go deeper and waste good men. He's skimping on timber and candles."

"Been union trouble here before," Zachary agreed, "back in the eighties. He pushes those men too much, they'll make trouble again."

"Yeah, and he'll replace them with Eastern Europeans. Plenty of mines failing these days. Plenty of men looking for work."

Gretel wished they'd talk about something else. Didn't they ever get tired of work?

"Excuse me, please," she said at last, with some effort to conceal the curtness. She stood and the men stopped in mid-sentence to find out what she wanted. Johnny smiled at her but she did not return it. Instead she walked quickly to the door and outside, closed the door and leaned back against it to breathe deeply of the fragrant, dusky air. She walked away from the house, into the meadow, halfway across. Behind her the cabin door opened, then closed softly, and she heard the squish of footsteps on moist ground.

She felt his warmth near her back and his hand on her shoulder, lightly, tenderly. She looked sideways, as though to turn, but did not. His fingers were warm like the sun, though the sun had gone now, even the fringes of pink from the clouds.

"Would you like to go to the opera?" he asked, his voice quiet, his Spanish accent as subtle as always, but seductive. It weakened her. He weakened her.

She turned to him, to this body that had drawn her to it all day, but still, somehow, managed to stand apart. "Yes," she told him. "I would."

The next morning and all during the two weeks until the performance, she wished she had refused. She woke with the dawn, ate a quick breakfast of strong coffee and oatmeal with dried fruit, and remembered how after she had said yes they had walked slowly back to the cabin, his hand gone from her shoulder, and the warmth had filtered away.

She hated town, mostly because of the mines that supported it but also because it violated a valley as beautiful as her own. She hated the way people glanced furtively at her clothes, the way the north-side ladies wrinkled their delicate noses at the south, the conventions that prevented women in the saloons (not that she'd ever want to go to one) and forced them to enter even the most respectable dining room through a side service door and remain in a waiting parlor until their male escorts were ready to dine. She detested the men who tipped their hats and shuffled their feet shyly before a lady yet slapped a token on the dresser so they could slap a whore on the butt. She wanted to whip the mule skinners who whipped the mules until they screamed, turning them into abject creatures no closer to mules than ants, just so people could get their wondrous ore down from the holes they fired into the mountain. And she hated the way the mines had stripped the mountains of trees, and the consequent avalanches and floods that carried off whatever the men forgot to cut. The only good thing about the avalanches was that sometimes they carried off the buildings, too.

But she did not hate Johnny Torres. Last night she would have said yes no matter where he offered to take her. Still, why town?

"Folks are getting into a regular fever over this opera," Zachary said when he arrived the following Sunday. A light rain had left him dripping. Gretel turned from her loom and glanced at the floor, where the drops collected and spread around his booted feet. He seemed oblivious. "It's supposed to be the best traveling troupe yet."

"The best? Out of how many?"

"Okay, so it's only the second," he said, and poured himself a beer from the frosty jug.

"I hate opera."

"You've never been to one."

"You've never been to the North Pole, but I don't think you'd like it very much."

He laughed. "Probably not a whole lot colder'n here, and sure not half as crowded. Plus which they ain't got opera. You'd love it. Wanna go?"

"I have nothing to wear. I don't even own a dress."

He rubbed his jaw through his thick, graying beard. "Little cold up there for a dress."

She had to smile.

"Make a dress," he said. "Why not? Go on into town and get some cloth and lace and whatever else you need. Perfume, too. One of the boys told me Oliver Wells just brought a new kind in from Paris or some fancy place for his store. All the girls are asking for it. Costs a fortune. Why not try some of that?"

"Because it's too much trouble. And too expensive. Maybe I should just tell Johnny the whole thing's off. Why couldn't he have asked me for a walk, anyway?"

"You said no to a walk, Gretel." His tone was softer now, and serious. Uncomfortable, she wished they'd never begun this conversation. But he went on: "Don't you want to have beaux?"

"Oh, for God's sake!"

He finished his beer, then pulled a cigar from his pocket. One of Johnny's, from the looks, long and fancy.

"Why do you want him to court me?" she asked.

Zachary struck a match on the door frame and puffed on the cigar. Its aroma was surprisingly mellow and pleasant. "Make that dress," he drawled, rolling the cigar between his finger and thumb. "You won't have to pretty up for him but once, because he already likes you in your trousers and shirt. Though he says you need a hat, too."

So she made the dress. She borrowed Zachary's old brown horse and rode the five miles into town. The beast plodded along so slowly, stumbling now and again over a rock, that Gretel wondered how many more times he'd be able to make this trip. At the edge of Telluride, she steeled herself against the assault of traffic noise, the ever-present odors of butchered meat, unwashed bodies, and trash. In the relative calm of the dry-goods store, she paid the exorbitant price for light green satin and white lace, though not the perfume, and carted it all home and started to stitch.

She finished the dress on the day of the opera and laid it on her small bed that was crowded against the wall by the loom. She remembered with some reluctance how her mother had set up the loom in the front room and that she, Gretel, used to share this bedroom with Cole, when he'd slept in the cabin. Often he'd camped out at night. Once she'd sneaked after him, found him lying on his back with his hands folded under his head and his long legs crossed at the ankles. The air had chilled after sunset but he had no blanket and the grass must've felt wet against his back. He had hiked up to the pass, as usual. He watched her slip off the horse and walk toward him with a blanket in her arms.

"Go back to the cabin," he'd said quietly, as though his voice might disturb the starry sky. She guessed, looking back, that he'd said it kindly. She'd wanted to argue, then to plead, but instead she'd turned and walked the horse down from the pass. That was a long time ago, before Anna got sick.

Now she stood in what had been their room, naked. She thought she had the body of a boy, though her female parts said otherwise. So did her skin, ivory white except below the elbows and above the neck, where it was newly golden brown and freckled from the strong mountain sun.

She put her hands on her chest and slipped her palms down over herself, slowly, sucking in her already flat belly. Men's clothes were more comfortable and protective, but Johnny Torres had seen right through them. For an instant she wondered what he would look like naked.

She fixed her hair on top of her head and fastened on the dress to the sound of Johnny's horse trotting up the valley with a wagon rolling behind. She was sure the bustle under the dress made her look like a duck, and the lace itched. The wagon creaked as Johnny jumped down. The grass muffled his footsteps as he walked to the door. Suddenly Gretel realized she had no shoes, only heavy, muddy boots that had once been Cole's.

"Son of a bitch!"

"Does that mean I can't come in?"

She yanked open the door with her face flushed and her long toes, which she had always considered bony, sticking out from under the light green dress. Johnny held out the biggest bouquet of wildflowers she'd ever seen. She took them and cooled her red cheeks against their earth-scented petals.

"No," she said. "It means I don't have any shoes."

He looked solemnly at her toes, then walked past her into her room. Soon he returned with her corduroys, boots, and shirt. She stood stock still, watching. He strode outside to the wagon and, through the window, she saw him unhitch it from his palomino, take out a box and bring it back in. Then he took the flowers from her hands and laid them on the table. She noticed for the first time that he wore a well-fitted black jacket, creased slacks, and brocade vest, with a silk tie at the neck of his pleated white shirt, that the clothes suited him as well as they would suit any gentleman, a nobleman even, and that he wore them as though he had dressed this way many times before. She did not switch worlds with such grace.

The box he had given her was light, tied with a string. She pulled off the string and lifted the lid. Inside was a hat, an old blue felt hat with a rounded crown and a brim that drooped on one side. She tried to put it on but her hair was piled too high. Johnny reached around her head and pulled out the pins, and his hands sent shivers over her scalp and down her back. He loosened her hair, took the hat and put it on her head. Then he gave her her clothes.

"Your dress is beautiful, but you won't need it where we're going," he said.

So she changed, right there in front of him. She wore no corset and no chemise, but she felt no shame either, though he watched. If he'd looked hungry or embarrassed, the spell would have broken, but he simply watched, and his eyes told her he liked what he saw, with the dress, with the flannel shirt and corduroy trousers, and without either.

They walked outside. He grabbed a sack from the wagon and swung onto the horse. There was no saddle and the frisky horse stood still, for once. Johnny reached down and she took his hand and he drew her up behind him. Then he pulled off his necktie, tossed it into the wagon, and unbuttoned his vest and the top of his pleated white shirt.

Her arms snapped tight around him as the palomino bolted forward. They rode into a stand of aspen behind the cabin and the horse settled into a lope, fast but smooth. Gretel could feel Johnny's body shift with the three-beat motion as they reached the back of the valley and began to climb, slowing to a walk, and with her face near his neck she could breathe in the smell of him. She gripped the horse with her knees and enjoyed the ride up the steep, winding, escarpment trail, from which the sun was already hidden. They topped out on a road that paralleled the railroad tracks, for the moment clear of trains, and continued, the way wider and less steep. She took off the blue felt hat. The sun shone here, golden with the waning day. The wind blew Gretel's loosened hair off her face, and the light felt warm and good.

It took an hour to get from the cabin to Lizardhead Pass. The broad meadow stretched before them, awash in yellow wildflowers. The tiny brook threaded past and mountain peaks still veiled in snow rose all around. The rock formation called the Lizardhead thrust from behind the peaks, and evergreens clustered in the lee of the slopes.

Gretel put the hat back on and slid off the horse. Under her boots the grass was as thick and spongy as in the valley. Johnny hobbled the horse; he said the animal would run off otherwise. As daylight slipped away, he and Gretel rustled up some wood and started a small fire.

"You knew we would come here," she said as he opened his sack.

He shrugged. "Maybe." He took out tin plates and cups, a pan, two T-bone steaks, some mushrooms, and a bottle of red wine. She shook her head, still hardly able to believe what was happening, what she was allowing to happen. The steaks sizzled with the mushrooms, and delicious-smelling smoke rose from the frying pan.

"What would you have done with the meat if we went to the opera?"

"I don't know. Good thing we came here."

She nodded, taking in the last of the sunset, now a pale peach light behind the toothlike peaks.

"Thanks for the hat," she said.

"Sure."

"Where did you get it? It must have a story."

"It does."

"But you don't plan to tell me."

"No, not now."

She sighed. She felt deeply relaxed and happy, the foreboding and the regret having flown off into the mountain wilderness beyond the pass.

"What about you?" she said. "You've never told me your story, either."

He stared beyond the snowy peaks. "That's long and involved, and not all pleasant. You don't want to know."

"Yes, I do."

He was silent for a moment. Finally he said, "Okay. I'm a prince."

"No you're not."

He cocked an eyebrow. She smiled.

"Well, it's partly true. A long time ago my family was titled in Spain." He poured a cup of wine for each of them and raised his. "To the Torreses of Seville, wherever they are now."

She joined the toast. "I thought you were Mexican."

"I am. Or at least I was until I came here."

He cooked the mushrooms in the pan with the steak juice. The sky turned a velvety, cloudless blue dotted with stars, and the evening moisture brought out the fragrance of the meadow grass and wildflowers. A couple of mule deer turned up to graze not far off. Johnny told her a little about his childhood in Mexico, and how he helped his father run the mines when he got old enough. He spoke sparingly of his father, as though discussing a public figure he'd never known personally, and Gretel figured this was how he put distance between himself and a man he probably disliked. He said nothing of his mother, or of any siblings. In fact, he said little more than usual of substance, except that as a youth he'd missed what he recalled of Europe from his early years. Soon after that his words trailed away, and he only stared across the meadow, over peaks whose snow now gave off the faint blue glow of evening.

"I'm sorry," he told her. "I said you wouldn't want to hear it."

"You haven't told me that much. What happened next? Did you go back to Europe?" She sensed that she was prying, but she wanted to know the rest, if he would tell her.

He shrugged and gnawed at the steak bone. "Yeah. I traveled and I played. I got to like opera. It wasn't the way I remembered it, though." He looked at her. "There's no way to go back."

"No?"

"I don't think so. Not if you've really left."

"I wouldn't know. I've never left."

"I don't think you ever will."

"No." She paused, inhaling the moist fragrance. "I'm sorry you had to miss the opera."

"No matter. I wish you could see it, though." He fell silent again, as if working on an idea.

"What?" she demanded finally.

"Maybe you can."

"Can what?"

He stood. "*Sappi chi'io sono innamorato d'una bella dama . . . e son certo che m'ama. La vidi, le parlai: meco al . . . al casino questa notte verra: zitto! Mi pare sentir odor di femmina.*"

She had to laugh.

"You laugh! And it was such a nice perfume, too."

"What are you talking about? Was that Italian?"

"Yes. A line from *Don Giovanni,* spoken by the bad boy himself. No, not spoken, sung. Now wait, I'll sing the next one. Okay?"

"Okay." She laughed again.

"Gretel, I love your laugh."

"That's not the next line. And you didn't sing it."

"I know. *Scusa.*"

He put one hand on his chest and stretched the other toward the stars. He opened his mouth. He was clowning, but serious, too.

"She said, "In English.""

"Wait a minute!"

"How can I enjoy it in Italian?"

"It would've been Italian at the opera house."

"And you would have translated it for me."

"True."

"So?"

"So I've only heard it once in English."

She smiled and shrugged, waiting. After a moment he started singing in a voice that rumbled through her and carried across the

meadow to the wilderness. The mule deer raised their heads, then
returned to grazing.

Señorita! Here are valid statistics
Of his conquests from border to border
In the best alphabetical order.
They are listed from A down to Z,
If you want to, go through them with me.
There in Italy, three hundred and forty—
One hundred in Greece, which is plenty.
Germany's share is two hundred and twenty—
But look at Spain here,
Spain supplied him with a thousand and three.
There are peasants by the dozens,
Here's a queen and all her cousins,
Here's a countess and a duchess
Who have fallen in his clutches—
Ev'ry type of female gender,
Stern or tender, warm or cold,
Plump or slender, young or old . . .
Weak or healthy,
Short or tall—
Don Giovanni loves them all!

She jumped up and clapped. He reached for her, pulled her
against him, and kissed her on the mouth. No one had ever kissed
her before. She pulled away, but not before the muscular warmth of
his body, the rise and fall of his chest, and the gentleness of his mouth
sent a ripple through her depths.

"Johnny—that's the same as Giovanni. Are you like Don
Giovanni?"

He laughed, and she could not help but love the sound: rich and real and even a little wise. "I hope not. He got burned alive by a marble statue."

"Oh."

He still held her, though not so close. Before letting go he kissed her again, on the forehead. "You don't need to be afraid of me," he said. "I will never hurt you."

Not on purpose, she thought, searching his dark, dark eyes.

They sat cross-legged in the fire's small aura. He reached again into his sack, pulled out an orange and gave it to her. She peeled it carefully, showing only a little of the inner fruit at the time. Finished, she pulled it apart, spraying sweet-scented juice over her hand. She gave him a section, which he accepted but did not eat. Instead, he took her hand and sucked tenderly at her fingers, and she felt a smile tug at her lips. Then he let go and popped the orange section into his mouth.

She gave him more and ate some herself.

"Thank you," he said, and smiled.

She thought he had a magnificent smile.

4

Pacific Avenue

He wanted to tell her where he got that hat. And all about Linda, his older sister, and Spain, and why his family left, without Linda. He wanted to tell her more about his life when he'd gone back to Europe, about France and Italy, Vienna and Seville. About the divas after the operas, and the late, late nights, and sleeping through the mornings, and then, later, the search for Linda. He'd never found her, only the hat. He'd found the hat in a trunk in the villa in Mexico when he was twenty and remembered her wearing it, and then he'd gone back to Europe. He wanted to tell Gretel about his mother, who wept when he left, and who made him want to weep for leaving her, and about his father, whom he had come to despise.

But why dredge up the past, even for Gretel? The day after the missed performance of *Don Giovanni,* he raced up the slopes at the east end of Telluride's valley. His legs pounded the earth until he thought his heart and lungs would burst, until he stood gasping atop the mountain, above the Bridal Veil Falls that tumbled to Pandora.

He coughed, years of mine dust unsettled by the climb. He looked down at Telluride and beyond it toward Gretel's valley, and made himself think of Gretel rather than his sister. Last night he had wanted to hold her against him, taste her lips with his tongue, open her man's shirt button by slow button and find what was woman underneath. She had made him wait.

He went to work that night and all that week, fighting the dangerous distraction of thinking about Gretel Coleman while striking a hammer and loading explosives. He succeeded, did his job well, and often added to his work by practicing double-jack drilling with Zachary. They had entered the Fourth of July drilling contest, less than a month away.

In the mornings he dreamed of Gretel, of her body and his, together. He did not so much want to see her again immediately as to think about her. He would see her on Sunday, and if he knew her at all, he knew she would need time to herself after that night on Lizardhead Pass. As did he. He dreamed of the others, too—the women in Europe, the women in New York, the women in Colorado. They all returned to him now, except Rosasharon, the one from Leadville who died. Even in sleep, or maybe especially in sleep, he refused to let her return.

He saw Gretel the following Sunday, and the Sunday after that, for pleasant dinners and light talk. But in the evenings before work he still went with Zachary to Marie's Fallen Idle, or to the dance halls, to drink and gamble and dance, and to follow the girls upstairs.

Marie looked unwell these nights: tired, with some of the glossiness gone from her red hair and a new gauntness to her doll-like face, which was pretty but aging fast. She drank more than she had a year ago, and always from the same bottle, unmarked, which she shared with no one. She also snorted from a tiny metal box, more of a locket, which dangled between her full breasts from a gold chain. Zachary seemed not to see, or else he ignored it. He was gentle and good to Marie, and Johnny often wondered why they had never married. He had heard that Marie used to dress like a man, in the clothes of a drifter who'd gotten her pregnant and married her, only to run off before the baby came. She'd supported her daughter by tending bar at the Fallen Idle back when it was made of logs and mud. After her daughter left Colorado, she'd bought the place and rebuilt it into the brick saloon of today, complete with a fine cherrywood bar and quality liquor. There were no whores and no second floor; Marie treated the barmaids decently and wore dresses now, simple cotton dresses with proper high collars and hems that hid her ankles.

Some days, between enormous dinners at Emma Stotter's boardinghouse and evenings at the Fallen Idle, Johnny saw Gretel. Most days he and Zachary had to practice, now more than ever, and the valley was a long ride. And Gretel did not always welcome him. At times she seemed downright withdrawn, as though shocked at his presence.

She would not kiss him with Zachary there, but she would when they were alone, at least on the days when she wanted to see him. Apparently she had learned that she enjoyed kissing, and being held, and walking arm in arm; it was easier than talking. She wasn't like the whores, who flaunted their bodies, or the north-side ladies, who disguised theirs in Victorian finery and manners, both seeming somehow cheapened and ashamed. No, Gretel was comfortable with her body and spare with her words.

One Sunday Johnny and Gretel climbed three thousand feet above the pass, up to the giant, rearing Lizardhead. When they got beyond the timberline, grasses and flowers splashed the ground, and lichens dotted the rocks. They found an abandoned field of corn, then a field of snow. They threw snowballs at each other, chasing and laughing and rolling in the cold whiteness until their palms were redskinned and dripping with melt. On the way back down they paused to watch a golden eagle swoop behind one of the jagged peaks. They walked on through the tall, thin-spired Engelmann spruce to the meadow below and soaked their feet in the freezing stream, then took off their clothes to lie in the strong mountain sun. They did not touch each other, just watched the clouds puff by. In his mind, Johnny touched her all over, and for once was pleased she looked at the sky instead of at him.

"There is no place like this," she murmured, drowsy.

"None," he agreed, and realized he had become attached, not only to her but to the place, to the valley and the pass and even Telluride. He had stayed with Braunn Mining much longer than his usual four months, with hardly a thought of leaving. He thought of it now, lying next to the only woman he'd ever known who would take off all her clothes right in front of him on their first night alone without flinching, and yet hardly bare herself at all. He realized, too, that he was coming to love her.

He rolled to his side and studied her face, freckled and golden brown. She looked at him and smiled, then laughed a little, a private laugh. She reached out to wind her agile fingers through the coarse black hair on his chest. He leaned over and kissed her, long and deep. His hand traced the curve of her hip, the dip of her waist. She covered it gently with her own, to hold it still. He wanted more. But she only kissed him again, quickly, and then she got up. The late-afternoon sun lighted the curves and shadowed the hollows of her body. Inwardly, Johnny sighed.

"One of these days we'll give the Southern a show," she said as they heard the train top the escarpment and chug toward them. It was still a fair distance off; they dressed without haste, and walked away.

The Fourth of July in Telluride was one of only two holidays the miners got—that and Christmas. Less than a week remained. Johnny and Zachary had increased their number of strokes per minute with the double-jack hammer to sixty and sixty-one. They still tried for sixty-two, but had not made it. Sixty was probably as good as any team could hope for; most would strike more like fifty-eight. They used Zachary's hammer, which weighed exactly the nine-pound maximum, with a well-seasoned, long-grained hickory handle and a narrow face like Johnny's dago.

They planned to sharpen and temper their drill steel themselves, at the Bonne Chance. Each drill team would have fifteen minutes, and during that time most would use fifteen steel of lengths increasing by three inches. Johnny and Zachary decided to prepare twenty steel, each two and a half inches longer than the former, with ten extras on five-inch changes in case one of the twenty chipped a bit or broke an ear.

On July 3, the first of three days off, they rode to the valley for dinner with Gretel. Over fresh-baked wheat bread, home-grown peas, and the possum that was Zachary's favorite, Zachary told Johnny he thought they had a good chance to beat Buck Daunt and his friend MacMurray, longtime champions. Johnny had noticed that Zachary was slimmer at the belt and more enthusiastic than he'd ever seen him, but then Johnny had gotten to Telluride after last year's Fourth.

"He always get this whipped up?" he asked Gretel.

She seemed faintly disdainful today, as though she'd rather be alone. "No, not this much."

"Our chances are better this year," Zachary said, enjoying Gretel's beer and wolfing down twice as much possum as Johnny. Normally Johnny beat him out for appetite, but not today.

"The hardest part will be sleeping," Johnny said. "I don't remember the last time I slept in the dark."

Zachary laughed. "You won't get much sleep tonight, unless you stay here—" He stopped, reddened, then waved his hand, laughed it off, and downed the last half-mugful of beer.

"Don't worry, Gretel," he said, already a little drunk. "I'm not dropping him at your doorstep."

"You did that a long time ago," she responded, with an attempt to smile at Johnny, and got up to clear the table.

"You coming to town tomorrow?" Zachary asked her.

"No. I hate the Fourth."

Johnny took a deep breath. He should've known. Should've known her at least that well by now. But it would have been nice if once in a great while she'd compromise on something, particularly something for him. He left soon after that, with Zachary. He'd thought of staying, but he wanted to drink and dance and could only do it in town. From what he could tell, Gretel hardly seemed sad to see them go.

As sunset streaked the sky, the men stopped at Emma's for Johnny's gun. Zachary said he had never owned a six-gun, and that this was the only time of year he wanted one. People had already begun shooting off fireworks, or firing shots into the air; these holidays could get a little rough. Johnny had not worn his Colt in town for months, and it hung heavy against his left hip. Sometimes when he went into the wilderness on foot and didn't feel like lugging his Winchester, he took the Colt and shot small game for Emma. He had to hit his quarry in the head or there wasn't much meat left.

Emma was doing her best to keep her sons in for the evening, but she fought a losing battle. Johnny and Zachary hid their grins and headed for Pacific Avenue to join a packed crowd at the Fallen Idle. A dark-haired girl greeted Johnny warmly while Zachary went to find Marie. The girl's name was Elizabeth, and he had taken her out for buggy rides a time or two. He had never slept with her, though one afternoon they'd come close. Now he wondered what she was doing after work, and then he thought that would be at least 4:00 A.M., and he needed several hours' sleep before the festivities began at dawn.

He thought about Gretel, not with any guilt, simply wondering over his first whiskey when she would give him enough of herself to make him give up seeing other women.

Zachary found him at a table with Elizabeth and said Marie had gone home, sick.

"Want me to go to her place with you?" Johnny asked him.

"Naw. They say it's just a bad cold. Girls been taking her soup and such but she wanted to sleep. I'll check on her and then maybe I'll be back. Don't drink too much."

Johnny nodded and said good-bye to Zachary by downing his whiskey. If they wanted to win this contest tomorrow he couldn't get drunk. He hardly ever got drunk anyway, though he did like the warmth of a good bottle. Zachary was the one who got drunk, probably more than he should but never on the job.

After Zachary left, Elizabeth put her hand on Johnny's upper arm and squeezed.

"What's that for?" he asked.

"Just seeing if you've got enough muscle to win. I have to decide whether to bet on you or Daunt and MacMurray."

He laughed. MacMurray was the day-shift boss at the Flossie, a huge, ruddy Scotsman with giant hands and a reputation as the best double-jack man in the San Juans. Daunt had a whole hard-rock crew's strength coiled in his wiry body. But Johnny felt lucky. He'd already pulled most of his sizable stake from last year's cave-in out of the bank and put it on himself and Zachary. The odds were close to even, so he stood to make a fortune if they won.

"Put it on us," he told her. "That'll get us up to sixty-two strokes."

"No one's ever gone over sixty."

He thought of the ten-ton block of granite sitting on the high platform built in the middle of Colorado Avenue for this event. The platform resembled a gallows at first glance, but then there was the granite, its once weathered face chiseled smooth by an expert stonecutter.

"We'll do sixty-one, anyway."

She got him a second drink and a cigar, then left to serve the other customers. Most of the men were miners and no women except the barmaids dared visit the saloons. Some of the men and all the girls stopped at the table to wish him luck. A bunch of Scandinavians sat down to talk and play a game of stud for a while. Johnny drew several bad hands and threw it in, hoping this was no omen for the contest. After an hour he left, and when he got outside in the noisy street he ditched his cigar in favor of the clean, crisp night air. Through the shouts and popping fireworks he could hear a group of Cornishmen singing. It made him think of London, which he'd only visited once, and how different life there was from here, though really no better or worse, and certainly no cleaner.

He strolled over the less crowded side streets toward Colorado Avenue and stopped on the boardwalk beneath the merchants' signs to stare at the platform with its giant, square monument of granite. Vermont black, hauled in on the Southern. The hardest anywhere, much harder than what he drilled in the Bonne Chance. How strange it would feel to swing a hammer with the sun beating his bare back, in front of thousands of onlookers, while Zachary turned the steel, switching off every couple of minutes, and all this with Buck Daunt and MacMurray next to them. He wondered what Daunt would do if he lost.

He walked slowly back along the boards to Pacific Avenue, then a couple of blocks along Pacific to Spruce and through the wide, swinging doors of a dance hall called the Senate. The noise hit him like a blow to the face. Big Billy, the oversized proprietress, who was popular with everyone in town, even the ladies on the north side, took him in hand at the bar, demanding the first dance before he lifted his first drink. She danced lightly for such a fat lady and laughed heartily as he whirled her through the smoke and stomping bodies. He'd been here many times, and she always cheered him up.

"Who you want tonight, Johnny?" she asked when the song ended, mopping her brow with a lacy handkerchief. "Anyone you want, she's yours. I and most of my girls got money on you boys."

He smiled. "I don't know yet, Billy. Maybe no one. I can't swing that hammer if I'm half asleep."

She nodded slyly. "Sure you can." And left him to dance with her girls while she caught her breath behind the bar.

Dancing worked him into a better mood and worked off most of the whiskey. He danced for a long time. Big Billy had added a couple of horns from the Telluride Cornet Band to her usual piano professor, plus a fiddle, and the odd mix of instruments blasted its way through everything from barroom stomps and Virginia reels to polkas and waltzes. The girls disappeared upstairs one by one, leading a miner or shopkeeper or young laborer by the hand. The men stumbled on the stairs, drunk, only to return in a half hour or so, their shirts carelessly stuffed into their pants, their suspenders twisted. They smiled, satisfied for the moment. The girls left them for the dance floor; they all danced with Johnny and they all invited him upstairs, but even when the whiskey the girls brought him (on the house, they all said) started to outpace the dancing, he turned them down. He liked the feel of their tight, satiny costumes under his hands, the way their corsets shoved their breasts toward his chest, the rub of their stockinged legs, but he said no. Tonight of all nights he could have said yes, he even should have, seeing as how Gretel hardly wanted him around and they owed each other no fidelity. But he said no, and as the night deepened he saw through the haze brought on by drink a mystified look coming into the girls' eyes, followed by a more knowing look and a slow shake of their curly-haired heads.

The band took a break finally, and Johnny rested his elbows on the polished wood of the bar. Big Billy was serving. She threw him the smile of an actress playing temptress, only kidding. She reached under the bar and came up with a bottle of deep amber whiskey, uncorked it, and poured a glass for him and another for herself.

"To winning," she said.

Johnny clinked his glass against hers and downed the toast, which was fine stuff. She left him the bottle and he poured some for the men on either side, who were too far gone to notice the quality.

The noise had numbed his ears: men gambling, shouting or singing many songs at once, and swearing drunkenly in loud voices. He was used to noise from the mine and blocked it out. But after a while a couple of voices penetrated. He heard a phrase or two and began to listen, filtering the words from the din. At first he thought they just talked, then he realized they talked about him. He went on drinking.

"Seems to me a man oughtta have a whore every now and then." The voice was deep, slurred, unfamiliar. "Gets all bound up if he don't, then can't enjoy hisself at all."

"'Specially them Mexicans. Hell, y'all ever seen a chili pepper with less than two *señoritas?* Must take a lot to keep them boys in practice."

A volley of fireworks from outside blocked the next words, then one of the men guffawed. "Maybe they don't like the girls. Shit, maybe they's all like them funny fellas we heard about that run the opera. Them fellas with no balls."

Johnny noticed that the other men around him, even drunk, had quieted and were watching. He turned to lean back against the bar, his right boot resting on the footrail that ran along the floor behind him, his left leg straight. By their clothes he figured these two for miners; he thought he had seen them asking for work, and would bet it rankled them that they were jobless while a Mexican earned a steady wage at the Bonne Chance. It looked like they'd bought a shave and a bath for the holiday, but already the dance hall's heat and the sweat of liquor and dancing, and maybe nerves, had carried their odor over the smoke.

"No what?" said Johnny.

The one man's face broadened into a jeering smile. He was older than the other, with gray in his dirt-colored, slicked hair. "Oh, Torres. We was just talking about you, sort of. Maybe you could clear up something for us, you being so innerested in opera. You do like opera, right?" He leaned forward, his breath foul with liquor and bad teeth.

"I like it all right," said Johnny.

The two men traded grins. Then the older one said, "Them boys over yonder really got no balls?"

"Over yonder?"

"You know," said the younger one, who could've been the other's son, from the looks. "Over to them places where we get these singers from."

Johnny knew he should get this over with and leave. He realized as the mild drunkenness drained from his mind that he was angry about Gretel, that he'd like nothing more than a good fight. But he also thought of Zachary and of the contest tomorrow.

They roared with laughter, their faces red. Some of the other men joined the laughter; they were too drunk to know what was going on. Johnny felt a body behind him and smelled strong perfume, and knew Big Billy would rather he ended this while he could.

"What about you, Torres?"

He let the old man have it in the nose. The man flipped back over tables to land dazed amid a game of faro. The roar died for a second and Johnny saw someone duck out the door. He was ready for the younger one to attack, but instead his eyes got big and his red, freshly shaven throat rose and fell as he swallowed.

"Shit," he said. "Why'd y'all have to do that? We was only funning."

Johnny shrugged. "Just answering his question."

The man's face deepened a shade. His jaw worked and his fingers twitched. Both he and the other wore handguns. He looked from Johnny's face to the Colt hanging along his straight left leg and the hand that, though relaxed, hung near it.

"Next time, Torres."

With his right hand, Johnny touched his forehead in a mock salute. The kid backed off and picked up his father, or whoever the old man was. He slapped the man's bleeding face a couple of times and the man groaned his way awake. The other drinkers had written it off and gone back to their games or girls or drink, and the band had begun to tune up. Johnny felt Billy pat him on the shoulder, but he kept watching as the young man dragged the old man to his feet. The old man wiped off some of the blood that dripped into his mouth from his smashed nose. He seemed able to walk on his own, and they both made for the door. Johnny scanned the place for further signs of trouble, found none, and turned to the bar to order another drink. Maybe now he would take one of the girls upstairs.

He glanced around. Out of the corner of his eye he saw the dance hall doors swing open and two men walk in. Then he heard Big Billy's voice, though she had to shriek his name twice before he understood.

He wheeled and drew and the heel of his right hand crashed down on the Colt's hammer. The gun bucked once, and again. The two men who'd just walked in lurched backward. One flew through the door, the other hit the door frame and spun before dropping.

The bar was suddenly silent. Men and women craned their necks to see the dead miners, the old one and the young one who had smelled of liquor and dance and maybe nerves. Johnny stood still and closed his eyes. In his hand the gun felt heavy and dead. He opened his eyes, holstered the gun. The people began to whisper, then to babble. He'd never seen those two men draw; he'd heard it in Billy's voice. Now the acrid stench of gunpowder mingled with that of beer and blood.

Johnny took a step forward, and another: his legs were firm beneath him. He walked to the door, glanced at the body inside it, held the door open and glanced at the other one. The younger man was inside and the older outside. Johnny walked back to the bar. Big Billy stared at him through narrowed eyes, her lips pursed, her chubby hands on her broad hips.

"Sorry, Billy," Johnny told her. He needed a drink but saw she had removed the bottle, probably before the fight to keep it from getting broken. She pulled it out again and poured him a long one.

"Somebody better go for the marshal, if they haven't already," he said.

"They have."

"We should leave the bodies until he gets here."

Billy nodded toward the door and Johnny turned to see the marshal shoving his way through. Like Johnny he glanced at the bodies, then stepped over them, not bothering to check for a pulse. His name was Luke Halloran. He was gaunt, slope-shouldered, and chinless, with a young face scarred by acne, an uncooperative shock of hair the color of barn straw, and hazel eyes that searched the room in a hard, flat way before coming to rest on Johnny. He was nervy enough and good with a gun, but maybe corrupt, too. Supposedly the mayor and most of the town trustees wouldn't have minded replacing him, if anyone would take the job.

Halloran worked a chaw inside his left cheek; it formed a bulge as large as the hollow in the right cheek was deep, so that his face appeared shoved to one side. He questioned several men, then sought one of Billy's brass spittoons. Finally, he walked up to Johnny.

"Nice shooting," he said. He had to shout, because the band had started up again and a roomful of booted feet banged against the wood floor.

Johnny said nothing. Billy poured a drink for herself and downed it. She could have told Halloran it was self-defense, but instead she set down her glass and wiped her rubied lips in silence. Johnny and the marshal jostled through the crowd and stepped over the bodies to the street, where things were marginally quieter.

"I've got to take you in, Torres."

"Why?"

"You just killed two men, that's why. No two people in there are telling the same story, and I need time to straighten it out. Besides which the whole town is exploding and I ain't got the patience to clear this up tonight. You think you might come with me or do I need a posse?"

"You saw their guns."

"Yeah, they never fired a shot and you fired two."

Johnny could tell he'd get nowhere this way. He could also tell the marshal believed him. "I'll be around in the morning," he said. "I can go back to Emma Stotter's now, talk to you tomorrow before the contest." He did not feel tired, but he'd rather go to Emma's and get some sleep than spend the night behind bars with drunks puking all over him.

"Unh-unh. The way some of the men in there are talking, you might not be around in an hour. You might be a hero with a hammer, Johnny, but when it comes right down to it this town ain't real partial to Mexicans." He sprayed the dirt with tobacco juice. "Damn, but I hate these nights when everybody has to wear a gun."

"I can defend myself."

"That's what worries me. You coming or not?"

"The jail have more than one cell?"

Halloran smiled. "Of course. You can have a clean one all to yourself, long as the drunks don't overflow. I'll even give you my pillow."

Soon after dawn a powder blast rocked Telluride, laying spurs to the day's festivities, and Johnny waited, wide awake, impatient to get away from the rancid drunks who, of course, had overflowed. An hour later Luke Halloran dragged in, bleary-eyed and pale, though not from drink. Word had it he never drank. Maybe dope, or just too many women. He would not have worked all night; the deputies had brought in the drunks.

Buck Daunt followed Halloran. He stood in front of Johnny with the bars between them, his sinewy arms folded across his chest and his thin lips stretched into a grin. Like the marshal, he had a chaw in his cheek.

"How are me and Mac gonna beat you today if you're in jail?" Daunt drawled. "I heard you're one hell of a shot, buck." He turned to Halloran. "You gonna let him out or not?"

Halloran looked from the super to Johnny. "Why'd you have to shoot those boys?" he asked.

"Why do you think?"

"Come on, Luke," said Daunt. "You don't care that he killed those men, you just hate having to get up so early. Charges dropped?"

Halloran's acne-scarred cheeks stretched with a yawn as he unlocked the door. Johnny took his gun and walked outside with Daunt. After the dim jail, he had to squint at the sunlight that spilled over the mountains into the street. Silhouetted against the light, the mountains looked black and forbidding. They walked over to Colorado Avenue, where Daunt stopped in front of the platform with the ten-ton block of granite and spewed a stream of brown juice at the platform's base.

"Where'd you learn to shoot like that?" he asked.

"I'm a miner, not a shootist."

Daunt's jaw jutted stubbornly and he snorted through his kinked nose. "You're a blaster," he said. "You may be good with a single-jack, but I've never seen anyone handle powder the way you do."

"Yeah, so?"

Daunt lifted his sweat-scarred hat to scratch his wire-haired scalp. "So I'm moving you to the Flossie. Want you to take over as night-shift boss there, but keep your hands dirty, too, like your buddy Zachary. Too much highgrading in that old whore. I want it stopped." Highgrading meant stealing high-grade ore, a common enough practice but one that could bankrupt an operation whose mines were playing out, like the Flossie.

"Maybe, but I can't stop it for you."

Lightning flickered in Daunt's dark eyes. "Sure you can. Just by being there."

"I've heard they don't like Mexicans."

"That don't bother you and you know it. Flossie or nothing, Johnny."

"Nothing, then."

Daunt smashed a platform post with his two-fingered left fist. The whites of his eyes showed all the way around the dark irises, and his voice rose in a screeching curse.

"That's just what you'll get," he screamed. "Nothing. Not even from the goddamned contest, because I can have you back in that jail before you draw your next breath. Who the hell you think paid to get you out?"

Men had begun to stagger into the light for the day's first event, a parade, and children scampered in the summer sunshine, raising dust puffs from the street, shepherded by women. Dogs gathered to forage where trash heaps remained from the night's revelry. The people and even the dogs had grown used to Daunt's rages; they barely turned a head.

Johnny knew the super wanted him in that mine precisely because they didn't like Mexicans. His presence could bring the trouble to a head, and someone might get hurt. But someone might anyway, and he had an idea.

"Take it easy, Buck," he said. "You make it worth my while, maybe I'll take your offer. Give me five percent of the Bonne Chance's profits."

It must have been a revolutionary proposal, because Daunt calmed right down. "I'll have to cable Heinrich Braunn," he said.

"Do it, then."

Again the lightning: volatile. Anything could happen with this man, and Johnny wondered if he should just draw his time and go to work for the Sheridan or the Smuggler-Union. But Daunt stopped short of anger, this time, and instead glanced at Johnny's gun with a slow smile cracking his hawkish face. Johnny figured he might as well take the job if it meant getting rich off the Bonne Chance. It was the first time anyone had ever bought his shooting arm, though, and inside he felt uneasy. Then he heard Zachary's voice booming along Colorado Avenue, and saw his former shift boss ambling toward them with a fat melon in each hand.

"Hey Johnny, what the hell happened?" Zachary demanded. "I'm looking all over town for you, then Big Billy tells me you're in jail. What you been doing?"

"Getting promoted," Daunt shouted back, and Zachary joined the two men with his grin fading fast.

5

The Fourth of July

She stood among the packed, pushing crowd on Colorado Avenue and wanted to strip off her heavy clothes. Sweltering, suffocating, she wanted to run; running would cool her, even with her heart pounding.

People hemmed her in on all sides. Most of all, she wanted to cover her nose against the odor of so many bodies, against the dust disturbed by their shuffling feet; they had no room to truly move. Only the children could make any headway through the crowd, and they darted in and out among thousands of trousered or skirted legs, playing tag, giggling shrilly, some picking pockets. Gretel had nothing in her pockets. She'd brought an apple and a hunk of black bread in a small sack tied at her waist, but the smell and feel of bodies baked by the beating summer sun left her too queasy to eat.

She looked out from under the brim of her blue felt hat at the block of black granite sitting in the middle of the platform in the middle of the street, rising out of a sea of upturned faces. The granite

64

looked like an oversized grave marker. No one pounded it; the mayor stood in front of it, wearing a suit and tie, of all things, and mopping his brow after every ponderous sentence. He tried to be funny, but only the politest onlookers laughed. Then he tried to raise a cheer for Telluride, which drew a better response.

Gretel wished she'd stayed home. Never mind the look on Johnny's face and that long, slow breath he took when she'd said she wouldn't come. Never mind how after he'd left, she'd walked slowly through the meadow, watched the sunset, thought about him, and her. He was waiting, she knew, and probably wouldn't wait much longer. But still, she wished she could have stayed home.

The mayor finished his speech, mopped his dripping brow one last time, and left the podium to climb down the steps, leaning heavily on the railing. Another important-looking man, probably a mine owner, hauled up his lanky form and announced the start of the drilling contest, which raised the biggest cheer yet from the crowd.

Zachary had said that he and Johnny were scheduled near the end, and Gretel could not stand waiting in the heat. She attempted to escape, find some fresh air, but found all avenues blocked. She waited until the first teams set up their steel and hoses. The crowd jostled closer and the shift allowed her to slip through to the boardwalk, though where she'd find fresh air within Telluride's confines she could not imagine.

She walked the south-side streets away from Colorado Avenue; she could have walked the north side, where the ladies bought her weavings, but she went south. She walked past Emma Stotter's boardinghouse to the edge of town, where the mountain loomed. The trail to the Bonne Chance and the Flossie began somewhere nearby, but she had no desire to go there and anyway she needed to keep an ear on the contest. She turned back toward Pacific Avenue, back along the boardwalk, and wrinkled her nose at the stench of beer and vomit that had seeped through the cracks in the wee hours.

As Gretel walked she heard the metallic sound of hammers striking steel, men's voices shouting the number of strokes per minute, the rising chant of the crowd counting down the time. She also heard singing, which sounded Cornish or maybe Irish, and children laughing, and dogs barking. The dogs rooted through the garbage behind the saloons and dance halls and restaurants, occasionally snarling at each other over a choice bit but mostly gorging themselves: there was plenty to go around.

The number of people away from Colorado Avenue surprised and frustrated her. Some were having tug-of-wars, others playing pick-up games of baseball in the street, most milling around, stopping to talk to each other, ducking into the bars. Why wasn't everyone watching the contest? She kept getting jostled, and though the men tipped their hats in apology, she could not bear it. She decided to visit Emma's. She liked Emma, and maybe the landlady would let her rest in Zachary's room. It would probably be improper to ask to stay in Johnny's, though she would like to see how he lived.

On Pine Street, she entered the tidy house. Heavy drapes preserved a cool quiet that muffled the noise from the contest. Gretel found Emma in the kitchen, kneading bread, her arms white with flour to the elbows and her gray hair straying from its bun.

"Want some help?" Gretel asked, after exchanging hellos.

"Sure. Here's a loaf."

Gretel took it, patted it with flour, and began to knead.

"You came in for the contest?" Emma asked.

"Johnny seemed to want me to."

"John Torres?" Emma's cheeks colored a bit. She was a sensitive woman, of high principles. It would embarrass her to discuss Gretel's relations with a man, especially one of her boarders.

Gretel said no more.

"It's awfully hot out there," noted Emma, giving her loaf a final pat and starting another.

"I can't stand the crowd."

"I can't stand the drilling. The sound bothers me."

Gretel nodded, took another loaf herself.

"But I hope the men do well," Emma added. "I hope John's nerves hold up all right. And Zachary's. I hear his friend Miss DuBois is ill."

Gretel's hand stopped moving. "Very ill?"

"No, just a cold. But I don't think she's a well person. She has not looked well."

Gretel wanted to ask what might have affected Johnny, but apparently Emma thought she would already know. Her way of calling him John sounded foreign, like they were talking about two different people. They went on kneading for a while.

"I'm sure they'll do fine," Emma said. "They've practiced every day. Maybe last night's incident will help. I don't know. Men respond differently than we do to things like that."

"Things like what?"

Emma looked at her and away, coloring again.

"It's not important." Her voice faltered and she cleared her throat. "I'm sure it won't matter."

Gretel wanted to ask more but Emma's color remained and she did not want to press the woman, who clearly thought she had hinted at a secret better disclosed by someone else.

"Do you know how many there will be before Johnny and my father compete?" Gretel asked instead.

"Quite a few, I'm sure. Would you like to sit and read in the parlor? I ordered a wonderful book by Charles Dickens. It's there on the side table by the settee. Help yourself."

"Thank you. After these loaves."

They finished the last loaves in silence, though Emma hummed every now and then, only to realize it and stop. She had a soothing low voice, and Gretel wished she would keep on: anything to cover the street noises that filtered through the drapes. After a half hour she settled herself with the book, a long one called *Bleak House,* and tried to read. Emma busied herself upstairs, cleaning. Thumping noises and the snap of fresh sheets mingled with the distant pounding of the drill teams. Gretel found her eyes slipping shut and finally leaned her head against the back of the chair, where one of her tapestries hid a worn spot, and gave in to a nap with the book resting open on her lap.

A thunderous cheer brought her awake and she leapt up, dropping the book.

"Oh my goodness!" said Emma, startled by Gretel's sudden movement.

Gretel blinked a few times and saw that Emma had been dusting the table by the chair. Gretel picked up the book, inspected it for damage, found none, and laid it carefully on the dusted table.

"I was about to wake you. They've just announced your father and John."

Gretel made it back to Colorado Avenue in a hurry but could not penetrate the crowd, which was thicker, noisier, and hotter than ever. She balanced on a hitching rail in front of the boardwalk, holding a signpost for support. Buck and MacMurray stood on the platform, shirtless, along with two other men, who from this distance at first appeared unfamiliar. Johnny and Zachary had shaved off their beards. Zachary had not done that in years and she had never seen Johnny without one. Their faces were paler on the lower half than on the upper, as though their beards had changed color. They shook hands with their rivals and got ready to drill. Hoses squirted water on the granite block to clean the mud from the holes. Drill steel were laid out next to the teams.

Zachary and Buck, respectively, started off holding the steel, which they would have to turn carefully and point just so, while

Johnny and MacMurray hefted the heavy double-jack hammers. The teams would go for fifteen minutes, head to head.

The official fired the starting gun and the strikers began swinging. Their hammers smashed against the steel with a ringing crash that sent out a small spray of muddy water. The blows traveled through the ground and up along the hitching rail into Gretel's legs, like an electric current. A man next to each team called the number of swings after each minute: sixty, sixty, one minute down, with Johnny and MacMurray swinging in unison. Sixty-one, fifty-nine, two minutes down, with Johnny leading. The sun glistened off Johnny's dark back and shoulders, and off MacMurray's paler skin. MacMurray was taller and broader, but older, too, by a good fifteen years. His hair, gray streaked with white, soon darkened with moisture; three minutes down, and Johnny's hair hung wet and black against the back of his neck.

The teams switched off. Zachary and Buck took the hammers. Four minutes, five, six. Buck hit two sixty-ones and a fifty-nine. Zachary hit three sixties, but his blows sounded more true, if Gretel heard them right. The sound echoed off the buildings, rang in her ears. She realized as the teams switched again that the crowd had hushed, straining to see. Then, over the striking and the bellowing callers, Gretel heard men talking in low tones behind her. She heard Johnny's name, which came as no surprise, but she heard something else, too, something about a shooting. She turned her head partway to listen.

"He's about as fast as anyone we've had here. Plugged those boys like nothing."

"Yeah, but wasn't it self-defense? They were about to shoot him in the back, I heard."

"Self-defense, hell. Why'd Buck Daunt have to pay his way out of jail this morning if it were self-defense? Tell me that."

The crowd roared and Gretel missed the next words. She returned her attention to the platform.

"Sixty-two!" she heard an excited child shout. "No one's ever hit sixty-two!"

"Sixty-two!" bellowed the man calling Johnny's numbers.

Johnny's whole body swung with the hammer. It had become part of his arms—a rock-hard hickory handle growing from thick muscle and glistening skin. Sweat poured off his back and chest to darken the waistline of his pants. He had a red bandana tied around his head to keep the moisture from getting into his eyes. The caller must have tied it there, because none of the drillers had stopped moving.

"Keep going!" Gretel heard her father yell, and when Buck and MacMurray switched off Johnny continued to drill. The crowd hollered. Some of the men raised a fist in approval.

"Sixty-two!"

But she could see the heat and the extra round of striking take their toll. The next minute he only made sixty, which was as much as any man ever made before, and then he and Zachary switched. She saw the quick flash of his white teeth as he and her father traded grins.

Eleven minutes down, four to go. Zachary hit sixty-one this time, but so did MacMurray, then they both hit sixty, and it was Johnny and Buck to finish up. The number of strokes was not everything: the striker had to strike with respect for the steel, and he had to strike accurately. The turner had to hold the steel steady against terrible blows and turn it perfectly, and all the while ignore the possibility of losing a hand should the striker miss. And the bits and steel had to be tempered and sharpened to perfection.

"Sixty-one!" the callers hollered in unison.

Sixty seconds. Johnny's back tightened. His dripping arms moved a fraction faster. His chest heaved. The blows rang louder, dissonant with those of Buck Daunt, whose wiry body jerked so fast it was hard to pick up his motion. Gretel watched Johnny, anyway. And counted the seconds: thirty, twenty, ten, five, four, three, two—

"Sixty-two!"

"Sixty!"

The sixty-two was Johnny's.

The gun went off and both strikers held their hammers over their shoulders, their arms quivering as they fought to stop the next blow. They succeeded, and lowered the hammers. Zachary jumped up and pumped Johnny's hand. The crowd hollered some more, then quieted as the official slid the measuring rod into the holes, one after the other. He said something to the teams. Gretel saw Buck Daunt snort and thrust a pointing finger at the holes. The official stuck the rod in again, pulled it out and shrugged. Apparently the numbers stood. Daunt started to flare a second time but the official spoke to him and he calmed down. Gretel could see the looks that passed between the two teams, and the animosity worried her.

"He drills as well as he shoots," said one of the two men on the boardwalk behind her.

The official announced the results: Johnny and Zachary by a quarter inch. Both scores destroyed the previous record, the official told the crowd, whose roar rose, deafening.

Gretel watched, neither clapping nor yelling. The teams shook hands, Buck grudgingly, and the losers headed down the steps. Buck called a parting shot over his shoulder but no one could've possibly heard it. Zachary grabbed the hose and sprayed water over Johnny's already soaked head, then over his own and down his throat. Johnny whooped and leapt into the air, laughing, clasping Zachary's hand and holding it high. Whatever had happened last night hardly seemed to bother him now, and that bothered Gretel.

She had to find out. The men behind her still cheered wildly; no use asking them. Instead, she shoved her way along the boardwalk to Emma's and hurried inside. No sign of Emma. She ran upstairs. Still no sign. From a back room she looked down into the yard to see Emma hanging out wash. She ran downstairs and outside.

"Emma!"

"What is it? Did they win? They must have won."

"No. I mean yes. They won."

"Oh, that's—"

"Listen. Please." She managed to catch her breath. She could still hear the crowd roaring and wanted to press her palms to her ears. More, she wanted to run from the festering town this instant, never mind whatever Johnny had done last night. But an old anger, or maybe an old wound, drove her to ask. Cole. After she found out she could run, as far as she wanted.

"I heard some men talking," she went on, hearing not the woman she had become, but the voice of the nine-year-old girl she thought she had banished. "About Johnny. About a shooting. Emma, you have to tell me. What happened? Please. What happened?"

6

Hired Guns

She had her knife. She always carried it, had learned long since, as a girl, how to throw it, to defend herself with it. She needed no other weapon and her traps provided enough food. The Sharps carbine remained at home, and she'd be damned if she'd ever carry it or any other gun again. Carbine, pistol, shotgun; it did not matter. They all shot bullets. They all killed. They all defined who a man was in this land, no matter what else he could do or how well he could do it. The gun ruled, even now, even in 1892. Even these San Juan Mountains, once inaccessible to all but the hardiest (or most fool-hardy) because of winter snows that could fall as late as July, once hostile with Utes (no wonder they fought the white man's ways), once thought bare of the treasure that finally lured the westbound tide past all other obstacles: even these San Juans had become civilized to the point where a man should no longer need to prove himself with a gun. Opera. Electricity. So civilized that Heinrich Braunn deigned to spend his summers here, had nearly completed building the lordly stone castle that towered over the mesa, and over Gretel's valley. So civilized, or so she had thought.

Reaching a spot where the slope above the valley leveled a bit, Gretel peered through the trees at the first of her string of snares and saw a length of limp fur: a rabbit, a good dinner, if she could eat. Of course she could eat. Nothing had changed for her. Today had only reminded her of that, and the disappointment must fade. She could deal with it as before: her valley, her cabin, her pass, her garden, her loom—her father. Well, perhaps her father had changed a little, with his new friend, his new drilling partner, this man who killed. He looked so different now with those long, aromatic cigars in his teeth. He might have changed, but then again, once he finished the cigars he was still Zachary: no gun, no greed, no pretenses.

She could lay traps and throw a knife as well as anyone. She could do without the gun. She would never fire it again. She reset the trap, picked up the rabbit, and started toward home.

From the escarpment she could see that the Braunn mansion had a roof now; during the last few weeks she had not heard as much banging, so the men must have been working inside. Last summer the decorator had begun asking Gretel for counterpanes and tapestries, an endless supply of them, and recently his orders had doubled. He came by the cabin every few weeks with generous payments and carted her work off to the mansion. She did the work, but was offended by the acquisitiveness, and the wealth that paid for it. She had no desire to ever set foot in the place.

"Why can't they get along with what they've got?" she said aloud, forcing her gaze from the mansion, descending the escarpment.

A train lurched past as she walked along the South Fork of the San Miguel, through the woods behind the cabin. She tried to focus on the trees and the clean, uncluttered dryness of the air. After the train passed, Gretel stopped several times and listened to the stillness, to the shrill song of a locust, the startled cry of a jay as it lifted from a branch. The rabbit hung heavy and warm from her hand: life feeding life, not like the men who lived off death.

It was dusk when she walked out of the woods and around to the front of the cabin. The air stirred, fragrant as always here, and she sniffed at the scent of the flowered meadow. She sighed, and then she saw Johnny, and froze. He sat on the doorstep, his head tilted back, as though waiting for the moon to rise, but his eyes were closed. His knees were drawn up and his arms rested on them, hands dangling, relaxed.

He opened his eyes and looked at her. Even in the dimming light, she could see how tired he was.

"Town is too noisy," he said.

She stood silently, the rabbit hanging. Finally she turned and walked off, to the back of the cabin, sat and pulled out her knife and butchered her game. She worked slowly, carefully: she could barely see. He did not follow, did not call, did not pester her. She thought he had gone. But when she returned to the front of the cabin she saw him there, his head tilted back, his eyes closed. This time he did not wake up, or not so she could see. She could not get into the cabin without opening the door and letting him fall backward into her home, so she went away again, made a fire, cooked the rabbit and ate. Finally she got up and stalked around front to tell him to get lost, but he was gone.

Now she was mad he was gone. She yanked open the cabin door and stomped inside, hauled off her boots, snatched up a tapestry frame. Jewel-colored yarns hung in a seeming snarl from the piece, but she could put them in order, make them beautiful. She took the tapestry to the settee and found Johnny there, sleeping, breathing slowly and quietly.

She made her voice hard. "Johnny Torres, wake up. You can't sleep here."

He stirred.

"Wake up. Now."

He raised his head and then his body, with a groan. He was barefoot, like her, his boots beside the settee.

"What do you think you're doing?" she snapped. "You can't sleep here."

He stared at her for a moment. She saw he was more alert than his half-closed eyes would indicate. He was not looking at her to figure out what she meant, but to figure out why she meant it.

"We won," he said in his tempered Spanish accent. "Your father and I. You should have seen it, although I guess you would have passed out from the crowd."

She held the tapestry in front of her like a shield.

He shrugged and stood up. "I would have liked it if you were there. But you knew that already. I was hoping we could celebrate together, here where it's quiet. Now I don't know what more to say to you."

"What more do you want to say?"

He shook his head, ran a hand through his hair, which she realized was clean and trimmed. He must have bathed, too, or else she would have smelled the contest sweat a mile off.

"Do you know how I feel about you?" he asked. "Or are you walled off from that, too?"

"I told you you can't stay here. I don't think we need to talk about it beyond that."

"You've been telling me that in one way or another for nearly a year."

"Right. So why don't you listen? What am I, the one woman in Colorado who won't fall all over you? If I let you stay, if I let you in, what then? I know: you'd take off. Not that I'd care, but why go to all the trouble? Listen to me now, Johnny. It's not worth it to go on.

Can't you see I'm happy the way I am? Can't you listen when I tell you that?"

He smiled a little. "I could if that's all you were telling me."

She wanted to go outside again, but it was her house and he was the one who had to go. She had a panicky sense that he might be right. But so what?

"Go," she said.

After another minute he pulled on his boots and walked to the door. His expression was sad, even helpless, and she remembered feeling that way, a long time ago, alone, and recently as well, with him.

At the door he began to speak, stopped, tried again. "I hope you are happy," he said, and walked out. She stood at the open door and watched him go. She wondered where he had put his wild palomino horse, since he walked toward town, not the barn.

She stepped from the cabin to the doorstep. "I saw you win," she said, unable to help it. He turned; she could just barely make out his face against the shadowy trees beyond the meadow.

"I saw you win. You were . . . " She wanted to tell him that the way his body moved was beautiful, or splendid, or exhilarating, but she could not.

He came out of the dark slowly, like a ghost, as though pulled by her unspoken praise. He stopped in front of her, not close.

"You are too much like him," she said instead. "I thought you weren't, but you are. I guess I owe you at least that much explanation."

"Like who?"

"I know about the shooting."

"Yes."

"Well, I think it was wrong."

"It wasn't. They were about to shoot me in the back."

"They never could've hit you."

"But they would have hit someone."

"You are too much like him. That's all. I'm entitled to keep that much for myself, Johnny."

He did not ask again. He knew.

"Why do you hate him?" he asked instead. "What did he do to you?"

"It's not what he did. It's what he is."

He stepped closer to her, not close enough to touch. "You hate people because they hurt you, not for what they are. Not this much hate."

"He's a hired gun, like you. I know about the Flossie, too. I know Buck Daunt bought your gun for the Flossie."

"Buck Daunt hired me as a night-shift boss. What was I supposed to do, refuse the promotion? I don't wear a gun in the mine, Gretel; it's whatever reputation this shooting gives me that Daunt's counting on. And as for your brother, I haven't heard his name in years. He's retired. He's probably married somewhere, or living quietly alone, like you." He glanced away, then back at her face, at the tapestry clutched to her breast, and at her face again. "I'm not your brother," he said. "I'm not a hired gun. And if you let me stay, I won't leave."

She felt tears begin to burn and turned her head away. She started to close her eyes, to blink the tears back, but it was too late. She blushed, deeply ashamed, naked as she had never allowed before. She could only hope the light silhouetted her, but knew otherwise. He could see. She looked back at him and saw he waited patiently, but also saw beneath that, through the layers. She set the tapestry aside and he came to her, held her in the doorway, between light and dark.

They walked into the meadow together, holding each other by the hand, no more. They lay on the dewy grass, and he traced a finger over her face: her brow, her eyelids, her nose, her lips. He kissed her lips. She opened her mouth, tasting.

His fingers slipped the top button of her shirt through its small hole. And the next. She had always undressed herself before. Now she undressed him. She opened his shirt and ran her hands over his chest, over the coarse, curly hair and pleasantly rough skin, kneading to feel the muscles there, hard but yielding, warm. She felt his hands on her own body, on her breasts, and then his mouth, searching, finding, searching for more. His fingers moved to her pants, inside, over her hips, out again, caressed her belly, tickling. They laughed, for the first time.

She found what he wanted her to find, touched without timidness or boldness where she had not touched before, where she had only looked, wondering, perhaps wanting. Certainly dreaming. She touched now, with the meadow grass wet against her back.

7

Buried

Gretel told him she feared having a baby, so he promised to bring
her a little cap like the ones used by the dance hall girls. He did not
tell her where he learned this method, but she knew. It did not seem
to bother her, nor did the possibility of getting pregnant the first
night. After making love in the meadow they slept, then woke to make
love some more. When the air chilled they moved to the cabin. They
lay on top of the blankets on the bed that had been Zachary's and
Anna's and made love again. When they woke in the morning he
rubbed her gently with oil, knowing she must be sore. She smiled,
and her happiness warmed him. It made him rise, too, but they
laughed at the idea.

"I love your laugh best," he told her.

"No you don't. Not anymore."

They ate breakfast with her afghans thrown around their shoulders. Even in the cool dawn they did not want to dress. He watched
her walk barefoot to the barn to collect eggs, and when she returned

he dried her dewed legs with his blanket. Her legs were long and slim and tanned now from the times she'd spent lying with him in the sun on the pass.

She cooked an omelette and brewed the bitter, black coffee they liked. She toasted her coarse home-baked bread and spread it with fresh butter and wildberry jam. She said she had collected the berries herself.

"They're as good as the beer," he commented.

"You like the beer better. You lie to me this morning."

"No, I don't." He finished seconds of the eggs and toast and jam. She made thirds. He ate even more than usual, as though a new chamber had opened inside him.

"Let's do it again," she said when he finally finished.

He could only stare at her. Then he laughed. He stood and dropped his blanket, pulled hers off and picked her up. She was slim but nearly as tall as he, not light, but he loved the weight of her resting on his arms.

"Don't drop me!"

He dropped her on the bed. He did not enter her again, but showed her other things, things he could tell amazed her, things few men would share with their wives. She did not know these things were reserved for encounters with women who had many teachers, or were teachers themselves, and he could see she enjoyed them.

They dressed at last and climbed the escarpment for a swim in the lake, where the frigid water was all that kept him soft. Swimming underwater, through filtered sunlight, he caught Gretel's long legs and pulled her under with him. Laughing, gasping, they surfaced together.

"I needed this ice," she said.

"Me too."

They dried off and dressed and returned to the cabin. He felt drowsy now, which was bad because he had to start work at the

Flossie tonight. Well, the Flossie would bring him around. And he'd bring her around, too. For now he rested in the meadow's late-afternoon sun with Gretel, until the mountain cast its shadow, when they shared a meal of cheese and bread and more of the wildberry jam.

"I'll feel strange when you leave," she told him.

"You'll want to run again."

"I might."

"But you won't. You don't have to."

"No."

And so he left, with no parting kiss, only a good-bye, satisfied for now. She walked partway down the valley with him, then left him alone, in a sense, and he walked to town and to the Flossie, which was not far from the Bonne Chance. A smile kept stealing to his lips, until he found Daunt waiting at the shaft.

"Where were you last night?" the super asked in his Georgian drawl. "Thought you'd be collecting your winnings."

Daunt's voice had an edge; the contest still rankled. He would have made the official take ten more measurements and still refused to admit the loss. MacMurray had handled it better, but Johnny liked him less than Daunt. The Scot was often churlish and even brutal, not hotheaded but always eager for a fight, and though he laughed easily enough, the laugh sounded sadistic, as though he had just played a dangerously cruel joke. More than once he'd used his huge, calloused fists to enforce his will, even in the mine.

"Zachary weren't around either, once it got dark," Daunt continued as the cage descended into blackness deeper than the Bonne Chance's deepest drift. The Flossie had an eleven-hundred-foot shaft, one of the longest anywhere. It was narrow and poorly reinforced, unlike the older shafts in the Bonne Chance. A solitary tommyknocker began to tap.

"He quit," Daunt told him. "But I expect you knew that. And I hear he's tied up night and day with Marie DuBois. Hear she's taken a turn for the worse. But no one knows where you been, Johnny."

Zachary quit? Suddenly the tommyknocker had friends.

"You didn't know, did you," said Daunt, scratching his wire-haired scalp. "Well I'll be go to hell. You must've been shacked up with some special girl."

"What's wrong with Marie?" Johnny asked.

"Pneumonia, I heard. She ain't exactly a strong woman, you know. Been nipping that laudanum too damn long. Beautiful lady, too. I bet Zachary's gonna turn right inside out if she passes on. He loves her something fierce. Never loved Anna that way."

Johnny wanted only to get out of the cage. The tommyknockers had given him a headache by the time he and Daunt reached the end of the shaft. Through the pounding he recognized Daunt as the danger, much more than the mine. Daunt was why Zachary quit, probably after another run-in over the Bonne Chance. The Flossie was worse. They continued deeper in, turned down a crosscut, picked up another cage. The surveying was poor: tunnels failed to meet where they should and air pooled in heavy, stagnant pockets, stinking with mine gases, rotting wet wood, and powder gas from oversize explosions—all poison to workers who stayed here long. No wonder men asked for jobs at the Bonne Chance.

Everyone knew the Flossie was merely a parasite on offshoots of the other mine's rich vein. Her ore had always been pockety, but only lately had Daunt slashed expenses. In town, at the bars, the men complained of two-candle rations when they should have had three or four. Bad lighting, bad air, MacMurray's brutal daytime management: no one could get a decent shift out of a man under these conditions. No wonder, too, that Emma Stotter fretted so about her husband, the only man who ran his shift with any good sense. O'Hearn, the night-shift boss before Johnny, had been as bad as MacMurray; worse, because he was lazy, too.

"What happened to O'Hearn?" Johnny asked.

"He's at the Bonne Chance. Took over Zachary's shift."

The tommyknockers pounded louder. Best to ditch this job, right now. Then again, he'd never been a shift boss. Maybe he could improve things. The Flossie brought back memories of touring his father's mines, of the laborers with their heads ducked, their shoulders hunched, their wheezing breath—and his father, spine erect, pace brisk, heels clicking, chin up and jutting, black eyes forward, always forward, even after the biggest mine collapsed. No, especially then. "Seal the adit," he had said, "there is no one left alive." But Johnny could hear them breathe, ragged, full of mine dust as ever, yet still breathing. It was a strange thing to hear, strange and impossible, but he swore he could. For a time, anyhow.

He could not let that happen here.

Ahead were voices, which ceased at Daunt's approach—a crew of miners on a drift face. Their faces showed the strain under which they worked: creases around their eyes from squinting in the dim, flickering light, their mouths set in hard lines. They eyed him suspiciously.

The walls were unstable, with too much loose earth, not enough rock, scanty timber. He had to skirt around a recent slough and wondered if anyone had gotten hurt by it. There was water here, too, acidic water. When the men moved, their boots made small slapping noises against the wet floor. Their flannel shirts hung damply, clinging to their shoulders.

The miners had been overloading the drill holes here for some time. Johnny ran his hand over the drift face, which had been blown smooth. At least they'd drilled and shot this round well, but they would have done so at the end of Stotter's shift. Now the graveyard team had begun to sink new holes. These also looked good, so far.

"Who's pointing these holes?" he asked the men. He saw one with a double-jack hammer, but none holding steel.

"I am," said a short, balding Cornishman with a bent back and swollen knuckles. "Name's Brody."

"I'll show you the other faces," Daunt said impatiently, and they moved on.

The rest looked worse. Johnny suspected they all had orders to work faster than they should, but Brody must have been able to do that and still point the holes right. He hardly seemed up to it.

Daunt finally left. Johnny watched him go and hoped he seldom worked late. He helped drill and load a round, rotating among the crews. Then he cleared the men out for meal break, and spit one set of fuses himself while blasters spit the others. He joined his crews several levels up. While they ate, the blasts from below rocked the deep mine. No one spoke to him and few spoke to one another. Several glanced at him now and then, wary of this Mexican shootist, but less hostile than he'd expected.

"The Flossie is a pit," he told Zachary the next morning. Johnny had skipped his usual morning's sleep and gone to Marie's house, but a woman he recognized from the bar had told him at the door that Zachary had just left. He'd found him at the Fallen Idle, a beer cradled in his big right hand.

The women had kept the place neat and profitable while Marie was sick: the worn wood floors were scrubbed and polished, the glasses shined, even the bottles dusted, not that they had much chance to gather dust. But a pall hung over the Fallen Idle. The dark-haired woman called Elizabeth brought Johnny a cup of coffee and some oatmeal, and greeted him somberly before returning to the kitchen.

"You knew it was a pit," Zachary drawled, his voice rough and hollow. "You shouldn't've took that job." He was already half-drunk, even with the morning light slanting through the bar's windows.

"She's ripe for a cave-in," Johnny said. "Somebody has to do something."

"Don't have to be you, Johnny. You almost got killed once. Weren't that enough?"

Johnny shrugged and worked on his oatmeal, which was hot but full of salt and lumps. "I'm sorry Marie's so bad."

"Yeah." Zachary laughed shortly. "She told me to get lost. Said I was making her nervous."

"She wanted to give you a break."

He nodded slowly, drank his beer, waited for more. "I got a pretty good stake for you from the bets. Collected it with my own. You don't have to work at all if you don't want to."

"I want to."

"Yeah."

Johnny drank his coffee.

"You were with Gretel, weren't you?"

"Uh huh."

Zachary managed a smile. "That's good. You two are okay together. Got any of them fancy cigars?"

Johnny produced two from his shirt pocket and they smoked in silence until Elizabeth brought another beer.

"I think I'll maybe do some prospecting," Zachary said after a while. He rubbed his jaw through the stubble of his returning beard. "Up high, above the valley. Where the slides've kept folks out. Been a long time since I poked around these hills, too long underground. Never stay too long underground, Johnny."

"I never do."

"Except this time."

He said nothing.

"The Braunns'll be coming back, now. Maybe you can take up the Flossie with Heinrich Braunn. I got no idea what sort of man he is, but who knows? He might listen."

"Why would they come back now? The mansion's only half-finished."

Zachary puffed his cigar and squinted at the bar, or maybe beyond it. "Don't matter," he said. "Marie passes on, they'll be back."

Zachary, Johnny, and four others from a large group of volun-
teers lowered Marie DuBois's mahogany casket into Telluride's
summer-baked soil. Gretel was there, along with what seemed like
half the town. The *Journal* gave the funeral and Marie's life a full page
of coverage, blessedly without any sermons on the evils of Pacific
Avenue. Marie had run a reputable saloon, and if her girls slept with
the patrons, or got paid for it, they did so on their own time.

When the casket rested in the earth and the Catholic priest
started up in Latin, Zachary stood apart. Afterward he left for his
room at Emma's, without a word for the men and women who knew
him or had known Marie.

"We should stay in town," Johnny told Gretel.

Reluctantly, she agreed. They sat in Emma's parlor, pretending
to read. After a bit Zachary came downstairs with a bulging canvas
bag.

"I want to go back to the cabin," he told them. He paid Emma
an extra month's rent and they all rode out, Gretel sitting behind
Johnny on his palomino and Zachary on his ancient brown gelding,
leading a laden mule.

8

Prospects

Eight days later Heinrich Braunn and his wife arrived. The Southern stopped near Vance Junction to let Mrs. Braunn off as close as possible to the nearly completed mansion. Once on the mansion's grounds she never left.

Zachary had already retreated to the slopes above the valley. He stayed nights at the cabin with Gretel, though he came in too late for dinner or conversation, and walked off each dawn with pick and shovel over his shoulder. He only stayed in long enough to help move the cumbersome loom to the front room so he could sleep in what had once been Gretel's narrow bed. She now slept in the double bed in the bedroom her father and mother had shared.

"He says nothing and barely takes a drink anymore," Gretel told Johnny after a month.

"Let him grieve," Johnny said.

He worried more about the Flossie. He had watched Heinrich Braunn closely, on the few occasions he'd been able to watch him at all, and tried to pick up indications as to whether he could go to the mine owner about conditions in the mine. He got nowhere with Daunt, though they argued often, probably more than Daunt had argued with Zachary. At this point, Johnny did not care if Daunt fired him, so he pushed hard for more timber, more candles, better management from MacMurray on the day shift. He almost did lose his job over the last.

"I should fire you," Daunt snarled.

"Go ahead."

"Nah. That night shift's producing too well. You go on with your mission of mercy, buck. I don't give a shit. Ask all you want, but there ain't an extra scrap of timber going into that mine. Or any more candles. Just stay the hell off MacMurray."

The night shift was not producing well, just more—increased tonnage of low-grade ore. Johnny had seen the assays. He got much more out of his crew than the previous boss had, once they got used to the idea of working for a Mexican. With his help the men could drill faster and use the maximum powder without overloading the drill holes; he refused to let them follow Daunt's orders about overloading. But the ore contained nothing of value, even with the cheaper shipping afforded by the trains, and the slag heap grew. The question of highgrading rapidly became a joke, since the miners had yet to hit another of the high-grade pockets that obsessed Daunt. Johnny suspected the vein had pinched out entirely, but the super still had all three shifts pursuing their fruitless way deeper into the mountain, which threatened every day to close up and kill them unless they held her back with timber.

When Johnny took time out to climb the steep trail to Zachary's prospect sites one day, the older man treated him cordially and showed him some spots of promising color. Johnny could see his friend wanted to work alone, and that he had been right: Zachary knew how to grieve. So Johnny left him to it. On the way down he had to watch his step, but once or twice he glanced up at the mansion on the mesa across the valley. No workers there now; it even looked deserted, except for a groom leading a horse toward the large stone barn. The horse wore a blanket that caught the sun, a scarlet patch on the mesa's wide green expanse. The groom led the horse into the dim entry, and the scarlet light went out.

Back in town, Johnny found that the best place to keep an eye on Heinrich Braunn was the recently completed Baroness Hotel, which Braunn had financed along with his mansion. He'd also financed the opera house, though he may have expected more opera for his money. The Baroness offered large, plush rooms, an ornately decorated bar with liquors from around the world, a fine restaurant, a lobby with a glass case full of sterling ornaments, and a single long stairway that climbed from lobby to top floor.

Braunn often stayed in his suite at the top, living away from his new mansion, and his wife, for days at a time. He'd had a telephone installed, as well as his own telegraph line. He usually took his meals in his suite, but early in the evening he sat at a table in the corner of the bar, listening to the classical music trios he imported from the East, and drinking.

On these evenings Johnny drank, too. He sat on a stool at the cherrywood bar with sterling rails, and made conversation with the north-side gentlemen and travelers. He traded his work clothes for a suit and tie, here: the Baroness was no saloon.

Braunn knew who he was, and they had a nodding acquaintance. Neither had spoken to the other, and Johnny could find out little about how the owner might take criticism of his company. Braunn visited the in-town office daily but never the workings. Like Zachary he'd passed fifty several years back. He was shorter, though, with a bulldog build. He had a long mane of thick gray hair, a bronzed, squarish face, and eyes so clear and light they looked silver. He dressed well: precisely fitted silk jackets, brocade vests, slacks neatly creased down the front, soft leather boots. He conversed easily with hotel employees, those he had imported from his country as well as locals who certainly knew no German, yet he spoke in a voice so discreet that Johnny could detect neither words nor accent. Above all, he seemed absolutely in control of himself and whoever came near him, from his crisp, concise movements to the way he signed his papers or fingered his Cuban cigar.

Late in August, Johnny went back up the mountain to talk to Zachary. As after his first night in the Flossie, he skipped his morning sleep and even his breakfast, figuring to catch a nap and a meal later. He rode his palomino this time, though the climb would have better suited a bighorn sheep. The slope was rough and dangerous, with the mountain towering above as though threatening anyone who dared to scale it, or worse, to mine it. He found Zachary at yet another prospect site.

"I can't figure Braunn," he told his friend.

"Look at this color," Zachary said, pointing to an outcrop of quartz in the sandstone. He was stripped to the waist, noticeably thinner though not gaunt. The sun had tanned his skin nearly as dark as Johnny's and his beard had grown back full and shaggy. Johnny had let his own beard begin to grow, too, against the Flossie's cold, stagnant air. Only when he swung a hammer did he feel warm in the mine's clammy depths, and every night the wetness worked its way deeper into his bones. Even Gretel could not massage it out of him.

But Zachary seemed to have traveled back in time, to before the mines sank beyond forty feet, before the whites cleared out the last of the Utes, to when the San Juans were new to the Americans, and Zachary was young. The pick fit well in his big hand as he tapped expertly at the sand-colored rock. He worked on a long, wide ledge well above any previous sites, close to the treeline, overlooking yellow- and red-tinged treetops that reminded Johnny of the first time Zachary had brought him to the cabin, and Gretel. Rock rose vertically from the ledge for fifteen feet, then leveled to a narrow lip, then rose again to the peak, a thousand feet higher, a spike that drilled the blue sky.

Johnny figured this slope never held its snow for long in winter, and getting men and supplies up on a regular basis would give a manager fits. But he studied the color and agreed it held promise. "You'll never get men or equipment up here without a tram," he said.

"So? Put in a tram. This is gold color, Johnny. Anyone would put in a tram for a gold mine."

Johnny shrugged. He had enough mining headaches for both of them. "Braunn is a mystery," he said after a moment. "I have no idea how he'd take suggestions on the Flossie, and she's getting worse by the day. Daunt won't budge; it's no sense trying anymore."

"So quit. Come up here with me. I'm telling you, this is a real prospect."

Johnny had to laugh. "You want company?"

Zachary tapped the mountain with his pick. "Sure. Why not? Don't you want to get away from Braunn Mining? And from Daunt? Between us we have enough grubstake to put this hole down sixty feet. Then who knows?"

"I don't think so. Maybe later."

Zachary shrugged. He chipped off a few chunks of likely looking rock with his pick and handed them to Johnny. "Here. Do me a favor and get these assayed."

Johnny stuck the chunks in his saddlebags.

"And how about bringing some powder out from town? Caps and fuse, too. I can get what timber I need for a shack from these trees."

"Okay," said Johnny. "But I'm not in on this. Not yet. Not till I'm through at the Flossie."

On the way back to town, he decided to talk to Heinrich Braunn. First he took the ore to the assay office, the one in town rather than at the mine, and agreed to return later for the results. Then he ordered Zachary as many explosives as a mule could carry. At the livery he arranged to rent the mule tomorrow, and all the while he thought about what abuse MacMurray might have doled out on his shift today, and about Heinrich Braunn. Early in the evening he crossed the busy main street and walked into the Baroness Hotel. His eyes adjusted to the cool, velvet light of the bar, and he remembered three things: he was not dressed for this place, he had not eaten since meal break at the Flossie last night, and he had not slept since yesterday morning. But then he saw Heinrich Braunn sipping his schnapps and peering through reading glasses at a sheaf of papers, occasionally dipping his fountain pen into an inkwell and making notes.

Johnny approached Braunn, who looked up over his half-glasses.

"Yes?" the owner said.

"I'd like to talk to you."

"Now?"

"Now."

Braunn removed his glasses, wiped his pen and set it in a silver stand. "You are Johnny Torres, correct? Night-shift boss at the Flosshilde."

Johnny nodded and took a seat opposite the owner. Braunn had a strong German accent and a soft, gravelly voice, and he said the name of the mine as it should be said, as it would have been pronounced in the Wagner opera that must have inspired it. Johnny figured any man who chose a name from *Das Rheingold,* with its magic gold ring, must have some brains, some taste, or at least a sense of humor. The first would come in handy, now; the rest counted for nothing, except maybe to help bridge a gap.

A waiter in a starched white shirt and black tie asked Johnny if he wanted a drink. He declined. "I think you should know about conditions in your mines," he said to Braunn after the waiter departed.

"I have not yet toured either property, nor have I felt it necessary. The Bonne Chance has always produced well. The Flosshilde has produced in spurts, as you know, but the ore is rich."

"The Flossie has produced nothing since before early July."

Braunn tapped the sheaf of papers. "Not according to these reports."

"Then those reports are false."

Braunn raised his thin brows, but his eyes remained as calm as ever. "These mines have paid well. I would have sold them otherwise." He sipped his drink. It was obvious he wished to end the discussion, but Johnny stayed in his chair, waiting. "If the Flosshilde is indeed losing money, the losses will show up sooner or later," Braunn said curtly. "In the meantime I can have someone double-check the books."

Johnny pressed. "Our crews have opened a whole bunch of new drift faces in the Bonne Chance. Daunt could cover the Flossie's failure by shifting profit reports. He could go on doing it for quite a while, especially since he thinks the next high-grade ore is just around the corner. He'll hang on to that mine forever rather than admit she's tapped out, but he'll continue to sacrifice safety while he's doing it. It's not that hard to doctor the books."

Braunn cleared his throat and signaled to the waiter for a refill. "Drink?" he asked Johnny, without hospitality.

"All right. Scotch."

Braunn told the waiter, who quickly brought their drinks. The Scotch was just below top drawer, and from this Johnny learned as much about this man as he had in the whole last month: Braunn would never take his word over Daunt's.

"So you suspect Buck Daunt is cheating me?" The tone verged on mocking.

"He's lying to you, anyway. And he's cheating the workers, maybe to death." Braunn evidenced no concern over this. "The Flossie is ripe for a cave-in, and even the Bonne Chance is more dangerous than a year ago. Daunt refuses to timber in all but the softest spots, and men have already been hurt by sloughing walls. He also cuts corners in surveying, which means it doesn't ventilate well and it's harder to get out, and he cuts corners in lighting, which means more mistakes. The Flossie's day-shift boss beats his men for making those mistakes."

"The day-shift boss. MacMurray?"

Johnny nodded.

Braunn lifted the stack of papers, neatened them by rapping them on the table. Johnny rose to go, leaving the drink. He saw Braunn glance at the glass, then back to him, his clear, silver eyes wary for a second. Then he stood and smiled and extended a blunt-fingered hand. Johnny returned the iron grip.

"I will look into it," Braunn said, without conviction.

"Good."

Braunn sat. Johnny turned to go, but Braunn tapped the table with his pen and said, "You are a friend of Zachary Coleman, are you not?"

"Yes."

"Please offer him my condolences on the death of Marie DuBois. Do you know why he left the Bonne Chance? Does it have anything to do with what you've told me?"

"Not directly. He beat Buck Daunt in a drilling contest. I don't think Daunt took it very well."

"I see. Were you not Mr. Coleman's partner in that contest?"

"I was."

"But Mr. Daunt has not fired you."

"He didn't fire Zachary either," Johnny said, and left Braunn at the table with his false reports and the glass of less-than-perfect Scotch.

He hurried across Colorado Avenue, back toward Emma's, his belly growling. With luck, supper would still be on the table. But someone shouted his name. He turned to look: the assayer, excitedly leaning out the door to his office. Johnny sighed and backtracked.

"Where the hell you getting this stuff?" the assayer demanded before Johnny even got in the door.

"Why?" His tone came back impatient. At the moment he cared a lot more about Heinrich Braunn, and supper. But he might as well find out about Zachary's prospect now as tomorrow. "It's good?" he asked.

"It's gold," said the assayer. "You better file a claim, and quick."

PART TWO

Flosshilde

September 25 to October 15, 1892

9

Homecoming

His body swayed with the rocking of the Rio Grande Southern, a swaying he no longer noticed after days on trains, broken only when he paced the railroad stations at the big junctions, waiting for the next locomotive, the next leg of the boring, tiring, cinder-choked journey from Montana to Vance Junction at the end of the valley where his father had lived, where he supposed his sister lived now. He did not know for certain where Gretel lived. He had not exchanged a word with her, written or otherwise, since leaving fourteen years ago, before Vance Junction existed, before Otto Mears built his toll road from Dallas and Dave Wood built the cut-off from Montrose, well before the Rio Grande Southern, when Telluride was still called Columbia. And he despised all of it except his father and Catharine. He still did, only now his father was dead.

Soot had blackened his shirt, once light blue; his jacket and pants were black already. Soot had dusted his short, dark hair, thickened it, tarnished his face so that he looked unshaven, even though he'd shaved with cold water each morning. If he didn't shave every day, he'd soon have a beard as thick as his father used to. He wouldn't mind looking like his father, and did, mostly: the set of his features, the dark hair, even the way he rubbed his jaw now and then—it all mirrored Zachary. But he had grown taller, leaner, and he'd always had his mother's blue-gray eyes. His father had never worn a handgun, either, but Cole wore a well-used, well-oiled Peacemaker, snub-nosed, nickel-plated, with a large hammer spur and cutaway trigger guard. He also carried a Winchester '73 rifle, one like Zachary might have bought if he'd thought it necessary for hunting; chances were he'd used the old Sharps until the end.

Cole had not turned out like his father. He was not as genial, or as inclined to want other people around. He had never minded solitude, never needed drinking or gambling partners, or a dance hall girl every Saturday night. Even so, he'd gotten married, well after retiring from the shooting trade and taking off for Montana. That he should marry had taken him by surprise. It amazed him even more, though, that he should so deeply cherish his wife and stepson and the ranch he'd begun building when he first got to Montana four years ago, but really never brought to life until he had her help. He still held a large piece of himself, including all of his past, apart, but so did Laura. They were happy in the present; so far it had been enough. Cole had long wondered when the rest would return, and how—gently, through gradual fading or even acceptance, or violently, through a survivor's revenge. He'd always taken it for granted that the past would catch up with him, but he'd never expected himself to return to it like this, voluntarily.

He could not believe his father had died, and maybe he was going back to set it straight in his mind. Naturally he still saw Zachary as a young man, not much older than Cole was now. He'd not had to watch his father age; few Westerners did, though as the land got more and more settled, families stayed closer. He expected to ride into the valley and find Zachary there as on the September day he'd left, jabbing his shovel at the ground with Buck Daunt sweating next to him—Zachary calm around the thoughtful brown eyes but sudden in his motions, Daunt spasmodic with a depth of grief that shocked Cole but probably shouldn't have.

Cole had left that day before they'd brought Anna's body out and tossed the dirt on top. He had frozen his father's warm, sad handclasp in his mind, and Buck Daunt's angry refusal to shake his hand at all. He remembered Daunt's words when he realized Cole meant to leave without helping bury her: "She was your mother, you bastard!" He remembered that Zachary had said nothing, only smiled with regret that he should leave and shook hands, and in both ways wished him well.

Now Cole wished he had come back before this, while Zachary had still been alive. Or no—he wished he'd seen Zachary, but not here. Never once in the last fourteen years, or in the years before that, had he had any desire to be here. He'd missed his father, wondered what kind of woman his sister had grown into, and spent years of nights thrashing through unwanted dreams of Catharine DuBois. But never had he wanted to come back.

Now he looked out the window of the rocking train as it belched a high column of black smoke into the sky, which changed every half hour or so from gray, spitting clouds to blue with sunshine winking through. The black smoke plumed high, then bent back to trail above the train like a giant shadow, dropping the cinders that soiled the clothes and skin and made the eyes smart. Cole looked out the window at the red rock mountainsides of the San Miguel River valley, dotted with spruce, pine, and aspen. The aspen glittered a bright gold when the sun hit them, but under the spitting gray clouds they tarnished quickly: they were dying, as they must every year, their leaves weakened, brought to earth by the tiniest drop of rain or breath of wind, to make way for the new green of next spring. Between now and then would come a winter, and Cole hoped to beat the first snow out of here. He wanted to spend that first snow cozy and at peace in his ranch cabin back home in Montana, like he'd spent breakfast four days ago, laughing with Laura and Sam over steaming flapjacks, before the telegram came.

He forced his gaze away from the dying aspen, tried to rub the weary ache from behind his soot-smarted eyes. He dug the wire out of his jacket pocket and read it twice. For some reason he always read it twice.

PA DIED YESTERDAY. WILL BURY HIM TODAY. NO NEED FOR YOU TO COME. GRETEL

No condolences, no further explanation, no promise of a letter with details. She'd never send one. Even Zachary had written only a few times before he died, and Cole had done no better. She did not even say how Zachary had died, which of course he wanted to know. He had tried convincing himself that if she'd told him more he might not have come. But he could have cabled her for details; instead, he had come in person. He folded the wire.

The first time he'd read it (twice), when one of the hands had brought it out from town after a morning supply run, he'd folded it and stuck it in his pocket. He was in the cabin with Laura. Sam was hanging on the corral fence as he often did, watching the wrangler gentle the horses, and Cole could see him through the window. He stuck the wire in his pocket like a fire he was trying to snuff out. He tore a small hole in the middle by sticking it in there so fast. Laura glanced at him, then went back to the apples she was cutting for cobbler. He listened to the knife chopping through the apples on the wood cutting board and watched his stepson out the window, and wondered how Zachary had died. If he could wonder this then the telegram had to be real. He could feel it burn in his pocket, so he dug it out, smoothed it, and read it again, twice.

He was embarrassed to show it to Laura. Color rose to his cheeks, just like when he'd caught the influenza last winter and finally had to admit his need to rest in bed. She had faced the loss or estrangement (Cole did not know which) of her parents, the divorce from her first husband, the stillbirth of her second baby, Cole's child, a son whom they would have called Zack. Cole's illness was no major challenge to her after all that, and neither would this be. But he was embarrassed.

When he did show it to her, after she got the cobbler into the oven, she read it solemnly and looked at him with her tender gray eyes. Her angular face was flushed from the stove and her long, wheat-colored hair fell in wisps. She searched his face with uncommon lack of regard for his embarrassment, and he knew she saw that the telegram's last sentence disturbed him beyond his father's death.

"Will you go anyway?" she asked.

"I don't know."

Later they lay in bed, face up, not touching, each alone with the same thoughts. They could hear Sam's breathing in the next room.

"I think I'll go," said Cole.

Laura shifted toward him and he slipped his arm around her.

"I knew you would."

"How? I didn't know."

"Yes, you did."

He kissed her forehead.

"It will be hard for you," she said.

"It might."

She was silent for a while. When she spoke he sensed fear in her voice, and that scared him because she was afraid so seldom.

"Why have you stayed away so long, Cole?"

He took a deep breath.

"Your family?"

He made no reply.

She told him gently then that she was sorry for asking and he told her it was all right, but he lied. The present had cracked open, and the past had begun to sear through, just as the telegram had burned in his pocket.

Now the train drew closer to Vance Junction. Cole would not have known about this stop except that when he'd said he wanted a ticket to Telluride (first he'd said Columbia), the man behind the bars in the station house pegged him for green to the area and asked exactly where he wanted to go. He said there were a bunch of stops near there. So Cole bought a ticket to a place he'd never heard of called Vance Junction, where the narrow gauge line branched to Telluride six miles farther on, or to Ophir and Rico, beyond the valley.

On that train he put an elbow on the windowsill, rested his forehead on his hand, and closed his eyes. He remembered how Laura had left their bed quietly, believing him asleep. Her scent had lingered, a faint reminder of sunwarmed sage, chopped wood, freshly baked bread, a scent he wished he could have bottled and brought with him on this trip, to keep at least one of his feet on Montana soil. He'd lain in bed and pictured her sitting on the stool by the wood stove, her knees drawn up, her bare feet resting on the stool's rung, paper on a book on her lap, pen in hand. She never showed him her diaries; they were her windows on the part of her life she chose to keep separate from him. He did not regret that they had kept their pasts to themselves, because by keeping their secrets they'd bought the peace he'd thought he could never have, incomplete and vulnerable but peace nonetheless.

The train lurched to a stop. Cole opened his eyes and his right hand stole instinctively to his Colt. He looked out the window and found the same tree-dotted red rock, rain-speckled for the moment.

No depot, no bandits. The other passengers began chattering, but no one sat in the seat next to Cole and he only watched, waiting; ready, he hoped.

After a moment a man strode into the car. He had a long mane of thick silver hair, a bronzed, squarish face, and a barrel-chested, hard-muscled body. He wore an expensive-looking leather jacket, a clean white shirt, and gray wool pants neatly creased down the front. His eyes were clear, light, silvery; his gaze stopped the flutter of conversation among the passengers, except one woman whose last words soon trailed off. Cole watched, his hand still on his gun, as the man drew a deep breath and opened his mouth to speak. Then his eyes fell on Cole and he walked toward him.

"Zachary Coleman?" he asked in a voice discreet enough that no one else would hear. His German accent reminded Cole of Anna.

When Cole stood, he realized the man was half a foot shorter than he. His expression bore no malice and he extended a hand.

"I am Heinrich Braunn," he said, still discreetly, with the entire coach of passengers straining to hear. "Please accept my condolences on the death of your father. Now, would you mind coming with me? I'll explain outside."

Cole returned the vicelike handshake.

Braunn exchanged a few words with the conductor, too low for Cole to hear. Braunn and the conductor moved toward the end of the car and Cole figured he might as well follow. They descended the steps to the ground. After a minute another trainman brought Cole's Appaloosa, who tossed his head and tried to back away until Cole took the reins. A fair-complected man, mounted and presumably employed by Braunn, held Braunn's horse, a big, clean-limbed gray that looked like a thoroughbred. Cole wouldn't have had much use for a thoroughbred on his ranch. The horses danced as the train blew steam, its wheels spinning on the tracks.

"You are safer here than at the depot," said Braunn, and years of staying alive by reading the meaning behind a man's words led Cole to believe him. But the change in plans made him uneasy. Gretel's wire had mentioned no trouble, and he had never considered that Zachary might have died of anything other than an accident or an illness. Five years ago, perhaps. But on a ranch, struggling against the weather and the land, a person could forget such things—could forget how men struggle against one another, how they kill one another.

He rode with Braunn and the silent hired man alongside the train until it picked up speed and chugged away, trailing the awful smoke.

"What's so dangerous at Vance Junction?" Cole asked as the din receded.

"You, Mr. Coleman."

"Me?"

Braunn chuckled softly. "You do not know about the strike, do you."

"No." He pulled the Appaloosa to a stop: he meant to go no farther with this man before finding out what was going on. Braunn halted, too, but his patience was forced and his horse pranced.

"Your father opened a gold prospect before he died. Apparently, your sister, whom I assume cabled you, did not tell you that many people believe he was murdered for it."

Cole understood now. The crack in the present turned into a gaping hole and his past tumbled through. Here he was the shootist—not the rancher, not the husband, not the father. Here people expected a different kind of force from him than the kind it took to bring down an ornery steer or fight back a Montana blizzard. He understood, but Braunn said it anyway: "If you get off the train at the depot, the whole town will think you came here to fight. You look remarkably like your father, so they will know you at once, and whoever murdered him will try to kill you, too."

Cole urged his Appaloosa forward, and the other men moved

along also. He stayed a little ahead for the moment, digesting Braunn's news and trying to hide how angry it made him. He was angry with Gretel, angry with Telluride, angry that Zachary was dead, angry that no one knew whether he'd been murdered, and angry with himself for coming back here. No wonder Gretel wanted to keep him away, though she should have told him why. Then maybe he would have stayed home. He was no longer the gunfighter who would ride to his father's rescue; his father was dead, and revenge was deadly. He'd kept his Colt cleaned and oiled, but these days he loaded it with five bullets, not six, leaving the first chamber empty.

A sprinkle of rain had dampened their clothes and darkened the horses' hides, but now the sun snuck through. Cole felt his shirt begin to dry. A light breeze followed the sun, waving the tree branches, bringing leaves off the aspen in a flutter of gold.

"How do I know you didn't murder my father?" Cole asked Braunn. "You've told me nothing about who you are."

The older man chuckled. "You will, of course, draw your own conclusions. But the fact is that I did not do it. My wife and I own the Bonne Chance silver mine, where your father worked. He did a fine job for us, and he was well-liked. I suppose it would seem that with the silver market uneasy and the possibility of our other mine failing, I had every reason to take the Anna Strike from him. But you would not have come with me if I had. You would know."

The Anna Strike. Zachary had named the mine after Anna. Men did strange things for women. He wondered what had ever happened to Zachary's lover, Marie. And Catharine—what had become of Catharine?

They turned onto a wide trail blasted out of the side of the broad, high mesa that formed the western border of the valley where Zachary had settled sixteen years earlier. The trail was more like a road, big and smooth enough for a wagon, and not graded too steeply, which meant someone had settled on top of the mesa. The weather blew fierce up there, Cole recalled; only a strong house could keep a man warm in winter. Braunn could buy such a house.

The three horses trotted up the trail. As the way flattened the mesa spread before them, a broad grassy field tending from green to brown with autumn. Cole's fingers tightened on the reins as he saw a mansion rising mirage-like from the meadows—more castle than house. In the slanting sun its great, gray shadow was cast far across the mesa.

"This is my home," said Braunn.

It was built of stone, like the mountains that rose all around, and everything about it reached toward the sky. The main entry was at the northern end; the crest of the sharply pitched central roof ran north and south. The east wing had turrets and many windows, and a portico connected the west wing to the center. Cole looked twice at the west wing. The stone walls rose to the roof and the roof met in the middle, but the windows lacked glass and the black, shadowy interior had never been brought to life. This castle was unfinished.

The three riders dismounted and walked their horses to the stables, part of a large stone barn set apart. A boy took the other two mounts, but Cole unsaddled his Appaloosa himself: the horse was skittish around anyone else. The tall man with the white-blond hair stayed behind in the barn while Cole climbed the granite steps leading to the mansion's main entrance, a massive oak door, stained dark, ornately carved, and ornamented by a heavy silver knocker shaped like the face of a wild boar. The door swung inward before Braunn could open it.

Catharine DuBois stood on the threshold.

Cole's breath caught. Zachary had never mentioned Catharine in the few letters he'd sent, and Catharine had written only once, a message he had long tried to forget. Now he felt Catharine's fire as he'd felt it the last time he saw her, felt it when he got that letter he'd opened with shaking fingers and then burned in fury. Silver and gold. He hated what silver and gold had done to everyone and every place he'd ever known as a child, but even more because of the power of the memory of this woman, her choice of silver and gold. But the memory was nothing compared to the woman in the flesh.

He thought for certain her love of finery would have long since borne her far away: to San Francisco, to New York, to Paris, to anywhere but the gritty life of this mining district that still smacked of the frontier. But she was here. He had been prepared for the memory, but he was not prepared for this: the tiny body with its rounded breasts and hips, the blue satin dress that shimmered with every breath, the red-gold hair piled in gently looping curls, the leaf green eyes, the little full-lipped mouth, the pearly skin above the white lace on her chest, the spicy, exotic scent that enveloped him as, in his imagination, they embraced.

She smiled. "I'm sorry about Zachary, Cole. My mother died, too, last summer."

He had a sudden, laughable urge to ask if she still painted her toenails. What color today, Catharine? Rose red, oyster-shell pink, orange marmalade? Instead he returned her condolences, while her husband looked on. He was certain Braunn saw. He did not care. She would have to pay for this, not he. She could have warned him, but of course she would not. She would want him here, to tour her castle, to eat her food, to drink her wine. She had everything she'd ever craved. After the toenails he wanted to ask if maybe it wasn't enough, if maybe she had regrets. If he could only despise her as he should, he would hope she regretted it all.

She turned and Cole followed her into the cavernous central vault of the house. His eyes swept over the incongruous blend of sealed crates and richly carved mahogany pillars, oriental rugs, isolated marble sculptures of naked children with wings and arrows and equally naked adults that seemed erotic, even sinister. He looked up a level and along the mezzanines, the one side with unhung paintings leaning against the walls behind the railings, the other side with boards crudely nailed over doorways to block the unfinished west wing. He looked toward the far end, where an enormous bowed window commanded the view to the south, east, and west. The window reached to where the walls sloped inward to form the roof, whose inner ceiling had strapwork of the same dark wood as the mezzanines. From above the big window, in the triangle formed by the roof, a circle of stained glass scattered blue, gold, and crimson light. Cole looked again at the crates, and wondered whether the Braunns were coming or going.

"The decor is Gothic," Catharine told him, as though they were touring a museum. A servant silently took his jacket and Braunn's. Cole walked with his hosts to the southern end of the room and up wide marble stairs to a landing mostly encompassed by the giant bowed window. The landing alone was larger than most houses. On it were two heavily ornate armchairs upholstered in tapestries, and between the chairs a small, marble-topped table with carved legs. The chairs faced out the window rather than toward each other. The window took in the back of the Coleman valley, the escarpment that rose above it, the precarious network of trestles called the Ophir Loop, and the mountains that surrounded it all.

Braunn's gaze met Catharine's for a moment, fencing with her, it seemed to Cole. "Ah, yes," he said. "My wife and I are, in our humble way, students of architecture. I borrowed the landing from the Renaissance. I saw such a stairway in Würzburg, Germany, once." He shrugged. "But I am sure you have other things on your mind."

"Would you like a drink?" Catharine asked. One servant brought a third chair and another brought the drinks: what looked like schnapps for Braunn, sour mash for Cole, and white wine for Catharine. Cole declined Braunn's offer of a cigar from a silver box on the table and took half his whiskey at a swallow. Braunn lit a cigar for himself. The servant had left crystal decanters of whiskey and whatever Braunn drank.

They sat and watched the sunset in silence. Clouds remained, heavy and gray with fiery linings. Cole felt the last of his earlier rush drain off with the sun. Light washed the valley and the mountains, turning the evergreens nearly as golden as the bright swatches of aspen. But the light faded quickly, the valley disappeared into shadow, deepening, bottomless, and the eastern mountains dissolved to brooding silhouettes against the evening blue sky.

On the landing, they sat saying nothing; only the tinkle of ice against crystal or the faint sputtering of tobacco made any sound. Braunn leaned forward to light a small oil lamp, and the scent of kerosene mixed with the cigar smoke.

"I can't hide out here, you know," Cole said, breaking the silence, finally, as Catharine refilled his glass.

"You should stay at least until you figure out what you want to do," said Braunn. Every time the man spoke Cole had to listen through his German accent for the words. The accent distracted him, warned him. It was as though the frost of his mother, the ghost who had always been a ghost to him, was in Braunn's voice, a voice as bleak as the hard silver of his eyes.

"Do you have any ideas?" asked Catharine.

"No. Not yet." He saw that some of her fire had died: around the mouth he saw a tightening that most women would blame on passing thirty. With her it was more—her fire could not warm her husband, but neither could his chill extinguish her. He must have known that when they married. He must have married her for it. A man like that would want to play with fire, to challenge it, to freeze it eventually, but not until he'd had his fill.

"You could sell me the prospect," said Braunn.

"Who says it's mine?"

Braunn chuckled. Catharine sipped her wine.

"It is yours," said Braunn. "You are his son."

"Okay, so then what, go back to Montana?"

"If you like. Or stay here and help us secure it. We would pay you well."

"I gave that up," he said.

"Yes, but this time it is your father's murder. And your gold mine, if you want it."

Cole shook his head, finished his drink and held the glass so Catharine would not pour him more. He could feel her green-eyed stare, feel the way she leaned forward slightly, feel how her breathing had quickened. Unless the opulent mansion lied, she and her husband did not need the wealth of another mine, nor the headaches and risks of developing it. She wanted Cole, not the mine.

He remembered her thrilling to the early drilling contests, the first powder blasts, a runaway carriage on Colorado Avenue; she used to tell him of street fights with her cheeks flushed. She had enticed him from the start, enticed him still, and he knew he should leave her now while he could, as he'd left her before, to her own games.

"Who do you think murdered my father?" he asked her husband.

Again the chuckle. "Perhaps no one. Then again, perhaps someone he knew well. An old enemy? A friend? Perhaps Buck Daunt, a name you should find familiar. He is our superintendent, the man people think forced your father out of the Bonne Chance. That is not what I hear from Johnny Torres, who is one of our shift bosses and was your father's closest friend. He claims your father quit on his own, after many disagreements with Mr. Daunt. Your father and Mr. Daunt were once partners, were they not?"

"They came west together, and my father helped Daunt open the Bonne Chance. You think Daunt killed him because they couldn't agree on how to run a mine?"

Braunn puffed on his cigar, then held it out, studied it. "No, I think he killed him for gold. I think he knows he has made a mess of our other silver mine, the Flosshilde. The silver industry is shaky at best. What other reason could there be?"

Catharine lifted her nearly empty glass, as if in toast, and tipped it up to swallow the last. As she tilted her head back her throat curved, pearly smooth, almost translucent. And Cole watched, silent and still. There were always other reasons.

10

The West Wing

She had married Heinrich Braunn for his money and what she thought it could buy. Columbia meant little to her, one way or the other, and she never told Cole that what she detested was not the plundering of the mountains or even the greed, but rather the hounding discomfort, the struggle to obtain life's essentials, let alone a few meager luxuries. Dried apples just weren't enough.

She knew from the start that Cole would leave while she stayed behind. Even after she let him have her body, she knew that. Naturally he did not. Typical, she thought, of Columbia's men. More brains and ambition, perhaps. But not enough ambition. The thought of serving dumplings to a cadre of ranch hands somewhere in hot, dusty Texas made her wince. She never told Cole this, either. That he left should not have bothered her. She only fell in love with him after he left.

Was she so arrogant now? She married her husband for his

wealth, figuring they would eventually fall in love, as she had with Cole. Only Heinrich never fell in love with her at all. Heinrich was incapable of falling in love.

No one had seen through their businesslike union until today, when Cole re-entered her life. He certainly saw. It infuriated her that he saw, but it challenged her, too. As she sat across from him at dinner, she remembered the way they used to make love, remembered insisting he show her how the whores did it. He complied, hesitantly at first, then happily, then insatiably. She suffered no guilt for having wanted only a male body from him, because he wanted only a female body from her. They came at it differently, though: he thought they were falling in love, she simply had fun. Then he left, and if she could have gone after him with a gun and shot him dead she would have, because along with his seed he planted in her the kind of love he thought she already felt. He made her feel it. She damned him for the seed and for the love, and married Heinrich Braunn.

The marriage was not wholly empty. Catharine shared with her husband a passion for travel, for the hearty German menu, for gambling. Not for business, though, an unfortunate thing that rendered her merely one of Heinrich's cherished ventures, bought and paid for. But cherished. At least she could credit herself and him with that.

Each day they bathed together, with sex afterward—adventurous, inventive sex. If they got a little bored, they took several months off, sometimes traveling to opposite sides of the earth. Once Heinrich climbed the mountains in Alaska while Catharine shot elephants in Kenya, donning a boy's trousers and shouldering an elephant gun as tall as she. Then each wanted to see where the other had been, so she went to Alaska and he to Kenya. They crossed paths in New York City, spending a week locked in their suite at the Aster House while room service sent in clean silk sheets and champagne three times a day. Then Catharine boarded the train and Heinrich set sail. They barely kissed good-bye. They rarely kissed anyway; it would hardly have been proper, considering they were not in love.

They had planned to return to Telluride in 1893, to spend summers there when not traveling elsewhere, now that the region offered refinements other than dried apples. When news of Otto Mears's intention to build the Rio Grande Southern reached them, they bought the mesa overlooking the valley where Cole had lived with his family, and began building their mansion. Then Catharine's mother died.

From Marie's letters, Catharine knew the gunman that Cole had become. It excited her well beyond ranching, though Marie wrote a year ago that he had finally settled down to that. And got married. Catharine could not accept this, even when he sat next to her on the landing with that gold band around the third finger of his left hand. Could his wife answer some need in him that Catharine would never care to meet? Did that mean his wife couldn't begin to satisfy what Catharine could? Was it with them as it was with her and Heinrich? Heinrich could never satisfy all of her; even so she had not slept with another man since marrying. She had never slept with any man except her husband or Cole.

Now she had returned to Colorado, where suddenly, through the empty eyes of the west wing in which she frequently strolled, her heels clicking, echoing, on the naked granite floor, she saw the barren side of her life. It came as a shock, then as a relief. She had failed to see it before, or shoved it aside. But through those windows, through eyes that stung for days after her mother's death, she saw the bleak gray mountains with their ancient snow at the tops, and she thought her life was lived above the treeline, with only pale green lichens attesting to life at all. And the travel, the food, even the sex with Heinrich all became as hollow as the west wing of her new home.

When Zachary died, Catharine had known Cole would return as

well. Heinrich had found her in the courtyard deadheading her yellow rosebush, and as she listened quietly, he told her of Zachary's death and his suspicions about Buck Daunt, whom she had not met since her return to Telluride and only remembered as the distasteful but resourceful man who eyed all the women lecherously and sold Heinrich the Bonne Chance. She made the mistake of pricking her ring finger on a thorn when she heard about Zachary, but permitted herself no further visible reaction. Heinrich saw enough, though.

"His son will come back now, will he not?" he said, his eyes without expression.

So he knew, and for the first time ever, she feared him.

He had left her in the rose garden. After finishing the yellow bush and a pink one that splayed across the mansion's gray stone wall on a whitewashed trellis, she had returned to the house and walked the east wing's long hall to her boudoir at the end, where tall, narrow windows framed the slopes across the valley. She entered her dressing room, a large interior chamber with windows only on herself. The mirrors tossed back her image from every angle. The fear inside made the woman in the mirrors look excited. It had parted her lips and quickened her breathing and brightened her eyes.

The longer she stood surrounded by the mirrors, the more she had thought of Cole, and the more she knew he would not have changed any more than she.

After dinner, Catharine and the men retired to their separate quarters. Catharine changed into a kimono, leaving her blue dress and underclothes in a crumpled heap on her dressing room floor, her stockings inside out, her slippers kicked into a pile in the corner. She took more care with her purse, setting it as always on the table by her bed. Inside it she kept her derringer, a ladies' edition, small caliber but enough to do the job, properly aimed.

With the velvet curtains of her boudoir drawn to shut out the night, she reclined on a settee that had been her mother's, trying to relax. She had not yet gotten around to reupholstering the settee and the flowered chintz had worn badly. One of Gretel's weavings, this one in a uniform, shimmering violet with flowers raised abstractly, was draped over it to hide the chintz. Though these fine weavings pleased her eye, Catharine lacked patience with the details of adorning her castle. She left arranging the artwork and furniture to a staff of decorators, dealing only grudgingly with their polite inquiries about her preferences. She cared little how they did it, desiring only beauty in the end. All the same, the way the crates sat waiting in the mansion's central vault pleased her as much as the weavings, as though she might move again soon, or set off on another long voyage. She had always wanted to visit China.

As she reclined, her personal maid removed the pins from her hair. The maid was a devoted girl named Freda, born of German peasant stock and looking more like she belonged in a beer hall muscling heavy mugs among singing drinkers than brushing out Catharine's long, fine, red-gold hair. But in her own way Freda was gentle and demure. Catharine leaned her head back, closing her eyes, as Freda's brush strokes sent shivers along the length of her body. She felt her nipples harden under the pale green silk of her kimono, and pictured Cole as he stood on her threshold, as he strode through her mansion to the landing, as he lifted his glass of sour mash. At dinner, over hearty brown sauces and roasted beef and crusty rye bread, she had wanted to slide from her chair under the table, find him. She'd had to hide a smile behind her glass of wine at the comical image of herself crawling around under there. But the desire was almost overpowering. She had not shared her bath with Heinrich today, for once, and the food reminded her of her hunger.

"You have not asked about our visitor," Catharine said to Freda in German.

The brush paused. "He is well?"

"He is well."

She sensed Freda's smile. A peasant with the perception of a fortune-teller, the maid was short but large-boned, blond, round-faced and small-eyed, though the blue irises were so big and circular they scarcely left room for the whites. Her smile was intelligent and enigmatic. She was only fifteen, and Catharine thought of her as the daughter her body had never been able to bear.

Freda finished brushing and Catharine sighed.

"Bedtime?" the girl asked.

"For you, yes."

Freda smiled, shy but knowing.

"Go," said Catharine, pretending strictness, and after Freda left she walked back along the hall toward Cole's room, where she raised her hand to knock, then lowered it and noiselessly turned the knob. The door swung open without a creak and she found him sitting in the chair by the fire looking at her, his hair still wet in the front from when he had washed his face, his shirt hanging on a rack behind the chair. There was more hair on his chest than she remembered and the skin there was as dark as his face. She imagined him working outside without the shirt, under the hot sun.

"I should have known I couldn't sneak up on you," she said.

"Why did you try?" She liked the sound of his voice: older now, rather quiet, with an enticing depth.

She shrugged, tracing her fingernails over the bedspread. He glanced at her hand, then at her toes. She thought she saw a touch of disappointment in his blue-gray eyes, or a slight drawing together of his fine, dark brows. She had given up painting her toenails when he left Telluride.

"Your sister wove this bedspread," she told him. "She does beautiful work."

"Really."

She nodded slowly. "You're a cool one, Zachary Coleman."

"I was just thinking the same about you."

"Thinking about me? I'm flattered. Haven't you got other things on your mind?"

"Should I?" Hostility mixed with his sarcasm. "Tell me, Catharine, did you get everything you wanted? Is all this enough, or aren't you through yet? I see you remembered I like blue."

She told herself the anger would make him vulnerable, but he had her now. And the desolation she'd felt looking out from the hollow west wing had her, too. Her knuckles whitened against the bedpost.

"That's not fair."

"Who's fair? You? You throw me out for someone like Heinrich Braunn, then when my father dies you wait for me to come home so you can use my gun to add a gold mine to your trophies. You could've at least cabled to let me know what I was walking into here."

"You might not have come. I wanted to see you again. Maybe I was wrong, but now it's done. Are you so perfect?"

He laughed, biting. "Hell no. I let you go."

"You left, remember?" Now she felt the pain herself. She let herself show it, too, unlike him. "Cole?"

"What?" Still terse. Still angry.

"We haven't even said hello."

He looked into the fire, which had climbed, and stared at it, saying nothing, until she was about to leave, to try again later. But then he rose from his chair, to stand so much taller than she, and she liked the tallness, the strength. He embraced her and she returned it, not timidly, and she found herself finally welcoming the return of the love she'd felt after he rode off to Texas. I did love you, she wanted to tell him. You left me no other choice.

She tried to hold him tighter but he let her go. "We're married, Catharine," he said, with a thickness in his voice.

"You don't need to say it."

"Yes, I do."

Behind the hearth a small tongue of flame licked around a pair of charred logs, swelling as it swallowed one and feasted on the other.

"I should go now," Catharine said, watching the fire, and Cole nodded. Neither said anything more.

She returned, though, later, after she had lain in bed for hours, after she could lie alone no longer, but also after she was certain weariness from his long journey would have driven Cole to sleep.

She returned to kneel by his bed, to watch him, to watch him frown in his sleep the way a mother might watch when her child broods, caught up in his own anguished world. She wanted to hold him, to love him as she had never allowed when he'd given her the chance, in a way physical but not sexual. Instead, she skimmed her fingers over his body.

He began to dream. She watched in the blue moonlight, while her fingers traced his lips, his neck, the curled, dark hair on his chest and belly, and moved down, over the silk sheet that covered the lower half of his body. She hesitated, feeling it too much a violation. Her touch did not comfort: he murmured indecipherable words, agitated, and began to toss. She drew away, back to the door, hands behind her, groping. His mouth opened as if to scream. Catharine gripped the doorknob tightly, ears steeled.

No words came, no sound, except the thrashing of the sheets and the rapid, horrified breathing, hers and his.

She rushed from the room. The hall stretched before her, lengthening with every step. Her suite was miles away, the hall as long and dark as a tunnel in a mine. Viscous liquid sucked at her legs. Her ears steeled again, this time for the sound of his door opening and his footfalls behind her. Her skin tautened, ready for his hands to grab her shoulders, whip her around. She could almost hear his voice snarl his fury. She willed her legs to move faster, dragged herself toward her room.

She reached her door at last, breathless, clamped a hand on the knob. She froze. Through the still-closed door at the other end of the hall, Cole screamed, enraged: *"Anna!"*

Catharine ran into her room and slammed the door behind her and buried herself under her covers, under the counterpane woven by Gretel.

11

The Cauldron

Cole left before breakfast. He sat on his Appaloosa in front of the mansion while Catharine and Heinrich Braunn stood on the granite doorstep to see him off. The morning sun shone wanly, through a trace of mist, and the breeze blew clammy. Braunn put his arm around Catharine and she pulled her pale green kimono tight; Cole thought she looked tired and anxious and chilled.

"I hope you will reconsider my offer," said Braunn.

Cole touched the brim of his hat in farewell and rode away, while the mist gathered around his horse's withers. His brain was misty, too; he'd slept poorly last night and felt more tired than yesterday. He'd had trouble falling asleep to begin with, despite his weariness, and so tried to think about his sister rather than Catharine, tried to picture her, to hear her nine-year-old voice that was lower and older than nine years. It did not work; his mind was too weary. Instead of her voice he heard the shuttle strumming back and forth across the loom, heard with a shiver the toneless whirring and the gently thudding rise and fall of the heddle frame: back and forth, up and down, rocking him into an uneasy sleep because it reminded him of his childhood, and his mother, and her death, and leaving Catharine behind.

He dreamed Catharine returned, deep in the night. He felt rather than heard her enter the room. When in the dream he opened his eyes, he saw the fire had gone out, leaving only the moon's quiet blue light. He raised himself on his elbows, watched her move toward him, felt her warm, smooth hands on his shoulders, urging him back to the pillow. Without a word, she drew away the sheet and, untying her kimono, lay with him on the bed.

Her body pressed along his side, and the silk of the kimono draped over both of them in its own caress. He felt her full breasts against him, the nipples hard.

They kissed, then her lips moved over his face, his chest, down his side, almost tickling, and across his hip. He let her love him, knowing it gave her pleasure, taking pleasure himself from holding off the desire to make love to her until it swelled and nearly burst. When he could stand it no more, he lifted her like a doll and she sat atop him, twisting, clutching, releasing. He closed his eyes, tilted his head back, and they came together in soundless, drowning waves.

He looked up at her. Revulsion merged into rage and finally terror when he saw his mother, not Catharine. Wildly tossed blond hair framed the accusatory stare in that ever-young face, but below it the body had decayed. The skin hung in shreds, the breasts had shriveled, the sex grated.

He tried to scream but could not, and in desperate silence heard again the rhythmic loomsong, back and forth, up and down. He looked to the loom as if for help, but Gretel wove on, her back to him. Slowly, while her hands and feet worked the loom, her head turned on its long neck and she stared at him like Anna, only with eyes as black as hell. Then he did scream, and woke up. He thought he heard a door slam, or something bang. He was sitting, sweating, exhausted as though he had just ridden all night stopping a stampede back in Montana. He dropped back to the pillow and off to sleep, but the night gave him no peace.

Now he rode through the faint mist at a lope, across the grassy mesa toward the valley, satisfied to leave Heinrich Braunn, whom he did not trust; less than eager for the reunion with his sister, from whom he expected scant welcome; preoccupied with Catharine, and his father's possible murder.

He was not entirely sure about the murder. Braunn clearly wanted the mine; Cole did not. If he could figure out how his father had died, if Braunn had not killed him, perhaps he'd sell to the German. But Braunn had said Zachary left no will, and that Buck Daunt had jumped the claim. As Cole reached the eastern edge of the mesa, he thought that Daunt probably assumed he had a right to the mine. He probably still thought of himself as Zachary's oldest friend.

Cole slowed the Appaloosa at the top of the road down from the mesa, the same road he and Braunn and the hired man had ridden up yesterday. The valley yawned below him, awakening, a giant cauldron of fog that reached halfway up the eastern slopes and almost all the way up the mesa to boil and roll beneath his horse's hooves. He could see nothing through the fog. On the eastern side treetops floated above it; on the western side it obliterated the road. The horse, usually anxious to run in the morning, halted willingly, hesitating to proceed, even at a walk, when Cole touched spurs to the speckled hide.

Cole spurred the horse again and they descended. The fog swirled around them, thickening, and wind sighed through invisible evergreens. Cole's eyes never stopped searching through the clinging grayness, but he was almost blind: he could see ten feet, sometimes five, no more. In particularly dense pockets the horse's head began to dissolve, like a mirage.

In his mind he saw faces. Catharine first, of course. The leaf green eyes twinkled, the small, full lips curled in a teasing smile. Her face distended, taking up the whole trail in front of him, fluid like the fog. Her lips parted to laugh. He heard a magpie's raucous call and jumped. The horse jumped too, danced sideways.

Catharine's face faded into Braunn's, squarish, tanned, the eyes sterling lights, like two rays had penetrated the fog to bounce into Cole's mind, stinging. He continued to descend, and Braunn's image chased Catharine's to vanish in the mist.

He rode on with no further hauntings, reached the bottom of the trail, and spurred the horse into an easy trot, toward the sound of the river. He could tell the animal felt relieved at leaving the road: here at the bottom the fog masked the whistle of the wind above, and they heard the reassuring sounds of water flowing over rocks, of aspen and cottonwood and willow leaves fluttering. At the river Cole saw willow trunks rise in front of him. He could not see the branches, only the tips of the lower stems, drooping toward the water, swinging as though dangled from a hidden giant's arm.

He forded the river, which burbled slowly now to wash the horse's fetlocks. The Appaloosa picked his way through the rocks, surefooted, and they reached the other side. The image of Buck Daunt came to mind, materialized in the gray.

This one was more vivid; this valley was, after all, the last place Cole had seen Daunt. He saw him now, not bereaved as then, but fluid like Catharine and Heinrich Braunn, with thin lips parted to show tobacco-browned teeth as he cackled or cursed. Daunt had never really been a friend to anyone, not even Zachary. He called everyone "buck," as if to lump the world together against himself, so the world called him Buck, too. Cole had never known his real name. He'd never married and had no acknowledged children.

Cole listened to the sounds around him—the horse's soft foot-falls on the valley grass, which was thicker and greener than the mesa's; still the leaves fluttering and the South Fork gurgling, though fainter now; still an occasional squawk or buzz. He continued to search around him, turning often in the saddle, wary, increasingly spooked by the fog. He heard nothing unusual, but listened with more than his ears. The horse walked among stands of trees, larger and fuller than Cole remembered, the aspen burnished, the evergreens with sweeping boughs ready for snow. It was as though the boughs held up the fog, or tried to. As he put more distance between himself and the river, the sounds deadened. The breeze stilled, the red and gold leaves hung, fading in and out of his vision, listless, waiting to fall.

Finally he stopped the horse. Noiselessly he slid the Winchester from its boot on the saddle and laid it across his lap. He nudged the horse forward. The fog was even more dense; Cole could hardly make out the worn trail that led to the meadow in front of the cabin. He could not remember how much farther he must ride, and thought his memory had expanded the meadow. The cabin felt very far away.

He heard a new noise. No, he felt a noise. It traveled through his hands on the reins and his legs gripping the saddle. He could not identify it. It felt like something alive, though. A horse, or a man. Maybe a deer. He cocked the rifle with a click.

The click echoed. Only it was not an echo. The horse's soft footfalls echoed, only they were not an echo. A minute tug on the reins brought the Appaloosa to a standstill and the echo did not repeat. The Appaloosa did not shift as most horses would. He made no sound at all. Cole listened hard, barely breathing.

He thought the other click had come from his right and a little behind. He thought it was the click of another person cocking a gun. He hoped it was Gretel.

The snort of a horse startled him. He laid spurs to his own horse's sides and bolted forward. He rode maybe four strides before three mounted figures appeared through the gray, sitting like statues, blocking the trail. Cole hauled on the reins and his horse reared, scared. There were more riders to his side and behind. He jerked around as the horse danced, jerked back to face forward.

There were seven riders and they all wore sack masks over their heads, with ragged holes for eyes. The riders were all men, and all laborers—he could tell from their grime-stained trousers and heavy boots and flannel shirts. They all held handguns, and all the guns were cocked and aimed at him.

The Appaloosa spun and danced. Cole eased the reins and spoke to the horse in a low tone, until he settled.

He looked from man to man, man to gun. Their heights and builds varied, and so did their eyes. Through his fear he forced his mind to study the eyes, memorize them. He would not forget: they all had the same look, a hunger, a frigid hunger for pain and blood and probably death. And gold. He knew they wanted the gold. He studied them with care and found neither Buck Daunt nor Heinrich Braunn, but maybe they worked for one or the other, or both. He wondered fleetingly if Catharine could ever know how these powerful men really did business.

"What do you want?" he asked.

The one straight ahead flicked his gun, indicating Cole should drop his own. Cole did. They wanted his Colt next, so he dropped that, too. They let him keep his knife.

He watched silently as a man with heavy-lidded brown eyes dismounted to retrieve the guns. He was short and stocky with muscular thighs and clumsy, work-blackened hands. After handing the guns off to another, he took a short rope from the pommel of his saddle and tied Cole's hands behind his back, winding the rope many times and cinching it tight. He remounted.

"What do you want with me?" Cole asked again.

He could tell the one in front of him smiled inside his mask, because his blue eyes crinkled at the corners. He seemed to be the leader. None of them said a word. The leader jerked his head westward. Another took the reins of Cole's horse. The three men in front turned their mounts slowly and touched their sides with spurless hobnailed boots, and the horses moved out, tails swishing, oblivious to whatever would happen next. The Appaloosa tossed his head and tried to pull back from the man tugging on the reins, until Cole spoke to him. He moved then.

They rode through trees, skirting the meadow, along the valley floor, where no trail flattened the grass. The mist still swirled, a prison. Cole tried to think of a way out but there was none, for now. He could tumble off the horse and run or roll into the trees, or spur the horse, either way hoping the fog would hide him. But the men all had their guns cocked: they would drill him before he covered a foot. If not for the masks he might have tried it anyway, because that would mean they intended to kill him. No need for masks then. So maybe they would let him live. If he tried to get away now he would die.

They reached the western side of the valley and started to climb. Still no one said a word. Ahead and above, the fog thinned and brightened until it smarted the eyes. Another hundred feet and it gave way to the early warmth of a September day.

Cole wiggled his fingers. He could barely feel them. Catharine popped into his mind again and he wondered what she was doing now. Sitting down to a poached egg and a cup of coffee, strolling in her courtyard. Something routine, familiar. But she would be thinking of him, not as he was now but as he had been last night, as he gave in and held her. She could not know about these men in masks; Braunn would never take the risk of sharing this with her, if it was Braunn. Cole had given too much away to Braunn; Braunn saw he would not fight for the mine, whether he owned it or not. Knowing this, Braunn would think him a liability, but so would Buck Daunt. It could be Daunt.

A half hour later the procession turned left and wound toward a group of peaks called the Ophir Needles on a steep, rocky trail that

Cole recalled vaguely. Now they were a good ten miles out of Telluride and well above the valley, much closer to Ophir. Several times the horses slipped, and Cole had to grip tightly with his knees to stay in the saddle.

They climbed through the spruces and firs to an elfin forest, where winter's bitter winds had twisted aged trees into dwarves. Some of the trees grew to only three feet. The trail cut back on itself repeatedly; Cole figured that if it led to a mine, the location would support only a small crew. It might be the Anna Strike.

They reached a ledge and Cole saw the prospect at the far end. It must be the Anna Strike. It looked deserted, except for a supply shack out front, with pine timbers so new that the sap still glistened yellow in the sun.

Through sparse trees, the ledge commanded an expansive view of the valley, the Braunn mansion beyond, and the surrounding peaks, some still snow-clad, most naked gray. The fog below had cleared, and Cole could make out the cabin and barn two thousand feet down. Smoke threaded toward him from the cabin's chimney, a pathetic welcome. He surveyed the ledge, which was about thirty feet at the widest and twice as long, with the mountain towering above, the ascent broken only by a narrow, sloping lip fifteen feet higher than the ledge. At this elevation air bit the lungs and made the head spin: fighting or running would be hard, if it came to that.

His captors dismounted, keeping at least four guns on him all the time. Here he was the Texas gunfighter, never mind his move to Montana, or wife and stepson, or the ranch they were building. Never mind that he had not drawn his handgun with any deliberate speed in years, that he rarely fired it, that he often left it at home when he went hunting with the Winchester. Never mind that civilization had supposedly conquered the West.

The brown-eyed man with the heavy lids dragged him from the horse. He landed on his shoulder with a grunt and his black Stetson tumbled off and rolled away. The man kicked him onto his belly, bent over him and cut the ropes.

Cole moved fast, before they could react. He spun onto his back, caught the man around the neck with his forearm and wrenched it tight until the man's eyes bulged and his mouth opened and closed in futile gasps for air.

"Drop your guns or I'll kill him." The man's throat gave.

The leader's handgun boomed. Half the hostage's liver splattered across the ledge and blood sprayed Cole's clothes. He shoved the writhing body off him. Another bullet, and the man's eyes stared lifelessly through the mask.

Cole sat up. He was stunned, and scared: he saw no way out. He did not understand the masks, except maybe to trick or frighten (as if the guns weren't enough), because sure as hell it looked like these men meant to kill him.

"What do you want?" he demanded for the third time, but still they said nothing. He understood that their silence was calculated, too, like the masks. They wanted something and would hurt him to get it. It would not be something he wanted to give, maybe not even something he could give. If they only wanted him dead they would have killed him, not their own man. He became acutely aware of his body, as though haze lightning sizzled through him. He did not want to be aware, not now. He needed to be numb.

At a signal from the leader, two others yanked him to his feet and pinned him tightly by the arms. The leader handed off his pistol and approached Cole until they were only a foot apart. Up close, Cole saw gray lashes and eyelids creased with age, but the man stood tall and broad, and his hands were huge.

"Who told you to come here?" he asked in a deep voice all the more menacing for its quiet Scottish timbre.

"Who's asking?"

A rock-hard fist slammed into his gut. His body caved at the middle, strained to double over as air choked from his lungs. The men held him upright. He fought to catch his breath.

"I'm asking. Who sent you?"

He could not speak at first. Then he said, "No one." The man's right arm twitched. "My sister," Cole added, still breathless. "She sent word my father died. She told me not to come. I came anyway."

"You're lying."

For an instant anger blocked the pain in his stomach. "The hell I am. What do you care why I came? Who are you?"

"Answer my question, man!"

Cole said nothing. The man slugged him in the jaw. The muscles in his neck pulled as his head snapped back. Anger flared into rage. He swung his feet up and into the man's chest, knocking him onto the rocky ledge.

The man rolled instantly to his feet and came at Cole with both fists. Cole caught a glimpse of his blue eyes blazing and then the clenched fists crashed into his belly, his ribs, his cheek. Three blows. That made five. He saw nothing but red, black, blinding gold light. He felt nothing but the five blows, over and over, five, ten, twenty-five, though the man had stopped. He wished the other men would let go of his arms. He needed to double over. He needed to throw up. His stomach cramped. He'd eaten no breakfast, nothing came.

He heard the Scotsman laugh, a deep, sadistic belly laugh. Cole squinted through the bursting lights behind his eyes to see the man's knuckles: bright pink, raw. Only five blows and they were raw. Any of those punches could have crushed something vital inside him. Maybe they all had. His left cheek throbbed, the skin and probably the bone split. He heard footsteps but was too weak to look. He saw arms hold out a single-jack hammer and the raw-knuckled hands wrap around the handle. He shuddered.

"Who?" the Scottish voice demanded. "Tell me who!"

He forced his head up on his sprained neck and looked into the bright blue eyes. He could feel blood dripping past the side of his mouth.

"No one," his voice said for him, wearily.

The reddened hands hauled the hammer back and hurtled it forward. Cole heard his ribs crack. He yelled, guttural, choked, and squeezed his eyes shut. "No one," he gasped. "I swear it."

The hammer struck again. Cole's legs collapsed. He tasted salty blood. He heard himself yell another time, the voice not his own, an animal's, beyond reason, comprehension. He lost count of the blows. As his head jerked and rolled, the ledge turned grainy, then warmth rushed into his tingling arms as he felt the men let go. He fell, and the sky turned dark.

Icy liquid showered his face. He opened the only eye that would open and saw five forms above him, blackened by sunlight, and above them the yellow of the sky, glaring, cloudless. He lay on his back and his whole body throbbed.

"Get up!" commanded the big Scotsman, but his body would not roll over, his legs and arms would not push him up. One of the masked men grabbed him and dragged him to his feet. He stood, swaying, and noticed through his one open eye that they all had their guns out again. Without two eyes the world looked flat, the guns closer, nearly touching him. He did not want anything to touch him. A gun barrel would poke. He would scream.

The Scotsman waved him toward the pine shack. Someone had opened the door. Cole staggered inside, his body a disjointed jumble of bones and muscle that used to work. The Scotsman and two other men followed. One of them carried the corpse.

Cole stumbled to the far wall and turned around to fall back against it. He had to work to focus his open eye. The fog had returned, this time inside his head. He made out tools and provisions piled on one side of the shack, while neatly stacked wooden cases of dynamite formed an inner wall on the other.

"No traces, huh," he muttered through split lips.

The Scotsman laughed. "There's enough here to blow up this whole mountain."

"Or bring it down."

He shrugged. "Less to dig through later."

Another man assembled a fuse with a professional blaster's expertise. He trailed it across the top of the wall of dynamite, beyond reach, on to the door and out.

The Scotsman leveled his gun at Cole's chest. Cole felt his aching throat rise and fall as he swallowed, but he also felt relieved. Come on you mining bastard, he wanted to say, pull the trigger and get it over with. He tried to call Laura's face to mind, but could see only the man's blue eyes, narrowed now, hungry for the kill. Then the face changed to Catharine's, and Cole wanted to cry out against her. He wanted to see Laura. He wanted never to have left Laura. But he had been the one who'd chosen, chosen to travel back in time. Laura now hid in a future he could not reach.

Over the Scotsman's shoulder, Cole saw another man come to the shack's door, where he stood watching, pale eyes narrowed. The Scotsman cocked his gun. "Don't kill him," the other said. His accent was German.

The Scotsman lowered the gun and fired. The bullet tore into Cole's left thigh. It spun him around and into the wall, then drove him to the floor. He lunged at the Scotsman but collapsed, grasping air. The man stepped neatly away, laughing with his head thrown back. A flash of ignited fuse rounded the door frame at the top and sped toward the dynamite. The Scotsman strode outside, leaving the door open.

Cole could not move. The sound of the sputtering fuse mixed with that of receding horses crashing down through stunted trees. Lying on his belly, his arm stretched along the floor under this head, blood pooling under this leg, he stared dully at the fuse. Only a few feet now. He lifted his head and looked to his other side at the brown-eyed man's body. Flesh hung where the bullet had torn his side away.

Cole let his eyes close. He thought of death, and how it would take away the pain. But the dead body slithered behind his eyelids and into his mind. His brain told him he did not want to die next to that man, with both their insides scattered all over this mountain above the valley, across from Catharine's castle.

He could still hear the fuse. It seemed to have slowed. He could hear each sputter, and each one sounded like the click of a gun's hammer. He did not want to die hearing that sound, though he figured he deserved it. It fit.

He opened his eye and looked at the corpse again. He turned his head and rolled his eye in its socket and saw the fuse had hardly moved any closer to the cases of dynamite.

Time had slowed. Time was pretending to give him a chance to live.

He thought, So be it, you bastard.

He put his arms under his chest and began to drag his body across the floor. The rough wood made it slow going. Only bruised muscle held his ribs together, and his body seemed to stretch. He dragged on and reached the sunlit rectangle of the door. He rolled out onto the rock. So time had let him get this far. It was crueler than he'd thought.

His body wanted him to lie still. Instead, he looked toward scraggly evergreens at the outer edge of the shelf and kept sliding along the ground. Once he looked behind him. The wide ribbon of blood his leg left on the rock made him move faster. Fucking time, he kept thinking, I'll beat you. For Laura, for Laura. And Sam. And Catharine.

The shack exploded.

A wall of air hurled him against a tree, whipped his body around it and dropped him. He tumbled down the steep slope. Every rock and tree smashed him like the hammer. His right forearm, his left ankle, his ribs, his collarbone all took the blows in turn. Then the hammer smashed his head. Agony surged down the mountain and over him like a molten avalanche, a searing current that arched his back and stiffened his limbs before it thundered away toward the valley.

The thunder faded. Cole hung for a moment, devoid of thought, emotion, sensation. He hung in a void as black as any mine, and for once, with what may have been left, valued the blackness. Then even the void slipped away.

12

Will and Testament

"**H**e's dead. Zachary's dead." Gretel had walked all the way up the mountain in the middle of the night and gotten him out of the Flossie to tell him this. "He died in the Anna Strike. I think it happened yesterday. I think something went wrong with the explosives."

Johnny had looked away, swallowed, wrapped his arms around his body, bare of a shirt. Showers had dampened the mountain, leaving the air close and clammy by the start of the night shift; now the last straggling clouds scudded past the moon, which shone cold and white in the windy sky.

He had watched the clouds, unable to speak. How could she speak so easily? His eyes smarted, yet in the reflected gold glow from the Flossie's workings, he saw no moisture in hers, no tears on her cheeks. Chilled, he rubbed his arms with his hands. Zachary, he'd thought. Christ, Zachary, you and that damned metal cleaning spoon. It had to have been the spoon.

"Johnny."

He was your father, Gretel, he'd wanted to tell her. Your father. Cry, damn it. Cry and let me hold you. And hold me.

But she had not cried. "Will you come to the valley tomorrow?" she'd asked. "To help me bring him down?"

"I'll come now."

She'd shaken her head. "Go back to work. It's too dark. In the morning we can bring him down." And she hurried away.

Alone and shivering, he'd stood on the mountain outside the Flossie while her graceful form receded into the night, and the wind had whipped around him. He'd felt as naked and cold as he imagined the mountain must feel without its green cloak.

The cold drove him back into the mine, where he finished his shift. He said nothing to his men about Zachary's death; he would tell them tomorrow, though by then they'd already know.

The next morning he'd done as Gretel asked and helped her retrieve the bits and pieces left of the man they had both loved. He checked every inch of the demolished shaft and, except for the twisted remnants of Zachary's metal cleaning spoon, found nothing to indicate whether the charges had been set off prematurely, or intentionally. When he told Gretel this, it made her angry. She thought he had accused her father of suicide.

"No," he said. "That's not it. Not him, someone else."

Her anger had vanished, as a rock does in a mirrorlike lake, with a ripple and then again no sign. He'd been surprised she showed any emotion at all, given her steady reserve since the previous night. Working next to him, sifting through charred ruins, collecting what looked human, she'd seemed as cold and black as the inside of a mine, she who hated mines.

Against her wishes, the area coroner and Marshal Luke Halloran also checked the site.

"Impossible to say," the coroner had agreed. Halloran had

avoided Johnny's eyes, spattering a rock with tobacco juice, and Gretel had stared icily across the valley, ignoring them all. "Old boy like him ought've known better than to use a damn metal cleaning spoon. Seen too many cases just like this."

"This one has a motive," Johnny said.

"They all do," the coroner replied, packing his things, preparing to go. "Gold makes one hell of a motive, Mr. Torres."

He left and so did Halloran.

"I'm going home," Gretel said, and did, so that once again Johnny had stood alone on a cold, windy mountainside with a mine in it. He thought of calling them all back, of telling them about Zachary's will, which might or might not have made a difference in the coroner's verdict. Probably not, and so Johnny let them go.

Zachary would have wanted it this way, because Zachary had written the will for his son, no one else. It was hidden now in Johnny's room at Emma's, behind one of Gretel's more recent works of art, a framed tapestry of the candy cabin from the fairy tale that bore her name.

"I want to write a will," Zachary had said one night, late, sitting at the homemade pine table in his cabin with his hands wrapped around a cup of Gretel's bitter coffee. Gretel was sleeping in the next room. "You know how to write a will, Johnny?"

The floor felt suddenly colder under Johnny's bare feet. He set his own coffee down, though his hands felt cold, too. "Are you all right?" he asked.

Zachary laughed softly. "Of course I am. Been doing some thinking, is all. I guess losing Marie set me to it. And maybe Catharine DuBois coming back here, too. You probably know I have a son, Cole, and that he's been gone a long time. Well, before he took off, he and Catharine were close, I mean real close. But he went his own way and she went hers, and Marie and I let them go. Maybe we ought not've let go so easily, but we did, and now Marie dying has set me to thinking that I want to give Cole something. I want to give him the Anna Strike."

Johnny took a deep breath. "Okay, Zachary. You want to write a will, I'll help you. If Cole is why you want to write it."

"He is."

"Okay."

"Johnny?"

"Yeah?"

"I don't want Gretel to know. I want you to keep it for me. Hide it somewhere safe, you know, like your room at Emma's. All right?"

He'd agreed, and Zachary had dipped the pen.

They'd talked some more, afterward. Zachary hemmed and hawed about it, but finally he told Johnny he wanted Cole to come back of his own accord, and if he stayed away Johnny should burn the will. He said this in some pain, but Johnny knew it was his way of repaying his son for leaving home so completely. Then, as if to make up for this small punishment, he got another piece of paper, dipped his pen again, and wrote Cole a letter. He sealed it with candle wax and addressed it simply, My Son. He did not give it to Johnny to read, merely to hide.

"All right," he'd said when it was all done. They turned in, Johnny to the bed where Gretel slept, murmuring in her dreams, Zachary to the room his son and daughter had shared as children.

A week after Zachary's death, Johnny still had the will and Cole still had not shown. The whole town was sure Zachary had been murdered, and incapable of understanding why Johnny hadn't done something about it. They heaped no responsibility on Halloran or the coroner, but they'd seen Johnny use his gun, and those who missed seeing had heard. No one had told him exactly what he should do, nor even discussed the case with him beyond offering condolences, but he knew they wanted justice, or at least a fight.

He considered riding out. Gretel did not want him here; she had yet to share tears with him. Three days ago she had said she wanted him to stop calling on her at the cabin.

"I know you want to help me," she'd said, "but you must understand that I need to be alone." He did not understand but neither had he gone back.

Yesterday he'd sat at the Baroness Hotel bar, openly but absently watching Heinrich Braunn's corner table. It was empty; Braunn hadn't been to town in days. The violin, cello, and piano slogged forth some obscure adagio, the instruments neither well-tuned nor well-played. Johnny drank Scotch, top drawer this time, more Scotch than he would have put away before Zachary died, before Gretel shut him out, before Cole failed to honor Zachary's memory with a visit home. At the back of his mind was the aggravating admission that he would not return home to honor his own father, either. His mother, well, he would go home for her, if anyone could find him to let him know. And his sister Linda—he would go home for her, dead or not, except that she had cut herself free from the family even more thoroughly, though less willingly, than he. He would go anywhere for his sister, if he only knew where to go.

Instead of leaving Telluride, he sat at the bar and thought of cabling Cole, because Zachary was dead and could no longer care whether Cole came on his own, and because something had to give. Then he looked at the glass of Scotch, his sixth, empty, and almost smiled. He would not cable Cole. Give him one more day. He set the glass down, paid in coin, as always, and tried to walk steadily out of the bar. He also walked all the way to work, in order to sober up before entering the mine.

When he got there he remembered he had on his suit and clean white shirt. And that it was Saturday, his night off. He sat on the flat expanse of mountain outside the dark, quiet workings, with the beams of the hoist rigging a series of black slashes against the half-clouded, half-starry sky, and put his head in his hands and wept as Gretel would not. A long time later, in the wee hours, he walked back to town, and drank and danced at all the dance halls until near dawn, when he reached the end of the line and found himself ready to throw up in front of Silvia's. With head spinning and stomach doing flips, he staggered back to Emma's, hauled himself up the stairs, and toppled into bed.

He'd slept until now, suppertime on Sunday, when the scent of a woman and a timid voice brought him around. His eyes opened, swollen and unfocused, to the blur of someone familiar.

"Emma?" His voice sounded more like a croak.

"I'm sorry to wake you, John. I would never have come into your room, but you slept through my knock and I thought you should know."

He started to sit up, groaned and fell back.

She must have seen him blanch, because she blanched too, and rushed through her message: "There's talk in town. Folks are saying someone tried to murder Zachary Coleman."

His eyes opened farther and he tried again to sit up, made it to his elbows. "What?" His voice had graduated from croak to rasp.

"He never got to town. They say he went straight to Mr. Braunn's mansion—"

Confused, he cut her off. "What do you—" Then he knew. Not Zachary: Zachary's son. Cole. Cole had come home, or tried to, finally. "You mean Cole," he said.

She nodded, rushed on. "Some say Mr. Braunn stopped the train and took him off. The servants say he left the mansion in the morning, that would be early this morning, and he was killed."

"Where?"

"Wherever the Anna Strike is." She smoothed her apron nervously. "I'll be tending to supper now."

He nodded and fell back as she shut the door behind her. His belly hitched and he rolled out of bed to his knees and grabbed the basin. Then, somehow, he stood and walked to his door, with the world curiously tilted, first one way, then the other. Once there he decided he'd better wear his Colt, so he got it from the dresser and buckled it on, having a little trouble with the catch. He made it to the door again, and managed the stairs, no easy trick. In the dining room, Emma's three teenaged kids were sitting down to supper with two new boarders who worked the day shift.

Emma scurried to a chair and pulled it out for him. He would've felt embarrassed if he'd had the strength.

"Just some bread, Emma," he said, declining the offer of the seat and hot food.

"You need more than bread, John."

He attempted a smile. "I need to get going."

So she got him half a loaf and some water, and he headed for the stable. The palomino tossed its head and snorted at the odor of whiskey.

"Shut up," Johnny said, and cinched the saddle.

The horse danced as he mounted and he told it to hold the hell still. It ignored him, as always, but he climbed on. He dropped one rein, had to lean forward to retrieve it, and cursed the drill steel in his head. Finally he rode out, hoping the evening air would help.

It did. Around dusk, when the sky had softened to purple except for one whitish streak behind the western mountains, the palomino lurched up the last few yards to the ledge.

Luke Halloran was there already, wrapped in a bulky, soiled overcoat that seemed about to slip from his sloped shoulders.

"Howdy, Torres," he said in his bland voice.

Johnny touched the brim of his hat. His headache had begun to disappear, but now it clawed its way back. "Evening, Marshal. Been up here all day?"

Halloran grinned his chinless grin, which stretched the pock-marks in his cheeks. "I wouldn't put it that way, no. You? This your first trip?"

Johnny nodded and leaned forward on the saddle horn. "Find the body yet?"

The marshal eyed him a moment before replying. If he doubted Johnny's right to check the ledge, he at least knew Cole's sister was Johnny's woman. Everyone knew that, since Zachary's funeral. He shrugged and held out a broken handgun and a black Stetson. The Stetson was well-worn but intact.

"Found these. And bones, blood, and supplies scattered every-where, all burnt to a goddamned crisp."

Johnny took the gun. Its handle was charcoal. He handed it back to Halloran.

"So what's next?"

"Give a few of these bones and the hat to his sister, tell her as much as I know. See if I can find out who did it."

"Really?"

"Don't matter a whole lot, does it?"

"I'm sure it does to someone. Maybe Buck, huh?"

He could see Halloran rein in his temper. "If Buck knew anything about this, he would've told you, Torres. You're his number-one gun these days." So the marshal was not in on all of Daunt's secrets. That's what Johnny wanted to know.

"Maybe. You through here?"

"Yup. You?"

Johnny hesitated. "Yeah. I just wanted to see what was up."

"Good, then let's get moving. Too damned dark riding down that trail at night."

13

Remains

Consciousness returned slowly, a whisper stealing into a dream, hinting that the world waited, that oblivion was not all. It whispered his name first: Zachary Coleman. You are Zachary Coleman. They call you Cole. Consciousness stopped there, for a moment that could have been an hour.

Then sounds drifted in, mutterings, not whispers, to lap at his shore. Mutterings—faint, unidentified. No, human voices. You are not the only human being, consciousness told him.

The mutterings withered as thoughts intruded. Where am I? God, my head pounds. I feel like I am lying upside down, like all the blood has drained from my body. Everything is numb but my head. Where am I?

The thoughts told him to open his eyes. He tried. One opened but the other stuck shut. The open one saw a blur. He began to wonder what happened. The question faded. The mutterings returned; he heard the voices again, indistinct, far off.

Not far off, far above. And he *was* lying upside down, or almost. And on something freezing and wet, though he did not feel cold inside; he felt nothing inside.

His one-eyed vision cleared and he saw a tangle of gnarled arms against fuzzy purple. Trees. Sky. Dusk. He was outside. He tried to raise his head. Pain flooded him, rushed uphill to his toes and fingers. His head fell back and his breath came in gasps.

Jesus Christ, what had happened?

He remembered. The horror of the memory stirred his voice, raised a scream, which emerged guttural, choked. He clenched his fists, felt bruises on his wrists.

The voices! He lay still, listening, heard only his own breathing, slower now but ragged. Even the wind had died, and the evening creatures with it. He waited. The voices came again, farther off, to his right. Still indistinct. He struggled to focus his sluggish mind, recalled the trail over that way. So they were leaving. If they were searching, they had finished with the ledge. So he had to get to the ledge.

He tried to move his arms and groaned at the pull on his ribs. Every motion assaulted him with terrifying, enraging memories. He saw the bright blue eyes with the crinkles at the corners, smiling before the fists slammed home. He saw the raw knuckles, the hammer clenched in the long, blunt, calloused fingers. He saw the fingers grip the hammer whitely. He saw the hammer draw back. He heard a crack: his ribs, crunching.

"Jesus," he pleaded, whispering. "Go away."

He rolled over and scrambled around so his head was up and his legs down. The pain obliterated the memories; the blood drained from his head, which made him dizzy. The leg wound must have cost much blood. A thought poked through, a tiny, inconsequential reassurance: lying upside down had probably saved his life. For now.

The slope was steep. He considered going down, but the ledge was closer than the road below and the people with the voices had gone down. He worked gradually toward the top, grabbing rocks and stubby trees when he could, until his arms burned with the effort. He pushed against the ground with his right leg; his left was useless. What must have been a half hour passed and dusk with it. The moon rose and he'd covered only twenty feet. His leg started to bleed again, streaking the moonlit mountainside glossy black.

"Listen Luke," said Johnny, "let me go alone to Gretel's." They had reached the spot where the trail met the road to town.

"What for?"

"What do you think? Cole was the last of her kin."

"I should ask her some questions. Maybe Cole went to her place before they got him."

"Maybe, maybe not. If you think you need to talk to her, I'll send her into town. Let me go alone."

The marshal sat his horse and scratched his left ear. Johnny figured he'd rather let the case die anyway, and the longer he waited to question Gretel, the more likely it would.

Halloran dropped his hand from his ear and held out the oily, dirty sack of remains, along with the hat. He kept the gun, which was all right with Johnny, then loped off toward Telluride while Johnny trotted down the trail to the cabin. Johnny wanted to turn and race back to the ledge, but he trotted on, holding the edgy palomino with a tight rein. He was as edgy as the horse. The moon would set well before dawn, and his chances of finding Cole in the dark were slim. He pulled the horse down to a walk, slowly picking his way into the valley, his ears tuned to the waning hoofbeats. A moment more and he reined in to listen. Seconds passed. The hoofbeats faded.

Johnny dropped the hat and sack, wheeled his startled mount, and charged back up the trail.

Cole climbed slowly, fighting delirium. He wanted so much to rest, just for a minute, or not even that long. But if he did he'd never finish. He looked toward the ledge and his neck muscles cramped. Only another ten yards.

Then he heard the click of hooves on rock. It came from the ledge. He saw the rhythmic sweep of lantern light and wanted to call out. Maybe someone up there could help. Like hell, he thought.

The light traversed the slope, back and forth, skimming toward him. He scouted for whatever might cast a shadow and rolled behind a rocky protrusion a few feet to his left. He came to rest on his back and wrapped his arms around his ribs. His body pleaded with him to call out.

The light darted over the rocks at his head, then hesitated. He held his breath. The light moved on and finally flickered away.

Cole heard the horse leave and resumed his climb. Ages later he reached the ledge and hauled himself onto it. Sweat soaked his hair and skin and clothes, and he shivered with pain and the chill mountain air. You can't rest now, he told himself. Especially not now.

Johnny searched for hours. After the ledge and the prospect hole, he covered every trail that led to the valley, and the entire road along the valley's east rim. He thought of going to Gretel's now, but from what he'd seen on that ledge there was no way Cole could have made it that far. He also thought of giving up, because there was really no way he could have survived the blast, either. Unless he got out of the shack.

Johnny stopped in the middle of the road, frustrated, weary, hungry. Emma's half loaf was still in his pocket, but though he felt as gaunt as Luke Halloran he did not want to eat. He did not want to sleep, either; he wanted to find Cole. The moon drew ever nearer the southwestern peaks. Soon it would cast blackness over the ledge and the trail and Johnny would have to wait until dawn, a waste of more than two hours.

He decided to try the ledge once more.

The moon had set by the time he got there. He swung the lantern toward the outer rim, pausing at odd, barely recognizable shapes: a beam from the shack, twisted charcoal; a length of heavy cable, still wound; the head of a single-jack hammer, its handle a withered twig. The light passed over a pile of something and he swung it back again. Cole.

He looked dead. He lay face down, with his legs hanging over the edge of the rim. Carefully, Johnny pulled him all the way onto the ledge and rolled him onto his back. His arm flopped over, his head to the side. His eyes were closed, his face and the front of his once light blue shirt darkened by blood and dirt. Johnny put an ear to his chest. At first nothing, then the faint heartbeat and intake of air.

"I didn't think you'd give up that easily," he said.

He felt for broken bones. Cole began to come around: his breathing quickened and he murmured a word or two. As Johnny checked further, he knew the broken ribs, lacerations, and multiple swellings resulted from more than the explosion. Then he found the leg wound.

Cole opened one eye. The other was puffed shut and patched with blood from a cut on his temple.

"I'm going to take you down the mountain to your sister's," Johnny told him. "We'll take care of you there."

Cole stared at him vacantly for a moment, then whispered, "Who are you?"

"My name is Johnny Torres. I was a friend of your father's."

Cole's stare turned vacant again, then his eyelid fell shut. Johnny called to him to make sure he was out, then lifted the torn body and draped it over his horse.

14

Waking Dreams

The pounding began while she slept. She hoped it came from her dream, but in the dream she lay next to Johnny at Lizardhead Pass, languishing in the sun, the breeze, the caress of his hand, with only the wind for sound.

The pounding persisted, forcing her awake. She let the dream go with a sigh: Johnny dissolved to the grainy darkness of her room as she opened eyes crusted with sleep. Johnny dissolved; he had dissolved weeks ago, after the Fourth of July, dissipating like the smoke from the fireworks and the popping six-guns, his own popping six-gun that killed two drunks and got him promoted into the Flossie and in its own way killed first Marie and then Zachary, and now Gretel. She lived in her dreams.

She swung her long legs out of bed. Her toes touched the cold floor and she shivered. She wore a nightgown these nights, without Johnny, a flannel that should have kept her warm. While the pounding continued, she groped for her shawl, and threw it around her shivering shoulders.

"Gretel!" It was Johnny's voice, strained—the voice of her dreams. Yet now the cold of the floor was a shock that the dream would have muffled. I was dreaming of you, she wanted to tell him. I dream of you all the time.

"Gretel!"

She reached for a lamp, carried it to the door, and lighted it as she stood on the other side from him, inches away. The flame flared; the kerosene odor filled her nose, singeing. She unbarred the door, the door she never used to bar, and opened it halfway. Johnny stood there with a body slung across his shoulders. A head dangled from one end, booted feet from the other.

"Johnny?" She was confused. "What—"

"Please just open the door, Gretel."

"But who—" She stalled; she could not open the door. Since Zachary's death, she had been keeping everybody out, but mostly him.

"Open the door!" he ordered, angry.

She obeyed.

He walked past her to Zachary's room, laid the other man on the bed. Blood and grime covered them both.

"He's still alive," Johnny said. "Get some water and clean rags, will you?"

She stood frozen.

"Gretel, please."

"Tell me what's going on."

So he stood and faced her. She looked past him and the confusion lifted. She walked toward the bed. Johnny stepped out of her way. Revulsion rose in her like bile.

"It's my brother," she said. "Why did you bring him here?"

"You can see why I brought him."

"I can see he needs a doctor. Take him to town."

Johnny shook his head and leaned over Cole again, pulled off the filthy boots and clothes, took his knife and cut away the bloodstained woolens.

"Get me some water."

"Johnny—"

He shoved past her and out of the room. She heard rattling pans, then the slosh of water.

She looked at Cole, who stirred. Johnny returned with water and cloths. He began to wash off the blood, starting with the left side of Cole's face. Cole resisted his touch, but never fully woke. Gretel watched. If possible, she would have bodily removed both men from her house. It was hers, now. Zachary's death left her nothing else.

From the bruised flesh around her brother's ribs and the ragged bullet hole in his leg, Gretel knew he needed more help than Johnny could give him. She had a wagon; Johnny could get him to town easily enough and maybe he would live. She watched him squirm and realized she did not want him dead, only out of her life.

"You don't have to help," said Johnny, "but I'm not moving him again."

"You don't and he'll probably die."

"Would that bother you?"

She had never felt so angry with him. He deserved it, for bringing it all back, that part of her past she despised most. She stalked from the room.

God damn her brother. You bastard, she wanted to scream. You refused to bury your own mother, you rode off to a life of murder without even wishing your father good luck. You bastard! I worshiped you, and you left without saying good-bye.

First light was breaking through the peaks outside. Not long ago this would have drawn her to the meadow, where she would have strolled, perhaps naked, with her fingers skimming the tall grass. Occasionally she had done this with Johnny, before he disappeared into the mine. It occurred to her that she'd really known him only a short time before he disappeared, but long enough to eclipse the rest of her life. She hated him for disappearing.

No sunrise stroll today. She sat on the hearth rug, drew her legs up under her nightgown and wrapped her arms tightly around her knees. After a while she heard footsteps. Johnny stood in the doorway to her father's room, looking twice his thirty years.

"What did you expect me to do?" she asked.

"Do you have any laudanum?"

"No."

"Whiskey?"

"I threw it out."

He sighed and ran a wet hand through his hair. "I can't take that bullet out if he's awake."

"You can't take it out at all. He needs a doctor."

Johnny shook his head.

"Why? What's going on here?"

"I have to take care of him first. I'll explain it to you after."

"You don't know how it was."

"I know he's your brother. That should be enough." He walked past her to the door. "I'm going to town after some laudanum."

"You're in danger, aren't you." She said this coldly, barring compassion and concern.

"We're all in danger. I'll get it from one of Silvia's girls. She'll keep quiet about it." He opened the door but paused before going outside. "Stay with him if you can stand it," he said. "I'll be back as soon as I can."

He left, and she stared bleakly at the closed door.

Cole groaned, so Gretel got up off the rug and walked across the cold floor to stand over him. He must have groaned in sleep, because now he lay still and silent, eyes closed, breathing a little better than before. Then he groaned again, twisted in the bed and stretched his hand toward his leg. Johnny had covered him with Zachary's blanket. Through it, he touched the bullet wound with his fingers.

Gretel saw moisture on his face and wondered whether he had a fever. Too high and it would mean infection. She resisted wondering this, but her hand reached to feel his forehead. She saw that Johnny had left a bowl of clean water on the pine table by the bed. A cloth floated in the water. Her hand wrung out the cloth and sponged the moisture from her brother's face. She looked at her hand, someone else's hand.

Cole murmured something. Gretel's hand put the cloth back in the bowl and she started to leave. Cole said it again. This time she understood, and turned back to him. His right eye was half-open, glazed.

"Catharine," he called. "Catharine." He reached weakly toward Gretel.

His stare caught her, like her mother's used to. She'd always thought he'd had Anna's eyes, frosted blue-gray. No, she thought now, Anna's eyes had been frosted, Cole's were more shielded. She wished he would let her go. Wished Anna would, too.

She weakened. She went to her brother, knelt at his side, took his hand and held it tight, though no tighter than he held hers. She bowed her head and pressed his hand to her forehead, and after a while tears ran down the back of his hand, over the raw bruises on his wrist, over the chafed skin of his arm, over the sinewy muscles, the veins, the wiry dark hairs. She kept her head bowed, kept him from seeing her cry. She doubted he could feel the tears.

His grip relaxed and she looked at him again, afraid this time, but he breathed evenly, sleeping or passed out. His left eye was bruised, but she saw laugh lines around the other, white in suntanned skin. He never used to laugh much as a kid.

I know you never cared for me, she thought. But I cared for you. Zachary might have needed you when Anna died, but I needed you worse before that. Zachary spent all his time at the mines or the saloons or Marie DuBois's. Anna stayed home with me but she was cold as a stone. I was so lonely, Cole.

Suddenly tired, she sat on the floor and leaned her head against her father's mattress, where her brother now lay. As she drifted toward sleep she thought she felt his hand on her hair, but then again it might have been a dream.

15

The Blue Habit

From the mezzanine Catharine could see Heinrich standing at the great bowed window, there on the landing. He usually sat, but now he stood, wearing the smoking jacket she had bought him in France, and she thought this unusual so early in the day. He held one hand behind his straight, broad back with the silver hair hanging below his collar. In the other hand he held a cigar. He never smoked at this hour.

Cole had not come back yesterday. She hoped he would come today, and the hope gave her an eager chill.

"Good morning, Heinrich," she said, with the eager chill in her voice.

He puffed on his cigar and gazed out over the valley. The edge of the mesa obscured the valley floor where Gretel lived, but the eastern slope rose in the view, with its velvet blanket of evergreen, speckled now and again with yellow aspen, until it reached the stunted forest and the place where Zachary Coleman had sunk his prospect hole, where he found gold, where he died.

"You should not sleep so late," Heinrich said. "You miss too much that way. The day happens at its beginning and end; the middle is but an adjunct."

She frowned. "It's only half past eight."

"We had a lovely sunrise this morning. You really should have watched it with me. Only then I would have missed it, because I would have felt compelled to watch you. When the first rays touch your face, they appear to penetrate several layers of skin, as they would filter through a brook or a lake. It's lovely, really. You could never know how lovely."

"Heinrich, what is it? What has happened?"

"Your friend Cole was killed yesterday."

It struck her that by facing out the window, he offered the greatest courtesy. It also struck her that perhaps he had, momentarily, lost his game, though this would not last. He would simply adjust the rules, to the extent his game allowed. She thought these things, not allowing herself to feel anything at all.

He did adjust the rules, just as she knew he would—in front of her, in a way imperceptible to anyone but her, in a shift of his spine, a lifting of his cigar, a flicker of a glance over his shoulder, the barest hint of a smile. Mother of God, she thought, a smile. And suddenly she had this awful fear that the game had caught her up again, too, the game of infallible self-control, that she would not be able to cry, or worse, that the tidiness she suddenly felt inside would keep her from feeling anything at all, especially grief. She would be like Heinrich, with their marriage consummated at last.

"He went to the supply shack near the Anna Strike," Heinrich said. "There was an explosion, but nobody thought anything of it because the miners at Ophir have begun blasting again and in any case everyone knows Buck Daunt will start deepening the hole sooner or later. Then someone let out a story in town. Luke Halloran rode to the shack. Coleman's horse was gone, but Halloran found his hat. Odd that the hat did not burn."

"His body?" she asked, her voice thin, her mind tracing the body she loved, the body she had traced with her own fingers two nights ago. "Was there a body?"

"No body. Only scattered remains."

Catharine realized she was clutching the back of the chair. "You said someone let out a story. What story?"

He turned on her. "They say I murdered him. That is what you wanted to know, is it not? That is what you are afraid of."

"You didn't."

He smiled and shook his head grimly. His eyes never left hers. "Your emotions color your judgment, Catharine. It happens to all of you. It is what kills you in the end."

She groped to the front of the chair and sank into it. She put her elbow on the chair's arm and bowed her head to her hand.

"I'm sorry," she said weakly.

He stalked past her and down the steps, and the soap-clean smell of him lingered with the smoke. He had already finished his bath, for the third time in a week without her. Slumped in the chair, she stared out the window and over the valley, to where the shack had been, to where Cole had died. The sunlight shone white, washing everything so clean.

She walked up the stairs to the mezzanine, where she turned down the corridor to her suite. What should she wear today? Perhaps the blue riding habit. Yes. She should ride down to the valley and offer her sympathy to Gretel. Yes. And take her some pastries or dinner or roses. She had white roses, though their thorns were the worst. A question pricked her mind: Why did people wear black for death yet commemorate it with white flowers?

And then she heard his voice, telling her he saw she remembered he liked blue. Only he'd said that sarcastically, because she'd hurt him by invading his perfect life so suddenly. His perfect life. Like hers.

She walked along the hall, into her room, to her closet and inside it, to look along the rows of perfect clothes. Perfect. She looked at the blue dress for a long time, to see if it could make her feel anything. Her eyes roved on until she reached the riding habits. Rose, hunter green, chocolate brown, charcoal gray, navy blue. She pulled out the blue habit and took it to her dressing room.

Sitting at the vanity, she brushed her hair, twisted it into a chignon at the back of her neck. She chose not to summon Freda. As a young woman, she had dressed alone for Cole, and painted her toenails. She remembered the flicker of disappointment on his face when he saw her nails two nights ago. Never mind the toenails, she thought: in the mirror her face painted a picture of its own, serene and very beautiful.

She removed her kimono, then dressed herself in white lace underclothes and a white tailored shirt and the navy blue split skirt and matching tweed jacket with the velveteen collar. She pulled on high-heeled boots and left her suite.

She strode past the guest room, then turned back and opened the door. The room was empty and neat. Tidy, like her. Gretel's blue masterpiece of a counterpane with the interlocking rings covered the empty bed. Gretel had completed no more weavings since Zachary's death. Catharine went into the room and shut the door.

16

South Side

Johnny rode down Pacific Avenue toward the end of the line, past Marie's Fallen Idle, Big Billy's Senate, and the countless other dance halls where he'd gotten blind drunk Saturday night. Now it was Monday morning, with the street as bleached and blighted as ever after a Telluride weekend. Never mind that yesterday had been Sunday, a day of motionless contemplation in some circles, priestly hellfire in others. Never mind that Johnny's mother had taken him every Saturday afternoon to confession and every Sunday morning to mass. He had neither confessed his sins nor accepted the host in years, not since leaving Mexico, except once in Spain when he'd gone back to look for Linda, at the cathedral where he was christened.

Here in Telluride a saloon or two might give way to a churchless minister's sermon on Sunday morning, a circuit-riding priest might dish out bread and wine and penitence for sins confessed, and the brand-new whitewashed Congregational church on Colorado Avenue might fill with singing women and the men they had dragged from bed. But come Sunday evening the revelry would recommence and come Monday morning this blight would hit. The miners would work intensely, even morosely, with heads ducked. The barkeeps would clean up.

Johnny should have worked last night; Daunt would give him hell, might even fire him, at last. He wouldn't mind. Maybe just ride out. Or no, not now, not after getting involved in this mess with Cole. Now he had to stay, and probably fight. Now the town would get its wish.

The palomino's head drooped as he walked down the line.

"I know how you feel," Johnny said.

Silvia's parlor house was one of eight. He did not want to see Silvia. Their paths had yet to cross here in Telluride, which meant she was avoiding him, still blaming him for Rosasharon's death. Rosasharon had been the only girl in the house with any chance of getting out. She'd gotten out all right.

Though Silvia probably hated him, Johnny figured she'd cooperate. Her code said she had to. So would Iris, Silvia's other niece and Rosasharon's sister, who was addicted to laudanum and always ready for extra pocket money. Up in Leadville, before Rosasharon died, the men still thought Iris was worth their ten bucks and Silvia cared enough about her girls to keep them clean and well-dressed. Her house there had been near the beginning of the line; now it was at the end.

Johnny dismounted and flipped his horse's reins around the rail in front of the peeling yellow frame building and knocked. A rustle and a grumble filtered to him and then Silvia opened the curtained door.

"God damn you, Johnny Torres, don't you know it's the crack of dawn? My girls need rest." Her green eyes flashed amid baggy flesh. She wore no makeup and her hair fell over her shoulders in a copper tangle. Once she'd been fat, but now her gaudy red kimono hung as loosely as her skin. Her unexpected alertness and lack of surprise at his arrival made Johnny uneasy. He forced a smile.

"More like halfway to noon than the crack of dawn," he said. "You gonna let me in or not?"

She stood protectively in the doorway with the door half-open. He thought of Gretel at the door to her cabin.

"Silvia . . . "

She let him in. In the morning light her face looked as haggard as the ravaged entry parlor of the house, where frayed gold fringe edged threadbare red velvet. At night the place would look less worn, but then nobody would care.

"What do you need, Johnny?" Silvia asked in her old, smoky voice. "You didn't come here for a romp. Well?"

"I need to see Iris."

She snorted through her small, fine nose. All her features were small and fine, but they got lost in the wrinkled pink skin and, later in the day, the makeup. She had aged since Rosasharon died.

"She's sleeping," she told him. "Damn girl sleeps all day, now. Men say she's as dried up as your Flossie."

"Let me see her, Silvia."

"I won't. Now now."

"Why?"

"You look tired yourself, Johnny. How about some coffee?"

He nodded. She pointed to an armchair, and as he sat back against velvet worn from red to rust, soft to scratchy, he decided to take it easy with her. He'd never gain any ground pushing, and he needed to find out why she resisted his request, whether she was wearing her grudge or had other reasons. Maybe someone had reached her already. He sat up.

Silvia brought the coffee, weak and tepid.

"Thank you," he said.

She sat in the chair next to his, reached to touch his shirt where dirt mixed with dried blood. "Been fighting, Johnny?"

"I guess you could say that."

"What else could I say about it?"

"Nothing much."

"Looks like you won. You ain't hurt."

"No."

"You kill someone else last night? Or yesterday? I hear you're one hell of a *pistolero*."

He set the coffee cup down. Damn her.

Silvia twined her fingers around the gold tassels on her chair. Her nails were long, chipped, and jagged, in need of a fresh coat of paint. "Iris been feeling poorly lately," she said. "I think she's pregnant again. Stupid girl won't take the proper precautions."

"Maybe she wants a baby. Maybe she wants out."

"Hell with you, Johnny Torres. She can't get out now, too far gone. So don't you go putting notions in her head. That girl is sick. She'd take on sixty a night."

"For the money."

"For the laudanum. It's all that makes her happy. And it don't make for heartbreak the way loving a man does."

"Leave it alone, Silvia."

"I know why you never stop here, Johnny. That beard and all the mining grit can't hide guilt, because guilt is in the eyes."

He did not want to hear this. "Let me see Iris."

"Why should I?"

"Because I need her help."

She sighed. "Leave her out of it. Let me help, though sweet Jesus knows why I should. Just leave her out."

"Out of what? What do you think I've done?"

"Never mind. I'll give you the laudanum, then you can go."

She untangled her jagged nails from the gold tassels, got up, and climbed the stairs like a fat woman. Johnny got up too, slowly, his flesh crawling. He felt watched.

When she returned with the bottle, he pulled a double eagle from his pocket, but she slapped his hand away.

"Think that little of me, do you?"

"Take it, Silvia, give Iris a night off. What I think has nothing to do with it. They can always pay you more."

She took the gold.

He made it from the parlor house to the boardinghouse and to his room without Emma seeing. At first he'd thought of going to her instead of Silvia, but he liked Emma too much to involve her in this. Now he could hear her making a bed in one of the other rooms on his floor, so he changed clothes and washed up quickly and quietly, then poured the laudanum into his canteen and left.

Halfway out of town, he heard a man hollering his name. He swore; Daunt must've had every off-duty miner looking for him. He looked over his shoulder, along the dirty, nearly deserted south-side street, which was little more than an alley. The backs of restaurants and saloons formed one side and the backs of cheap homes the other. The alley stank from the garbage tossed out of the back doors.

"Hey, Johnny Torres!" the man called again.

Johnny reined in the palomino and saw the man was a miner from the Bonne Chance evening shift.

"Buck Daunt wants to see you at the in-town office," the man said, and walked off, back along the alley, around the garbage.

Johnny thought about riding on. The miner wouldn't care, wouldn't even report relaying the message. Few seemed to feel any great loyalty to the super anymore, since he'd cut all candle rations to two and started letting the walls slough for lack of timber. But Johnny knew he had to see Daunt, or Daunt would come after him at Gretel's, and find Cole.

He walked to Daunt's private office through the cool, dim, granite building where he'd first asked for a job fourteen months ago. He had never worked anywhere for fourteen months, except at his father's company, where he'd learned it was better to leave after a short while, unless you ran the operation yourself.

Daunt was pacing behind his desk, his steps stabbing the floorboards, while a clerk went on about something to do with the books. The instant Daunt saw Johnny in his doorway he started screaming.

"Where the fuck you been?!"

The clerk ducked out of the room. Johnny stood still and silent, glaring at his boss. Daunt took a step forward, opened his twisted lips to scream again. Johnny turned and strode from his office, past the workers' desks and filing cabinets and wary glances, toward the door that led to the street.

"Torres!" Still screaming.

Johnny reached for the latch. Daunt's gun boomed. The latch splintered under Johnny's hand.

Johnny turned and drew. His gun was cocked, his finger on the trigger well before the latch finished sailing across the room and clanked to the floor. The workers stopped breathing. The air in the room stopped moving.

"Don't ever do that again, Daunt. Ever."

Daunt's dark eyes narrowed. He still aimed his pistol at Johnny. Only smoke from the blast and ten feet of charged air separated them. One of the employees coughed—the accountant, Mordecai Watt, who had first sent Johnny up to the Bonne Chance to find Zachary, and who was probably responsible for doctoring the books to please Heinrich Braunn and keep the damned Flossie open.

Daunt cackled a laugh and holstered his piece, and the rest of the men and women in their office clothes started breathing again. They even pretended to scratch at their pads and file their documents.

"You think you gonna kill me, buck?" Daunt said.

"You nearly blew my hand off. My left hand." He heard his voice come back: low, dangerous, the Spanish accent more pronounced.

Daunt affected a genial humor, but under it Johnny could tell he seethed. He showed no fear, though. "Damn latch's broke anyway. Needed a new one. Wouldn't want to do nothing to hurt that left paw of yours."

Johnny waited.

"Y'all can forget the apology, Torres."

"Then so long."

Daunt's voice rose a notch. "I got questions for you."

"So fucking what?"

"Torres—"

"Say you're sorry, Buck. I want to hear you say it. Then you can ask me why I didn't come to work last night to blow more holes in your tapped-out Flossie."

"Fuck you, buck."

"The same, Buck. Say it."

"What the hell, I'm sorry. Shit, you think I'd hurt you?"

Johnny put his gun away. Daunt returned to his office, and after a few seconds Johnny followed. Daunt shut the door.

"What do you really want to know?" Johnny said. "You don't care whether I showed up for work."

"I care why you didn't. Where you been?"

"With Gretel, where else? Where did you think?"

"I suppose you was there all night?"

"Yeah, so?"

Daunt shook his head, hawked, and spat a long stream at the brass spittoon in the corner nearest the door, leaving a brown stain on the whitewashed wall. The whole corner was stained.

"I caught your crew lightloading their holes. Ore tonnage was way down. You been cutting back on powder and picking up the slack with your champion drilling."

"What if I have? We're shooting three rounds a night and you're getting enough ore for ten tailings piles. The muckers in my crew have been turning up crap and the whole mine shakes after every blast. Overloaded charges might bring her down, the Bonne Chance with her."

Daunt wiped his bristly chin with the back of his maimed left hand. "Not like you to shy away from a little risk, buck. Y'all going yella on us?"

"Hell, why does the Flossie matter so much to you?"

"Right now it don't. Right now all that matters is what happened to young Coleman."

Johnny forced a sarcastic laugh, which was no easy trick considering he still wanted to plug the super with all six bullets in his Colt. "He's dead."

Daunt looked long at him, scratched his head, and finally spat at the corner again, short this time.

"You bring him here, Johnny?"

"No. You?"

He shook his head. "I think Braunn did. Murdered Zachary, too. Zachary and me was friends, a long time back. You know, buck, I think you and me got a common interest here."

"My gun's not for hire. Not that way."

"Not even for Gretel? Pretty girl under them trousers. I bet she gives a man plenty of reasons for going after the one that blew up her father and her brother."

"Forget it," Johnny said. "You and I throw in together against a man like Braunn and it's a bloodbath."

"You're a damn saint, buck."

Johnny shrugged and pulled the door open. The office workers hurriedly bent their curious eyes back to their desks, except Watt, who want on watching Johnny.

"I'm going back to Gretel's," Johnny told Daunt over his shoulder. "I'll be at work tonight, if you want."

Daunt spat, nearly hitting Johnny's booted left foot as he stepped away from the super's office, toward the front door with the broken latch.

"Don't be late," he said.

17

Commandments

Catharine sat in the chair by the fireplace, where the fire had burned out the morning Cole left. The blue bedspread intrigued her. She studied it thoroughly, learned every ring in the pattern. At first she thought more threads were raised than not, then realized her error: the raised threads simply dominated the subtler background. That anyone could work out such a delicate balance amazed her, until she thought of the mathematical precision of gambling odds, and how many times she had beaten Heinrich quite soundly at five-card stud. Weaving must be like playing the odds in every way except one: it left no doubt as to how the piece would end up. No chance. No game. Suffocating.

She sat there all day, until Freda found her. The door cracked open, and the round, peasantlike face with its enormous blue irises poked through.

"Perhaps you would rather be alone," the girl said shyly, in German.

Catharine shook her head.

Freda walked into the room, practically on tiptoe, and sat on the bedspread, hiding some of the rings. "I am sorry, *gnädige Frau*. Herr Braunn told me of your friend's death." She would call it death, not passing on. She would see it as death, would grasp the black and white. But then she did something Catharine did not expect: she crossed herself.

Catharine felt her own hand rise to her forehead, drop to her heart, move to her left shoulder and her right. It happened without thought, a mere imitation of a gesture that might have comforted, long ago.

"Blessed mother," she murmured.

"I wish I could soothe the hurt."

"There is no hurt."

"Oh, my lady. Have you been here all day?"

"I guess. What time is it?"

"Half past four. Time for tea. Would you like some tea? I can bring it right here."

"Thank you."

"You are awfully calm. Are you all right?"

"No. I seem unable to feel."

Freda frowned. "Perhaps you should take tea on the landing."

"Yes."

So they left the guest room, Freda closing the door softly behind them, and walked together, though not touching, down the long corridor with the other closed doors. On the mezzanine, Catharine stopped and looked out over the great central vault, with its statues and tapestries and unopened crates. A heaviness settled in her chest.

"It looks like a church," said Freda.

"It looks like a coffin."

On the landing she sat in the chair where Cole had sat, with the great bowed window nearly surrounding her and the gold-splashed slopes outside.

"Where is Heinrich?" she asked as Freda served tea.

"I do not know. He left no word."

Catharine smelled brandy. "No need for that."

"I brought the tea both ways."

"You are an angel, Freda."

The girl smiled, though without the usual enigmatic gleam.

"Did you see Cole?" She could even say his name without hurting.

Freda demurred.

Catharine lifted the tea. Borne on the steam, the sweet, thick odor of brandy filled her.

Freda said, "Well, maybe I did poke my head out onto the mezzanine. But I could only see a little."

Catharine sipped the tea. Too hot, it burned her tongue. "The tea is good."

"All right, so I saw a bit more than that. He seemed very nice, very nice indeed."

"He is." Was.

"He did not talk much."

"No."

"He was the quiet type."

Was. "Sometimes."

"I am sorry, my lady."

"Yes. Me too. Thank you." She looked out the window, across the mountains. She wanted to fly over them. What would that feel like? The brandied tea warmed her. "Would you not like some tea, Freda?"

"The brandy makes me silly."

"You said only one had brandy in it."

"That I did."

Freda sat in the other chair and took some brandied tea. Catharine did not think it would make her silly. She sipped her own. The brandy spread inside, warm, gentle, like holding a lover after sex. Like holding Cole.

"Cole," she whispered.

"Pardon?"

She looked at Freda, then out the window, above the trees, at the sunsplashed snow on the tips of the peaks. Perpetually peaceful, white, innocent. Not like her, but like she used to be. Like she so wanted to be.

She asked Freda to bring the bottle. Freda also brought a snifter, but Catharine continued to use the teacup, and after a while she got drunk. Wooziness wrapped her, her eyes puffed, strands of hair kept falling in her face. She took off her jacket and unbuttoned the top of her blouse. She was about to take off her boots but decided not to.

"Where is Heinrich?" she asked.

"I do not know, my lady."

"Maybe he left."

"Maybe. Or else he would be here watching the sunset."

"He is in love with the damned sunset."

"Oh—"

Catharine slipped into English: "'S all right, Freda. Ladies can cuss, too. You know my mama used to dress up like a miner and tend bar? Folks said she could cuss up a storm, but she never did it around me."

Freda leaned forward, listening carefully. Catharine did not understand why at first, then realized. "Yes, my lady," the girl responded in German. "You have told me about your mama."

Catharine reverted to Freda's language, but she had to work to maintain it. "Good woman, my mama. Took good care of me."

"Like a mama ought to."

"You do, too."

"No, my lady. If I did, I would have taken away the brandy. Do you suppose Herr Braunn will be upset with me?"

"Don't be afraid of Heinrich, he only goes after the big game." English, again. She sighed heavily. "That and the beautiful. I'm not so beautiful now, am I Freda?"

Freda brushed a stray lock of red-gold hair off Catharine's cheek and spoke in English herself, though haltingly. "You are always beautiful. You are the most beautiful lady I have seen."

Catharine studied her hands. The alcohol had bloated them, made the skin less translucent, but there were no wrinkles. She touched the back of one hand with the other, feeling nothing.

"Where is Heinrich?" she asked once more.

"I do not know, my lady."

"Probably with Krieg," she said. Krieg was Heinrich's personal assistant, a man of dark talents, imported from Germany. He had been with Braunn Mining Limited for years, in God knows what true capacity. These days, Heinrich spent more time with him than with Catharine.

"No, my lady. Herr Braunn sent Krieg away this morning."

"Sent him away?"

"Fired him. Do you want me to ask someone else? Franz may know where he has gone."

Catharine waved her hand. Her movements were sloppy. "No, no, no. He'll be back. I don't know why I want him anyway." English or German? The languages meshed. She started to pour more brandy.

"My lady, I do not think—"

"Oh, don't worry, Freda. You shoulda seen my mama put this stuff away. Only it wasn't brandy." She raised the teacup; some of the drink sloshed over the side. "Here's to laudanum, or whatever else kills the pain."

She retired early, without supper and before Heinrich returned, but sleep evaded her. Cursing the new mattress, the silk sheets that entangled her legs, the thick woven blanket that scratched her skin, she forced her eyelids closed but saw Cole's blue-gray eyes with the laugh lines at the corners. He had barely smiled here.

Finally she disentangled herself from the sheets, slipped into her green kimono and walked barefoot to her husband's room, where she found him reading in bed. He looked at her over his reading glasses.

"I want to have sex," she said.

"I think, 'What are you reading?' might be a more appropriate greeting."

"Heinrich, don't—"

"Or perhaps even, 'Hello, dear, where have you been all day? I have missed you.'" He chuckled. "I guess that would be asking a bit much."

"Heinrich."

"But, no, you just want to have sex."

"I'll go."

He chuckled again.

"You have no cause to be angry with me."

He sighed, mocking. "The dead can be so much more powerful than the living. You should know that. I suspect you feel it right now."

She would get nowhere asking for sympathy, which would be worthless, anyway, since her earlier numbness persisted. She had told the truth at the beginning: she wanted to have sex. It would help her sleep.

"All right," she said, "what are you reading?"

"Die Bibel. A particularly enlightening passage on adultery here in die Ausführung. Exodus."

"I know which book it is."

"You have never indulged in adultery, have you, my dear? No.

No matter how much you may have wished. Now fornication, well, that is another subject altogether, perhaps one better left alone."

"Yes."

"Then again, I am curious," said Heinrich. "It was Mr. Coleman, was it not?"

"Yes. He was in love with me, before you came."

"And you?"

She looked away. "I let him go."

"But you loved him, too."

She looked back into his eyes and said nothing. He already knew, anyway.

"How touching."

Still she said nothing. It was her right to keep this past for herself. It was all she had left, all she had ever won for herself without his money or influence.

"Come here, Catharine."

She stood by his bed. He closed the Bible and set it next to him on the sheet, and pulled her sash until the kimono fell open. His fingers stroked her waist, then her breasts.

"How do you want me to make love to you?"

"So I can feel it. I want to feel. I want to feel you."

"Me? Are you sure you mean me? Or will you feel Cole when I turn out the light?"

"I want it to be you."

"You have always wanted it to be me. But whom will you really feel? Whom have you felt all these years?"

"I have never made love to you and imagined you were Cole. That was a different kind of love than what I feel for you."

He laughed and withdrew his hand, folded it with the other in his lap. She thought he looked professorial with those glasses on and sitting that way, the smug smile playing across his lips.

"You have never loved me, Catharine."

"Have you ever loved, Heinrich? Ever?"

"What a stupid question. Of course. But I have never been in love, not in the way you mean."

His fingers resumed their course. He pulled her to him and kissed her body, took off his glasses and turned out the light.

"Why do you hate the idea of being in love?" she pressed, as the smoothness of the skin on his chest slid against hers.

"Because being in love means needing," he said, and kissed her mouth. She did not want him to kiss her mouth. She turned her head so he would kiss her neck instead, and as she did he chuckled almost inaudibly, in triumph.

18

Home Again

The red-tailed hawk dipped and glided, riding the wind. Cole reined in his Appaloosa, tilted his head back, spotted the bird against the vast Montana heavens. The hawk soared, spiraling higher and higher until it caught the setting sun and dwindled to a fleck of gold.

Home, finally. Coleman cattle ranged over every one of these grassy hills; this Appaloosa cow pony had covered nearly every acre at one time or another. Some of it was fenced, though not as much as in Texas. Here a man could still run his cattle on open land, and if that changed, well, maybe he'd just sell out and take his family farther north, into Canada.

It had been as warm as summer today; even now, at dusk, there remained a gentle balm with no hint of coming snows. The feel of the evening air through his shirt, the taste and smell of it, and the way it filled his lungs so cleanly brought a slow, contented smile to his lips. He flipped off his hat and let the air dry the sweat on his forehead and hair. It had taken some hard riding to make it home this fast from the depot in Springdale. Now he could pause for a moment, and cherish the coming Montana night as much as anything in life.

The Appaloosa dropped his head to munch on the sweet grass. What a perfect year for the grass: not too bad a winter, plenty of rain in spring, even enough in summer, but without the thunderstorms.

The hawk had disappeared. A star popped out in the east. In the silence of twilight, Cole heard hoofbeats. They came at an easy lope, thudding gently against the earth. Gazing in their direction, he smiled again. The rider topped the hill to the west, stopped, waved a hat broadly, spurred the horse, and came on at a gallop. Down one hill to vanish into a gully, fast up the next to reappear and gallop to where Cole waited. Sam looked small compared to his mount. But at seven years old he rode like a little man.

"Howdy, Cole!"

"Howdy, Sam. You and that horse are looking good."

Sam nodded. "Been working him every day, just like you said. Figured he was ready for a real run."

Cole grinned. "Looks fine," he said, and the boy could barely conceal his pride. He'll make a good rancher, Cole thought. He loves it like I do.

"You see that hawk?" Sam asked.

"Yup."

"Sure flew up high. I thought she might go away for good."

"How'd you know it was a she?"

Sam shrugged. "Just knew."

"Oh."

"You're teasing me, Cole."

Cole laughed. "How did you know I'd come back tonight?"

"Just knew that, too. See? I know everything. You can ask me whatever you want."

"Okay, then. How many stars up there?"

Sam turned his face to the sky. Sandy hair stuck out at all angles from his hat. "Can't say yet, 'cause they're not all out. Maybe in a while."

As they turned their cow ponies toward home, Cole reached out and gave his stepson a one-arm hug.

"Don't, you'll make me fall off."

"Never."

"I missed you, Cole."

"I missed you, too. How's your mama?"

"She misses you, too."

Not half as much as I miss her, he thought. And woke up.

Sam faded, and the hills, and the stars, and all of Montana, all of home. He clutched at the dream, but it turned to nothing and slipped away, leaving him with empty, clenched fists and a pain that wracked his entire body.

There was a sound—a groan, his own. And something cool and dry touching his forehead, a hand. He opened his eyes. Gretel. But different. The thick, dark hair, the long face with its golden brown skin and high cheekbones, the dark brown eyes and wide, full mouth with its slightly crooked front teeth, even the accusing hostility were all the same, but she had grown up, and she had changed inside. She had lost something.

"How are you?" she asked. Her voice was low the way he remembered, but older. Her eyes were hard. She put her hands in her pockets, and he noticed her clothes, a man's clothes. He'd missed that at first.

"I've been better." Talking was difficult. Hold still, for God's sake: moving hurt worse. Her face wavered. Stay awake, stay awake.

"Who attacked me?" He remembered the man torturing him on the ledge, but it seemed far in the past.

"We can talk about that later, when you're better."

"Did Daunt send them?" Worse, now. Every word hurt worse. God, my ribs, stabbing. "Tell me, Gretel."

"I don't know. Heinrich Braunn, maybe, or Buck Daunt. I don't know yet." She barely tolerated his questions; she would rather have left the room, now that he was awake.

He nodded minutely and wished he hadn't. Wished for something to stop the pain, too. He asked and she brought some laudanum in a tin cup, lifted his head so he could drink. He tried to move his hand to take it himself. She laid him back slowly, and the drug sat poorly in his belly.

"How long—" he began, and had to stop.

"You've been here since yesterday morning. We took the bullet out last night. It's Tuesday afternoon."

"Who brought me here?" Damn this exhaustion! And the pain! But sweet Jesus, my head hurts, and now I can't make out her face. Or her words. What did she say?

"Cole, I think you should rest. We'll talk later."

She straightened the blanket. He caught her wrist, and winced.

"Who?" he whispered.

"I told you, Johnny Torres. He brought you here. Cut the bullet out. Look, you really should rest. You're lucky to be here at all."

But her face, look at it: a pale oval framed in brown. Look at her shirt: plaid fused into a mishmash of color. Like someone left her out in the rain, and all her parts ran together, like his, jumbled, confused. Did she touch him, or fix the covers? She was all around him, yet he couldn't lift a finger to reach her. Hadn't this always been the way between them? Hadn't it? He should ask. But the words dissolved, and so did she.

19

Black Powder

The palomino climbed the steep trail to the Flossie without hesitation, yesterday's lethargy gone. He had yet to show Johnny affection or loyalty, and the feeling was mutual, but the horse would've treated anyone this way and Johnny needed his surefooted talents in Telluride's mountains.

The moon sat round and full atop the eastern peaks, glowing with the same pale color as the horse's hide. As the palomino climbed, so did the moon, whitening. At the stable, Johnny looked away from the mine, across the mountains, clearly outlined against the starry, cloudless sky. The moon shone so brightly that he could see the peaks above Gretel's valley.

He'd planned to stay away from there today, though through a disturbed sleep this morning and during the noon dinner, when his thoughts distracted him from responding appropriately to questions asked by Emma's sons about Cole, he kept thinking he should check on things at the cabin. In the end, Luke Halloran gave him an excuse:

he wanted to see Gretel in his office the next morning, first thing, eight-thirty at the latest.

"He's not strong enough to leave alone," she'd said when Johnny gave her the message. "What if someone comes by?"

"You just don't want to see the marshal," Johnny replied. "Or go to town."

"So what if I don't?"

"I'll be here first thing tomorrow," he'd told her, and then he left. In fact, he couldn't wait to leave.

Now he dismounted and stabled the horse. At the main shaft the hoistman greeted him solemnly, which was better than last night when he'd offered no greeting at all. Daunt must have dressed the men down royally on Sunday; they were as solemn as the hoistman. Last night Johnny had repelled their inquiries and treated them harshly, which they'd probably expected but not deserved. Now he stepped into the waiting cage and plunged into blackness. The tommyknockers started right off, but that was nothing new. It was all in his head, anymore; he could no longer trust them. He should've left this death trap months ago.

"I don't care what Buck Daunt said," he told his crew when they were all down. "Don't overload the holes." Last night the blasts had rocked the whole mine, rumbling from below, practically knocking the men off their feet.

"He'll fire the lot of us," one of the men challenged tonight. They called him Eldridge. He was one of the blasters, along with Johnny and a young, gawky Pennsylvanian named Isaac.

"He'll have to fire me first."

"So? What's to stop him?"

Johnny had yet to figure that one out. "Just lightload the holes," he said, and sent them off to the drifts. As the shift wore on he rotated among the crews. He did not work as hard as usual; he swung the double-jack hammer maybe fifty times a minute, not enough for three rounds. So they'd shoot two, and if Daunt fired him and the whole damned shift, so be it. If Johnny got his way and the mine closed they'd all be out of work anyhow, which would put the men at his throat faster than mistreating them, but at least they'd live to find another job.

The first round went all right. The blasts vibrated the workings and the rush of air even put out a candle, but that was normal for this mine. Johnny saw the questions in the men's eyes at meal break, saw they wondered why only two rounds. Because I'm worn out, he wanted to tell them. I can't keep drilling three rounds and right now I don't give a shit what Daunt does about it. Who the hell is supposed to rub the soreness from my shoulders when Gretel barely lets me in her valley, let alone her bed?

Something in his look, or the way he tore at his meat sandwich, must have put the men off, because no one said a word during break, not even Brody, the normally talkative Cornishman.

He wound up drilling the last of the second round with Brody and his crew, in a stope scarcely wide enough for the double-jack hammer, on the drift face with the hardest rock. At least the lack of timber posed no problem, he thought, as the hammer on the steel rang in his ears. They finished drilling the seventh hole and he tamped in black powder and primers, harder than he should. At least he used a wood stick, not a metal cleaning spoon like Zachary.

"Go on up," he ordered the men. They took off, except Brody, who hung back while Johnny worked.

"Go up, Brody," Johnny said, but sensed no movement behind him. Finally he turned to his drilling partner. He had grown fond of this man; at times they'd raised a glass together.

"Got something to tell me?" Johnny asked.

Brody narrowed his grit-ringed eyes, then shrugged his bony shoulders. "Taper 'er light, boss," he said, and headed up the drift.

Johnny sliced the V's, poured in the powder, and used his candle to spit the fuses. The backfire extinguished the candle every time. He kept relighting it as the fuses burned toward the powder, and he fumed all the while about Daunt's ridiculous two-candle ration. Not that more candles would change spitting the fuses; he'd only ever used one candle for that. But still. He spit the last fuse and started up the shaft.

Suddenly the mine shook, as if the mountain had coughed. A blast followed, knocking Johnny off his feet. He cursed the mountain. No, the mine. Curse the mine. He rolled to his front, covered his head with his arms. For an instant he could not hear: the blast had deafened him. But he was alive. He should not have been alive this close to the powder. He raised his head, looked toward the drift face. But it wasn't his drift face that had blown. His seven fuses burned toward the primers, as they should. He could see them, but at first he could not hear the sputter. Or even the tommyknockers. Only the echo of the blast.

The drift shuddered and gob splattered down from the ceiling. Johnny scrambled to his feet and snuffed the fuses, then ran. He jumped onto the ladder at the first shaft, skipping the bottom three rungs, raced up the ladder, ran along the next tunnel. A wall sloughed toward him; he leapt against the wall opposite, leapt up. The slough slid under his boots. He climbed past it and ran on. Another shaft, another ladder. At the top he nearly collided with Isaac, his eyes wide with panic.

"Where's Eldridge?" Johnny hollered.

Isaac started to bolt. Johnny grabbed his arms and jerked him back.

"Where's Eldridge?"

"I don't know. Down there. Let me go!"

He did. Isaac took off up the next shaft. Johnny knew he was too close to the remaining drift face, the one Isaac had set to blow. No way Isaac would have taken the time to kill his fuses. Johnny glanced up the shaft as the blaster's boots disappeared on the ladder, then down the crosscut toward the shaft that led to Eldridge's drift face. Eldridge never traded a pleasant word with anyone but he was a fine blaster. He could outdrill Brody and he worked hard. He also had a wife and three or four kids in town, on the south side.

Johnny turned down the crosscut and broke into a run. He reached the shaft and gripped the ladder with his hands.

"Eldridge!" he screamed down the shaft.

No answer. In his mind he could hear the fuses sputtering toward the powder in Isaac's drift.

"Eldridge!"

Nothing.

He began to descend the ladder. Powder gas and rock dust mushroomed up the shaft. He yanked his bandana over his nose and mouth, but it couldn't stop him from coughing. The dust thickened as he descended. His eyes smarted and ran in the choking fog. His candle was useless: it cast a tiny circle of smoky light that failed to reach the shaft walls.

He was halfway down the sixty-foot shaft when the other face blew. The blasts wrenched the ladder from his hands, pitched him backward against the wall and dropped him. He screamed again, not anything human. He had an oddly exhilarating sense of weightlessness as he plummeted. And something else: a fleeting awareness of two explosions, maybe three, not one.

Then his feet hit the mud floor below the shaft. The impact nearly drove his shins into his knees, his thighbones into his hips. His legs buckled and he tumbled full force into the mud. The heels of his hands sank deep holes. Then his arms buckled, too, and he lurched sideways. His legs began to quiver, then to shake violently. He drew them up, wrapped his arms around his knees, but the shaking persisted.

Still, he was not hurt. Numb with shock, soaked with sweat and acidic mud, deaf from the blasts, but not hurt. He got up, but had to support himself against the tunnel wall with an extended arm because his legs kept shaking. He wobbled farther into the mine along the pitch dark tunnel, toward where Eldridge should have been, through smoke and gas and dust.

He had trouble breathing. He could not see, and his hands lacked the steadiness to relight his candle, for all the good it would do. He tried to call Eldridge's name but a cough stopped him. He could not get a deep enough breath. The air hung thicker than the black dark.

Damn this fucking mine, he thought. I lived through the fall and now the air will kill me.

But he kept going in, working his way along the wall until his legs steadied a bit and he could walk without holding on. Utter blackness and smoky dust blanketed him, smothering. He coughed and coughed. Obstacles tripped him—rock, mostly, also supplies, broken track, small bits of timber, dirt, other unidentifiable objects knocked loose by Eldridge's blast. That blast had been heavy; Eldridge had overloaded the holes. But that wouldn't have sparked the charges early, or set off the other blasts. Sabotage. It had to be. Sabotage to trap him here. Or kill him. Either way, to keep him away from Gretel's.

Johnny tripped again and landed on his knees. Something big tripped him, this time. He fumbled in his pocket, opened a case, found the matches dry, and managed to strike one. His hands had steadied. He touched the match to the candle, barely a stub, and through the suffocating dust saw Eldridge's body, or what was left.

Sickened, Johnny dragged himself to his feet. Tripping and coughing, he struggled back toward the rest of the crew. Up the drift, up the first ladder. At the top of the ladder, he hauled himself out of the shaft and lay on the floor of the next tunnel for several minutes, panting between coughs. He felt weak and woozy. A new blackness beckoned, the black relief of sleep. Get up, get up, he told himself.

But he couldn't, not all the way up, only to his hands and knees. Okay, then, crawl.

Mud gave way to wet rock that scraped the skin off his palms. It ripped holes in his corduroys, scraped the skin from his knees as well. He wanted to stand and walk, but could not get enough air. He crawled for what must've been hundreds of feet, with his head lowered. The candle turned to a glob of wax and went out, leaving the hand that had held it empty of all but shredded skin.

His head hit a rock. He swore. He felt his way over the obstacle, dragged himself to standing by holding on to the piled rocks. Cave-in. He swore again, though a cough cut the words. He let himself collapse to his knees, his side, let himself lie with his cheek against the clammy, seeping floor. Damn the surveyors. Damn Daunt. Tunnels and shafts that didn't meet, that trapped the smoke and gas and dust could kill a miner as easily as a fall or a blast, but not so fast, not so mercifully.

His cheek began to burn: the water was too acidic. He forced his head up, forced his arm to move so that his head rested on it. Forget the faint burning along his side. Forget anything but trying to breathe. He strained for a gulp of air, got nothing but a harsh, choking cough. His stinging eyes closed; they burned almost as much as the inside of his chest.

He put one hand across his face to shut out the dust and acrid gas, and lay still, trapped in the black mine he'd hated from the first time he'd descended the main shaft with Buck Daunt. All he could see was that image of Eldridge, or what used to be Eldridge, but it flickered as his candle had flickered, the candle that had melted to a glob. He should tell the man's widow. Climb out of here and tell the man's widow. And then go to Gretel's. He was supposed to be at Gretel's by eight.

20

The Morning Mail

Gretel waited until the last minute for Johnny, trying not to worry. Now she would have to ride to town; walking would take too long, though Zachary's old brown gelding wasn't much faster. If Johnny got here now she would take his palomino. If she could control him. A vicious animal, the palomino, devoid of even a horse's loyalty for a caring master, but he ran fast.

She stood over Cole and called his name. He frowned and turned his head, winced, and slept on. His bruises had begun changing from black and blue to purple with some yellow at the edges, and the swelling had gone down. He had begun to look like Gretel remembered. He still looked an awful lot like Zachary, though leaner and more serious.

She touched his shoulder and called to him again. He opened his eyes and stared at her vacantly. Then he said her name.

"How are you feeling?" she asked. It was hard enough mustering any compassion toward him when he slept; harder when he looked at her out of their mother's eyes.

He started to reply, cleared his throat, tried again. "Better," he said.

"Do you think you can get up?"

"What for?"

"I need to go into town to see the marshal—"

"Why?" He was suddenly alert. She might have known: he would be accustomed to trouble with the law.

"Don't worry, Cole," she said coldly. "I won't tell him you're alive."

"Who is he? Is he dangerous?"

"His name is Luke Halloran. And no, he's not dangerous."

"You don't lie very well," he said, trying to smile.

"I'll do my best. Now you have to get up, and quickly. I'm late. You can hide in the barn."

She did not want to touch him, but he needed help sitting up and dressing. By the time they finished getting him into Zachary's old woolens and flannel shirt, and his own black pants, which Gretel had washed and patched, his face was pale and the clothes were dark with sweat. Gretel tried not to care.

He leaned heavily on her while they stumbled along. The barn was small, with three box stalls, one for the cow and two for horses, and a pen for the pigs. Except for the horse, the animals were outside. This day would be warm if the sun stayed out, Gretel thought, but the barn was cold and drafty from the night. She had forked a thick layer of hay into the stalls and spread a blanket along the side wall of one. Cole sank onto it and closed his eyes. Under the bruises his skin was bloodless.

"Are you all right?" Gretel asked. Some sour sense of family dragged the question from her.

He half nodded. "Sure," he said. "Cover me up."

She laid Zachary's old carbine next to him and gave him a handful of extra bullets. He wrapped his fingers around the gun and stuffed the bullets into his pocket.

On Colorado Avenue, Gretel tried her best to ignore the signs that cluttered the boardwalk, the false-fronted shops, the closeness of the crowd. The old brown gelding was blowing hard from the brisk ride. His hooves crunched through the crust on top of the mud.

Finally she reached Spruce Street and the jail. After looping the reins around the post in front—not that the horse would run off, the way Johnny's palomino would—she took a deep breath, and walked inside. Her heart pounded so loud she could hear it. Johnny had been right, she did not want to see the marshal. And so had Cole, she did not lie very well. She was afraid Halloran would find her out.

A deputy sat at a desk inside the small, cluttered office. "I'm here to see Marshal Halloran," she told him.

"Gretel Coleman?"

"Yes."

The deputy glanced out a barred window, then back at her. "He was called away. Can you wait?"

She looked out the window, too, but saw nothing remarkable. "I guess so," she said.

"Have a seat, then."

She sat in a spindle-backed chair and the deputy returned to his desk, where he wrote something in a ledger. Gretel had never thought of deputies as writing, but they must've had to file reports and whatnot. Her chair was uncomfortably hard. She tried not to fidget.

Her throat grew dry and her skin grew hot. Even after she took off her jacket, perspiration oozed under her arms. She longed to get back to her valley but worried about Johnny, and what had detained him; worried about Cole, too, though reluctantly. The deputy wrote intently, then every few minutes he looked out the window and tapped his pen on the paper. It must have made a mess of the page.

Someone called from a cell out back. Gretel jumped.

The deputy scraped his chair across the wood floor, and walked off jangling his keys. Gretel watched the clock: ten before nine. The deputy returned shortly, shaking his head. Gretel said nothing. She had nothing to say.

The minutes turned into a half hour, then three quarters. The deputy finished his writing, then took out his pistol and began to oil it. Gretel tried to look at something else, anything except a damned gun, but her eyes kept stealing toward the piece. It made her more nervous than ever.

"Do you think the marshal will be back soon?" she asked.

The deputy shrugged. "Maybe. He didn't say, exactly." He resumed cleaning his gun. Gretel realized her fingers were gripping the seat of the chair and forced them to loosen. Fifty-five minutes now. Her eyes fell on the gun again. Enough. She had to leave. She stood. The deputy looked at her sharply.

What excuse could she give? Coffee. She needed a cup of coffee. He had not given her one, and had none himself. But then the door opened: the postman, with the morning mail.

"Ma'am," he greeted Gretel. "Howdy, Beal," he said to the deputy, who nodded, rubbing the blued steel of his gun barrel with a rag. The postman set a small stack of envelopes on the desk.

"News today?" the deputy asked, without much interest.

"Cave-in at the Flossie."

Gretel's mouth dropped open. The postman was not looking at her. He did not know who she was. The deputy did; he glanced at her and back to the postman.

"Anybody hurt?" he asked.

"Johnny Torres went down to rescue a blaster name of Eldridge.

Both are still inside but that's all. MacMurray's crew and most of the night shift are digging out."

Gretel tried to swallow. On his way out, the postman nodded to her and touched his cap. "Ma'am," he said again.

Gretel cleared her throat, tried again to swallow. Her throat was too dry. "I'm going to the mine," she told the deputy.

She hardly heard what he said as she rushed out the door, failing to latch it but not caring. She jumped onto the brown gelding, who was standing motionless except for his jaw working around the bit. He snorted, startled. She kicked his old ribs, startling him more, and hauled the reins to the side. He spun and lurched into a gallop, or what passed for a gallop in him. His gait jerked her around in the saddle.

She made the southern edge of town, where the trail to the mine began, and pulled the horse in. He didn't dance as most horses would. He just stopped. Gretel sat atop him, her insides quivering. Johnny. She wanted Johnny. But she could not go to the mine. She had to go home. She had been about to race home when she'd heard the news. She swiped an arm across her eyes, finding tears there, tears she did not want to cry.

She wheeled the horse and laid in with her heels. He nearly leapt off the street. His fat old legs hit the ground so hard that the drying mud splashed the south-side hovels fifteen feet away, and he ran.

21

The Pitchfork

Cole lay under the straw, fading in and out, dizzy, his fingers clammy around the cold stock of his father's old Sharps. Fade in, and the scent of fresh hay called Laura to mind. He thought of forking hay with her, of dropping the fork and diving for her, tackling her angular body in the hay, laughing, rolling. Then checking furtively through the door to see who was about—one of the hands, a visitor, Sam? No one? He lifted her dress. She laughed.

Fade out, and Laura with him. Then in again, tingling. She was waiting. He thought how he had learned to laugh with her. And she with him. It was their greatest gift to each other. He was not like his father; Zachary had loved to laugh. Neither was Gretel. So serious, aloof, haughty in her hostility. Could anyone make her laugh?

If only he could write to Laura, tell her. How much gentler and compassionate her touch than Gretel's cool efficiency. When he was a boy, sick in bed, it had seemed like Anna's coldness made him worse. He used to wish she would leave his side, and she usually did.

There was always some excuse, whether she shared it with him or not. Often she just left. When she would stay any length of time he would tell her he felt better, so that she would leave. Often she saw through this. "If you are better," she would say in her clipped, accented English, "then get out and help tend the garden."

He faded out, and in again, to the sound of a rumble. Thunder? No, the sun shone through the cracks between the boards. What then? His senses were hazy. Cool, fresh air filtered to him through the straw. The haze lifted. The barn door, someone had slid open the barn door. Cole pushed some straw over his face.

Slow, quiet footsteps scuffed against the dirt floor. Heavy steps: a man. Not Gretel, anyway. Cole's fingers closed tighter around the old single-shot carbine that lay along his right side. The footfalls traveled all around the barn, climbed a few steps of the ladder to the hayloft. If the man could see the loft from that rung, he was tall.

Another sound, now, a rhythmic ripping, crackling sound. The man was jabbing the pitchfork into the hay in the loft. Cole picked up the rhythm and cocked the carbine on one of the jabs so the man would not hear it. The jabbing stopped and the man descended the ladder. The rungs creaked. Footfalls again, approaching the stalls. Breathing, too, slow, deep, regular, like someone trying to stay calm.

A gate swung open to the right and the ripping sound resumed. The man was forking the straw in the first stall. The gate squeaked closed and the next one opened. The ripping sound again. The man breathed faster now. He would have checked the cabin already. Cole hoped Gretel had hidden any sign of him. Or maybe she hadn't. Maybe he knew.

The second gate closed and the footsteps moved closer to the third stall, where Cole lay. The gate creaked open. Now he would have to kill this man or die himself. He would have to sit up and raise the gun and fire, one shot and that was all. With his ribs already screaming at him from the way his stomach muscles had tensed, ready to move, he could easily miss.

The fork speared the straw, thudded against the floor. It struck again, harder, moving toward Cole's booted feet. Again, farther to the right, then again, closer.

Cole squeezed his eyes shut and opened them, hiked himself halfway to sitting, saw the startled look on the man's gaunt face, swung the Sharps up, and jerked the trigger. The carbine's kick drove him back to the straw in agony. Long arms and legs whirled around in a blur as the man smashed against the gate and out of it.

The man scrambled to his feet with a grunt of pain. Cole rolled sideways as the man's gun boomed once, twice, three times, the bullets chasing as he rolled across the stall and into the stock of the pitchfork, stuck in the straw.

Cole grabbed the pitchfork and heaved it at the man's face. The man fired again. The bullet cracked into the wooden wall behind Cole's head.

The fork speared the man's neck. He screamed, choked on his own blood, sprawled backward. The fork fell out of his neck and landed on the dirt floor next to him.

Cole rolled onto his side and drew his legs up, holding his ribs. The haze descended again, and with it Anna, Gretel, and Laura. And Catharine. They merged: they traded features, hair color, figures. Their features on one another's faces did not fit; they looked like gargoyles. Cole faded, and took the women with him. He did not have room for all four of them, but they dogged him. At least they crowded out the man he'd killed, and the blood, and, finally, the pain.

22

Grave Markers

Zachary's old horse went lame a mile from the cabin. Gretel leapt off and ran. White-trunked aspen flew by in a blur, then cottonwood and willow as she neared the river. The willow branches hung low, whipping her face. Air raked in and out of her lungs. Finally the trees opened out onto the meadow. She raced across it. Tall grass snatched at her legs, twined about her ankles, crackled dryly as she ripped free, ripped through, toward the homestead.

The barn door was open. Breathing hard, she drew her knife and walked hesitantly to the barn. She could throw the knife if she had to. She'd always had good aim, though she'd never had to throw at a person. Scared, she peered into the shady dimness. Her eyes adjusted. A man lay on the floor with blood all over and all around him. Luke Halloran.

"Dear God," she whispered.

She walked into the barn like walking on eggs. Halloran looked dead. He had to be dead. But in its red pool, his head moved, turned toward her. She shrieked and jumped back. His mouth opened and blood ran out. More came from his neck. The pitchfork lay next to him. His eyes pleaded with her.

She stood riveted, her hand over her mouth. Look away, turn away. Now. She did. And stepped into the middle stall and peered over the side at her brother, who was curled like a child. There was no blood on him and after a few seconds she could see the rise and fall of his body as he breathed. Again she forced her head to turn, to check on Halloran. He was dead.

Sheathing her knife, she walked around the body and into the stall where Cole lay. "Cole." She shook him, timidly. "Cole." But he was unconscious, not sleeping. She glanced back at Halloran's body, at the bloodied straw that surrounded it. Nausea gripped her. She sank to hands and knees and vomited.

The earth was stubborn, stony, hard. Gretel hacked at it with Zachary's old pick. Hacked and hacked, after some time grunting with each swing, and wondered how Johnny could do this all day. After loosening enough earth, she set in with the shovel. She remembered watching from the window while Zachary and Buck Daunt dug Anna's grave, Zachary calm, quick, strong; Buck frenzied, a mystery to her at the time, Cole riding off. Buck had come to despise Cole, but Zachary would have wanted Cole's grave next to his own. Cole's, not hers. The shovel hit a rock. She worked it loose and tossed it away.

The hole was shallow, but Luke Halloran fit, guns and all. Gretel covered the gaunt body, then cut a cross with a point at the bottom. With her knife, she carved:

ZACHARY COLEMAN
1858–1892

She used Zachary's old hammer to drive the cross into the ground at the head of the grave. It was wrong, she realized—he was born in 1859. She wiped her sweaty face, only she found again that she was wiping off tears, not sweat. Above her the peaks slashed the graying sky. Even they had betrayed her. Last week they had murdered her father and today they were trying to murder Johnny. She raised the hammer high and smashed it down on the cross a last time, hard.

"I hate you!" she screamed, the words echoing out toward the mountain walls: "Hate you hate you hate you . . . "

The echo died. Gretel trudged slowly back to the cabin with the hammer on her shoulder, slumped like a miner after a long shift. Ha, she thought, a miner.

Cole was back in bed, dragged there with the help of Zachary's old brown gelding, which Gretel had found grazing where she'd left him. Luke Halloran's horse was in the barn, which Gretel had cleaned by burning the bloodsoaked straw. Only waiting remained. She sank to the front step of the cabin, too drained to go inside, check on Cole, wash her filthy hands, slake her laborer's thirst.

She was still sitting there halfway through the afternoon, staring at heavens now weighted with impending rain, worrying about Johnny and whether he was safe or even alive, bargaining with the God she viewed as created by Man, and in which she had theretofore never believed, bargaining nevertheless in desperation, promising to trade once and for all her solitude, her privacy, her own life for his, when Catharine Braunn stopped by. Catharine Braunn, the last person she wanted to see.

The fine surrey drew up in front of the cabin. Gretel stood while the driver, an older man, helped Catharine down and handed her a fat, full basket. Catharine walked silently toward Gretel, like walking in sleep, her face pale, the skin translucent.

"Hello, Catharine," said Gretel.

Catharine nodded and cleared her throat. "Heinrich and I want you to know how very sorry we are about Cole."

Gretel took the basket. On top were white roses, with the thorns removed. Under them were fruit, bread, cheese, pastries, even a bottle of white wine. Reluctantly, Gretel invited Catharine into the cabin.

"You can sit down if you want," she offered, putting the roses in water. She had not seen Catharine since her wedding to Heinrich Braunn thirteen years ago, but the woman looked little different from the girl. The wan complexion must have derived from recent losses, not from age; like Anna, she would never have allowed herself to age.

Catharine pulled a chair from the pine table and turned it toward the cookstove, sat, and leaned forward to warm her hands.

"I've been so cold these last few days," she said.

Gretel sat opposite her. She wished Catharine would leave. What if Cole woke up or cried out in his sleep? An awkward moment passed.

"Do you want some coffee?" Gretel asked at last.

"No. Thank you." She hesitated, studying her hands. "May I visit the grave?"

Gretel walked with her to the family plot. She glanced over her shoulder at the cabin. One of the windows in Cole's room faced this way, but the angle hid the bed. Catharine stopped at the foot of the fresh grave, where Luke Halloran's body lay.

"The date is wrong."

"I know."

"Then why—"

"Because I got tired after making the cross and carving his name there, that's why."

"Yes, of course."

She left Catharine at the grave site and retrieved the white roses from the cabin. They were exquisite: their petals curled open perfectly, unblemished. The water dripped off their stems as Gretel inhaled their fragrance, so terribly alive. She carried them outside and handed them to Catharine.

"Here," she said, "I think you brought these for Cole."

A short while later she watched from her doorstep as Catharine departed. The stately old driver helped Catharine back into her fine surrey, climbed onto the front bench, and flicked his whip over the haunches of the crisply built bay horse. The whip did not actually touch the rain-darkened hide.

Gretel sat on the doorstep, waiting, as afternoon shambled grayly toward evening, as rain began to fall, softly, as her mind, her body ached for nothing but him. She rose only to check on Cole, every quarter hour, then every half, then not at all. The rain glued stray curls from her hair against her forehead, weighted her braid against her back, wet her jacket and shirt and trousers. After a long time it tapered to drizzle. Mist rolled up the valley, across the meadow from the river, dank and raw.

She was still sitting there at dusk, when he rode out of the trees across the meadow, above the thin mist. The white of the palomino's forelock materialized first, then the milky mane, the yellow body. Then the rider, dark as ever, nearly swallowed by the backdrop of weather-tarnished trees.

Gretel rose and walked toward him through the tall, browning grass, now bowed by rain. She raised her arms, her stinging eyes, as he swung a leg heavily over the horse's neck and the pommel of the saddle, and pulled his other foot from the stirrup and slid to the ground facing her, with the rain dripping off his broad-brimmed hat. She had her arms around him, her lips brushing his cheeks, his eyelids, his mouth, before he could fully embrace her. She whispered his name, felt his arms enfold her, his hands on her back, not with any strength, as he leaned against her.

They moved toward the cabin, his arm across her shoulders, hers around his waist, his steps less than certain.

"I'm sorry," she told him. "I wanted to be there."

"It's okay," he said hoarsely, and coughed.

"You're all right?"

He nodded.

"Your voice—"

"The smoke."

"Oh."

"I would have been here an hour ago. They kept me at the bunkhouse. They wouldn't let me get up."

"They were right."

"No." He coughed again. "Halloran?"

"He's dead. He came here. Cole killed him."

He said nothing, but his step faltered.

"We'll talk about it later."

They reached the cabin and she pushed the door open. He stood in the doorway while she lighted a lamp. In the light she saw his clothes and hair were caked with mud: he had come straight from the bunkhouse.

"I need a bath," he said. His voice was raspy but still tinted with the Spanish accent she loved.

She put water on to heat and brought him a blanket. He peeled off his clothes and dropped them out the front door, then rested on the settee, wrapped in the blanket. She stripped, too, changed into her flannel nightgown. Then she brewed coffee, brought a steaming cup for him and one for her.

When the water heated, he helped her fill the wooden tub and sank into it with a sigh. She washed him, carefully at first, then more thoroughly as she found his skin remarkably free of cuts or bruises, except his palms and knees, which were torn and made him wince as the hot, soapy water stung them. He told her the scrubbing felt good, and she could see it brought life back to him. The steam helped clear his lungs.

"I quit," he told her.

A breath caught in her throat. "You did?"

He leaned his head back so she could rinse the mud from his hair. "Daunt was waiting when MacMurray's crew got me out. You know what he said to me?"

"What?"

"He said, 'You should've known better than to go down there.'"

She said nothing. She agreed with Daunt, but for different reasons.

Johnny closed his eyes. "The other blaster died. I wanted to see his widow. I should have gone."

"You couldn't."

He said nothing for a moment. Then: "I told Daunt to go to hell, and quit right then, when I first came out of the mine. It's only getting worse in there; I can't stop it."

She ran her soapy hands over his dark skin, liked the ridges of muscle underneath. They did not talk further until after the bath, when he wanted to know about Cole's battle with Halloran. She told him some of it, not all. Not the details.

"Will they send anyone else?" she asked.

They sat together on the settee with their bare feet stretched toward the hearth. "If it's Braunn, I'd say yes; maybe not right away. If it's Daunt, no. If it's someone else, who knows? I'll have to pick up a few things in town at some point, but until then I can stay here in case they do come. Did the deputy know where Halloran went?"

"I'm not sure. I don't think so."

He sighed. "Maybe not, but now whoever's behind all this knows Cole is alive. If it's Daunt, he'll want Cole for himself. He'll wait."

"You think he's the one?"

"I don't know. Could be. Could be him and Braunn together."

"Let's not talk about it anymore," she said, and he nodded.

She wanted to make love to him, to help him forget, help him rest. She leaned over his body, kissed the hollow where his collarbone met his neck, liked the roughness of his beard against her temple. She felt his hands on her back.

"Just lie still," she whispered, and he did.

23

Letters

Cole drifted in and out of his dreams, and all the dreams ran together. They usually began with the pitchfork arcing through dusty sunbeams to spear the man's neck. Then the man would become himself, clawing at his neck to get the fork out. This he would see from the loft, as though he were two people. He would leap from the loft to save himself, only to land on his injured leg. The pain would bring him down. He would lunge for the man who had turned into himself, but grasp only air, and the man would turn into the big Scotsman with the sack over his head, laughing from the door to the mine shack. The fuse would sputter toward the dynamite there, closer and closer. And the man would become Catharine. Cole would try to warn her away from the shack, but blood from his mouth would drown the words. Then he'd try to wake up, only to drift into the next horrifying dream.

Through the dreams he had a sensation of time passing. He fought repeatedly to wake himself. Sometimes he clawed his way close to the surface, struggled to open his eyes, only to descend again. Finally he descended deeper than ever, into the restful blackness of true sleep.

The sound of the loom brought him awake with a shiver; he would always hate that sound. Outside the window, sunshine slanted in a jewel-blue sky to brighten the trees, some evergreen, some with leaves of gold or red or brown, and naked limbs showing through. Close behind the trees a huge mountain wall climbed to the sky. The weather had turned crisp. Cole had hoped to leave before the season's first snow. He looked around the room, where he'd slept (when he'd slept inside) during his last years in Colorado. He could almost feel his family here, ghosts, a part of the room but more a part of him.

He tried to think of something else.

His physical pain had lessened and he felt refreshed. He wanted to get up, get moving, walk around, but that would be foolish. So he lay still, or fairy still. He did clench and unclench his fists and move his arms. He flexed his ankles and even tried moving his bad leg, which felt better than he'd expected. His ribs and head hurt the worst. He touched the tightly wrapped bandages around his ribs, then the side of his head that ached so.

At least he was healing. Heal enough and he could go home. Or stay here and take his revenge. Better to go home, but it may have been too late for that.

Again he tried to think of something else, and a new sensation hit him: hunger. The minute it hit he thought he would die of starvation. The smell of biscuits and gravy seeping under the closed door made it worse.

The loom thumped on. Maybe he should try to sit up. To hell with lying still. The window was open a crack and the breeze sneaking in on the sunshine smelled like crackling leaves. He wanted to walk through the leaves, feel them shuffle at his feet. He wanted to drink from a clear brook like the one on his ranch, survey the heavens for a hawk. He recalled that dream about the hawk, and Sam. He wanted to wrestle with Sam. But mostly he wanted to eat.

He propped himself up and turned back the covers: bruised and naked. Gretel had folded towels thickly under him, but they were dry. The bandages around his thigh looked fresh, with no bloodstains. He listened to the loom and, certain its rhythm would continue, swung his legs over the edge of the bed. The loom continued. He stood. His left leg gave immediately, but the right leg worked. With his weight on his good leg, he made water in the bucket on the floor by the bed, then opened the window all the way and tossed the urine out.

The loom noises stopped. The front door opened and shut, and then behind him his own door creaked open. Cole turned, expecting Gretel, but a dark man with long black hair and a close-cropped beard stood there instead. He looked Mexican. He was younger and shorter than Cole, though not by much. He had the compact, well-muscled body of a laborer and wore the clothes of a miner, but around the eyes he looked like he might have been out of place in a silver mine.

"Johnny Torres?" said Cole.

He smiled, showing straight white teeth. Cole worked his way back to a comfortable spot on the bed and adjusted the covers. Johnny came over and shook his hand.

"Guess you're the one who saved my life," Cole said.

"Along with Gretel." He had a faint Spanish accent.

"Well, thanks."

Johnny nodded.

"Where is Gretel?"

"Out for a walk."

It figured. No doubt she'd heard him rustling around.

"Are you thirsty?" Johnny asked him.

"Hungry, too."

"Good sign."

Johnny left the room, to return soon with a cup of water and a flannel shirt, which Cole pulled on painfully. Johnny left again, and came back with two heaped plates of chicken and biscuits drenched in thick gravy. He sat on a chair across the room from Cole and wolfed the meal down. Cole ate his more slowly. Johnny fetched seconds for himself and wolfed them, too.

"She's a good cook," he said after washing down the last bite. "Want some beer?" He grinned. "Maybe you should be drinking milk."

Cole smiled. "Beer."

Considering the size of the cabin, Cole saw surprisingly little of Gretel during the two weeks it took him to get back on his feet. It would take a couple of months to fully heal, but during those two weeks he managed to limp around the cabin and outside, staying close, with a walking stick, then without the stick, and to breathe without feeling like the man with the blue eyes was still hammering his ribs. He also learned that his sister had found someone who could make her laugh, though she never laughed in Cole's presence. Every so often, late at night or during a raw day when he was supposedly napping, he heard the subtle rustlings and soft laughter of a woman he'd never expected to know. He had always been sure she would become like his mother. Lying still, listening in his bed, he did not know whether to feel awkward or to smile. Often he ended up smiling, but other times the noises called Laura to mind, or Catharine, and he tried to shut them out.

Anyway, Gretel steered clear, and when he did see her, mostly at dinner, she responded to his questions curtly, and to his comments not at all.

He spent plenty of time with Johnny, and liked him from the start. Johnny may have lacked the comfortable roughness of a lifelong laborer, but he was adept at crossing from whatever other world he had lived in to the one he lived in now.

The men played cards, with beans for stakes, or smoked cigars together in front of the fire when Gretel went out. Johnny said she walked, or hunted, or fished. She gardened, too: Cole could see her from the window, crouched over her squashes and spinach. She had brought small pots of aromatic herbs inside, against the frost that blanketed the valley every morning. Johnny rarely strayed far from the cabin, though he looked out the window an awful lot and Cole would've bet he felt pretty cooped. His well-oiled Colt hung against his left hip whenever he did go outside, or from a hook on the wall when he stayed in. Johnny cleaned the gun carefully, always when Gretel was out. Cole felt guarded.

He'd asked Johnny after that first meal of chicken and biscuits if he was expecting trouble. Johnny shrugged and said anything could happen.

"Do you know who attacked me?" Cole asked.

"No. Could've been sent by Braunn or Daunt, or both, or someone else. Describe them for me."

So he did—the eyes, the clothes, the weapons, the builds.

"The big one's MacMurray," said Johnny, with no hint of surprise. "Runs the day shift at the Flosshilde silver mine. The others, who knows?"

Cole struggled to recall more. At first, nothing. Then, "One of them had a German accent."

"German?"

"Not Braunn."

"No."

Silence, while Johnny thought. Finally he shrugged. "Not too many German miners. They don't much like working underground."

"One of Braunn's men?"

"Could be."

"What about the marshal? It was the marshal I killed, right?"

"Yup. The trustees have already moved the senior deputy to the marshal's job, and he's doing nothing to follow up. Either he's in on it, too, or else whoever's behind this told him to hold off." He laughed sarcastically. "Awful lot of hushed cases these days."

"You think my father was murdered?"

"Hard to say. He got blown up in his prospect hole, the Anna Strike. There wasn't much left to go on." He hesitated. "I'm sorry."

Cole looked out the window, through the wavy glass that made the trees appear watery. "What a name, huh? Anna Strike. My mother's name."

"Yeah. Zachary told me."

"Braunn said you were friends."

"Close friends."

Cole said nothing, and Johnny took their plates away. When he returned he seemed to want to say something else, but held off. Maybe Cole misread him; he couldn't be sure, he had just met this man. Johnny asked if he wanted anything, and Cole said no, so Johnny left him alone. Tired after sitting, even for such a short while, Cole lay back and drifted off to sleep, and all he heard until the next morning was the front door opening and closing, and the murmur of Gretel's voice.

Two weeks after that, Heinrich Braunn came to the cabin. Cole and Johnny were playing blackjack at the pine table, with pinto beans for betting, and Gretel was out for one of her innumerable walks. It was nearly evening and supper simmered on top of the cookstove: a stew of squash, wild berries, and roast duck left over from the previous day. Cole's belly growled. He poured himself and Johnny fresh mugs of beer (he never would have expected his sister to make such fine beer) and dealt a pair of cards for each of them.

"Guess I'll stay," Johnny said of his cards.

Cole took one from the deck. The men placed their bets. When they turned over the cards, both had twenty, Johnny with a king high. He reached to rake in the beans.

The front door flew open and Gretel rushed in.

"Heinrich Braunn's coming," she said, breathless.

Cole and Johnny looked at each other. Johnny took his gunbelt from its peg and buckled it around his waist. Cole limped into his room and Gretel shut the door behind him with a pronounced thud.

Cole sat on the bed. He heard her close the other bedroom door, and then the scrape of chair legs on the wood floor as she and Johnny sat at the table, probably to resume the card game. Any other time, she stayed clear of cards.

He heard the knock at the door, then Johnny's stiff greeting, with more behind it than the suspicion of Braunn's involvement in recent assaults and murder. He heard an almost haughty disdain that would have taken him by surprise if he hadn't already figured out that Johnny had done more during his life than swing a hammer. He addressed Heinrich Braunn as an equal.

Cole heard lighter steps on the floor. Gretel had gone to stand by Johnny.

"May I come in?" Braunn said, his tone as cordial and compassionless as during the time Cole spent at his mansion. "I have something to discuss with you, Mr. Torres."

"Come in," said Gretel.

The door closed. The footsteps stopped inside the door; no one sat.

"What is it?" Johnny asked.

"I was pleased that you came through the Flosshilde cave-in in good health."

"So was I."

"Yes."

A silence passed, briefly.

Braunn cleared his throat. "I wanted to tell you before this, but I have been occupied at the mines. I fired Mr. Daunt."

"That's wise. A little late, though." Johnny's voice betrayed no surprise or wariness, especially no approval.

"You may not think I took your comments about the Flosshilde seriously, but I did. I had intended to release Mr. Daunt imminently, cave-in or no cave-in."

"Too bad Eldridge had to die first."

"Yes, it is. I saw his widow myself, though I expect that counts little with you at this juncture."

Johnny said nothing.

"I am disappointed you left," Braunn continued.

"I don't miss it."

"Perhaps not, but I came here because I hope you will return. I want you to take over as superintendent."

The ensuing silence told Cole that Johnny had not expected this. He would've bet Gretel had, though.

"And the Flossie?" Johnny said, finally.

"Should be closed."

Cole heard a shifting in the other room. He could not tell who had moved. Then Johnny said, "Thanks for the offer. You'll understand if I take a day to think about it."

"Certainly," Braunn replied, and then he left.

Again there was no movement. Then a rustle, then Gretel's footsteps toward the cookstove, the clank of a serving spoon on dishes, harder than it had to be, the slosh of beer in a mug.

"It's a good offer," Johnny said.

"Of course it is." No bitterness, no anger, merely resignation.

"I have to work. I can't live off the land like you. I'd go crazy."

"Yes, you would."

"And you won't leave here."

She said nothing. Cole heard the plates set on the table, three of them, with less force than the spoon had set the food on the plates.

"I won't start just yet."

Gretel walked to Cole's door and opened it. She was looking away from him, at Johnny.

"Start whenever you want," she said. "Cole will be fine." Then she looked at Cole, and he saw in her a reaching out that vanished as soon as he saw it.

The next day Johnny rode into town, and after he came back he gave Cole Zachary's will, and a letter that went with it.

"Gretel does not know about this," he said. "I've been holding on to it. I even thought of burning it. But it's yours, and Zachary's, and whatever gets done with it should be up to you."

Cole did not open it. Gretel was out, though icy rain fell steadily, drumming the cabin's tin roof. The two men had been peeling potatoes for her at the pine table, and drinking beer. They'd left a pile of potato skins.

"The Anna Strike?" Cole asked.

"Yours."

Cole nodded slowly.

"I'm starting back to work tomorrow," Johnny said, shoving the skins into a blue ceramic bowl. The bowl reminded Cole of his mother, how she used to stand with it clamped between her arm and body, beating vigorously with a wooden spoon.

"There's also a letter for you," Johnny continued, "from Montana." He handed this to Cole as well.

Cole smiled, though without mirth. "Don't worry, Gretel will be fine."

"Yes." Johnny hesitated. "You know, if you want help going after these bastards—"

"I know. Thanks."

Johnny set the bowl by the door to go out to the pile behind the garden. He wiped his hands on his corduroy pants. Cole stood, too, and put the peeling knives away and the envelopes in his pocket. He would read the will and the letters, one from his father, one from his wife, later. When Gretel got back the men drank another beer by the fire and she fixed the trout she'd caught.

"Kind of rainy for fishing," Cole commented.

"It's all right," she said, without the usual edge.

In his room after supper, Cole dug Laura's letter from his pocket, undressed, and sat in bed to read it by the light of the kerosene lamp. He would read his father's will tomorrow, or maybe after that. Maybe he would not read it at all.

October 3, 1892

My Dearest Cole,

Of course I had to write. Please do not take time to reply. I would far rather think of you hurrying your Colorado business along and returning safely home.

You must forgive my silly imagination. I cannot help but conjure notions of the danger such a long trip could hold. Gold country has always had its share of crime, and when you received the telegram from your sister, my first thought was of foul play. Have I read too many stories? Did you have the same thought? Truly, I was embarrassed to share it with you, but now from the safety of distance, I can.

I am afraid I have little to say, so it seems silly to waste your time, but just thinking of you reading this warms me, and how cold the weather has turned since you left. I expect it is a bit more balmy there. Oh, here I go discussing the weather! Have we not gone past that?

I write much differently from how I speak, don't you think?
So formal and dramatic. Here I sit, barefoot on my stool, happy
to be a ranch wife, writing like some fancy dame. What a laugh:
me, a fancy dame!

Cole rubbed his eyes. In the dim lamplight, the pages looked
yellow; against his fingertips, the paper felt brittle. Laura's tall,
slanted letters ran together, as though her pen had blotted. Cole let
his arm fall, his eyelids droop. The letter slipped from his fingers,
dropping to the floor with an almost soundless rustle.

"I'm going up to the pass," he told Gretel the next morning, after
Johnny had left for the mines.
She stopped cleaning the dishes and looked at him more directly
than during the whole time he'd been here. Dishwater dripped from
her reddened hands; she always washed with scalding water.
"You are?"
He put on his father's shearling jacket.
"If anyone like Buck Daunt comes around, tell him where I went.
Don't be brave."
She laughed, without laughter. "Take Halloran's dun. He'll only
cause me trouble."
He touched his injured thigh through the patched trousers and
thanked her. "You must have buried Halloran. What about his guns?"
"They're with him, where they belong."
For a last instant he thought of meeting her hostility head-on.
He stood still in front of her and she met his gaze. Finally she looked
away, toward the door.
"Shovel's in the barn," she said. "I'll fix you a sack."

By mid-afternoon, he was cooking trout in the wilderness beyond Lizardhead Pass. He rested by his fire's crackling warmth,

knowing his body would resist too much activity; his leg still pained him, and so did his ribs. The leg would improve soon, but the ribs would ache for weeks. He thought of revenge, of the man Johnny called MacMurray. He wanted to kill that man.

But he did not want the gold mine. Anna Strike. He did not want the Anna Strike. He did not care to take on Buck Daunt or Heinrich Braunn; let them fight each other for the damned mine.

His father's will held no surprises. Neither did the letter, except for the way it blurred before his eyes. He had not cried in years, except once, when his baby son Zack had come lifeless from Laura's womb. He did not cry now.

Maybe he should burn the will. Johnny had thought of that, too. Cole held the papers over the shrinking campfire, felt the heat on his fingers. A corner of the will began to blacken and smoke, but did not catch. He held it closer to the fire. It seemed he meant to burn his hand off with it, as though that would be fitting. To burn his father's will, his father's dying wish, would be to burn himself. He withdrew his hand. The fire popped hungrily and a flame leapt from the pop, brightening the pages, beckoning. Cole folded the will and put it away. He had not decided about revenge, but this will was no more his to burn than it was Johnny's.

Maybe he should've written back to Laura, but what could he tell her? Got half my ribs smashed in, my head busted, my leg nearly blown off. Doing fine. Be home soon, after I plug the bastards who did it. Or in a box, after they plug me. Or, Be home this week, on the run, Colorado business unfinished.

Why lie? She would not expect a response anyway. He had left to buy cattle before and never written then. She was right: he was a lousy correspondent. He'd never written back to Catharine, either.

24

A Most Deadly Game

The Braunns watched the sunset from their landing. Soon it would be time to leave for the opera, Wagner's *Das Rheingold*, to be performed by an acclaimed traveling troupe. They'd planned this evening weeks ago, but Catharine had forgotten. Heinrich had reminded her this morning, and now she sat with him, dressed in her finest gown, of saffron satin and black lace, sipping white wine. The great bowed window darkened around them; the sunset was fading.

Heinrich seemed eager for the diversion tonight's performance should provide. The return to Colorado, the deaths of Marie, of Zachary, of Cole had changed him not at all. He went on with his game; in fact, he appeared to relish it more. Catharine wanted no part of it anymore, though she kept up her façade. Why not? It fit her like the perfectly tailored gowns in her closets, but it did not wear well.

Heinrich distracted her by telling her something. Every time he spoke now, he distracted her. She lived far away, in a corner across the room from her fear of him, and her doubt about whether he might have been responsible for Cole's death.

"Pardon me?" she said.

"I hired Johnny Torres to replace Buck Daunt."

"What?" He had her attention. She reacted as she would to a bite of meat gone foul.

Heinrich chuckled. "Why so surprised?"

"I don't know. I don't like him."

"You have never met him, my dear. And you have said you disliked Mr. Daunt as well. Who is worse?"

"Don't mock me, Heinrich."

"Mock you? I was simply making conversation."

She said nothing.

"Have you a prejudice against Mexicans? Or I should say Spaniards—he hails from Spain, originally, and from the little I have been able to learn about his past, his father owned a number of mineral properties. Mr. Torres is the best shift boss we have, and the most resourceful and intelligent. It is highly unusual for these Westerners to respect a Mexican."

"I'm aware of that, Heinrich. I grew up here, remember?"

"Yes, Catharine, I remember."

She sighed. She should not care.

"So what do you have against our new superintendent?" Heinrich said. His persistence with this question put Catharine on guard, but his tone had gentled and he seemed to want to talk. He had always viewed conversation after sunset as a social given.

"Well?"

She avoided his eyes by sipping her wine.

"You think he should have avenged your friend Cole," he said.

"Would you have him come after me? Is that what you want?"

She took a larger gulp of wine than she meant to: her eyes

smarted and she almost sneezed. "Of course not," she said when she could, and wiped her lips with a lace-edged linen napkin.

He took a cigar from the box on the table, nipped off the end and lighted it. Still she could not look at him. Instead she looked out the window, or at it, since night now obscured the mountains.

"Mr. Torres might do better to come after you, Catharine."

She looked at him now.

He puffed smoke, making small rings. "Has it ever occurred to you that you play a most deadly game? Perhaps I play with money and the power it affords, but you play a game with much higher stakes. Think about it."

She said nothing, but her finger and thumb were pinching the stem of her fine crystal wineglass so tightly it hurt.

"Emotions can get you killed, my dear, and others as well if you stir them up enough. Love is even worse. It makes one so inexcusably vulnerable."

She rose, slowly, as if drawn by a string. "Are you saying I killed Cole? By not warning him? Are you saying that?"

"I would never say such a thing."

She stepped toward him. The wineglass felt like it would snap in her hand. If only it would. Then she could slash his throat with the sharpest piece. She flung it at the window. The crystal shattered. The panes of night remained intact. Catharine ran from the landing, her high-heeled shoes clattering against the marble floor.

Later, much later, with Heinrich away at the opera, she sat alone in her dressing room among the mirrors, still wearing her fine saffron dress with the black lace, and the dreadfully binding corset. She thought of Gretel in Cole's old clothes, and then of her mother, who for years had worn the clothes of Catharine's father.

She remembered going to the Fallen Idle to tell her mother that

Heinrich had asked her to marry him. She had never gone there until then because Marie had forbidden it.

The night had been clammy with mist and occasional rain that wanted to change to snow. As Catharine pulled her wrap tighter a drunken miner stumbled out the door, one hand over his mouth, the other over his belly. He saw her and froze. Then the liquor got the better of him, and he turned aside and threw up.

"Sorry, ma'am," he slurred, and wiped his mouth with his hand before lurching back into the bar. He opened the door and light spilled out like the glow from a potbelly stove, but the saloon emitted no heat. After the door closed, she stood in the street with mud seeping through her boots and wondered where the relief at saying yes to Heinrich had gone.

Catharine, I want you to marry me.

Yes, Heinrich. Yes, I want to marry you.

He wanted, she wanted. For themselves, not for each other.

She went into the saloon. Heads turned, men leered and whistled. Barmaids and whores averted painted faces. Smoke enveloped her, making her eyes smart and blurring the room into an opiate dazzle. Instinctively she put a gloved hand to her nose, but the stench of spilled liquor, stale tobacco, and sweating bodies flared her nostrils. Voices cut the blur.

"Hey, sweetheart."

"Over here, darling."

"Gotta be Marie's filly."

"Come see papa, baby. Let's see whatcher mama'd look like outsida them men's clothes, huh?"

She felt a hand on her butt and slapped it away, only to realize it was a pair of saddlebags hanging off a chair. She felt foolish and out of place and couldn't see Marie anywhere.

Then a prospector left the bar, which opened a space. Catharine glimpsed her mother, the hat pushed back on her head, her red hair disheveled around her face. She worked fast but with ease, tossing drinks into glasses, laughing throatily with her head thrown back, calling the men by name. Catharine worked her way through the throng to the end of the bar, where a sodden customer slept on one stool and another sang tunelessly next to him. She slid between them and tried to attract Marie's attention without drawing anyone else's.

Marie served a few more drinks, returned a few more handclasps, answered a few more obscenities in kind. She pretended liveliness, but Catharine saw through that. When Marie smiled at the men, her eyes squinted almost shut, and Catharine knew this hid the strain. She worked here so that Catharine could become a lady. She'd worked all Catharine's life. She'd never sold her body, but bit by bit she'd sold all else about herself that was valuable and worth keeping.

Catharine watched as her mother fished in her vest pocket for some coins and handed them to a man at the bar. The man gave her a tiny tin box. She opened it, closed one nostril and snorted deeply, closed the other and snorted again. Her eyes teared and she made a face and coughed. Then she seemed to brighten. Her laugh climbed to a shriller pitch and her hands sloshed the drinks across the bar faster than ever. Catherine bowed her head and made herself think of Heinrich.

The tone of the men ordering drinks changed, became impatient, belligerent. Catharine looked up. Marie was staring at her. Apparently she had been for several seconds. Now only the drunkest of the men continued to make demands. Marie ignored them. Her green eyes were wide, her expression bewildered, as though someone had dealt her a terrible, undeserved blow.

"Why are you here?"

"He asked me to marry him, Mama. I told him I would."

Marie's hands hung limp at her sides. Catharine wanted to take them in her own, shake her into realizing they were finally free. She saw they had acquired an audience. The men at the bar craned their necks to see and the noise level had dropped.

"But you don't love him," said Marie.

"I'll learn to, Mama. It's all right." She swallowed the growing lump in her throat. "I thought you would be happy. I thought this was what you wanted. Mama—" She felt tears coming.

Marie forced a smile and held out her hands and Catharine took them. "He wants to marry you?"

"I said yes, Mama. I said yes."

One of the men whooped, another attacked the piano, a third grabbed Catharine and whirled her around and around. As tables and chairs and a hundred ribald grins sped by, she saw her mother lifted over the bar. And she saw tears running down her mother's face, felt her own tears as they danced, pretending to laugh, then laughing for real because they were such fools to want something so much and cry when they got it.

At the wedding, Marie had stood ghostly white in pale pink and lace, dried out, dried up, old at thirty-six but not half as old as Catharine felt at nineteen. Zachary had stood with her, and Catharine kept thinking they should take the vows, not she and Heinrich. But Marie had turned Zachary down, just as Catharine had turned Cole down. Only Zachary had stayed.

How strangely life twisted its knife. Now, surrounded by mirrors in a castle above her old lover's cabin, Catharine rose and turned out the light, extinguishing her image. She left the dressing room for the bedroom, where she lay down, still bound in her corset and fine saffron dress.

25

Guarding the Gold

Heinrich Braunn walked to his box at the front of the opera house, his spine straight, his broad shoulders stiff, his silver-haired head immobile, looking at no one, greeting no one, though everyone watched. He was late; the overture had begun, Herr Wagner's chords swelling through the hall.

Johnny watched Braunn, too, wondering if Catharine would ever join him outside her castle. She had yet to venture into town. The seat next to the mine owner remained empty, so Catharine had intended to view this performance, or at least her husband had intended for her to view it. After all, it would be sung in German.

As the lights dimmed, the overture progressed and the heavy gold curtain rose. The stage manager must have held the lights for Braunn. Johnny had wanted to see this opera since finding out about it weeks ago, to escape if only for a while the mines, the killing, the straitjacket of Gretel's cabin. He had not expected to make it. Yesterday, after learning that Cole had left Gretel's for the pass, he'd managed to scare up a ticket.

The traveling troupe had set the scene elaborately: carefully situated props, greenish lighting, and cascading mist created an almost believable mountain river haven for the Rhinemaidens, who soon danced and sang among painted water and paper rocks. The Rhinemaiden called Flosshilde warned her sisters to guard the Rhinegold more attentively.

What a relief yesterday to bang nails into the boards that closed the Flossie forever. Many from the mine's crews now worked in the Bonne Chance, fortifying with square sets and lagging where Buck Daunt had skimped on timber. Johnny had fired MacMurray and O'Hearn, the night-shift boss who had replaced Zachary. Emma's husband had taken O'Hearn's place. MacMurray and Daunt had yet to retaliate, but Johnny had taken to wearing his Colt all the time.

On stage, the repulsive gnome Alberich pursued the three river nymphs, who teased him by offering themselves, only to flit from rock to rock just out of Alberich's lustful reach. Alberich became disgusted with Woglinde and Wellgunde, but then Flosshilde took over the enticement with sweetly sung insults. Her sisters laughed.

Johnny couldn't keep his mind from wandering. Waiting for Cole to decide was driving him crazy. If Cole chose revenge, Johnny would throw in with him. If he chose to go home, Johnny would go after Daunt or Braunn himself. It had to be one of them. It could have been both, except that now Braunn had fired Daunt.

Once again he attempted to focus on the opera. Alberich had managed to wrest the Rheingold from the Rhinemaidens by renouncing love. Johnny thought the gnome should find this easy, except that Alberich equated love with lust and so renounced lust. He could have renounced love, retained lust, and still had the gold. Buck Daunt did that: he spent his nights abusing Telluride's whores, or Ophir's, and during the day he and his men blasted holes in the Anna Strike. He had long since filed his claim, to the whores and to the mine, though of course Zachary's will invalidated the latter. Only Cole and Johnny knew about that will; if Daunt found out, he'd kill Johnny tonight, in this very seat.

The hours stretched on and the opera progressed. Johnny's concentration was shot, though—a shame considering the quality of the rendition. To hell with it, he finally decided, and left at the intermission. He'd check on the Bonne Chance instead.

Braunn nodded to him in the lobby.

"Quite a performance, no?" the mine owner commented, without conviction. He seemed preoccupied.

"A good troupe," Johnny replied, and they parted ways.

Outside, the night air had a bite to it. The first real snow of the year was overdue, though white had cloaked the high peaks already and frost lay thickly on the rooftops every morning. Colorado Avenue was crowded with a mix of promenading north-side residents and half-drunk south-side workers. On Pacific, old lanterns and new electric lamps turned night to day, while music from the saloons and dance halls clashed in a jumbled street serenade. Men and women already danced on the boardwalk; the saloons had filled to overflowing, as on any Friday. Johnny hurried past. It seemed like years since he had enjoyed a night in town, and he looked forward to returning here after checking on the mine. The night would be half-gone by then; no sense going back to Gretel's.

At the foot of the trail he started to climb. The palomino was stabled at Emma's. This trail was steeper than the more commonly traveled one, but also shorter. Johnny was thinking of Emma and her husband who now worked for him, when three men stepped out of the shadows into his path. He stopped, startled. His left hand went to his Colt. The men had their guns out already: moonlight glinted off the steel.

"What's going on?" Johnny demanded.

"Nothing much," one of them answered, his drawl as Georgian as Daunt's. All three had worked for MacMurray; now they were jobless.

Johnny looked past them up the trail. So Daunt was making his move tonight. His first move, anyway. And it had to be Daunt. Braunn would not move on his own mine.

"Buck Daunt tell you to keep me here?" he said to the men.

"What if he did?"

"He tell you to kill me?"

"Hell no, why'd we want to do that?" The Georgian drawl reeked of sarcasm. "We'd rather y'all stayed alive for the fireworks. Be much more fun than your danged opera."

Johnny studied each of them.

"Then get out of my way," he said, his hand tighter on the Colt.

"Can't do that, Torres."

"I said get out of my way."

The man on the right guffawed. It was the first sound he had made. "Or what? You fixing to shoot all three of us?"

The Georgian spoke again. "I think you better drop that gun, Torres."

He stood still.

"Drop the gun."

The Colt burned against his left palm.

"Drop it!"

He drew the Colt and slammed his right hand against the hammer. Fire flashed twice from the barrel. The Georgian and the one on the right jerked backwards, their screams choked off. Flame spouted from the third man's gun. The bullet drilled Johnny's shoulder and wrenched him sideways, which brought the Colt in line with the man's gut. He fired and the man doubled over, then sat down hard, screaming like the others, pressing with his hands while blood, black in the moonlight, poured from between his fingers. Johnny pulled the trigger again. The man stopped screaming.

Johnny dropped the Colt and sank to his knees, holding his left arm close to his body. *Dios me libre,* he thought. For once in this mountain hell, have mercy.

Blood pasted his shirt to his shoulder. He peeled it away and checked the wound. Moving his arm shot a current of pain through him, but only because the bullet had torn the flesh and still chafed inside: no broken bones, no severed nerves.

He ripped a section off one dead man's shirt, wadded it, and plugged the wound. Then he reloaded his gun and scrambled on up the mountain. Water trickling from above had turned the trail into a creek bed oozing with slippery mud. Every step gave him more trouble than the last. Dizziness made him halt several times to clear his head and press the wadded cloth farther into the throbbing wound. He was losing blood too fast.

He reached the area outside the mine. Amid a treeless expanse awash in moonlight, the bunkhouse, the stamp mill, the shops, and the office stood silent and grim, hulking as ever against the mountain. The powder house, too. A procession of trammers dumped their ore cars and headed back inside the tunnels. The adits swallowed them, glowing, three gaping mouths. All quiet, except for a whole fucking army of tommyknockers.

Johnny took off toward the mine at a run.

"Get everyone out!" he roared. Startled faces turned toward him. Men appeared at the doors of the buildings. "She's gonna blow! Everyone out! The buildings, too!"

All activity ceased. Even the tommyknockers. Johnny felt a deep rumble. The ground shook. The men outside staggered and fell. Johnny fell. A shattering roar burst from the adits, along with rock and timber. The powder house turned into a giant ball of light. The buildings exploded as one. A half mile off, the powder magazine burst into flames and rose into the sky, turning back the night.

Johnny pressed himself as flat as he could to the ground. Debris pelted him. The earth pitched and the pitching roared all by itself. Rock strained against rock. Johnny pressed tightly with his arms over his head.

The roar died away. Johnny raised his head and looked at the Bonne Chance. The adits were sealed.

PART THREE

Anna Strike

October 16 to 18, 1892

26

Storm Warnings

The wind woke Gretel in the wee hours. She lay shivering and tense, plagued by premonitions. Her father and Johnny had often talked of tommyknockers. Now it was as though the wind had blown them down from the mountains to skulk about the dark cabin, lost, tapping here and there.

The weather had changed. Soon it would snow. Any other year she would have rejoiced in the first snow. She would have tiptoed outside, making small prints, then run through the powder, white jets spraying at her feet. Then stopped and stood motionless, enraptured by the white frosting on every tiny twig, the gold of lingering leaves peeking through, the red of a berry, the green of a pine needle. She would have gulped the air, free of dust, the dust brought down by the falling snow.

Not this year. In the morning, with the wind moaning and the clouds hanging low, she got up and sat at her loom, still ill at ease, dreading. A blizzard, it would be a blizzard. Not today, but tomorrow.

231

She stared out the window, unable to force her eyes to the loom, from which she had finally removed the dead white nothingness of the piece she'd started when Zachary died, the piece so like the coming blizzard. Except the blizzard would not be dead; it would kill. It was too early for such a storm. The trees had not fully prepared themselves, the animals had not had time for that last deep drink from the river, or to hide that last stash of nuts. A blizzard would kill the weak, anyway, but this one would take the strong, too.

Cole was in those mountains. She thought he would've decided quickly what to do, and returned by now to tell her. He would recognize the signs of the coming storm: Montana must get hit worse than this. Maybe he'd come down today, Saturday, after two days gone. She had provisioned him for a little longer, but not for a blizzard.

The loom. Work the loom. Work on this blanket, rose and green, for Catharine Braunn's mansion. She tossed the shuttle to and fro a couple of halfhearted times. A blanket. Cole might want extra blankets tonight, if he stayed up there. Why should she care? No reason, except that he was her brother. He had spoken not one unkind word to her his whole time here. He'd spoken no unkind words to her as a kid, either; he'd spoken hardly any words to her at all.

But he was her brother. Maybe Cole wouldn't remind her of this, but Johnny hadn't hesitated. He simply wouldn't understand.

"He as much as disowned our family," she'd told him. "He rode out of here in a huff while Buck Daunt helped Zachary bury our mother. Then he became a hired gun. That should be enough."

"It's not enough, Gretel," Johnny said. Damn it all, why wouldn't he see?

"Look," she said. "Some folks make mistakes all the time and never pay at all. Not Zachary—he made two, and he paid for them both. The Anna Strike was a mistake. And it killed him. And he's the only man I ever cared about, until you."

"What was his other mistake?"

"Cole," was all she said. "Cole was the first."

Johnny had gotten her meaning, which was good, because she had no intention of saying more. Why should he care, anyway? Had he ever cared for anyone the way she had cared for Cole? How little she knew of him, even after all this time.

She worked a while longer on Catharine's rose and green blanket, then finally gave up. Cole kept intruding and so did Johnny, though both were gone and Gretel had initially welcomed this time alone. Well, she wasn't alone: worry saw to that, and the incessant tapping of the wind.

Late in the afternoon she collected a bunch of blankets and a tin of chicken soup, lashed the bundles to Zachary's old brown gelding and led the torpid beast through the wind. She fought her way up the escarpment, the weather holding her back, resentment making her movements angular, ugly. Even so, her steps were too fast for the poor old horse.

A light sheeting of snow had already fallen on the pass, but under the lowering sky it looked dull rather than pristine. The wind had dulled, too, leaving everything gray: the grass, the trees, the slopes, the peaks, the sky. Gretel walked in a fog, her agitated steps the only sharpness except the cold and an occasional startled bird taking flight.

No one else in the world would know where Cole had gone. Slackening the pace, she approached his old campsite cautiously; he would expect trouble. She found the fire kicked over, the ashes scattered, fresh prints on the new snow. She called her brother's name, quietly. Her rapid climb had left her breathless. The horse, too: he wheezed and coughed.

Cole limped out of the spruce trees around his clearing, holstered Luke Halloran's pistol, and leaned the rifle against a tree trunk. He cast a rueful eye at the fire.

Gretel unlashed the bundle from the horse, whose sweat had turned clammy, and dumped it on the snow.

"Here," she said.

He looked from the bundle to her. "You didn't have to do this."

"No, I didn't. Funny what family makes you do."

Cole laughed, startling her. "You don't owe me anything, Gretel." He squatted stiffly, retrieved the container of soup and the blankets.

"You can stay at the cabin," she said, without hospitality.

He stood, holding the blankets and the soup. Throughout his days at her cabin he had revealed neither anger nor hurt at her treatment. Now she thought his eyes betrayed a hint of both, though she couldn't be sure.

"I don't think so," he said.

"There's a blizzard coming," she said.

He nodded.

She remembered making this same climb as a girl, with blankets then, too. He'd sent her away. She remembered understanding his need to be alone as though it foretold her own future. She remembered the long hike back down to the cabin on legs shorter and more spindly, legs that needed a night's rest by her brother's fire, and creeping through her bedroom window, scared that her mother would hear. She'd made it into bed that night and lain there shivering. Tonight she could do the same, on stronger legs that nevertheless craved a rest by the fire.

Instead she scouted the clearing for more wood, picked up some kindling.

"You don't have to do that, either," said Cole.

She shrugged and he joined her in rebuilding the fire. They kept it small, on the off chance that anyone might come, but it was enough to heat the soup.

They ate in silence. After supper Cole told her the soup was good, which she accepted with a nod. He brewed coffee, bitter and black the way they both liked it. Zachary had liked it that way, too, but not Anna; Anna had liked it smooth and rich with cream.

Cole asked after Johnny, and Gretel told him how Johnny loved opera, and had gone to town to see Wagner. A silence followed. Cole was no more one to force conversation than Gretel, and she shied away from asking what he meant to do next, the only other topic on her mind. He would tell her when he decided, or maybe he would try to protect her by not telling. Instead he told her something else.

"You've never asked about Texas," he said, with his hands wrapped for warmth around his second cup of coffee.

"It's not my business."

He shrugged, and some of the coffee's steam escaped from under the brim of his black hat. "Maybe, but I figure you deserve to know."

She shrugged, too, and poured more coffee for herself.

He sipped, breathing in the heat, and Gretel wondered for an instant if he would change his mind. But he didn't. "Catharine wrote me a letter a few months after I left here," he said. "I was working on a big spread and had sent her word in case she changed her mind about coming with me. Did you know we were supposed to go together?"

"I found out."

"Well, she never wrote in those first few months, then she wrote to tell me she'd lost a baby, and that the baby was mine. She also said she still couldn't come to Texas and she didn't want me to come back here. She said there was someone else. Now I know she had started seeing Heinrich Braunn."

He cleared his throat. Gretel poked at the fire with a stick, threw the stick into the flames. She felt a little awkward, hearing all this.

"I was angry," he said, "and hurt, too. I got into a scrape with another cowhand, and had to use my gun to get out. He was mostly at fault, I guess, so the law left me alone. Word got around, though, about what I could do with a gun. Pretty soon folks were knocking at my door, and you know what happened after that."

He took his turn at jabbing the fire, which flared and settled back. "I've tried to forget the killing, but I can't. I especially remember the last one, before Halloran, that is."

He looked at her. She could see he wanted to tell her about it. It occurred to her that he had never told anyone else, and the awkward feeling deepened. But she wanted to know, as much as he wanted to tell her. "Go on," she said.

"Well, I'd like to think he was all bad, though who really knows. Anyway, every kind of law wanted him dead. Marshals, Rangers, vigilantes, maybe bounty hunters most of all, since he had over eight thousand dollars on his head, dead or alive. No one could ever catch him. He was crazy, they said, so they never knew what he'd do next.

"I heard he wanted to fight me. The Rangers heard, too, so they paid me up front and put the word out that I was gunning for him. I remember waiting for weeks in a water stop in west Texas. Seemed like every outlaw in the state and a few from outside passed through during those weeks.

"There was nothing to do. I read. I tossed the lariat and practiced shooting. I slept with the whores who were clean enough, and I thought a lot about what I would do next. I had never thought about that before, not in Texas at least."

"What did you decide?" she asked.

"Nothing. That's just it—what else could I do? All the doors were closed. I could move on, but I'd be the same inside.

"I kept thinking he was in town all along, just waiting for me to figure out where. My mind began to play tricks on me. I'd walk by a dark space between two buildings at night and hear him laughing, only as I walked on I'd hear it was just a whore and some other man.

I'd look at every face to see if it was him. Somehow I figured I'd know him if I could only get his eyes to meet mine. I guess I felt kind of a bond between us.

"It's funny, but a lot of my reputation probably came from those weeks when I never fought anyone. On the border, folks don't talk to each other much, and no one asks questions. You can get shot just for looking at a man too close, but I looked at everyone too close. No one ever moved on me, and they always seemed to look away first. I don't know who they were. The only description anyone had of most outlaws was hair, eyes, height, maybe a scar or two; sure not enough to tell one from the next.

"The man finally turned up one Saturday night. I was playing poker in the cantina with a couple of Mexican road bandits. This man walked up to the table and tapped the bandits on the shoulder, and they just cleared out. I looked up from my cards and it was him. I knew then that he'd just gotten to town; I'd never seen him before, and then there was the trail dust and the low-heeled boots. Thing is, he didn't look like a killer. None of us did. The men who passed through that town looked the same as folks in church on Sunday, except for their clothes. And their eyes. I could always tell from the eyes.

"So I set my cards down and stood up real easy. We weren't of a mind to waste time. We didn't say anything, but people knew what would happen. No one left, they just backed against the bar and the walls. The bets had been laid a long time ago. I never did find out who they favored." He stopped.

"So what happened?"

He shrugged and peered into the fire. "I killed him."

"And then?"

"Well, he made a real show of dying. I thought I hit him dead center, but he just kind of backed up and laughed and leaned against the wall. He could have fired again; he still had his finger on the trigger and he was waving the gun around, and he looked strong enough for all the blood. So I shot him again, and he lurched and closed his eyes for a second. Everyone stood still, though anywhere else but border Texas they would've run off real fast because he still had five bullets left. He pointed the gun at me and I thought maybe I should shoot him a third time, but it seemed like if he lived through the first two, he'd live through the third. So I figured this was why I couldn't decide what to do with myself after the job, because the bastard was going to kill me, and I thought maybe that's what I wanted."

He took a deep breath. Off a few feet, one of the horses stamped a hoof in the snow.

He told her the rest. "Then his knees bent and his eyes rolled back and he started to fall. After he was down one of the whores tapped me on the shoulder. I nearly shot her; she should've known better. She started kissing me and I could see the other women giving her nasty looks because she won the bet on who'd get to me first after the kill. And I could see the money changing hands all around. The chatter started up, Spanish and English, and both where the bets crossed over, but all I could really hear was this man I thought had died twitching on the floor. I know you can't hear something like that, but I swear I did. Then I heard him laugh. So I pulled out my gun and shot him again, and everyone cheered."

"You left after that."

"Yeah, north. I went north." He rubbed his jaw, remembering. Gretel remembered how often Zachary had done that, through his beard.

"Funny, I got to the Colorado border and realized I'd headed right for it without even thinking. All those days in the saddle, those nights alone with the coyotes and the snakes, and it never occurred to me that I was on my way back here. It was like I slept through the whole trip while someone else guided my horse, and I just kind of ended up here."

"But you ended up in Montana."

"I know. I changed course as soon as I realized where I was."

"You're going home, aren't you," she said.

He nodded.

"When did you decide?"

"Tonight, when you got here. Maybe when you said that about family."

She had said that to hurt him.

"There should be a train tomorrow," he said, "before the storm hits. I'll head out northwest and catch it in Placerville." He hesitated. "If you want me to wait for Johnny to get back from town, I will. If you're worried about him, I mean. I don't mind waiting."

"You wait and you'll stay," she said for both of them. "Better you keep your mind on Laura and Sam, and that train."

"I'm going to stop at Braunn's first."

She looked at him and he shook his head sadly, as if she didn't even need to ask the question. "I'm in love with my wife, Gretel. But I guess Catharine's got a pretty good hold on me, too."

"She's in love with you."

"That's not why I'm going."

They had nothing further to discuss, and the night's chill called for a blanket.

The next morning the storm had moved closer. Another light coating of snow had fallen, but the spruce trees and the warm blankets had protected Gretel and Cole. They crawled into the day, their faces pinched and white, their breath steaming in the gray wintry air, their arms slapping around themselves to break the chill. Again Cole brewed coffee, again bitter and black. They drank it with blankets draped around their shoulders, while oats softened over the fire. The coffee reddened their cheeks.

They talked a little about the storm. After breakfast they broke camp and rode out, Cole to the Braunns' mansion, Gretel to her cabin. They parted in the valley.

Cole touched the brim of his black hat. "Thanks, Gretel," he said.

"Yeah. Sure." Their horses took a few steps apart. Gretel turned on the brown gelding's old bare back. "Maybe you could come back sometime."

He turned, too. "Maybe." And then he rode away, toward the end of the valley, and the road up the mesa.

At the cabin Gretel stoked the fire and sat by the hearth with another cup of coffee and a hand loom, waiting for Johnny. She did not expect him early: he would have stayed out the better part of the night. She thought of him dancing, and of how she would like to see him dance, because he moved so well. She would like to dance with him, but not at the dance halls. She could never stomach the dance halls. Maybe at their wedding. Their wedding? What a thought!

She had an order from Catharine for a small tapestry, a foot-and-a-half square, a picture of Telluride. It would include a row of buildings, some clapboard, some brick: the Baroness Hotel, opera house, Congregational church, First National Bank, Telluride Club, county courthouse. Above these would rise the mountains, with the Bridal Veil Falls in the center. Into the border she would weave a chain of Catharine's white roses, which should spring well from the dark blue background. She had decided to leave people out of her picture.

She arranged her threads and began to work. Tapestries took a lot of time; each tiny line required the most painstaking attention, which suited Gretel fine: she needed a project to concentrate on, while waiting. But like yesterday, her concentration strayed, settling more often on the window, and the storm gathering outside it. She hoped Johnny would make it here before the blizzard. She missed him.

Late in the morning there was a knock at the door. Johnny. Flooded with relief, Gretel jumped up and threw aside the bolt, flung open the door, and found herself face to face with five men in sackcloth masks.

27

Hell

Royal blue satin surrounded him, blurred and expansive at first, then contracting into focused ridges of fabric, faded in some parts, worn to a silver sheen in others: Rosasharon's quilt, sheets, pillows. His thoughts came simply, with room for one at a time: first, blue; second, Rosasharon; third, Silvia.

Fourth: Bonne Chance. He raised his arms, crossed them over his face. Shut out the light. Make it night, make it a dream. If only it could have been a dream. But it hurt to move his left arm. No dream. Reality. Mother of God.

He groaned, not in pain but at the memory. The mountain: gray, dead, charred, smoldering. The mine: scattered debris, splintered beams, sizzling wires, shattered rock. The men: crushed, trapped, writhing, dismembered, one decapitated. The screams: ceaseless.

In the end it had collapsed again. After a whole night's work. After blasts set with fuses too short, to save time. He was half-deaf from the blasts. After clawing through walls of rock, rock that fell on their feet, bruising, bruising. After blasting and clawing nearly to the bottom. Almost there, and the mountain began to grumble, a giant at the edge of a nightmare, turning in sleep, about to wake with a shudder and a roar.

Through the ringing in his ears, through the deafness, he had heard the grumbling. Tommyknockers, too, though they'd been pounding all night. He'd raced down the tunnels, screaming, "Get out! Everybody out!"

The rescue crews dropped their shovels and ran, all except Emma's husband, who claimed he could still hear cries.

"Get out! Now!" Johnny screamed it over and over.

Stotter shook him, by the shoulders. Blood flowed fresh from the bullet wound, staining Stotter's hand. Pain cut him off in mid-word, and he heard cries, too. No—a cry, only one.

"Johnny Torres! Is that you, mate? Gawd, I never thought I'd be glad to hear your cursed voice!"

"Brody?" Louder: "Brody? Christ, are you alive?"

"Ain't no ghost talking, mate." A second's pause. "Ain't no one else alive back here, Johnny. Just me."

A nearby beam cracked. It sounded like a blast from a gun. Johnny whirled. Ten feet behind him, the beam splintered, crashed to the floor of the mine. Debris followed, blocking half the tunnel.

"What was that?" yelled Brody.

Johnny and Stotter tore at the mangled wreckage that separated them from the Cornishman. Falling rock buried their feet and ankles. The drift began to shudder. They worked harder. The rumbling of the workings had covered their labored breathing and grunts of effort, but Brody's screams cut through.

"Get out! Torres, get out! Man, I ain't got no legs, no, no—Johnny, mate, please please please, don't send me to my grave with your goddamn death on my hands."

Johnny had broken through, squirmed in and groped in the dark.

He found Brody's arms, but Brody grabbed his shirt at the throat and pulled his face in close.

"Leave me, mate," he pleaded. "I got no legs, I got nothing from my hips down. *Leave!*"

The nightmare had shaken the giant awake; Brody's cries barely topped the din of the collapsing mine. Johnny turned his head back toward the opening and hollered at Emma's husband to run. Then he wrapped his arms around Brody's chest and started out through the hole.

"Leave me! I told you. Leave me! Getcherself out!"

Stotter had waited outside the hole, holding the lantern. Johnny saw Brody's body was intact, though both legs looked broken. With Stotter he supported his fellow driller, who cussed them in a steady stream as they shoved through the drift, over the debris, toward the shaft. Johnny hoisted Brody over his right shoulder and began to climb the ladder, with Stotter below him. He did not dare look up: rocks tumbled from above. Stotter helped him support Brody along the next tunnel, and Johnny carried the Cornishman up the next shaft, again taking care not to look up.

At the top of the shaft an explosion rocked the workings, knocking the three men to the floor. Stotter dropped the lantern, which shattered a hundred feet below, the flames igniting a piece of wood. The explosion had come from down there, not above. More sabotage? Or just a delayed charge from the first round? The fire spread with a *whoosh,* but this upper tunnel was dark. It was impossible to tell whether they had a clear path or a mountain wall to seal their tomb. They pressed on, stumbling toward the light they could only hope still waited.

Brody saw it first, from the four hundred station of the badly sloughing main adit tunnel, and his demands to leave him switched to shouts of hope. They took another two steps. The right side of the tunnel sloughed toward Stotter. The force of the mountain against Stotter's body against Brody's drove Johnny into the left wall, crunching his shoulder.

The light at the mouth went out. The tunnel had closed. Johnny groaned. He wanted to scream. He could only groan. Someone else screamed: Brody. Johnny said something that he thought was Spanish. It came back garbled. Something stung his cheek: a slap. His head cleared; he had started to black out. He was slumped against the left wall, with Brody more or less on top of him. He looked over Brody at Stotter and saw only a hand sticking out of a pile of rock. But he could see, and it took light to see. He looked toward the adit. The way was clear, but behind him the mine pitched and roared.

He had struggled to his feet, slung Brody over his shoulder, and staggered on, at intervals collapsing to his knees, rising again. No one outside had noticed him. He could see the rescue teams milling about, recently disgorged from the tunnel, in chaos. He reached the mouth.

"Hey!" someone shouted. Another pulled Brody off him and dragged Johnny away from the mine. He heard it thunder at his back and felt an expulsion of hot breath as the giant jaws clamped shut.

Two men held him up with his arms across their shoulders. He tried to help them by walking, but his legs seemed to bend in both directions. His shoulder hurt so much he thought he would black out, all the way this time.

He had tried to tell the men to let go of his arms and that he just wanted to lie down and rest. Either the words came out wrong or in Spanish or the men ignored him. His head rolled back, so that he was looking at the clouds. Up here they were close enough to touch. Then his head rolled forward and he saw that the men had refused to lay him down because bodies covered every available foot of ground.

His anger burned. He had felt it all night, but now it renewed itself, coming into him as though from somewhere else like a germ, making him feverish. He thought of Daunt. God, the bastard. Daunt, you son of a whore—

"Easy, Torres," said one of the men who supported him. He must have shouted the words.

"It wasn't Daunt," the other one told him. "He's up at the Anna Strike. You know that."

Johnny's voice had bounced back at him: "You lie. You *lie!*"

"You're hurt, Johnny. Shut up. Worry about it later."

"*No!*" He wrenched away. "It was *Daunt!* God damn it, why can't you see? *It was Daunt!*"

The clouds descended on him. Or maybe it was the mine. The world darkened, but a voice penetrated the darkness. Johnny opened his eyes. He was lying on his back and cold wind lashed his right side. The doctor's face hovered above him. His lips moved. He had odd lips. Too thin. He had no lips at all. What was he saying? Johnny squeezed his eyes shut and opened them again.

"You'll be all right," the doctor had said. "I'm going to give you a shot of morphine and take the bullet out later. These men will put you on the wagon to town."

He had not wanted to ride on the go-devil with the corpses, so he sat up. He felt fine—strange, as though encased in a bubble of liquid—but fine. The anger was bottled, ready to burst again after he got to town and rested. He would go to town now, but not on the wagon. They'd tried to push him back but he fought them and stood.

"Johnny," said one of the miners.

"I'm okay." He sounded fine. He had to or they'd never let him off this mountain without morphine and corpses all around him on the go-devil.

They had shrugged and left him alone.

He had ended up at Silvia's not knowing how he got there. Silvia took his right arm and led him into the red parlor with gold trim.

"What time is it?" he'd asked Silvia. His voice sounded distant. His thoughts were muddled and he was clutching an unopened bottle of Scotch by the neck. He looked at the bottle. Top drawer, Torres, nothing but the best. Where the hell had it come from? The time since he'd left the mine was all jumbled.

Silvia led him to a chair. Where were the rest of the women? They should've been doing housework now. Where was Iris?

"Where are the women?"

Silvia took the bottle from his hand and started pulling off his jacket, the black suit jacket he'd worn to the opera last night, and into the mine. He winced. She went slower. When she had it off she opened the Scotch and poured half a glass. Holding it in his right hand, he tried to remember where he'd been but could only recall the clouds descending lower and lower and the cold wind sweeping down on Telluride from the mountains where the mines were and slashing through the streets and slashing him until his fingers turned blue and the bottle of Scotch felt like an ice cube against his palm. The weather here could change as fast as a man's luck.

He'd downed the half glass of Scotch at a throw and liked the way it seared his throat. Silvia poured another but set it on the table. Then she pushed him back into the chair, and it felt better not to sit up so straight. She took his hands and rubbed them. Warmth returned, stinging at first, then soothing like the Scotch in his belly.

"What time is it?"

She'd squinted at the banjo clock on the wall across the room. Her eyes must've been going, but her hands still worked very well. He'd never had sex with her, but her hands had comforted him when Rosasharon died. He'd tried to comfort her, too, but she would not have it.

"Twenty past one," she'd said in her thick voice. "Where have you been?"

"Outside."

"I know that. Your hands are practically frostbit."

"I remember the courthouse. The priest was just starting confession."

"Did you go in?"

He'd shaken his head.

"Who needs confession," she said.

"I killed three people," he told her. "Four, if you count Stotter. A hundred, if you count the rest."

She'd handed him the second Scotch.

Now, God knew how much later, the red and gold parlor was gone, replaced by Rosasharon's royal blue. Johnny uncrossed his arms. Water was dripping back along the sides of his face, into the pillow. He swallowed.

"Johnny?" Iris's voice rolled across the royal blue, sweet and sad.

He blinked.

She was sitting in a chair on the other side of the room. How different she looked when awake: older, scarred, tough yet brittle, like mistreated fabric. But she was only twenty-three, with the voice of a child.

Stiffly, he sat up. His shoulder was heavily bandaged.

"How do you feel?"

He shrugged, looked away. Outside, the wind hammered the curtained window.

"Doc said it weren't a real bad wound, just that you lost too much blood and got yourself all wore out at the mine." Her eyes narrowed. "How come you only stop here when you're in trouble, Johnny? You used to call all the time up in Leadville."

Leadville. More bad memories. "That was a long time ago, Iris."

"You still go to the opera?"

"When I can."

"Rosasharon liked going to the opera with you."

"Yes, she did."

"She had a pretty voice. She wanted to be a singer. You ever know that?"

"She told me."

"You used to teach her to sing. I should've remembered. You got a new girl now, huh?"

Gretel. He should check on her. Maybe bring her into town, maybe even here, to hide her from Daunt so he could return to the rescue effort, if the storm hadn't shut it down. Even the palomino couldn't climb that mountain in a blizzard.

"Yeah," he said. "Do you know what time it is?"

She shrugged. "Somewhere around eleven. Maybe noon. No clock in here."

He could see that. "You mean it's Sunday?"

"Sure. You slept the clock around, almost." She looked down at her hands and frowned. "I've gotten so old." Her conversations were always broken, flitting from one half-thought to the next. Her mind had probably never been keen; by now the drugs had fractured it.

"You still talk like a little girl."

"Johnny?"

"Yes?"

"How come you didn't wake me last night?" She seemed hurt.

"I don't remember last night, Iris."

"And now?"

"Now I have to go."

"Doc said you ought to stay here. Said you need a few days' rest. He—"

"Come here, Iris."

She walked to him on feeble legs.

"Come here," he said again, and she leaned over. He kissed her and tasted the staleness of death. "Thanks for helping me. Now go on."

He went looking for Silvia before leaving. Amazingly, men crowded the parlor, so he went down the back way and found her in the kitchen, surrounded by the smoky, herbal scent of hemp.

"Sneaking out the back?" she said. "Tell me, is that because you're too good for my place or too bad?"

"Probably too bad."

"Ah, so you're feeling better. I'm glad."

"The hell you are."

She laughed caustically and sucked on a pipe. Then she held it out to him.

He shook his head.

"Oh how virtuous! Really, Johnny, you ought to run for sainthood."

He handed her money to cover Iris's time off and left by the back door. Leaning into the wind as he walked past the kitchen window, he heard her laughter, thick and forced. "Saint Johnny Torres," she shouted, because she knew he could hear.

Icy flakes began to fall as he headed toward Emma's. He dreaded running into Emma even more than going back into the Bonne Chance. All he could think of was her husband, with his hand sticking out of the pile of rock. But the wind was bitter and buffeted him violently; without the warmth of his winter coat, he'd be frostbit halfway to Gretel's. Plus he needed his horse.

The few other people on Pacific Avenue, mostly men in search of a warm body with which to pass the storm, tucked their coats tightly around them and hurried along, heads ducked into upturned collars. Johnny reached Pine Street and turned north. Muddy ruts had frozen into slick ridges, which made for tricky footing. He still wore his boots from the night before, the expensive soft leather ruined by the Bonne Chance. Inside the leather his feet were swollen and bruised.

The boardinghouse was deserted. Johnny took the steps two at a time and walked down the second-floor hall to his room. The door was half-open. Colt drawn, Johnny stood aside and nudged the door, which creaked inward on battered hinges.

He gaped at a room turned upside down. The blankets had been ripped from the bed, the chair and washstand overturned, the basin shattered, the tapestry ripped from the wall above the mantle. Shredded fabric and his few possessions littered the floor, but the tapestry was gone. He tore through the wreckage, unearthed his coat, and raced back down the stairs.

Outside, sparse snow stung his face and the wind clamped his legs in lead. He ran around behind the house to the stable, where the palomino waited, unharmed, irritable as ever. Johnny grabbed the bridle, ripped open the stall, bridled the horse roughly, allowing no protest. He leapt onto the animal's bare back and rode out of the stable at a gallop, heading west, to Gretel's valley.

Riding hard made him hot, even with the wind. He had to hold tight to the slippery bare back with his legs. He was unaccustomed to riding without a saddle; the last time had been on the way to Lizardhead Pass with Gretel, months earlier, lifetimes ago. The horse wore a coat of lather and breathed in wheezes by the time they reached the homestead. The storm had worsened, now verging on a full-blown blizzard. Johnny could barely make out the cabin through the driving snow. He saw nothing unusual, but he was almost blind. At least there were no other horses out front.

He looped the palomino's reins loosely around a tree across the meadow from the cabin and approached on foot. Skirting the meadow, staying behind the trees until he reached the other side of the barn.

He checked inside the barn and found only Zachary's old gelding.

The horse raised his head dully. Johnny went back outside, heaved the door shut, and scouted the area. No horse droppings, no sign at all that anyone else had been here, but the snow would've hid the tracks. He crept around the cabin, peeking in the windows. The curtains were drawn and he could see little through the cracks. He did see Gretel, on the settee, weaving a tapestry.

Everything looked all right. Maybe Daunt and his men were waiting elsewhere. He would've bet they'd try for him here, though, and still felt wary. But the storm howled around his ears and bit his cheeks: he could not stay outside forever. He walked to the cabin's door and reached for the latch.

He paused. Something was wrong. He could feel it. He looked to either side and behind him. Snow, only snow. He looked up. Two black forms hurtled over the crest of the roof and plunged from the snowy sky. They crashed onto him, drove him to the ground.

He raised his head, dazed, as the front door opened. Firelight spilled over him and the two men, who now yanked him to his feet. A pale-eyed man in a sackcloth mask stood in the doorway, his pistol out and cocked. Behind him, two more men held Gretel by the arms. All the men wore masks. The first two forced Johnny into the room, holding him securely. He looked into Gretel's brown eyes to see if they had hurt her, but saw only tears.

"Now go to town and find your brother," the man with the pistol said to Gretel, his accent unmistakably German. "Tell him we have Johnny Torres. Tell him to meet us at the Anna Strike at the end of the storm."

Johnny struggled against the hands that pinned him. "You can't send her out there. The storm—" The butt of the pistol flew at his head. He tried to duck, but the others held him still. Gretel shrieked. The gun butt cracked into his left temple.

"Go!" the German yelled at Gretel.

Johnny shook his head. He saw two of everything. Two Gretels fetched two coats and scarves and two of Linda's blue felt hats. He shook his head again. Only one, now, and still crying.

Johnny opened his mouth but the German hit him in the jaw. He wanted to tell Gretel where he'd tied his horse, because Zachary's old gelding would never make it through this blizzard. But by the time he could talk, Gretel was gone.

28

The Baroness

West of Telluride, Cole rode past a herd of what must have been four thousand beeves, hunched into great red and white masses against the wind. He tried not to think of his ranch, or his family.

He reached town around noon and rode down a main street turned dusky by the coming storm. Darkness was still many hours away, but the thick clouds and the news the servant had given him at the Braunn mansion left him feeling like night. A pall hung over the town as well. Drawn by mules, huge wagons bumped over icy ruts, their iron wheels screeching. They stopped to unload the wounded in front of a stately red brick hotel called the Baroness. The name made Cole think of Catharine.

He stabled Halloran's dun at the livery, aware that it might be recognized. It hardly mattered now: the sooner Daunt found him, the better. He walked the short distance back to the Baroness, ducking his head against the wind. At the door, he had to wait for another load of stretchers.

The lobby was crowded and somber. A well-dressed young man directed those carrying the stretchers up the long, straight, red-carpeted stairway. They filed up in a silent procession and turned right at the first-floor landing. The hotel stairs were unique: they climbed in an unbroken line to the third floor, with a landing at each level. They were wide, with scroll-engraved, silver-plated railings. As Cole watched the men take the wounded up, he became conscious of people watching him. One of the stretcher-bearers glanced around and nearly tripped at a whispered comment from his partner. Cole walked to the front desk, which was tall and massive, ornately carved and stained dark. On the desk were a number of electric lamps and a grass green blotter in a leather desk pad. The desk clerk was dressed well enough for Montana's most formal dance.

"I'm looking for Catharine Braunn," said Cole.

The clerk showed no sign of recognition, but his detachment was studied. "She might be on the second floor helping tend the wounded," he said, in a German accent that came as no surprise. "If she is not there, check her suite. You will find it on the third floor, at the end of the hall. Turn left at the top of the stairs."

Limping slightly, Cole threaded his way through the crowded lobby. People averted their stares. He climbed toward the second-floor landing, wondering what would happen if he suddenly drew Halloran's pistol and waved it around. Partway up, he turned abruptly and caught many pairs of eyes in embarrassed or nervous surprise. To hell with all of you, he thought, you'll get your fight. They looked away one by one.

He limped along the hall, over cranberry-colored carpet. Most of the doors to the rooms were open; from inside some he could hear moaning and softly spoken reassurances. So many wounded; the infirmary must have overflowed. He tried not to consider how much of this blood might be on his hands. He had intended no harm coming back to Colorado, but intentions hardly counted now. He looked into each room. He had nearly reached the end of the hall without finding Catharine, when she stepped through a doorway, looking down at her hands as she wiped them on a towel. There were bloodstains on her white blouse.

She raised her head, saw him, and went pale. Even in the dim light of the hall, Cole could see new lines on her face.

She whispered his name. "I thought they killed you."

"They tried."

She stepped toward him timidly. Her hands reached out to him, feeling beneath the open shearling jacket that had once been his father's.

"Bandages," she said as though she would cry. She rested her head on his chest. "My God, what did they do to you?"

He returned her embrace. His heart quickened, pounded hard against ribs that still ached.

"Are you real?" she murmured. "Have you really come back? If you only knew the number of times I've done this, only to awaken in my room, alone in the dark. I even leave the light burning now, because the dark makes me see you when I know you're not there."

He touched her hair. Other women had emerged from some of the doorways, curious, but Cole did not care. At the moment he only felt her touch and saw the tears of relief and disbelief on her lovely face, and he had no strength to turn her away.

"This is a dream," she said. "It must be. I worked so hard to make myself admit you had gone. I never thought you could die."

"I'm here, Catharine. I'm here."

He was relieved when she took her hands off him and led the way to the stairs, past the women, who now slipped silently back into the rooms. He followed her to her suite on the third floor. They walked inside and she closed the door and held him again, and even through the bandages he felt a tremor. She looked up at his face.

"I love you, Cole."

"No—"

"I do. I love you. I thought you died never giving me the chance to say it."

"I can't love you."

"But you do."

He fought to regain his wits. He took her hands and put them at her sides, carefully, carefully. She started to reached for him again.

"I came to see your husband," he said.

She lowered her hands and shook her head. "You came to see me."

"I've got to see your husband. And Johnny Torres. Do you know where they are?"

She looked away. "Heinrich's at the office. Johnny got shot trying to stop the cave-in, though not badly from what I could find out. No one's seen him since yesterday. I think the doctor knows where he went, but he won't say."

"What about Daunt?"

"Gone. The man called MacMurray, too, and some others. When the storm clears and Johnny turns up, we'll find them."

Cole tried to focus on what Catharine told him rather than on Catharine herself. He failed. He looked around the sitting room, where the twilight before the storm cast a bluish glow. The furniture was upholstered in white, and the strange light made each piece look ghostlike. Cole's eyes came to rest on a painting on the wall above a heavily cushioned settee. It showed some trees and a house mostly obscured behind them. He walked toward the painting. Up close it was more like a lot of little brush strokes fading into each other.

He turned from the painting, walked to the window and leaned his arm on the frame. He watched the clouds outside and the mountains that rose to meet them. The mountain crests disappeared and reappeared as the clouds scudded past. It seemed that he stood there a long time before he got any words out.

"What will your husband do now?"

"He wants to return to Germany. Sell the mansion and what's left of the Bonne Chance. He wants me to go with him."

The wind moaned outside, and the windowpanes gave off a chill. "Will you?"

"A happily married wife usually moves with her husband."

"You're not—"

"Oh, but I am. Can't you tell? Look at this room. Look at the furniture, the art. I've got it all, Cole. I've had it all for years. How much happier could I get?" Such bitterness. No wonder her face showed new lines: the Bonne Chance was only part of it.

"So you're going. I guess you should."

"No, I'm not. It's tempting, but I'm not."

He nodded slowly. "If I hadn't come here today—"

"I decided yesterday morning, after hearing about the Bonne Chance, when Heinrich first told me what he wanted to do. I haven't told him yet."

"Then why? There's nothing for you here."

"Because this is my home. And because of you."

"But you thought I was dead. And you know I can't stay now. You know that."

Outside the window, snow had begun to fall. It swirled so fast that it all blurred together, but if Cole looked hard enough he could make out some flakes. It reminded him of the painting over the settee. Out of the corner of his eye, he saw Catharine walk to a white chair made blue by the light. She poured him a drink from a snifter on the table by the chair and brought it to him, then poured herself one and sat in the chair to drink it. He set the glass on the windowsill and continued to look out. She sat silently, with her legs tucked under her, sipping her drink. She seemed to be waiting. He had never known her to be patient, but now she sat as though she could wait the rest of her life. It occurred to him that she had already waited a very long time.

He turned from the window. She rose and came to him, and they stood in the storm's blue twilight facing each other. She knelt in front of him and unbuckled his gunbelt and set it on the windowsill by his drink. He took her hands and she stood, and he let go of her hands and put his arms around her. She raised her face and her lips parted and he kissed her longer and deeper and harder than he had ever kissed anyone before.

They tore each other's clothes off until the only things left were the bandages around his ribs and leg. They fell onto the settee, their fingers and lips and tongues silently searching out every hungry part of each other's body. They moved to the bedroom, tossed the thick, downy white quilt off the big, high bed, and lay on the silk sheets.

He thrust into her and they moved as one. In the spectral blue he saw her clutch the sheets in her fists and press her head into the pillow. She squeezed her eyes shut and arched her neck, then her back, and her mouth opened as if to scream, but only quick gasps came out. Cole saw the moisture on her skin and felt the heat where their bodies touched.

He thrust deeper and faster. But I love her, I love her, I love her, he kept thinking. And he felt himself begin to break away from some distant peak and slide, but it was not him, it was only a feeling. So he felt it come, felt it suck the air from him, the life from him as it thundered down, down, always down. Then it picked him up and tossed him so high on glittering white waves of ice, tossed him into the fiery sun where a million flakes of light burst apart and came together, came into him, burned him.

And the burning became the pain in his ribs and the bandages that bound the pain as Catharine let go of the sheets and clutched him instead.

29

Zachary's Old Horse

The cabin door thudded shut behind her and she had to wipe her face with her sleeve to keep her tears from freezing. A gust of wind drove her at a stumbling run to the barn and slammed her against its weathered wood. She slid along the wall toward the door, yanked it aside. Zachary's old horse raised his head and the dairy cow lowed. Chickens clustered in a corner, ruffling their feathers, and the pigs grunted nervously. The walls creaked.

The horse danced uncharacteristically as she saddled him. "I know," she said. "It's no day for a ride." Her voice was shaky; all she could think of was that gun butt smashing against Johnny's face.

The horse. Focus on the horse. He took the saddle and bridle all right and gnawed at the bit. She led him to the door. Snow sliced in. The horse backed. She held fast to the reins. He reared. Tug him down, tug him down. But not too close. Then too close anyway, close enough to run her hand over his neck and withers, or take a kick in the head. God in heaven, what if she died right here? Or got knocked out. She'd never find Cole, the men would never find her. And Johnny? What would they do to him then?

But the horse was old and more docile than most, and he calmed enough for her to lead him outside and slide the door closed behind her. You know you'll die, old horse, she thought. That's why you fought me. You may be old and gentle, but you'll fight death all right.

She mounted. The wind threatened to buck her off. Her scarf had loosened; the cold bit her skin, bit through her clothes. Tucking the scarf in, she touched the horse with her heels. The German had said Cole would head for Telluride when he found out about the Bonne Chance. If the wind kept blowing the same way, maybe she could find the God-cursed town. Otherwise she might circle the barn a hundred times and freeze to death.

The snow painted everything the same grainy, glistening white; at times it even obscured the horse's head. Gretel thought the wind was changing. If she followed it, she'd never get out of the valley. Once she thought she heard laughter and felt panic creep into the saddle. Why was the way still level? She should have reached the end of the valley. She should have begun to go up.

Then she did. She patted the horse. But the slope seemed too steep: the beast labored. If they climbed the wrong side and got too high, the blizzard would worsen.

The horse plodded slower. The snow was powdery, not slippery, but the trail had iced before the snow began. The mud had frozen, like Gretel was freezing now.

"Poor horse, no coat for you," she said, finding it hard to move her lips. "Poor old horse." She patted him again and felt him dying. Zachary had bought him before Cole left for Texas. He'd never been much of a horse, but he'd never done any harm, either. The hairs around his muzzle had grayed and his eyes were bluish with cataracts. "Poor old horse," she said again. "You never asked anything of anyone and now I'm killing you."

This is wrong, she thought, but nudged him on. Snow had turned his brown coat white. At first some had dripped off and steam had blown from his nostrils. Now he was so cold that the snow formed a heavy casing on his hide, and he barely seemed to breathe at all. His stout old legs stiffened until he could hardly lift them from the drifts, and through the saddle Gretel could feel his body shiver against the bitter wind. Another laborious mile and he stopped. She kicked him gently, then harder. His legs crumpled. She jumped free, crawled through the powder and fell over him.

"Get up," she pleaded. "You can't lie still! You'll die if you lie still! Don't die, please don't die. You die and I'll die and Johnny will too. Please . . ."

The horse had died already. Gretel rolled over and lay back against him as she would have lain in bed, only her pillow was a dead horse so frozen that the warmth had left his body long before the life. She closed her eyes. She let her mind drift. The cold began to thaw, melting into tepid liquid. She floated. Peace, it felt like peace. Let me sleep, she thought. I am warm now. I want to sleep.

"Don't die, Gretel." She imagined Johnny's voice, rich, like a song, a kiss, an embrace, rich with Spanish intonations, rich as his smile. I will live, she told him from the coldest part of her, the part only he could warm. I will rest here a little while, then I will find my brother and come back for you. I love you, Johnny. I love you.

30

A Paltry Sum

Lying in bed, Catharine held her eyelids closed with her fingers to preserve her dream. In the dream, Cole had come back to her and she had told him she loved him and they had shared that love on the big, high bed with the silk sheets at the Baroness Hotel. In the dream, Cole had been alive.

With her fingers over her eyelids, she remembered it had been real. She removed her fingers and opened her eyes. The room had been blue before the storm; now the blizzard outside turned it silver. Catharine was covered with the thick, downy white quilt, though she remembered falling asleep on top of the sheets with no covers, because all the warmth she needed had come from Cole. He must have covered her. Now he was gone.

She slid out of bed and dressed in a clean skirt and blouse. A shutter must have come loose somewhere outside: it banged irregularly, like gunshots.

She opened the door to the sitting room and found Heinrich waiting for her. He was smoking a cigar and reading *Faust*.

"Quite a switch from die Bibel," said Catharine.

He finished a passage, or pretended to, marked his place with a red satin ribbon, closed the book, set it on the table, removed his reading glasses, and studied her.

"Is he in one piece?"

"He seems to be. I don't think he has all his strength back."

He chuckled.

She held her tongue. "What's happening with the mine?"

"I sold it, subject to your approval. The Flosshilde, too."

"I'm surprised you found a buyer."

"Buyers: a British syndicate. They will hire an army of salesmen to peddle the shares one by one, far from here: Maine, Virginia, wherever. I believe you are familiar with that sort of operation." He smiled. "The world is full of fools."

She nodded slowly. "How much?"

"A paltry sum." He puffed on his cigar, rolled it between finger and thumb, pretended to study it intently. "I know he has the sort of looks that might catch a lady's eye," he said, "but tell me: what else makes a man like that so attractive? Is it the prowess with a gun? The challenge of confronting a murderer? Or is he just a virtuoso in bed?"

"He's not a—" She hesitated. "Don't try it, Heinrich. It won't work."

"Not a what? A murderer? Yes, I suppose that is a rather harsh term. How about a killer, then? Will you deny that?"

"Would it matter?"

He slammed his fist on the table and rose from his chair. "Listen to me," he said, low and threatening, the German accent strengthened. "You are still mine. And until I leave here, you will continue to be mine. After I leave, if you choose not to leave with me, all you will have in this world is half the pittance we make selling those mines. It is barely enough to run your precious castle for a day." He grabbed a fistful of her blouse. "Let alone buy the silks and satins and lace, not to mention the diamonds and gold. Gold, ha! You can go to Buck Daunt for that. Maybe if you prostitute yourself for him, he will give you a nugget."

She remained detached, out of the game. She had forgone contention; thoughts of Cole held her apart.

"Amazing," he mocked. "Such control. Too bad it failed you earlier today."

She said nothing.

He chuckled and resumed his seat, resumed puffing on his cigar.

"Cole came here to sell you the Anna Strike," she told him, smoothing her blouse.

"That is amusing. What makes you think I would buy it?"

"It's the first thing that went through your head when you heard he was alive."

"I have known he was alive since Luke Halloran disappeared. You would have, too, if you were not so blindly in love with him. It is too bad, really. That you love him, I mean. Your feelings will weaken you, and you will decide to stay here despite the fact that you will have nothing, and he will only leave you, too. It is really very sad. Such a beautiful woman, alone with no money. You will have to find a job or another husband; either way you will work for a living. Zachary Coleman's son will never support you, no matter how easy he finds it to betray friend and family in, shall we say, a moment of passion. No, he will return to Montana soon enough. He is too righteous to do otherwise."

"You love to think of me as a whore, don't you, Heinrich?"

"My, how easily you dismiss your own fate. Have you really let your emotions blind you so much? And yes, I do. Because you are a whore."

She slapped him, not because of any passion on her part, but, oddly enough, because he would have expected it.

He touched his cheek and clucked at her. "Very good. A command performance, though a tad lacking in conviction. You may sit down now."

"If I am a whore, I'm the highest priced in the world. And you haven't paid half of it yet."

He smiled. "Very well. I always expect to pay for what I get. And to get what I pay for."

"If Cole will help you secure that mine, will you buy it from him?"

"Naturally, but I want more than the mine."

"What else?"

"Buck Daunt. And may God forgive the analogy, but I want his head on a silver platter. Or no, a gold platter. And I want you. In Germany. With me."

She met his silvery gaze in silence.

"But I think you have made a grave miscalculation," he told her. "You have underestimated your friend Cole. He will never sell that mine to me now. He will never accept any help at all from me." He smiled with what might, to another woman, have looked like benevolence. "You have seen to that, dear Catharine, as only you could."

31

Deep Drifts

In a dreamland of snow, she lifted her right foot and put it in front of her left. It vanished from the knee down. Snowshoes might have helped, except that she needed the drifts to anchor her against the wind.

Town, at last, where gusts shoved her against buildings barely visible until she hit them. She trudged along Colorado Avenue, meeting no one, past stores and saloons shut down in surrender to the storm. It took a great deal of strength not to stop and bang on the door of each one, in hopes that the proprietor might be sitting by a hearth upstairs. She willed her feet to keep going, though between vanishing in the snow and having lost all feeling, they seemed to have split off from the rest of her body. She took one step after another, each a deliberate act. She did not walk; she took steps.

She reached a large building with a pointed roof and a spire. Driven snow cloaked its front, hiding the white clapboards and the sign. The Congregational church. As she stopped in front of it, the

267

wind stopped, too. Like a great, white curtain, the snow fell straight to the ground.

Light filtered through ice-glazed colored windows. Gretel's legs weakened. She tried to make them carry her on to the Baroness Hotel. They refused. She had an urge to sink to her knees, but her legs were too stiff. She stared at the church through the curtain of snow.

Through the curtain she saw images of the old horse, Cole, Johnny, Zachary, of herself. God was playing games with them, games in which they didn't matter.

"We don't matter!" she screamed, and the wind blew again. She felt her right leg move, and her left. Her body was heavy with snow. She lifted her feet and set them down one by one until she stood on the threshold of the Baroness Hotel. She opened the door and passed into the warm, well-lighted lobby, empty of guests but with a fire behind the hearth.

Suddenly lightheaded, she grabbed the back of a chair. Through a haze that reminded her of the blinding snow, she saw a man come toward her from behind the desk. He helped her to the hearth in front of the huge fireplace and started peeling off her hat and scarf and jacket. He sat her on a soft chair by the fire, pulled off her boots, and told her to wait there. He walked away quickly, and she sat motionless until he returned with a steaming drink that smelled of whiskey and coffee. She wanted to ask him where she could find Cole, but her cheeks had frozen.

He resumed his place behind the big front desk. Gretel's body began to thaw. She sipped the drink. Steam warmed her face and water dripped into the cup from the snow melting off her brows.

She stood and hobbled to the desk.

"Are you all right now?" the clerk asked. She noticed now his German accent. He had gray in his broad, rust-colored mustache and in the sparse hair he combed across the bald part on top of his head.

"Yes, thank you. I'm looking for Zachary Coleman. I'm his sister."

"He went out."

"When?"

"Not too long ago. Perhaps a half hour?"

She glanced at the clock behind the desk: ten past four. "Did he say where?"

The clerk hesitated. "Perhaps you should stay here, Miss Coleman. We have many victims of the mine explosion, but I do have a room available."

Gretel looked around at the front door, frosted over with the blizzard. Her feet were still thawing, but she could not wait any longer.

"Thank you," she said, "but I have to go. If my brother comes back, please tell him to wait for me."

The clerk nodded.

She put on her jacket and boots, pulled the blue felt hat over her ears, and tied the scarf around it. The clothes were sopping with melted snow. Shivering inside them, she left the hotel. The storm did not seem so formidable now that she had warmed a little, but her legs could only move at a leaded pace through the deep drifts. She made it to Emma's house, finally, thinking Cole might have gone there.

Finding no one downstairs, she climbed straight to Johnny's room. She opened the door and stood still. The blizzard seemed to have come right inside: the furniture had been blown all around the room. She looked at the wall above the mantle, where Johnny had said Emma had hung one of her best tapestries, the one of the marzipan cabin from *Hansel and Gretel*. It was gone.

She left Emma's. The parlor house owned by the madam Silvia was the only other place where Johnny might have gone, and Cole would have gone looking for Johnny. Hugging the leeward side of the buildings, she plodded through the storm to Pacific Avenue. She entered the first parlor house, where the women studied her curiously but directed her willingly enough. She walked on to Silvia's. The buildings didn't snuggle so close together, here; the wind whipped stronger.

She reached the last house on the line and went in. Gaudy red furniture and draperies with gold fringe and tassels adorned the parlor. Oil lamps emitted a musky smell and a sickly yellow light. She supposed it would look better than this to the two men who sat waiting. The line had not surrendered to the storm.

A woman in a feathery, tight-fitting green dress approached Gretel and asked what she wanted. Like the women at the first house, she was curious but not unkind.

"I'm looking for a tall man with blue eyes and dark hair. He walks with a limp. Has he been here?"

The woman asked her to wait, then ran up the steps with her skirt hiked. Soon she returned and asked Gretel to have a seat. Gretel sat in a red chair in her soaked clothes and waited. She had begun to shiver again. Her teeth chattered.

The woman took one of the men upstairs and another woman took the other man. Gretel sat alone, wondering reluctantly how it must feel to have everyone see through your clothes, see only below your neck, see only sex. She longed for her loom and the little tapestry of Telluride with no people in it. She longed even more for Johnny, and to know where Cole was. And Silvia. Where was she?

After a while, another woman entered the parlor through a curtain at the back of the room. She was too young to be the madam.

"Coffee?" she offered, holding out a chipped china cup.

Gretel accepted it. The young woman sat and tucked stick-thin legs under a spindly frame.

"I'm Iris," she said, in a voice like a child's.

Gretel tasted the coffee and found it watery and tepid. She set it on the table. "I'm here to see Silvia."

"You Johnny's girl?"

She hesitated.

"I always liked Johnny," said Iris. "He treats me real nice. He ever tell you about Rosasharon?"

"No."

Iris smiled. She looked different from Gretel's idea of a whore: her violet eyes were innocent and as childlike as her voice. But her face was lined, even haggard.

"She was my sister," Iris told her. "Johnny used to take her out."

Gretel nodded, wishing Silvia would get here.

"She died a couple of years back, up in Leadville."

"I'm sorry."

Iris shrugged but Gretel saw she still mourned. "Silvia thinks Johnny killed her. She died from too much morphine. Silvia says she done it on purpose, because she wanted something she couldn't get. But Rosasharon weren't like that. She was pretty and she could sing, too. Johnny never told you about her?"

"No, he never did."

"He's a good boy."

"Yes."

Gretel tried to drink some more of the weak coffee. Her shivering had lessened.

"He come here after the Bonne Chance," said Iris. "Silvia says he were a mess. She got him drunk so he could calm down, but I think she hurt him, too. I think Silvia likes Johnny, but ever since he started seeing Rosasharon she's funny toward him. Then since Rosasharon died she never treats him nice at all."

Gretel stood. "Where is Silvia?"

"What?" Iris seemed distracted.

"Is she going to see me or not? If not, I'm leaving."

"But—"

"It's all right, Iris."

Gretel turned toward the thick, smoky voice. A woman stood on the stairs. It had to be Silvia. She was older, with baggy flesh around her painted eyes, and brittle red hair done in loops around her face. She leaned on the railing, looking smug.

"You're here after your brother," she said. "My, girl, you do get tangled up with some dangerous men."

"Was he here?" Gretel asked.

"Of course he was. Looking for Johnny Torres. Every damn person in the world seems to want that boy, though God knows why."

"You have no right to hate him," Gretel said. "No one does."

"Of course not. Saint John: the purest man these parts've ever seen. God reserves a special place in hell for anyone who crosses Johnny Torres."

"Aunt Silvia—" Iris began.

"Hush, child."

"When was my brother here?" Gretel asked.

"Not long ago."

Gretel started for the door.

"Johnny will make you believe there's more, too," Silvia said to her back. "He'll fool you just like he fooled her."

Gretel stepped outside, back into the storm, which was for the moment less vicious than Silvia. She hurried toward Colorado Avenue, the wind blessedly at her back, anxious to get as far from the line, especially Silvia's parlor house, as she could. When she reached the Baroness, the clerk told her Cole had returned and was waiting for her in room 207. He told her to turn left at the second-floor landing.

She walked up the expansive stairs, dripping snow all over the red carpet, and down the hall until she found room 207. She knocked and called quietly who she was. Cole opened the door. He looked like he'd just gotten out of bed. He had: the bedcovers were rumpled.

"They have Johnny," Gretel told him, before he had a chance to close the door. "They want you at the Anna Strike as soon as the storm gives out."

"Who? Daunt? MacMurray?"

"No, the German. I don't know who else. They're all wearing masks."

32

The German

As soon as Gretel left, the men slammed him against the wall, took his gun and knife, and bound his hands behind his back. Then they dragged him to near the hearth and shoved him to the floor. One of them, not the German, yanked off the soft leather boots.

"What the hell happened to your feet?" he said.

"What do you think?"

The man laughed contemptuously inside his mask and made some comment about wearing expensive boots into a silver mine.

"Just tie him," said the German.

Johnny looked from one masked face to the next. He could not tell who they were from just the eyes, and he knew no Germans except Heinrich Braunn.

"Someone gimme a blindfold," said the man who was binding Johnny's ankles.

"What for?" said the German, taunting, and took off his mask. Which meant he planned to let Gretel go, but not Johnny, and certainly not Cole. The German's eyes were small and pale, seemingly without lashes or brows, and his thin, wispy hair was so blond it looked white. There was something strange about his skin, a pearly cast, unnaturally smooth and shiny, as though scrubbed too hard, or even burned. He was as tall as Cole, and broad across the shoulders, like MacMurray. Johnny had never seen him before.

The one who'd bound Johnny's ankles pulled his mask off next. More like he tore it off. Johnny knew this one, all right. Blade Garrett, a miner on MacMurray's shift, or he had been before the Flossie closed. He was darker than the German, though not as dark as Daunt, with a jagged furrow running from his right ear to the side of his mouth, the result of the knife fight that had given him his nickname. The scar stretched his lips into a permanent half smile that was anything but friendly.

The others pulled their masks off, too. A tough-looking lot—the masks had left their hair wild; their mouths cut harsh lines in their faces. One had worked with Blade Garrett; Johnny thought his name was Rink. The other two were drifters who had turned up in town just after Zachary died, supposedly in search of mining jobs. They were all well-muscled, neither young nor old, and not a one appeared nervous. They were hired killers as much as miners, who'd done this sort of thing before.

Garrett tossed his mask into the fire. "Enough of that damn thing," he said.

The German looked at him sharply.

"Who are you working for?" Johnny asked.

"Who says we work for anyone?" said Garrett.

"Braunn or Daunt?"

"Shut up," said the German, and kicked him.

"Where's Buck Daunt?" Johnny pressed. "And MacMurray?"

"I said shut up." Another kick. Not with soft leather boots, either.

It had to be Daunt. Braunn had every reason to want the Anna Strike but no reason to destroy his own mine. Johnny had read the assays: all fine. As long as they were true. He looked up at the five men standing above him.

"What difference will it make if you tell me?"

The German smiled, for the first time. It was more like a sneer. "None," he said, but that was all.

Hours passed, night came, though with the storm it might as well have been night all along. The men rustled some dinner from Gretel's stores. Afterward, Garrett lounged on the settee in front of the fire, which was stoked to roaring, and puffed on one of Johnny's cigars. The blizzard raged around the cabin, shooting drafts down the chimney to fan the flames.

"Tasty cigars," said Garrett. He had crossed his booted feet on the settee. Except for the pale-eyed German, the others were enjoying cigars as well, and the smoke from the blizzard fanning the fire mingled with the smoke from the cigars to fog the air. It was nearly as bad as the mines after a blast. The German sat alone and straight-backed at the pine table, playing with his knife. He kept flipping it over, alternately catching the handle and letting the long, curved blade stick in the table. Every so often he'd pause to carve something in the wood, or get up and look out the window, which the storm had glazed.

Johnny flexed his hands and feet. His fingers must have turned blue by now; his toes tingled. And he was famished: except for the Scotch, he'd had neither food nor drink since Friday night, over forty-eight hours ago. When he'd asked for water, Garrett had laughed.

"Dead men don't need water," he'd said.

By the fire the heat was fierce: Johnny's tongue had begun to swell in his mouth. Escape, he thought. Think of nothing but escape. Don't think of Gretel out there in this storm. Don't think of the Bonne

Chance, or Stotter, or the others the mountain has murdered or maimed. Don't think of food, or water. Only escape. But his captors all wore handguns and not one had touched Gretel's beer at dinner.

He sat another three hours and a couple of them dropped off to sleep. The German had assigned shifts to guard him: two men for two hours each. Wide awake except for his hands and feet, Johnny waited out the first shift.

"I need to go to the outhouse," he said in the middle of the second.

Blade Garrett was on duty. He guffawed. The other guard, one of the drifters, looked at the windows, plastered with snow. The German still sat at the pine table, playing with his knife. He must've carved a whole mural by now.

"Right," said Garrett.

"I mean it."

"So what if you do?"

"You don't want me to go in here."

The two guards exchanged looks. "All right," said Garrett.

"Try anything and you will wish you were dead," said the German, without looking up. Then, to his men: "Wake one of the others. Three of you go."

Again the guards exchanged looks. One of them woke Rink, who came out of Gretel's bedroom grumbling and digging grit from his eyes.

"Shut up and go," the German told him.

The three men pulled on their coats, cut the ropes around Johnny's ankles, dragged him to his feet, and shoved him toward the door. His feet were so numb that he stumbled and nearly fell. Rink caught him.

"Get my boots," Johnny said.

The German laughed softly and let his knife spear the table with a clunk.

The three guards opened the door and shoved Johnny outside, into the storm.

"Sonofabitch," said one as the gale coated them with snow.

Johnny leaned into the wind and plowed through eighteen inches of white powder to behind the cabin. His feet froze in seconds. His body, too—no coat. He made it to the outhouse and waited while Rink opened the door.

"You going to cut these ropes or take my pants off for me?" Johnny said, shouting above the wind.

Garrett cut the ropes. Life returned to Johnny's blue fingers. He went into the outhouse and closed the door behind him. He only had to piss, which he could have done closer to the cabin, but the men didn't know that. He made water and stood there a while, figuring it was just as well that he had no food in him, since he did not care to sit on the frozen seat. He stayed long enough to agitate his guards, more than long enough to freeze his feet to the floor.

A guard thumped on the door. Johnny waited longer. Another thump followed. The guard hollered something, which the storm whisked away. Johnny wiggled his toes: numb. His teeth clacked together as he shivered at the wind whistling through the outhouse's board walls.

Now or never, he thought, though God knew this was about as futile as looking for silver in the Flossie.

He kicked the door open and somersaulted into the snow. His back collided with a man's legs. The man tumbled. Johnny rolled through the blinding whiteness, to the side, halfway to his feet, crouched, lowered his good shoulder, rammed into another man. Over the storm he heard their startled shouts.

He fell on top of the second man, rolled over him, rolled through the billowing snow, again to a crouch, to a run. He charged toward the woods. The snow sucked at his legs. He heard shots. Forget it, screamed his iced feet and shivering body. You will die. They'll kill you right now. And if they don't, the blizzard will.

One of them jumped him, caught him around the waist with thickly muscled arms. Johnny shoved against the snow with his numb feet, still trying to run. The man slipped but held on. Johnny caught him around the neck. With his left arm, he clamped the man's head against his body. With his right hand he grabbed the man's head and wrenched, hard. The man's neck stretched, stretched. His body lurched and writhed. Johnny wrenched harder. The man's neck cracked. Johnny felt it crack. He let the body fall.

But the other two were on him now. One snared his legs, the other careened into his back. They flipped him over and he went down, into a drift. He crossed his arms against their blows. Their blows were sharp: pistol butts, not fists. The stitches in his shoulder ripped. Blood rolled down it, hot liquid amid the freezing coat of snowmelt.

"Get up!" ordered one, but the other kept slamming the pistol butt at him.

"Stop it!" the first one yelled above the storm. "It ain't our kill." The blows stopped. The snow had cushioned them, a little. Not much. The men grabbed his arms and jerked him to standing, hauled him back to the cabin, and tossed him through the door. He landed on his back, started to spring up, but stopped at the three drawn revolvers pointed at his face. Garrett and the drifters held them. So it was Rink he'd killed.

The German parted the group of men. He looked down at Johnny for a few seconds, working his jaw. His pale skin had reddened, his eyes glared, knifelike, but his voice was calm, frigid as the storm.

"One of you get me a meat cleaver," he said to his men.

With a grin, Garrett went to the kitchen.

Johnny said nothing. Blood seeped from the reopened shoulder wound, melting snow pooled under him, his hands and feet burned, thawing. He could hear Garrett ransack the kitchen, hunting. He did not take his eyes off the German.

Garrett brought the cleaver. It had an ebony handle and a big, heavy, rectangular steel blade. Gretel kept it sharp.

"Tie his hands," said the German, and they did. Two of them kept their guns out, cocked and pointed.

"Now hold him down. Tight," the German ordered, and the men holstered their guns. Johnny thrashed to get away from them. Their hands clamped his shoulders and legs. Especially his left leg. He thrashed harder.

"Hold him!" the German hissed.

The men tried. They grunted with the effort. Johnny felt a hand or two give way, then clamp down again. The men jerked and swayed as he moved. They couldn't hold him still; they could hardly hold him at all.

"Watch out for my goddamn hand," said the man nearest the German, the one who held Johnny's left foot.

The German raised the cleaver high.

"No!" Johnny screamed.

The German threw back his head and laughed.

33

Night Watch

Hours after Gretel reached him, hours into the night, Cole sat in the chair in his room, alone. Gretel had gotten a room of her own and gone to bed. Maybe she could sleep; Cole could not. The blizzard still surged against the hotel, rattling the windows and hissing through invisible cracks.

He held Luke Halloran's Colt in his hand, which rested on his lap, and his hand knew the gun belonged to someone else. He regretted losing his own Colt and the Winchester, too, though somehow it seemed fitting. In the grainy snowlight, he half smiled. How many men had he killed with those guns?

He thought about Laura, wondered what she was doing. Sleeping, of course. Dreaming, as she often did. Maybe talking in her sleep. He could never understand the words, but he always listened. She seemed to have only peaceful dreams. Not him. So many nights he would awaken sitting straight up, sweating, the image of some nameless man screaming for mercy. They all wind up in hell, he thought; I'll have quite a welcoming committee. Ha! I have it already. Ghosts.

If he made it through this, Catharine would haunt him like all the others, as she had all these years. He could never let Laura know, just as he had never really let her know all that he'd done in Texas. He had to protect her from knowing, because the saddest part of the whole thing was that he loved her best. And he knew she loved him. So the hell would be his and so would the ghosts. God damn the ghosts.

The wind paused, took a deep breath and started in again. Its hesitant rush rose to a shriek before settling back to a moan. It sounded like the cries of a woman belabored. Cole stroked the gun's shiny blued-steel barrel, so smooth and hard and deadly.

The night wore on and the blizzard seemed to slacken. As dawn approached, the room turned blue, like Catharine's suite before the storm, like a scene from a dream. Cole wished he could have slept. He was exhausted.

He heard a light knock at the door and said, "Come in."

Catharine, of course. "Your door isn't locked."

He shrugged.

She looked at the gun and at his face. She kissed him, but he did not respond. It would hurt too much later if he responded.

"You stayed up all night," she said.

"Yeah."

"Heinrich would like you to have breakfast with us. He still wants to buy the Anna Strike."

"Tell him no."

"I think you should consider his offer."

"He can take it himself. I don't plan on using my father's will."

"Your father's will?"

He nodded and studied the gun. The news silenced her. It had silenced Gretel, too, when he told her last night.

"Why did he send you to invite me?" Cole said at last.

"He didn't. I'm supposed to be having my hair done. He'll send you a note." She looked at the gun again. "So don't blow the boy's head off when he delivers it."

"I think you'd better get your hair done."

"I can fix it myself. We have time."

"That's the last thing we have."

She started to say something, stopped. "You shouldn't have stayed up all night."

"That ranks pretty low on the list of things I shouldn't have done."

She glanced out the window and back at him. "You regret it?"

"It was wrong."

"So are a lot of things. That's not what I asked."

He hesitated.

"Do you?" she said.

"Tell your husband no."

"That would be a mistake, Cole."

"Tell him no."

"I think you should consider his offer. So does he. In fact, we both think it would be bad form not to."

He sighed and got out of the chair, stiff from sitting so long. "The men who attacked me have Johnny Torres," he told her. "Gretel rode through the storm to tell me. Their leader is German."

Catharine's leaf green eyes widened briefly. She swallowed and smoothed her red corduroy dress, which was already smooth. "Just because he's German—"

"I know, Catharine. The man called MacMurray was with them before. He's not there now. Neither is Daunt."

"But the masks—"

"Gretel would know either of them, even masked."

"But still."

"Yes. Still. But I can't be sure." He paused, thinking. "You know, I couldn't figure it about the masks. Men don't wear masks if they plan to kill."

"You think they were supposed to let you live?"

"I did live."

Neither said anything for a moment. If they were supposed to let him live, they took a big chance handling it the way they did. If they were supposed to let him live, he would put his money on Braunn, not Daunt.

"But Heinrich would never destroy his own mine," said Catharine.

"As long as it was turning a profit. Right?"

"It was. I'm sure it was."

He wondered how sure anyone could be with Braunn.

"I thought for a while that Johnny reminded me of you," said Catharine. "Did I tell you that before?"

"No."

"It's true. Then, well, it doesn't matter now. Cole, they'll kill him. Whoever they are. They'll never let him get away. Please—"

"Don't fight?"

She looked down.

"I have to."

"I don't care. I can't care."

"I know, Catharine. But I have to anyway."

"Where do they want you to meet them? The Anna Strike?"

Cole shuddered inwardly.

"That's where they took you, isn't it?"

He nodded.

"Let us help. Please. Sell the Anna Strike to Heinrich and he'll help. He couldn't have blown up the Bonne Chance. He couldn't be behind all this." He saw how desperately she wanted to believe her own words. "You go alone and they'll kill you and Johnny and go right on with their butchery. It won't end when Heinrich leaves." She stopped abruptly, as though struck. "You mean for me to leave with him."

He said nothing.

"My God."

Still he said nothing.

"You want me to leave, and then you'll never have to see me again. You're willing to send me off with someone who may be a murderer—"

"I don't want you to leave." The truth, and a lie.

"And you're willing to risk death to get me to do it." She clutched his arms; her perfectly manicured fingernails dug deep. "Say something, damn it! Say it's not true. Say you'll stay, or at least come back sometime. Say you love me."

He swallowed hard and shook his head. He tried to avoid her eyes. "I can't," he said when he could trust his voice. "That's all there is to it, Catharine. Whether you leave with your husband is up to you, but either way I can't love you anymore."

Her arms fell, but she went on looking into his eyes. He stood still, silent. Only the blizzard made any noise, though even that was dying. Finally, she walked to the door and out, without looking at him again.

Cole felt his shoulders slump. He thought of meeting the German and his men on that ledge, of fighting them with fists or knives or anything but guns, because guns would bring the snow off the mountains and kill them all. He thought of what condition he'd find Johnny in when he got there and what more his captors would do to make them both suffer, and the thought of going through all that and maybe dying after turning Catharine away as she had once turned him away only made him feel like he had died already.

When a boy brought the breakfast invitation a short while later, Cole was standing at his window, looking at but not seeing the patterns the snow had made on the glass. He returned the invitation with his regrets. The storm would end soon, anyway. After splashing cold water on his face and buckling on his gunbelt, he limped down the hall to use the bathroom. As he crossed the landing on the way back, he saw Heinrich Braunn descending the stairs from his third-floor suite.

"Good morning, Mr. Coleman," Braunn said, smiling faintly. "I am sorry to hear you have refused my offer."

Cole nodded and continued toward his room.

"Mr. Coleman."

He stopped and turned. The smile had gone. The light eyes glittered like silver, hard and cold.

"She is going to Germany with me. In a matter of days."

"You know," said Cole, "you're amazing. Why don't you just put it to me straight?"

The expected chuckle never came. "Do not provoke me."

"I don't think I could. I don't think anyone could."

Braunn stepped toward him. "If you touch her again, she stays here."

"I won't, but the rest is up to her."

Braunn's cheeks flushed and his eyes narrowed. Cole stood his ground. Braunn turned away and continued down the stairs.

Cole limped to his room and prepared for the trip to the ledge. He would leave early, before the storm fully cleared. He cleaned and oiled Halloran's guns, checked the bullets in his gunbelt, and sharpened his Bowie knife. By then the storm had eased enough for him to start riding. Before leaving he reread his father's letter.

September 11, 1892

Cole,

If you are reading this letter, then what I figured would happen did. I gave this to Johnny and the will too because he is a good friend and a good man. I expect you two met up by now if you have this letter, and you are making plans to move on Daunt. I got no quarrel with that. The son of a bitch deserves whatever you can dish up.

Johnny has not read this and neither has Gretel. Go easy on your sister, Cole. She is a hard one to figure out, but I have come to like her real well. I think she is a good woman even if Anna tried to turn her.

Funny about your Ma. I must of gotten soft with the years. I used to hate her memory and all she done to you kids, but not any more. She just married the wrong man. Ought to of held out for some baron like Braunn. Expect you have run across him by now too. That means you have seen Catharine. There is another good woman. Hell, Anna married the wrong man and Catharine let the right one go. Guess we will never quite get the hang of women.

How I am running on. If I knew I could do this, I would of written you more. Truth is, I just wanted to make it clear about Gretel and Johnny. Plus I wanted to tell you that I left the claim to you because you are my son and that is how I wanted it. You might think about cutting Johnny and Gretel in on it, though.

I know you will not stay in Colorado, even though it is a good place once you get past all the lusting after what is inside these hills, so you ought to let Johnny run the mine if you decide to keep it. Me, I would sell it and divvy the money and buy up some more land. Then again, maybe I would keep it and smelt Anna a gold wedding ring like she always wanted.

Sorry I missed seeing you, but I know you are reading this in Telluride and that you came back mostly on account of me. Feels funny to write at all, so I am going to stop.

You done right leaving here, son.

The signature blurred and he had to blink to clear his eyes. After folding the letter carefully, he reread the part of his father's will about the mine: "To my son, Zachary, I bequeath the property known as the Anna Strike, for which I have filed a claim in Telluride, Colorado." It amazed him that one piece of rock could cause so much pain. He would write no will, himself; he hated the idea of doing that to Sam.

You're lucky you're only seven, Sam, he thought. You don't have to defend the honor and the life of a man you just met by trying to reclaim a mine you don't even want. I'm not leaving this God-cursed mine to you or anybody else. I ought to leave it to the mountain, which owns it anyway.

Then he sat at the little room's desk, took out a piece of hotel stationery, and wrote a letter of his own.

Catharine,

You will read this after I leave. Do not try to follow me. I may not survive, but neither will they. You can stop hoping, though that is not why I am going. Please believe me. I would give my life for you in a fight, but I will never take it myself. I am going for Zachary and Johnny.

Forgive me for turning you away today and leaving you fourteen years ago. I do love my wife, but if I had it to do over again I think I would stay here. Maybe it is better this way. We will never know if it could have worked out, but I think we were both smarter then.

I hope you understand why I could not leave you any of my possessions. You have my heart, and my love.

Cole

He sat back in the chair, fatigued from lack of sleep and the strain of facing death, but more from so much of life happening in such a short time. Less than a month ago he had repaired a weather-torn fence on his ranch and kissed his wife and heard his stepson's prayers before bed.

"Laura," he whispered, and closed his eyes. He sat still for a moment, almost praying himself, then got up and quickly left the room. He stopped to see Gretel, who fought with him this morning as she had last night about asking Braunn to help. He gave her the will and the letter for Catharine.

Downstairs, he glanced around the lobby and into the dining room, but could not see the Braunns. A movement in the bar caught his eyes, a patch of red fabric, a crown of red-gold hair. Catharine's laughter drifted to him, shrill, brittle, false. She raised a glass and acted drunk, but her crisp movements would have betrayed her to anyone who knew her well.

I know your every gesture, he thought. I memorized them all, years ago. I know how your eyes look just before you smile, or just before you kiss me. I know how your fingers curl when you lift a glass or caress me until I think heaven could never feel so good. If I walked into that bar now and asked, would you leave with me this time?

The beautiful red-gold head tilted back as she downed her drink. Maybe she was drunk. Maybe she would never leave again, with anyone.

34

Bargains

Cole had made Gretel promise not to go to Heinrich Braunn. He had gone to his sister before leaving to ride up to the Anna Strike. They'd argued about it the night before, when he told her about the will. The will: what a shock. What an infuriating shock.

She had been asleep when Cole came to her, sometime around ten in the morning. She had not slept all night, but in the morning, while he prepared to fight, her body had finally driven her into a deep, black slumber. His knock at the door brought her up from the depths: for a blessed instant she forgot where she was and everything that had happened.

Then he came in and said good-bye, and refused once again to go to Braunn for help.

"For all we know, Braunn might be responsible for all of this," he said. He handed her Zachary's will, and a letter. "Do what you want with the will, and the mine if you get the chance. Give this letter to Catharine. Wait an hour first. Don't let her know I've gone until then."

"Let Braunn help. He's your only hope." She must have said that fifty times already.

"No."

"Cole—"

"I said no."

"You can't win."

"I can kill the damned German."

"The others will kill you, and Johnny. You owe him more than that." It was all a repeat of last night. It was wearing her out, and him as well.

"I can't accept Braunn's help, and that's that. Now can I trust you or not?"

"You'll let Johnny die for your sin." No repeat there; she had tried to keep that inside.

"Jesus Christ."

"Cole, I love him."

"And I love her. Now promise me."

Her fingernails bit into her palms.

"Promise, God damn it!"

She whispered the promise.

He grabbed Luke Halloran's rifle and jerked the door open. But then he turned, and the look in his blue-gray eyes was gentle and sad. "I might never see you again," he said, "so I think we should make our peace now."

She nodded slowly.

Cole's limping steps faded down the hall. Sitting on the bed, Gretel clutched Zachary's will in one hand and the letter for Catharine in the other. She sat for ten minutes of the promised hour, trying to feel angry at her brother, and failing. She sat another ten minutes, with teeth clenched and fists tight and sweaty around the paper.

It was no use. Fighting Cole, sitting here, making promises, trying to keep them—no damn use. Gretel smoothed the will and read it. Though written in her father's hand, it had Johnny's mark all over it. So had Zachary, with those long cigars, that drilling contest triumph, that final drive into the mountain after treasure. And so did she. No use at all. So she slid off the high bed, walked out of her room and up the stairs to the Braunns' third-floor suite, where she knocked nervously on the door.

Heinrich Braunn opened it. "Why, Miss Coleman."

"I'm looking for Catharine."

"Of course you are. Come in."

The two doors on the other side of the room were closed.

"I'm looking for Catharine," she said again. She meant to give her the letter now, a half hour early. "If she's not here, I'll—"

"Please come in. Sit down. You seem wrought up. May I get you a brandy? Come in. Let me close the door." His accent gave her gooseflesh.

She walked in, though not too far.

"It's still morning," she said in response to his offer of brandy.

"No matter. Here, take my coffee then. I have not touched it." He held out the cup and saucer.

"Is Catharine here? I must see her."

He set the cup down. "No, to my knowledge she is with your brother."

"My brother is gone. He just left."

He sat in a white chair. All the furniture was upholstered in white, which made the room look surprisingly sleek, not at all like the cluttered opulence of the north-side homes.

"Then I expect," Braunn said, "that you want to see me, not my wife. Am I correct? You wanted to reach me through Catharine, because you know she is in love with your brother, so she would throw herself at my feet and beg me to save his life." He chuckled. "I doubt Cole would approve of your scheme. Not such a virtuous man. Am I still correct, or is there more? I seem to recall your affection for Johnny Torres. I suppose that has more to do with your desire for help than any sisterly concern."

"I love him," she said. "And he needs your help."

"A dangerous habit, love."

"Don't—"

"But it is. I have tried to tell my wife that, but she refuses to listen. It is so unbecoming to fall in love, just as it is unbecoming to beg. It is all a loss of control, do you not agree?"

"What do you want from me?" she said. For God's sake, get it over with.

"Ah, now there is a question! Let me see. You are an attractive girl. Tall, lithe, very pretty. Suppose I wanted to take you to bed?"

"You don't."

"Well, at least you have some spunk. Love usually makes such simpering fools of women. Men, too. It is particularly pathetic in a man."

"Tell me what you want."

He chuckled. "What do you have to give?"

35

Herr Braunn

Drink and laugh and drink some more; act drunk.

The sandy-haired bartender leaned on his elbows on the polished cherrywood bar, and the muscles in his chest and arms made Catharine want to feel him without the shirt, to roll laughing under the sheets while he did things to her body that could block the memory of Cole. Like many of the Baroness Hotel's employees, he had once been a miner. Heinrich's German hotel manager had hired him, and like many other ex-miners, he had proven better at this than at mining. Few made out at mining.

"Another one?" he teased. "Mrs. Braunn, you've already had—"

"Five. I know, I counted. And I'm not drunk, see?" Act it, though. Make him think you are. What the hell, it's all a game. "And please, it's Catharine." She smiled and ran her forefinger slowly around the rim of the empty glass.

The bartender poured her another shot. Tequila. As she lifted it, some sloshed onto the front of her dress.

"Oh!" she said.

The bartender offered a damp cloth.

"Wipe it for me."

He cocked an eyebrow.

"Please."

He leaned across the bar and the cloth touched her breast through the red corduroy. She set her glass down and took his wrist. "I'm sorry," she said. "I shouldn't have done that." Shouldn't have done that? Shouldn't be here at all.

He regarded her levelly.

"Please excuse me," she said, and slid off the stool. As the liquid evaporated, the spot cooled.

He nodded. She started to walk away.

"Mrs. Braunn?"

She turned.

"You're a very beautiful lady. You ought to be careful whom you tempt."

She smiled. "It's a little late for that, but thank you."

She walked up the long, wide, red stairs to the third floor, and turned left down the hall. She opened the door to her suite and found Heinrich talking with Gretel. He sat in the white chair by the table with the decanter, and Gretel stood just inside the door.

"Hello, Catharine," said Heinrich, getting up. "We were just discussing you, in a manner of speaking."

Catharine barely heard him. "He's left already?" she said to Gretel, who nodded. Catharine turned to her husband.

He held up his hand. "Save your entreaties, my dear. What have you to suggest that I have not asked already? Gretel has just offered me the Anna Strike. She showed me her father's will, in which he leaves the property to Cole. She believes that if Cole lives he will feel obligated to honor any bargain she might make with me. If he dies, well . . .

"I was considering her offer when you came in. Perhaps if you sweeten the pot with your undying devotion—or some similarly ridiculous euphemism; in any case, more than your mere presence in my bed and my homeland—I might consider helping. Though I must say the odds would still weigh heavily against you."

Catharine glanced from Heinrich to Gretel. Gretel's face had a pinched look, as though she had just come in from the cold. She would not be one to plead.

"I will agree to your terms if you will help fight Daunt," Catharine told her husband. "Even if Cole survives."

Heinrich puffed on his cigar.

"So will you help us or not?" Catharine said.

"You should have known better than to ask."

Catharine heard the breath catch in Gretel's throat. She held out her hand to keep Gretel from speaking. "That is not an answer. Will you or not?"

"Why should I?"

"We've already given you all the reasons you need."

"You have yet to beg."

"If we did, especially if I did, you would say no."

"True enough."

"And now?"

He looked at Gretel and at Catharine. His eyes traveled down Catharine's body to her crotch and lingered there. She slapped him. He hit her with the back of his hand, hard in the cheek. She lost her balance, caught herself on the table by the white chair. The table toppled and the decanter shattered on the floor.

Gretel took an angry step toward him. Catharine stood in her way, facing the man she once vowed to love, honor, and obey, for better or for worse, but not for this.

"I loved you once," she said, her voice a snarl. "That's what you wanted, to make me love you and not have to love me in return. To win a whore's love."

"That is ludicrous."

"What would have made you help?"

He chuckled.

She resisted the urge to hit him again. No, to kill him. Gretel had a knife at her belt; Catharine had the derringer in her purse, the one that had saved her from other men in the past.

"Nothing," he said. "Why should I help, when the situation is finally playing out as I wanted it to all along? What do you plan to do, anyway? Sell yourselves to Daunt and his men, as you would have to me? What a bargain for them, just knowing what it would do to Cole and Johnny to go free while they had their fun. The Anna Strike could never compare with your splendors, Baroness Catharine DuBois Braunn.

"Help? Good heavens no! But you do as you must. And hate me, if you will. I shall have what I want: Buck Daunt, dead. The Anna Strike, too. And I have had what I wanted of you all these years, Catharine."

Catharine turned to Gretel, who glared at Heinrich with the blackest hatred. Another instant and she would draw that knife. She would become her brother, as he had been in Texas, as she hated him. She was not torn, she was driven. She would use the knife. Heinrich might die, but so might she. Heinrich would never go easily.

"Gretel," said Catharine.

Her right arm bent at the elbow.

"Gretel."

She looked at Catharine. Her hand stopped moving but stayed

near that delicately carved handle. "Go get your coat. Wait for me in the lobby."

Gretel stood still.

"Let me speak to him alone, Gretel."

She lowered her hand and stood there a moment longer, and Catharine thought she trembled slightly, with rage, not fear. Gretel did not say a word; she did not have to. She looked from Catharine to Heinrich, and then she left them alone.

For a moment Catharine watched her husband in silence. Then she said, "I want three things."

"Only three?"

"Yes. Only three. Answers. Three answers."

"She took a deep breath. "Did you murder Zachary?"

The inevitable chuckle. "Now why would I murder a man when I planned to invest in his mine? Like Johnny Torres, he knew considerably more about working underground than I do. Really, my dear, are all your questions as obvious as that?"

She ignored the slight. "Did you sabotage the Bonne Chance?"

No chuckle, this time. But the hint of a smug smile, as though he'd kept back a last secret, as if Daunt's death and securing the Anna Strike were not enough.

"Did you?"

He looked at the painting on the wall, the one of the house mostly obscured by the trees, and made rings of the smoke from his cigar. He was deciding, she knew, deciding how much to tell her, calculating the risk. When he turned back to her, his silver eyes gleamed. "Let me tell you about the Bonne Chance," he said. "After all, why not? As of July, it was not profitable. And the latest assays were false."

"False?"

"You have long made the mistake, or so one might call it, of

staying out of our business affairs. So you could not have known their
true state. A lifestyle such as ours, particularly such as yours, could
never survive on the proceeds from this hotel and its adjacent opera
house—and I use the term opera in the loosest sense—nor on the
ore pulled from our mines. You knew the Flosshilde had failed. Any
knowledgeable miner could have told that from looking at the ore.
With the Bonne Chance, the failure was not so obvious. The mine
was still breaking even, but no more. No more."

She felt weak. All those men, dead. And all those wounded,
whom she had held while they moaned, or prayed for death, or died.

"I considered ordering the mine destroyed," he said. "But why
risk it, when another was all too ready to do it for me, without even
being asked. How considerate of Mr. Daunt. And how foolish to
oblige me, when what he really wanted was revenge."

"But you wanted to sell it. Surely you got less for it this way.
Why—"

Again the gleam. Catharine's blood ran cold. "Insured?" she
asked, barely above a whisper.

"Insured. A fine London firm. A much better claim. You see,
liebchen, the only way I could back the Anna Strike was with the
money we made from the Bonne Chance, and simply selling it would
never have given me enough. Developing the Anna Strike will take
tremendous resources, financial and otherwise." He paused. "Which
brings us to your third question."

"Cole."

"Yes, Cole."

She swallowed. Suddenly she did not want to know, and did, all
at once. "And?"

"I did not order him killed. That was Daunt's idea."

"You wanted him left alive to go after Daunt," she said. "How
kind. How terribly compassionate of you, Heinrich, to want him alive.

But Krieg ruined it, didn't he? Krieg couldn't control MacMurray. MacMurray told Daunt. So you fired Krieg. Needlessly, as it turns out."

She thought he had lost a hand there, but in his eyes she saw bemusement, not defeat. What else was there? How much else could there be?"

"Fire Krieg?" he said, puffing on his cigar, making rings of the smoke. "Perhaps it looked that way. I intended it to, in any case."

Catharine shook her head slowly. So he had meant for Cole to die, at MacMurray's hands, not Krieg's, and for the Bonne Chance to be destroyed. For the insurance, and the Anna Strike. He had intended it all, but didn't have to do any of it himself, didn't even have to issue a direct order. He'd left it to Cole and Daunt and MacMurray, under the watchful eye of Krieg. Perhaps he hadn't counted on Cole surviving, or on Johnny Torres joining the fight, but now Johnny had been injured, and captured, and Cole's survival had only given Heinrich another shot at Daunt.

He had lost her in the process, though. No matter what he said, she knew that stung.

"I think you are a coward," she told him finally. "And a fool."

"Oh? How so?"

"It's an odd combination, really. Usually fools are brave men, and when they die it's sad because inside they know their acts were foolish. But when a fool is also a coward, there's no excuse."

"Profound."

"You'll never risk it, will you?"

"Risk what, my dear?"

"Falling in love, what else?"

Once more, the chuckle. She wanted to rip it from his throat.

"Love is a creation of the heart in need of more than it can accomplish on its own," he said. "Or no, not of the heart; more of the mind. The heart is merely an organ that pumps blood to our bodies so we can do what we must. Those who fail fall in love, and I suppose if I had a void to fill, I would as well.

"If I am a fool, as you claim, it has nothing to do with this Anna Strike business. It is only in that I misjudged you, and the depth of your lust for wealth, of your . . . passions."

His cigar had gone out. He relighted it and waved her away. "So go. Take my knife. And let Gretel take my horse if hers is too slow. I know yours is fast enough. God forbid you should miss watching your treasured Cole die."

Perhaps he expected her to respond, but she saw no need. She had loved him once, and not long ago. Because she had loved him she pitied him, and because she pitied him she let him live. Otherwise she would have taken the gun from her purse and shot him right here, in the head, not the heart.

She put on her coat. Heinrich stood and continued to puff his cigar, his brocade jacket and perfectly creased pants as immaculate as his long, silver hair and the expression into which he had molded his face: disdainful, untouchable, controlled.

"Good-bye, Heinrich," said Catharine.

"*Auf Wiedersehen.*" He lifted his cigar.

36

Burning Threads

They had let him keep the foot. The German had brought the meat cleaver crashing down into the wood floor, sinking it deep.

"We are supposed to keep you alive," he said. "And this time, we will. You should be thankful that Mr. MacMurray is not here."

Johnny was not sure what he meant by that. Unless they'd been ordered to keep Cole alive, too. Well, they had, in the end. That would explain a lot, but right then he hurt too much to think straight.

They tied his ankles again and left him lying in the middle of the floor, and he gave them no trouble the rest of the night. He could not sleep and so listened to the storm. It howled around the cabin like ghosts, and after a while he could make them out if he closed his eyes: Zachary, Rosasharon, Linda, his mother, weeping; the men murdered by his father's mines, the men murdered by the Bonne Chance, the widows and children of them all. And someone else—a fragile, pretty, blond woman, or the shell of one, porcelain, hollow, with translucent skin rouged at the cheeks. He opened his eyes and looked at the daguerreotype on the mantle: Anna Streich.

This morning the men had slung him over his palomino's bare back and hauled him to this ledge, to the prospect hole named after the ghost he'd seen in the night, up the trail made more treacherous than ever by the blizzard, through the storm's final flurries. They'd given him no coat, no water, no food, but at least they'd put his boots back on. They'd tied him to this stumpy tree and after a while the German had told the man with the scar that he could start the beating.

The sun had come out, at last, stinging at eyes grown accustomed to darkness, but the wind swept up over the rim and through his shirt. When he was not gasping from the punches, he could hear the snowfall shift above and below, on rock that strained against its first blanket of the season. One gunshot could bring it all down, or one word spoken too loudly; this mountain never held its snow for long. It's alive, Johnny thought, it's just waiting for us to make the wrong move.

"Hit him again," said the German.

Garrett drew back his right fist. Sweat glistened on his face and forearms, and the furrow in his cheek had turned angry and red. Johnny looked at his hand. The knuckles were red, too. The fist came over again and it was like someone rammed a pole into his gut. The left followed fast. Johnny nearly passed out.

Garrett grinned.

"Enough for now," said the German. "We need him alive a little longer."

"Torres got plenty left before he's dead, don't you, Johnny?"

Johnny spat out a mouthful of blood and said nothing. Behind and below him the Coleman valley spread. If he could see it, he could think of Gretel and hold on. But if he were still alive enough to feel when Cole got here, it could be very bad for both of them.

Shortly after Garrett stopped hitting him, he heard horses coming up the trail and looked over that way. Daunt and MacMurray, topping the ledge.

"It's about time," muttered the German.

They left their horses with the others at the far end and walked over to where the German and his men stood around Johnny.

"Well look who's here," Johnny said.

Daunt's harsh mouth parted in what might have passed for a grin. MacMurray grinned for real.

"Looks like you had a rough night," drawled Daunt.

"Never slept better."

"I bet." He looked around the circle of men. "Where's Rink?"

The German's chin jutted. "Dead. Broken neck."

Daunt spattered Johnny's left boot with tobacco juice, then worked the chaw around in his mouth, his dark eyes narrowed. Almost gently, he reached out and touched Johnny's temple, swollen from the German hitting him with the gun butt the night before. Johnny flinched. Daunt dropped his hand, started to turn away, then suddenly spun back and landed a left hook that split the bruised skin. For a moment Johnny's legs started to give way, but he held on.

"You never should've taken my job, buck," said Daunt. "Pissed me off for sure. I expect Gretel weren't too pleased, either." He laughed. "And what about Cole? He give up living by the gun when he left Texas. He was on his way back to Montana when we got to Gretel. Maybe he kept right on going, huh?"

"I saved Cole's life, remember? Your number-one asshole here had a little trouble finishing him off. Even with help." MacMurray took a menacing step forward. Johnny smiled, which took work. Blood was running down the side of his face from where Daunt had hit him. "Easy when we're tied, right Mac?"

"I'll kill you, Torres."

"Sure you will. A tick can kill a man any time, with an army to help."

Daunt hit him in his already cracked jaw. Again the snow faded.

"Leave it, Mac," he heard Daunt snarl, and he regained his senses in time to see MacMurray back off. Daunt gripped Johnny's shoulder and gouged his thumb into the bullet wound. "I can make you scream in ways Krieg here never even thought of," he threatened, "but I need you alive for Cole." He let go of Johnny's shoulder, wet again with oozing blood.

Johnny looked at the big, pale-eyed German. "Where the hell'd you dig him up?"

"Braunn Mining Limited, where else? Ole Heinrich got it in his head to rough up Cole a little, make him mad at me. Wanted Cole to help him take the Anna Strike, see." He spat, hitting a rock this time. "Hell with roughing him up, I says, kill the bastard. So Braunn fires Krieg, and I get one damn fine fighter all to myself. Worked out great, except that Cole went and survived. As for you, buck—" He walked to his horse and took a piece of fabric from the saddlebags: Gretel's tapestry. He scraped a match into flame and held it under a corner. The threads caught. The flames ate through the valley pictured there and worked toward the candy cabin. He dropped it. It sizzled on the snow and finally turned to wormlike bits of charred thread.

"Your turn, Mac," said Daunt. "Just keep him tied and make sure there's enough left for when Cole gets here. And Torres, don't ever cross me again. Not that you'll get the chance."

MacMurray's beefy red face deformed into a grin. Johnny looked at the blackened remains on the snow and tried to remember the last words he'd said to Gretel. If only he could have told her something to help her return to the life of peaceful solitude she'd once had, before Zachary brought him home to Sunday dinner. If only he could tell her now.

MacMurray moved toward him.

37

An Honorable Man

There was no back trail to the Anna Strike, just the steep, slippery needle of a mountain. Cole tied off Luke Halloran's dun horse near the road and started up on foot. After ten yards he fell. He hit a stunted tree halfway down and scrambled back up, his ribs and leg throbbing, his body hot inside the jacket. He turned south, and for a while followed a more lateral route.

The way steepened again. He fell once more and had to lie still before resuming his climb. He kept seeing flashes of the last time he'd climbed this mountain, with blood streaming from the hole in his leg. There was a faint memory of a face at the top: young, dark, bearded. His father . . . no, saying something about his father. His father's friend. Johnny had saved him then. Now he had to save Johnny.

He climbed the last several hundred yards, the going smoother where the wind had swept away some of the snow. He crested out on the small shelf above the mine, which was at the near end of the ledge. Freshly cut timbers fortified the entrance and he could just see the top of the hole. He moved a few paces farther along the narrow shelf, staying low, until more of the ledge came into view.

On the far edge he saw Johnny. His hands were tied behind a tree and his bearded chin rested on his chest; Cole couldn't see much of his face. There was a large smear of blood on his left shoulder but most of it had browned, drying, and he stood on his own.

Cole saw none of the masked men, only Johnny and the rebuilt shack, its wood again the yellow of pine still full of sap. The men could have been on the other side of the shack, or inside it, or in the adit tunnel. They would have seen him if he'd come up the trail. He drew his gun.

"Hey!" he called, not too loudly because anything could dislodge the snow.

Johnny raised his head and squinted at the sunlight that bounced off the slope. His lips were cracked and his right temple and cheek were a palette of bloody, bruised colors. Cole raised his hand, and the others came into view. No masks, now. And Daunt leading, with a huge, gray-haired man who could've only been MacMurray not far behind. Surprise, surprise.

"Af'noon, buck," said Daunt. "Looking mighty robust for a ghost, ain't you? Hell, I hope you ain't planning to use that Colt. This whole damn mountain's just itching to come down."

"Let Johnny go."

Daunt's laughter cackled until he clapped his three-fingered left hand over his mouth. "Jesus, I almost forgot: nothing too loud. Get us all killed."

"Let him go or I'll pull the trigger."

"You're crazy, buck. Pull it and both y'all die."

"Nothing to lose, Buck. Let him go."

At a nod from Daunt, MacMurray moved to Johnny and cut the ropes. Johnny nearly collapsed. MacMurray caught his left shoulder. Johnny winced.

"Can you make it all right?" Cole called.

Johnny nodded and took another couple of steps, but his skin was gray and MacMurray still held him up.

"Get him on his horse," Cole ordered.

Daunt spat. MacMurray shoved Johnny back against the tree and hit him in the right side. Johnny started to double over but Mac-Murray held him.

"Drop the gun, buck," said Daunt.

Cole felt like he'd taken the blow himself. "Let him go."

MacMurray swung again. Johnny fell to his knees. MacMurray slugged him in his bruised right cheek. He fell to the ground. Blood from his mouth spotted the snow. MacMurray raised his fist.

Cole pointed the gun at one of Daunt's men and pulled the trigger. The man flipped backwards over the edge of the ledge and disappeared down the slope. MacMurray froze. Daunt froze. No one dared move. At Cole's back, the mountain rumbled. No one even breathed. The rumbling ceased.

Daunt's face flushed and his dark eyes widened until the whites showed all the way around. He seemed to quiver for an instant, as though trying to control his rage. Then the flush died and he shrugged. "I had to know, buck," he said.

"Get him a horse."

Johnny pushed himself up with his arms, then stood. One of the men walked to the southern part of the ledge, out of Cole's sight, and returned with the palomino. Johnny checked the bridle and pulled himself onto the dancing animal's bare back.

"Awright," said Daunt, "now we got him a horse. You want him free, you come down here. I ain't letting you go, too. And listen, both of you: Don't get any ideas about pulling the same stunt to get

Cole out. You can fire them bullets 'til every mountain in this district comes bare, but you and me, Cole, we got a score to settle. You understand that, Torres?"

Johnny said nothing. He looked like he would fall off the horse.

"Git down here, Cole."

"Let him go first."

"No deal. It's you I want, not him. You come down and he walks. You gotta trust me, buck."

Cole surveyed the nearly vertical fifteen feet of rock that separated him from the ledge. Snow clung to it and lay deep at its base. He could slide down, but his bad leg would make for a defenseless moment at the bottom.

"Tell your men to back off."

"Do it, boys." They took a step backward but drew their knives.

"Farther," said Cole.

They moved almost to the rim of the ledge. Cole knew he should put the gun away. He had gambled once against great odds; he couldn't risk it going off when he landed. He kept it out and jumped into the slide. At the last second he took his finger off the trigger. His fist clenched tight: the gun would have gone off.

"Good," said Daunt. "Awright. Go on, Torres."

The man who held the palomino let go and Johnny rode toward the trail. Before disappearing below the rim, he touched his forehead. Cole returned the salute.

Daunt walked to Cole and stood with the gun barrel against his belly. "See? I'm an honorable man, buck. I just love standing here with the legendary Zachary Coleman holding a gun to my gut, and he can't even pull the trigger. And here I tried to get you killed, blowed up, at this very spot. Now it's your turn. Come on. Murder me. Cold blood." He spread his arms wide. "See? I won't even go for my gun."

Don't.

But his body will muffle the shot. The snow will hold.

Don't.

It held before.

It won't hold now.

He'll kill you. Or MacMurray will. Johnny is in no shape to come back and help. Shoot now.

"Go on, buck. Do it."

Cole shoved him away with the gun. Daunt's hatchet face twitched, and for a moment Cole thought Daunt would come at him right then. Instead he laughed.

"Round one to the shootist."

"How do you want to die, Buck?"

Daunt spat his whole wad of tobacco into the snow and handed his gunbelt to one of his men. Cole looked at the man's pale eyes: the German. The same man who'd ridden up the trail from the train to the mansion with him and Braunn, what now seemed so long ago. He looked at another man's eyes and another's—all here, except the one he'd just killed. He looked finally at MacMurray, and turned the gun on him. He wanted to shoot him almost as much as he wanted to shoot Daunt. MacMurray met his gaze evenly, silently; this was very much Daunt's show.

So Cole holstered the gun and unbuckled the gunbelt and set it aside. Daunt took off his jacket. Cole did, too. Daunt unsheathed a Bowie knife. The fourteen-inch blade flashed in the sun. Daunt touched it to his palm and a line of red appeared. He grinned, and his dark eyes burned.

Cole unsheathed his knife as well. Daunt's men stood around them.

"Tell them to put the knives away," said Cole.

"Nope."

"Then you can't win."

"Hell I can't! You kill me, you kill me. They'll only kill you after."

He tossed the knife from hand to hand. "Won't be no after, though. You can shoot, but this is my way."

Daunt crouched and moved sideways, stalking. A trace of the grin still twisted his thin, dark lips. Cole tensed. In his hand the knife felt alive. He waited for Daunt to lunge. Daunt waited for him.

"Did you murder my father?" Cole asked, circling low, ready.

"Nope. Would have, but he beat me to it."

"Why'd you jump his claim? You can't have it, now. He wrote a will, you know."

Daunt's face registered no surprise. He flicked his knife and again it caught the sun. "To get the gold," he said. "To get him for crossing me. Maybe to get you. You're his son."

"He never crossed you."

"Like hell. Dug up the gold mine without telling me."

"He owed you nothing."

Daunt snorted. "He owed me Anna."

"*What?*"

Daunt lunged.

38

Sacrifice

Riding next to Gretel, Catharine rounded a bend in the road above the valley and saw a dark-haired man coming toward them on a tall palomino horse. The man's head was bowed and he sat unsteadily on the horse's bare back. The horse seemed eager to break into a trot, but the man held the reins taut.

"Johnny—" Gretel's voice was a strained whisper. Then louder: "Johnny!" She kicked Heinrich's big gray into a gallop. Catharine hung back.

Johnny raised his head. Catharine grimaced when she saw the right side of his face, the split lips, the blood on his shirt. Gretel reached him, touched him timidly with long fingers. He leaned against her, rested his head on her shoulder, and all Catharine could think of was Cole. She spurred her mount, caught up. Johnny let Gretel go and looked at Catharine. They had never met, but he seemed to know her.

"I need some water," he said, with difficulty.

Gretel opened her canteen and handed it to him. He rinsed blood from his mouth, then poured a couple of swallows down his throat, without touching his lips. Half spilled over his beard and down his chest.

"I have to go back up," he said, though Catharine wondered how he'd ever make the climb if he could barely sit his horse. His body was bent, as though someone had caved him in at the middle.

There was panic in Gretel's eyes. "You can't!"

"Cole's still up there. I have to."

"Is Cole all right?" Catharine asked. "We heard a shot."

"He killed one of Daunt's men." Johnny urged the palomino forward.

"You can't," Gretel said again.

But he rode on, heading back the way the women had come. Catharine turned her horse and followed. After a few seconds she looked behind her at Gretel, who sat still on Heinrich's horse, her expression desperate.

"Come on," Catharine said gently, and Gretel did.

Johnny rode to a spot off the road, a small clearing behind a jagged outcropping and some trees. A broad-chested dun was there already. Cole's? Johnny slid to the ground, landing with a wince, and the women dismounted too. Catharine saw nothing resembling a trail.

"What are you going to do?" she asked.

"Climb the mountain, like Cole did. Daunt's men will see me if I go up the trail."

"And then?"

Johnny turned to Gretel. "Give me your knife."

"No." Her chin jutted stubbornly.

"I don't think you should come," he told her. "Or you," to Catharine.

"We'll come anyway," Catharine said. "You can have my knife."

Gretel looked at her sharply. Catharine handed him Heinrich's stiletto.

The three of them started up the slope, following what must have been Cole's bootprints, grabbing tree trunks and giving each other a hand when the snow took their footing. By the time they reached the first lateral part of the route, Catharine and Gretel were breathing hard and Johnny could barely walk. He seemed to regain a little strength before the way steepened again, only to lose it as they continued.

Finally, they reached the narrow shelf on the slope above the ledge. They could see Cole and Daunt, with Krieg and the other three standing around them, knives drawn. Catharine, Gretel, and Johnny stayed as far back near the mine as possible so the men wouldn't spot them.

Catharine pulled her derringer from the purse she had tied at her waist. Johnny touched her shoulder, shaking his head, and she put the gun in the pocket of her coat. Gretel saw the gun and glanced up the mountain at the snow.

On the ledge, Cole and Daunt circled, each with a Bowie knife, already red. They wore no jackets and sweat glistened on their faces. Cole's flannel shirt was ripped across the chest, cut cleanly and darkened with blood. Daunt had a gash on his right arm near the shoulder, deep enough that blood had dripped to his elbow. They had fought a long time now, with much of this taunting, though neither one looked tired.

Daunt's men watched intently, except for Krieg, who looked impatient, even bored. He was Heinrich's man, anyway, though only Catharine and Gretel knew that. Neither had had a chance to tell Johnny. The big man with the gray hair had to be MacMurray, Catharine shuddered. In her pocket, her fingers curled around the derringer.

Johnny sat down heavily on the shelf and rested his head on his arms. Catharine wondered if he was about to faint. Gretel squatted by his side and whispered something to him. He looked at her and put a finger to his lips, and Gretel said no more. Relieved, at least a little, Catharine returned her attention to the fight.

Daunt thrust his knife at Cole, who ducked and rolled and came up slashing. Daunt jumped back, but not before the blade kissed his side. He lunged. Cole moved toward him instead of away. Their knife arms crossed. Cole knocked Daunt over and they tumbled across red-flecked snow. Each seized the other's wrist.

Daunt rammed his knee into Cole's side. Cole closed his eyes and his mouth opened but he made no sound. Daunt raised the knife. Catharine gasped. Johnny stood. Daunt brought the knife down. Cole opened his eyes and knocked it away.

The two men rolled again, giving Cole the momentum he needed to get back on his feet. Daunt followed, then jumped clear as Cole swung at him.

For an instant, Catharine got a clear view of Cole's eyes. In them, she saw how much he wanted the kill. It meant more to him than revenge or survival. He wanted the kill. That's what he hated, what he'd tried to leave in Texas, what he'd come back to here. Not for Zachary, not for Gretel, not even for Catharine. Well, maybe a little for Catharine.

He should've stayed home, she thought, home with his wife. Laura must be his only weapon against this, the past. Which meant he needed her, not Catharine.

But right now he needed to stay alive; this fight wasn't over yet. Daunt danced to the side and attacked from there. Cole leapt away, but too close to one of the others. The man's knife drew blood. Enraged, Cole turned and slashed his throat.

Daunt flew at him. Cole took the blade on his left side. It laid open flannel and bandages and flesh. Catharine choked back a cry. Her fist tightened around her gun until her fingers ached. Cole brought his knife up from his hip and into Daunt at the center, and wrenched it. The thrust lifted Daunt off the ground. Daunt's eyes bulged and his face turned purple. He dropped his knife and clamped both hands around Cole's neck. Cole brought his arms up between Daunt's and apart.

Daunt staggered back. His rage dissolved to disbelief. Then he laughed, and the cackle danced off the mountain, into the Anna Strike and back out again.

"Her son!" he shrieked. "Her son killed me!"

He dropped to his knees, still laughing, holding the handle of Cole's knife. Cole hit him and he toppled, dead.

Catharine closed her eyes and let go a long breath. A bellow brought her back. MacMurray tossed his knife aside and charged. He hit Cole in the back with his shoulder. Cole yelled and went down hard. Catharine yelled with him, yelled at Johnny, to do something.

Johnny was already leaping up and out and off the shelf. He landed in the drift on the ledge, kicked his way free of the snow. One of the others, a big man with a jagged scar across one cheek, rushed at him. Johnny dove, rolled, came up with Heinrich's stiletto thrust forward, into the man's gut. The man pitched sideways, into the drift.

Johnny collapsed to his knees, gulping air, pale as death. Get up, Catharine wanted to yell at him. You can't stop now. Cole. Cole needs your help. For God's sake, *get up.*

MacMurray pinned Cole by the throat with one huge hand and brought the other crashing down into him. Blood from the wound in Cole's side colored MacMurray's fist. Cole struggled under the massive hands, twisting, trying to break loose. MacMurray held on. Johnny made it to his feet and lurched toward them. MacMurray saw him coming, released Cole, and tackled Johnny instead, knife and all. Cole rolled to his knees, his hand pressing his side. Blood trickled through his fingers. He got one foot under him but then collapsed again to lie on the snow, breathing shallowly and fast, close to passing out.

MacMurray and Johnny tumbled across the pink snow to the outer edge of the ledge. Johnny broke free, rolled to his back, tried to get up but couldn't. MacMurray could. He kicked Johnny in the ribs, once, twice. Johnny screamed, trying to roll away from the heavy boots. A tree stopped him. It also kept him from falling down the slope.

Cole groaned and turned over, shook his head as if to clear it. He began crawling toward Daunt, to get his knife, but he kept slipping. He meant to help Johnny, if he could. Catharine looked from him to Johnny and MacMurray, then to the bodies of Daunt and the man with the scar and the other one Cole had killed.

"Krieg," she said aloud.

She'd forgotten him, and Gretel. She looked sideways. Gretel stood where she had from the start, only a few feet away, watching Johnny and MacMurray, clutching her knife, terribly afraid.

But where was Krieg?

Cole still crawled toward Daunt. Catharine did not think he could get there in time. Johnny had dropped Heinrich's knife. He made a grab for it but MacMurray slugged him in the face. MacMurray snatched up the knife, lunged. Beside Catharine, Gretel shrieked. With his side to her and thirty feet away, clear on the other side of the ledge, MacMurray made a poor target.

Gretel sprang off the shelf, took three long strides and threw her knife. It caught MacMurray in the arm. MacMurray swore, clutched the wound. Heinrich's stiletto landed in the slush. Weakly, Johnny groped for it. He'll never get it, Catharine thought. He'll never get it and now MacMurray's going for it, too, and he's got it and he's raising it and Johnny's trying to hold him off but he's too weak.

Gretel ran toward them. Catharine looked from her to Cole. Still crawling toward Daunt, closer but not yet there.

The stiletto bit into Johnny's shirt and he screamed again, screamed for Gretel, then just screamed, with his head pressed into the snow, and even from thirty feet away Catharine could see the veins standing out in his neck.

Then Cole reached Daunt, pulled his own knife free, hauled back his arm, and threw. MacMurray's back arched. He dropped the stiletto. Gretel shoved him off Johnny and he tumbled sideways, off the ledge, down the slope.

But where was Krieg? Again Catharine scanned the ledge. Then she looked straight down. He was there, at the mouth of the Anna Strike. He held two guns, one a forty-five, the other a pocket pistol. Catharine glanced up at the snow. No witnesses, no one left to contest the claim. He'd kill them, and the shots would bring down the mountain, and he'd hide in the mine until it passed. No one else had seen him. He pointed the forty-five at Cole, drew back the hammer.

Catharine yelled: "Krieg!"

Startled, he turned toward her. She aimed the derringer at his face. They were only a few yards apart. He swung the pocket pistol up with his other hand. The two shots sounded as one.

Krieg's body lurched back, hit the ledge with a muffled thud, leaving only the echo of the gunshots to break the snowy silence. Catharine stood frozen, her eyes closed and her derringer dangling from her fingers.

The echo died. The mountain stayed silent. Catharine was afraid to hope that they had won. Krieg was dead. Daunt was dead. MacMurray and the others were dead. Cole was alive and so was Johnny. She began to hope.

And the mountain began to rumble.

39

Spring Leaves

Cole sat up. The snow and the sky looked strange and he could not see who had fired the shots. But he knew. And he could feel the mountain shudder. He shook his head, tried to clear his vision. Now he saw Krieg, dead in front of the mine. And Catharine, standing on the shelf above the ledge. And Gretel and Johnny and the three dead men. They all seemed to be encased in ice. Cole looked toward the peak. The sunlight hurt his eyes.

Near the peak the snow began to lose its hold. It slipped, came alive, struggled to cling and lost. Slowly, slowly it began to descend, a great solid block of white. Its last fingerhold broke and the block became a churning mass.

Cole struggled to his feet. Dragging Johnny with her, Gretel stumbled toward the Anna.

"Catharine!" Cole staggered toward her. She still stood above the ledge. Now he could see a tiny spot of blood on her coat, just below her left breast. The spot was spreading.

"Catharine!" Cole stopped where the ledge ended beneath her. "Jump!" She was staring across the valley. He followed her gaze. The mansion: haughty, majestic, watching from its San Juan throne.

Cole threw himself against the face of the mountain. His fingers clawed the snow, his feet scrambled against it. The snow came loose in his hands.

"Catharine!"

Something grabbed his arm. He looked and saw his sister. He yanked free. Gretel grabbed him again. Cole tried to hit her but she ducked. Then pain exploded from Cole's side and he crashed to the ground. Gretel fell next to him and yelled something. The roar took her words.

They began to crawl. The ground shook. They kept crawling. Cole closed his eyes and started to lie down. Just to lie down would feel so good. He remembered lying next to Catharine at the Baroness, waiting for her to fall asleep. He would not sleep, he would just rest. Just for a little while. Now as then. Catharine had fallen asleep and he had covered her with the thick white quilt and left her there, alone. Catharine, Catharine.

He felt hands on his arms and opened his eyes. Gretel tugged at him. She was shrieking but he could not hear her. He tried to crawl but kept slipping. She pulled him along. He thought he would go deaf from the roar. It went inside his head and pounded his brain and bellowed: "Catharine, Catharine, Catharine."

He looked over his shoulder. She stood watching him, smiling, with the snow close to her back. Gretel gave him a final shove. As he made the last foot toward the mine, he saw Catharine's smile vanish and her mouth open wide to scream his name.

Gretel pushed him into the Anna and piled on top of him. The snow thundered over the ledge, engulfed the shack and the dead men and the ledge itself. It tore the shack free and hurled it to the valley floor. It went on and on. Then it was gone.

Snow drifted deep at the mouth of the mine, and a fine snowy mist hung in the air. The mist caught the sun's rays and burst them apart into a million flakes of light, dazzling. Cole leaned his head against one of the timbers that framed the Anna's mouth. He thought the light was beautiful. So very beautiful.

"Will there be any more?" he murmured.

"Don't go out yet," said Gretel. He ignored her. "Cole, don't go out."

He pulled himself up by the timber and leaned against the mountain. The rock was bare and sandy gray.

The avalanche had carved away the outer part of the ledge. Cole worked his way across what was left, using the mountain for support. Catharine was gone, but he could see her in his mind. Her eyes shone very clear and green, and amid the white of her face they looked like spring leaves against the snow.

EPILOGUE

October 23 to November 1, 1892

At the Baroness Hotel, Gretel carried a tray to Cole's room: beef Wellington and a similarly extravagant red wine. She fluffed a second pillow and stuck it behind him so he could sit up in bed with the tray on his lap. She took her own plate from the tray, sat in a chair across from the bed. This was all on Heinrich Braunn, she thought sourly; neither she nor the men would pay anything but the doctor's fee.

Braunn had taken off for God knows where as soon as word of Krieg's death reached him. Gretel had held off telling Cole and Johnny about the true extent of his involvement in the Bonne Chance disaster and the contest over the Anna Strike. It would make no difference to Cole, and Johnny was in no condition to hear it. Even when Johnny got better, Gretel might not tell him. If he got better. The doctor thought he'd pull through, but the way fever still drove him to thrash and rant had Gretel worried.

She picked at her dinner, pushed the meat around the plate with her fork. Her appetite had long since departed.

"He'll be all right," said Cole.

Mutely, she nodded.

Cole was right, though. Within another day the fever broke, and soon after that Johnny was sitting up, wolfing down his meals, cursing the Baroness and demanding to be let out of bed. He made such a wretched patient that Gretel forgot her initial concern and fled, leaving others to care for him.

Two weeks after the fight at the Anna Strike, Cole was well enough to make the long trip to Montana. Johnny insisted on going with Gretel to see him off.

"But the doctor—" she protested.

"To hell with the doctor!"

"I give up," she said.

"Good. Then let's get out of here."

And so they did.

Another snowfall had blanketed the town, though not so viciously as that first blizzard. The sun was out now, and Colorado Avenue glistened. Snow formed small ridges across the tops of the store signs, and made frosty cuticles along the windowsills. At the station, Gretel and Johnny waited while Cole led the dun horse that had been Luke Halloran's aboard the train. When he returned to the platform to say good-bye, Gretel thought he looked a little haunted around the eyes, yet somehow relieved at the same time. He shook Johnny's hand.

"You sure you want to develop the Anna Strike?" he asked, his breath making steam in the wintry air.

"Why not?"

Gretel would've bet Cole could come up with plenty of reasons, but he only smiled. "All yours," he said, and turned to Gretel.

She felt a lump form in her throat. How silly, she thought, but even so avoided his eyes. She waited for him to say something. In-

stead he gave her a hug. "Come back," she managed. "Sometime."
And felt him nod.

The conductor called and Cole boarded the train. The engine
blew steam. The wheels spun, caught the rails, and the train pulled
slowly away. It picked up speed, chugged out of Telluride, heading
north.

"Home?" said Johnny.

"Home." They climbed aboard her wagon, which was hitched
to his palomino. She lifted the reins but he took them from her, flicked
them against the horse's golden hide. The beast hardly needed the
encouragement. He set off at a fast trot, too fast for Telluride's busy
streets, but Gretel didn't care.

"I have something to tell you," she said as they left the town
behind.

"You do?"

"Yes. About Heinrich Braunn." Despite her hesitation, she told
him all that Catharine had told her. When she finished he said nothing,
just looked ahead, at the snowy peaks that rose all around. His skin
was still pale, his cheeks still gaunt, and there were new lines around
his eyes. It was impossible to read his thoughts.

"Well?" she pressed. "What do you think?"

He smiled, then, thoughtfully, and Gretel realized she hadn't
seen him smile in weeks. Or heard him laugh, that laugh she'd once
thought was rich and real and a little wise. She missed his laugh.

"I think I should cable the insurance company," he said finally.
"If they want, I'll go back into the mine for ore samples to prove
Braunn defrauded them."

"That's all?"

"Sure, why?"

She shrugged, looked away.

"You thought I'd go after him, didn't you?"

"No—"

"Yes you did." He flicked the reins again and the palomino broke into a canter. "And you were right. I knew he was behind all this when Krieg stayed clear of the fight. And I thought there was no way the law could touch him, which meant I'd have to track him down myself. But I didn't know about the insurance."

"So now you can leave it up to them?"

He hesitated, but only for an instant. Long enough to make her wonder, though. "Maybe someday I'll get back to Europe," he said. "Try one last time to find my sister. If I run across Braunn, we'll see what happens."

So she was stuck with him, at least for now. She couldn't help but smile.

"Your sister?"

"My sister. Linda. Guess I've never told you about her, have I?"

"You've never told me much of anything."

"Maybe it's time I did."

They had reached the valley. With no need for direction, the palomino turned down the trail that led to the cabin.

"You know that blue felt hat?" said Johnny.

Gretel nodded.

"I found it in a trunk at my parents' house in Mexico. It was Linda's. A long time before, when we lived in Spain."